THE PELICAN BRIDE

This Large Print Book carries the
Seal of Approval of N.A.V.H.

THE PELICAN BRIDE

BETH WHITE

THORNDIKE PRESS

A part of Gale, Cengage Learning

GALE
CENGAGE Learning®

Farmington Hills, Mich • San Francisco • New York • Waterville, Maine
Meriden, Conn • Mason, Ohio • Chicago

GALE
CENGAGE Learning®

LIBRARY OF CONGRESS CATALOGING-IN-PUBLICATION DATA

White, Beth, 1957–
    The pelican bride / by Beth White. — Large print edition.
        pages ; cm. — (Gulf coast chronicles ; book 1) (Thorndike Press large print Christian romance)
        ISBN 978-1-4104-6947-2 (hardcover) — ISBN 1-4104-6947-6 (hardcover)
    1. Mail order brides—Fiction. 2. Fort Charlotte (Mobile, Ala.)—Fiction. 3. Large type books. I. Title.
PS3623.H5723P45 2014b
813'.6—dc23   2014007321

Published in 2014 by arrangement with Revell Books, a division of Baker Publishing Group

Printed in Mexico
1 2 3 4 5 6 7 18 17 16 15 14

For Robin, Katie, and Kim —
my sisters, my best friends.

1

Massacre Island
Mobile Bay, 1704

The fifty-six-gun frigate *Pélican* lunged as Geneviève Gaillain dropped six feet over its side before the canvas sling jerked her to a stop. Clutching the sodden rope above her head, she looked up at the dark-skinned mariners straining to keep her from plummeting into what they charmingly called "the drink." The sling swung with the motion of the ship, setting the sky tilting overhead in rhythm with the ocean's slap-slosh against the hull.

Queasy, she searched among the women still aboard until she found her sister leaning against the rail, cheeks as pale as the belly of a sea bass. If Geneviève yielded to her own terror, Aimée would refuse to get into the sling when her turn came.

And if her sister didn't get off that pestilential ship soon, she was going to die.

Geneviève looked over her shoulder at the scrawny, wind-twisted pines staggering along the shore like teeth in a broken comb. She'd begun to wonder if she would ever see this Louisiane that she was to call home — the New World, God help her.

She shut her eyes as the jerky, swaying descent resumed.

"Hang on, miss!" shouted the mate in the longboat below. "Almost down."

The seamen above chose that moment to release the rope, dumping her unceremoniously into a pool of seawater in the bottom of the longboat. Laughter erupted from the ship, but she caught her breath, ignored the merriment at her expense, and began the awkward business of untangling herself from the ropes.

The mate in the longboat reached down to help, grinning. "Welcome to Massacre Island."

She resisted the urge to jerk from his grasp. "Thank you," she muttered, recovering her dignity by scooting onto one of three narrow planks crossing the center of the boat. As the sling was hauled up, she looked up and cupped her hands around her mouth. "Aimée! Come on."

Her sister recoiled from the sailor waiting to help her into the sling. "I can't."

"Don't be ridiculous." Geneviève forced sympathy from her voice. "You can and you will!"

The sailors grabbed Aimée, stuffed her into the sling heedless of petticoats and shrieks, and dropped her over the side. Geneviève supposed they had little choice, but it was maddening to see her little sister treated like just another item of goods for sale. Although, essentially, she was.

After swinging through the air like a sack of sugar on a string, Aimée fell into the boat with a solid thump and a muffled squeal. "My skirt's wet!"

The mate chuckled as he extricated her from the sling. "You'll get a lot wetter than this before the day's out, *m'selle.*"

Aimée's blue eyes widened as she struggled to keep her balance in the reeling longboat. "What do you mean?"

"Sit down before you pitch us all into the bay." The sailor shielded his eyes against the sun and gestured for the sling to go up for another passenger.

"Geneviève, what does he —"

"Aimée, sit down." Geneviève grabbed her sister's clammy hand. "You're going to faint."

Aimée crumpled onto the seat. "I wish we'd never come," she whispered, leaning against Geneviève. "I want to go home."

Geneviève put her arms around her sister's quaking body. There was no home to go back to. Tolerance in France for Huguenots had come to a flaming end. Here in Louisiane there was at least the promise of marriage, a chance of gaining independence, a home and children. The pouch of coins in her pocket pressed against her thigh, reassuring her. So many unknowns about this venture. She had promised to marry one of the Canadians who had already come here to explore and settle, and Aimée, as young as she was, had promised as well.

Yielding herself was inevitable, part of the bargain she had struck, as was hiding her faith. She and Aimée would have to make the best of it.

Another girl landed in the rocking boat, displacing her anxious thoughts, then one by one, with varying degrees of noise and struggle, four more. Finally the mate in charge roared, "No more room! We'll get the rest on the next trip."

The sailors hauled up the empty canvas seat, tossed it onto a pile of rigging, and noisily saluted the departure of the longboat.

Thank God she and Aimée had been chosen to depart with the first group. They would have the choice of accommodations for the night — though who knew what that would be like. *Massacre Island.* She shivered. What a name for their landing place. But at least they would not have to stay here long. Tomorrow they were to travel up the river to their final destination, Fort Louis.

By the time they were halfway to shore, she and Aimée were both soaking wet from salt spray. Still, incredibly, her sister's cheek against her shoulder burned with fever.

Geneviève anxiously brushed her hand across her sister's damp, curly blonde head. Poor baby, she was lucky to be alive. One of the sailors had been buried at sea only yesterday. Geneviève herself still trembled from the fever they'd all picked up in Havana, but at least she was upright.

As the longboat drew closer to the beach, she lifted her hand to block the stark glare of sand as white as spun sugar. She began to make out human figures — male figures — gathered to watch their arrival. Her stomach tightened. Was her future husband among them? Some unknown Canadian with pots of money as they had been promised?

With every stroke of the oars she came closer to meeting him. Would he be like her father, a good man who had failed to protect his daughters? Or would he be like the rude and vicious dragoons who had been quartered in their home? Could she be so lucky, so blessed, as to find a man as kind and resourceful as Father Mathieu? As brave and principled as the great *Réforme* warrior Jean Cavalier?

Still several yards out from the beach, the boat grounded against sand with a bump. Aimée whimpered and stirred in her arms. Geneviève looked up and found herself encircled by grinning, bearded men standing hip-deep in the water. Her overpowered gaze took in a variety of faded, ragged clothing, sunburnt faces, and twinkling eyes.

The young man closest to her, the only one in uniform — the blue, white, and gold of the French marine — removed his tricorn and bowed, all but baptizing himself in the chopping surf. He rose, plopping his misshapen headgear back into place, and scanned the passengers of the boat as if surveying goods in a market. "Welcome, *mademoiselles*. We've come to carry you ashore."

Geneviève stared at the boy. He couldn't be more than nineteen or twenty years of age, his cleft chin emphasized by a dark beard still thin and fine. Indeed he was broad of shoulder but built on lanky lines.

12

They were all slender, she realized, looking around at the other men. Gaunt in fact. Another sliver of apprehension needled her midsection. "I can walk, *monsieur.* But I would be grateful if you would help my sister. She isn't well."

The young man transferred his gaze to Aimée, who lolled against Geneviève like a rag doll. "We'd hoped the fever in Havana would be gone by now." He slid his arms gently under Aimée's knees and around her back, lifted her with surprising ease, and turned to slosh toward the beach.

Ignoring the rough voices and equally rough, reaching hands of the men surrounding the boat, Geneviève hauled herself over the side.

And found herself underwater. She thrashed, tried to find footing as she sank under the weight of her skirts. Just when she thought her lungs would burst, a pair of steely hands clamped her around the waist from behind and hauled her into sweet, blessed air. She coughed and vomited.

"Let go!" Choking, she shoved at the sinewy arms around her middle. "You're squeezing the life out of me!"

"Stop kicking," the voice rumbled against her back, "or I'll let you swim."

"I *can't* swim!"

"Then relax and enjoy the ride." He hoisted her over his shoulder and turned toward the beach.

Geneviève shoved a hank of sopping hair out of her eyes. She had lost her cap in the water, and her braid had come loose. All she could see was a rough shirt of a faded, pink-tinged brown, plastered against hard lateral muscles flexing as her rescuer half waded, half swam with her. He gripped the back of her thigh with one large hand to hold her in place and extended the other for balance.

Lifting her head, she peered at the *Pélican* floating in the distance, sails flapping against the steely sky in a brisk northwest breeze. No more worm-ridden hardtack for breakfast. No more briny bathing and drinking water. No more malodorous cabin shared with three other fractious women.

She realized she had much to be thankful for.

A noise must have escaped her. The man halted. "Pardon. Are you uncomfortable?"

She hung upside down with her hair dragging in the water, her thighs tucked under a strange man's chin. "Oh, no, monsieur, I was merely wondering what time tea will be served."

A rusty chuckle erupted against her knees.

14

"Forgive us, mademoiselle. No one thought to warn you about the sinkholes." He continued slogging his way toward shore.

Sinkholes. What other unexpected dangers awaited her in this alien land? As the water got shallower and clearer, she could see sea creatures swimming amongst bits of brown, foamy algae. The gentle roll of the surf was wholly unlike Rochefort's rocky, choppy seashore, as were the long-legged, wide-winged white birds swooping in the distance. They were big enough to carry off a small child.

The bay was big, the wildlife was big, the men were big. She and Aimée would be swallowed whole.

The man stopped. "You can walk from here," he said, shifting her into the cradle of his arms. He held her a moment, looking down into her face.

Boldly she returned his stare. His bony, angular face was outlined by a neatly trimmed dark beard and mustache, with black eyebrows slashing above a pair of fierce brown eyes uncannily like those of the boy who had carried Aimée ashore. Dark hair curled to his shoulders and blew back from a broad, intelligent brow.

"You should know," he said, "that I only came to pick up supplies. I'm not here for a wife."

It had been a long time since Tristan had held a woman in his arms. This one was thin, bedraggled, and exceedingly wet. But she held her arms clasped across a nicely shaped bosom and stared up at him with black-fringed eyes the color of the ocean sloshing around his legs.

Stiff as a wet cat, she fairly hissed. "As if I would want to marry a presumptuous oaf who hoists me over his shoulder like a barrel of flour and then insults me without bothering to introduce himself."

"I am Tristan Lanier," he said with as much dignity as he could muster. "I'm s—"

"Put me down. I'll take my chances with the sink holes."

And then he saw the tears. Pity curbed his initial impulse to dump her onto her curvy derriere in the sand. He released her legs but kept a steady arm across her back. "The sand is firm here. You'll be fine."

"Thank you." She would have stepped away, but her legs buckled. "Oh!" she gasped as he caught her, pulling her hard against him. "The ground is heaving up and down!"

"It will do that for quite some time. Give yourself a minute before you try to —"

But she had already pushed away, staggering onto dry sand, where she stood peering up and down the beach. She had to squint against the sun, which had abruptly come out from behind the clouds.

Tristan followed her gaze. "What's the matter?"

"I don't see my sister."

Each of the men who had flocked to the aid of the women in the longboat had collected a prize and headed for shade. The longboat was already on its way back to the ship for another load. Tristan and this woman were alone on the beach.

"Come," he said, softening his voice. "I'll take you to the warehouse. That's where she'll be."

She nodded and picked up her soggy skirts to follow him. As they rounded one of the large dunes lumped along the beach, he glanced at her. She looked like a woman who had just awakened from sleep to find herself face-to-face with her nightmare. The fine sea-green eyes darted right and left at the seagulls wheeling in search of food, and she visibly struggled to maintain her balance. Her small leather boots, cracked and thin, must be little protection against the hot sand.

Halfway up the beach, a tall stand of sea

grass blocked the way. Tristan went ahead to hold it back so that she could pass without getting slapped in the face. On the other side of it, she stopped, putting a hand briefly on his forearm.

"Monsieur Lanier, I must beg your forgiveness. I have been unkind in the face of your assistance." She bit her lip, looking away. "My — my distress is no excuse for lack of gratitude."

"Apology accepted, mademoiselle."

A faint smile curved her lips and found her eyes, turning her from a pinched-face harridan into a starkly lovely young woman. Her hair was drying in dark waves that gleamed in the strong sun with umber and bronze lights, and there was a charming sprinkle of freckles across her straight nose. She couldn't be more than seventeen or eighteen years old.

She grabbed the blowing tresses with a self-conscious yank and twisted them into an impromptu knot at the back of her head. "In the absence of correct social protocols, m'sieur, I must introduce myself. I am Mademoiselle Geneviève Gaillain, late of Rochefort." She dipped a curtsey whose grace was marred only in the slightest by an unsteady step backward into the sea grass.

Tristan grabbed her wrist before she could

go rolling down the hill. "It is my very great honor to make your acquaintance, ma'm'selle."

She peeked up at him as if gauging his sincerity, but allowed him to help her up and over the dunes. She was quiet as they trudged the remaining distance between the beach and the warehouse at the top of the rise. He could not fathom what had brought such a pretty, engaging young woman to the wilds of Louisiane to find a husband. Were the men in Rochefort blind, deaf, and dumb?

This largest of the structures erected during the French occupation of Massacre Island stood between two open-air sheds and contained, at any given time, varying quantities of consumable products such as flour, sugar, barley, molasses, wine, lard, and meat. Also stuffed under its twelve-foot-high roof one could find piles of wooden shingles, miscellaneous cooking pots, axes, guns, and butcher knives; available as gifts for the Indians were red stockings — the preferred color — as well as handbells and glass beads.

But as Tristan shoved open the warehouse's warped front door, his supply list fled his mind.

Holding court on a rough three-legged

stool just inside the door, hands clasped de-
murely in her lap, was the most beautiful
young woman he'd ever seen. She blinked
up at Tristan's brother Marc-Antoine with
eyes the color of gentian violets, her flaxen
curls spilling onto her dainty shoulders from
under a white ruffled cap. Her oval face was
thin from illness, but the ivory skin gleamed
with the purity of a cameo.

Then he caught Marc-Antoine's dazed
eye. His brother looked like he'd run
straight into a wall.

Geneviève rushed past him. "Aimée!"

The two women embraced for a scant
second before the beauty squealed. "Ooh,
Ginette! You're making me wet again!"

Geneviève pulled away, searching the
younger girl's face. "Are you all right?"

Aimée nodded. "I've been well cared for,
Sister." She pursed her sweet lips and
flicked a glance at the male audience observ-
ing the exchange with slack-jawed interest.

"Indeed?" Geneviève tucked her arm
around Aimée's shoulder and faced the
crowd like St. Jeanne d'Arc confronting the
English at Orleans.

Clearly Geneviève Gaillain was capable of
taking care of her little sister, which put his
responsibility for them at an end. And at
the moment he had more pressing concerns

to discuss with his brother.

Tristan slapped Marc-Antoine's shoulder. "Come, you promised to help me transport supplies to my boat."

Marc-Antoine blinked. "Ah. Yes." He bowed to the two young women, a jerky, little-used courtesy. "Mademoiselles."

Tristan grabbed his reluctant brother by the sleeve and towed him toward the open doorway of the warehouse. "You'll have all the time in the world to fix your interest, once the ladies settle in at the fort."

Marc-Antoine looked over his shoulder. "But what if some other fellow takes up with her before I go off-duty again?"

"Yours was the first face she saw, is that not correct?" His brother had taken the drooping Aimée from her sister's arms and carried her ashore as gently as a mother with a newborn babe. And the girl's blue eyes had flickered to Marc-Antoine's face each time he looked away.

Marc-Antoine shrugged. "Women's affections, I have noticed, are often swayed by proximity."

Tristan chuckled. "Then let us hope she will return to your proximity at a more convenient time. I have news from the upper river."

"News?" Marc-Antoine glanced at him

sharply. "What is it?"

Tristan lifted a hand. "Not here."

Stepping outside the warehouse, Marc-Antoine switched to the tongue of the people among whom he had spent a year as a teenager. "The Alabama? Has something happened to them?"

Tristan answered in the same language. "No, why would you assume that?"

Marc-Antoine's expression cleared. "What then?"

Tristan lowered his voice. "The British have sent agents to the Koroa — maybe the Kaskaskians as well. If Bienville wishes to protect trade on the upper river, he'd better find a way to convince those Indians that their best interests lie in alliance with us."

"So they still think to take our territory? We were here first!"

"They'll never be satisfied until they control the rivers and ports." Matching his brother's angry pace, Tristan shrugged. "But neither will King Louis and Pontchartrain. It's going to come down to war."

"We'll have to send agents of our own to renew Indian alliances." Marc-Antoine's expression shifted to a mischievous, engaging grin. "There's nobody better at that, brother, than you and I."

Tristan halted. "Oh no. I'm no longer

responsible for keeping Bienville out of trouble."

"You know your own safety depends on the fortunes of Louisiane. Besides, how can you abandon us to this British thievery?"

"You'll figure it out. In the meantime, how do you plan to get twenty-five women and all their fripperies transported to the fort in two little barques and a fishing boat?"

"We had to send the pinnace to Veracruz for gunpowder." Marc-Antoine started walking toward the beach, where the long-boat could be seen debarking another load of passengers from the *Pélican*. "By the time we got word of the *Pélican*'s arrival, I was the only officer available to meet her." He waved a hand in irritation. "Well, me and Bienville's little hound, Dufresne."

Tristan nodded, grateful that he no longer had to deal with colonial politics. "You should keep an eye on young Dufresne. He's definitely got something up his sleeve besides his elbow. He was sniffing around La Salle's office earlier this afternoon — walked off and pretended to be looking for something on the ground when he realized I'd seen him — but there's something, I don't know, *off* about the fellow."

Marc-Antoine rubbed his forehead. "Bienville hired me as an interpreter, not a babysitter."

"He sent you down here because you can be trusted to do your job." Tristan threw an arm around his brother's shoulder. "So quit whining and do it. And who knows, little brother — you may end up with a wife!"

"It could happen." Marc-Antoine gave him a sideways look. "Why don't you visit the settlement? It's been a long time since you lingered in civilization."

"Yes, and for good reason. I've planted corn this year, and I don't need to be away for more than a few days."

"If you cleaned up a bit, there might be a woman crazy enough to go back with you."

Tristan laughed. "*I'm* not crazy enough to take a Frenchwoman to Lanier Plantation, so get the notion out of your head. You're all the heir I need."

"Tristan —"

Tristan stopped him with a cuff on the arm. "Leave be," he said lightly. "I'm happy with my independence. I come and go as I please, and have to answer to no one but myself. It's a good life." As he reminded himself ten times a day.

Marc-Antoine shook his head. "The least you can do is lend your barque to help us transport the young ladies up to the settlement."

Tristan frowned. "No one takes my boat but me."

"Then *you* captain her. Tristan, we can't leave any of those women to fend for themselves here on the island. We haven't enough men to protect them from . . . well, from the men." Marc-Antoine laughed. "You know what I mean."

Tristan looked away, picturing the Gaillain sisters, one damp and flushed with righteous indignation, the other pale and delicate as a butterfly. Neither should be left to the doubtful care of a handful of bored and randy young soldiers.

Conscience defeating pragmatism, he chanced a look at Marc-Antoine and found him grinning. Reluctantly Tristan laughed. "All right. One trip up the river with as many parakeets as you can fit onboard — and that's all! Then I'll be on my way — and don't ask me to stay."

2

Geneviève swayed upon the rough wooden bench to which she had been assigned for dinner, her eyes closing of their own volition. Her skirts crackled with dried salt, the nape of her neck itched as if ants had crawled under her collar, and her underarms were chafed raw. In short, she desperately craved a bath.

On the way to dinner, however, Father Mathieu had informed his dazed charges that there would be no time or opportunity for niceties until they reached Fort Louis. And maybe not then. August rains could be "unpredictable," the priest had admitted, avoiding Geneviève's gaze.

Squeezing her eyes shut now, she pictured the little mountain creek in which she and Aimée had waded as children, imagined its icy rush wetting her petticoats and turning her bare feet blue with cold. Perhaps she'd never feel cold again. Probably never walk through fresh snow or pick poppies or eat wild chestnut honey . . .

Resolutely she opened her eyes and focused on the sunburnt face of the young soldier seated opposite her at the table. He gave her a shy grin and went back to gobbling his stew.

Neither, she reminded herself as she lifted her own spoon, would she face the horror of watching her home burn to the ground in the aftermath of civil war. All she had to do was keep her personal beliefs private.

One could live without snow.

"Ginette, when are we going to our beds?"

Geneviève glanced at Aimée, who sat to her left, food untouched. "Soon, *cherie.*" She leaned close to whisper, "They have tried to make us welcome, so we must eat what we can. Besides, you need food for strength."

"I'm not hungry." Aimée's voice wobbled. "I'm tired."

"Just a little longer, then we can retire."

"But they keep staring at me."

Geneviève glanced down the length of the table and found, sure enough, several men with rapturous eyes fixed on Aimée. A young officer notable for a mop of ginger-colored curls, apparently feeling her gaze, nodded without embarrassment and returned to conversation with the man next to him. "They haven't seen young white women in a long time. They'll get used to us."

"I hope so." Aimée grimaced. "Do you suppose they speak French?"

"I assure you, mademoiselle, we can understand every word you say. We Canadians are Frenchmen, not barbarians."

Oh dear. Geneviève looked over her shoulder to find a tall, dark-haired man emerging from the shadow of the doorway. With a flood of relief she recognized Tristan Lanier, the man who had carried her ashore this afternoon.

Aimée seemed not to notice the humor in Lanier's eyes. Her face flushed with hectic color. "I'm very sorry to have offended, monsieur, but one tires of dining like a bird in a cage, with eyes peering at one through the bars."

Geneviève touched her arm in reproof. "There's no need to be rude."

But Lanier smiled and executed a rusty bow. "*Touché,* little canary. You must forgive our collective admiration. I am Tristan Lanier."

Aimée's small pointed chin remained elevated, but she graciously extended her hand. "I accept your apology, monsieur. I am Aimée Giselle Gaillain of —" She scowled at Geneviève, who had pinched her. "And this is my sister, Geneviève."

Geneviève managed to rise against the edge of the table and dip a mortified curtsey. "We met earlier today."

Lanier bent over Aimée's fingers as gallantly as if she were seated in a grand Parisian dining hall instead of a thrown-together adjunct to a warehouse on a windswept island. "Mademoiselle." A twinkle lingered in his eyes as he released her fingers and straightened, but the continued silence in the long, narrow room brought his gaze to the ginger-haired officer. "Dufresne, are you going to allow these men to sit here all night gawking at our guests? Surely Bienville has made provision for their lodging."

The redhead's expression darkened. "Of course he has, though it is no concern of yours, Lanier." He rose and snapped his fingers. "Come, men. We are to clear out of the barracks and turn it over to the ladies." Picking up his trencher and spoon, he led the way out of the room, catching Aimée's eye as he passed. "Mademoiselle Canary," he murmured with a silky undertone that made Geneviève uneasy. Bowing to her, he quitted the room, followed by a straggling rank of reluctant soldiers.

Geneviève indicated the empty seat across the table. "Would you join us, Monsieur Lanier?"

Lanier folded himself onto the bench, his amusement dissolving into lines of weariness. "Mademoiselle Gaillain, if you are going to ignore this fine meal, please pass it across the table so that I may deal with it."

Aimée blinked but complied, staring at the Canadian.

In the confines of this dark, squalid little room, Lanier seemed to Geneviève even bigger and wilder than he had appeared on the beach. His worn, reddish shirt had dried against the contours of his shoulders, his dark hair falling in thick waves against its open collar. Both sun-browned hands bore heavy white scars across the knuckles, and she couldn't help wondering how he had injured them.

Transferring her gaze to his face, she found him watching her. She probably appeared to be sizing up his potential as a mate, despite his claim of disinterest. Hurriedly she glanced away, but not before his lips curved.

"You two have made quite an impression on the men from Fort Louis — including my little brother." Lanier turned to confiscate a tankard left on the table behind him.

"He could not stop talking about the blue-eyed angel he carried into the warehouse this afternoon."

"Captain Lanier was most kind," Aimée said stiffly.

Her sister was clearly annoyed with his tone of amusement, so Geneviève attempted to steer the conversation into less personal waters. "We are anxious to complete our journey, m'sieur. Will you and your brother travel with us to the settlement?"

Mild irritation darkened his expression. "I'm afraid so."

Geneviève waited for him to explain, but he continued to eat in silence. She tried again. "How early will we need to be ready to leave in the morning? I understand we've half a day's travel ahead of us."

He sighed and glanced at her. "That's right. My brother has instructed your priest to be ready by daylight. The journey will be much more pleasant if accomplished before the heat of the day presses in." His lips tightened. "Besides, you'll have much to do once you land at Fort Louis, and I must get home before sunset."

She wanted to ask him where "home" was. Presumably not Fort Louis. "Where shall we reside? No one was able to prepare us for the details of life here." She touched the itchy upstanding collar of her dress. "I suspect we all brought wildly inappropriate clothing for the climate."

Lanier's dark eyes skimmed over her. "Certainly less . . . confining attire will be more comfortable." He scooped up the last of his stew and said offhandedly, "I imagine you will be housed with families in the settlement who have made room for you."

"But we were promised homes of our own!" Aimée had apparently overcome her determination to maintain a dignified silence.

Lanier eyed Aimée, his expression unreadable. "Bienville won't be concerned about promises made by those without the power to fulfill them." He shrugged. "When you marry, your husband will provide as well as he is able — and you must learn to make do with that." He stood and bowed with more than a hint of mockery. "But don't rely upon my word alone. After all, I will not be staying to find out."

The sun was no more than a strip of pink chiffon along the eastern horizon as Geneviève followed Father Mathieu's black-robed figure across the damp sand toward what looked like a glorified fishing boat bobbing in the dark surf. She looked around to make sure her sister followed. Aimée had had the nightmare again last night, her scream jolting Geneviève from a sound sleep. She'd managed to wake Aimée and soothe her gasping tears without creating a scene, but she'd gone back to bed with a bite mark in the side of her hand and a renewed rage toward the dragoons who had invaded their home.

To her relief, Aimée rounded a sand dune just then, enfolded in a gaggle of the four youngest girls. They were giggling at the galumphing gait of rotund nursing sister Marie Grissot, who marched ahead of them with more determination than grace. Sister Gris, as they called her — to distinguish her from her companion, Sister Marie Linant — held her billowing habit off the sand with one hand, and with the other struggled to keep her wimple from blowing off.

Geneviève congratulated herself that her own cap was tied snugly beneath her chin and her skirts too short to tangle around her ankles. She'd thought about keeping her Bible with her, to while away the long trip up to the fort, but had decided not to risk unnecessary questions. It lay at the bottom of her trunk — which, along with the rest of the baggage from the *Pélican,* had already been trundled to the beach on a cart pulled by a spavined ox. The poor animal's indignation at this task expressed itself as a series of grunts only exceeded in their ferocity by Sister Gris's snoring last night.

"What gives you a smile, little one?" Father Mathieu had dropped back to match her steps, one arm extended for balance like the wing of a glossy blackbird, the other clutching a painting of the Madonna and Child he had brought all the way from Rochefort. His button-brown eyes crinkled with teasing affection.

"The joy of walking on solid ground, even for a few more minutes." Geneviève offered her elbow for support, and he took it with a grateful look. The priest rarely showed his age, which, judging by the sparse fringe of gray hair which brushed his shoulders, must be over sixty. She studied the shadows beneath his eyes, the yellow tinge of the leathery skin. The fever had hit them all hard, and Father Mathieu had helped with nursing duties during the most difficult hours of the nights at sea.

He sighed. "Do you suppose we could simply walk the rest of the way to the fort?"

She chuckled. "Not unless you have a mind to emulate Saint Peter and walk on water."

"And we know how well that ended," he

said drolly. "Massacre Island, they call it. I can't help wondering how it got that terrible name."

"I'd rather not think about it." Geneviève made out three vessels bobbing in the water. They looked alarmingly small. "Are we all going to fit on those little boats?"

"We made it this far, my dear. The good God will surely see us to our final destination."

Geneviève nodded, reflecting not for the first time that God's will could be a capricious thing. Several of their original party had perished at sea, and there was no guarantee the rest of them would reach the settlement without further incident.

Perhaps she was being unduly cynical. Perhaps her faith was weak. But she couldn't seem to control the questions that assailed her in unguarded moments.

She squared her shoulders and smiled at the priest. "And thus far the journey has been . . . interesting, has it not? What do you think of Monsieur Lanier?"

Following last night's uncomfortable dinner conversation, Tristan Lanier had abruptly left the dining hall just as his handsome younger brother entered. Acquainting himself with each of the young women and the chaperones, Marc-Antoine bowed deeply, his engaging laughter ringing out loudly and often. He had remained talking to Father Mathieu when the women excused themselves to their quarters for the night.

"He seems a man of strong appetites," Father Mathieu replied dryly. "You would be wise to keep your little sister out of his sights."

"Why? Do you think he would . . ." Geneviève couldn't finish the sentence. Had they escaped France only to thrust themselves into a worse predicament?

Father Mathieu shook his head. "It is not the young captain's behavior which bears watching, my dear, so much as that of our little Aimée."

So, he'd meant Marc-Antoine, not Tristan. Geneviève bit her lip, absurdly relieved. "I agree Aimée is too forward, but only because she is so innocent."

"Perhaps it's time she learned what you and Jean Cavalier have done for her. It was he who broke you out of prison, and when he told me how you were treated there —"

"And *you,* Father. We wouldn't be here if you hadn't been willing to listen to Jean."

"Pssh. Child, I wouldn't sleep at night knowing I'd left two orphans behind to face that nightmare in the Cévennes — and all of it in the name of religion. It's my hope to create a climate here where all Christians, whether Catholic or Reformed or something in between, will be free to worship together." His voice rose above the roar of the surf, and he sounded stronger than she'd heard him in days.

"A noble dream, Father." She patted the trembling hand on her arm. "But I would not speak it within the hearing of Captain Lanier — nor anyone else in authority. We are yet a Catholic state, as long as Louis is on the throne."

"His Majesty thinks to keep the faith pure." Father Mathieu shook his head. "But such excesses of materialism — and down-right barbarism — I have never seen. How can it be right to murder one's countrymen just because their interpretation of Scripture does not line up with that of the Pope? And how is it right to live in gilded halls which house at least one mistress and numbers of illegitimate children, when innocents like you and your sister are deprived of parents and driven out of their homes?"

"Please, Father, have a care!" Geneviève stopped, clutching the priest's arm. They had reached the shore and were within earshot of soldiers and sailors milling about, hoisting kegs and boxes and trunks onto their shoulders, splashing toward the boats.

He gave her a sheepish smile. "You are right, of course. Besides, the sermon is wasted on the righteous. I shall save it for the audience who needs it." At her alarmed gasp, he laughed. "Don't worry, I *can* be subtle when necessary."

Geneviève eyed him with mock severity. "Wise as a serpent, hmm?"

"Quite." He drew her toward an officer supervising the removal of luggage from the cart. "Pardon, m'sieur, can you advise us as to the procedure for boarding?"

The officer turned and removed his hat to wipe his forehead, revealing a curly mop of red hair. Geneviève recognized the young officer from the dining hall.

He bowed. "Good morning, Father, mademoiselle." Rising, he gestured toward the swarm of activity surrounding the lading process. "As you can see, we are not quite ready for boarding, but your punctuality is commendable." His gaze found Geneviève's. "And how did you ladies pass the night? I hope you fared well on your first day in the New World."

"Tolerably," she said without much enthusiasm. The scuttling nighttime noises had been different from, but no less disconcerting than, that of the rats which infested the *Pélican*. And Aimée's nightmare couldn't

38

be mentioned. "I must thank you again for your men's willingness to sacrifice their beds in our favor."

"It is no sacrifice when one reflects that those beds may soon be jointly warmed." His sly tone was mitigated by a twinkle in the greenish eyes. "Within the bonds of matrimony, that is, begging your pardon, Father."

Father Mathieu laughed. "No offense taken, my son. I'm sure you young men have been looking forward to the company of our gentle beauties."

"And the reality far exceeds the hope. But we have not been properly introduced." The officer bowed once more, this time with a flourish of his plumed hat. "I am Aide-Major Julien Dufresne, at your service."

Geneviève dipped a curtsey. "I am Geneviève Gaillain. This is Father Mathieu."

Dufresne took her hand and kissed her fingertips. "Mademoiselle, I am enchanted." His gaze flicked over her shoulder as he rose. "One of these young ladies is your sister, if I'm not mistaken. I see the familial resemblance."

Geneviève turned and found Aimée and the other three girls clustered in a tittering knot a few paces away. "Yes, come here, girls. I wish you to meet Aide-Major Dufresne."

All four spilled forward and introduced themselves with a rush of giggles and curtsies.

"Barbe Savarit!"

"Ysabeau Bonnet — *bon jour,* m'sieur."

"Élisabeth le Pinteaux." Poor Élisabeth, shy and still weak from the fever, looked as if she might faint.

Aimée took the girl's arm and gave a regal nod. "We are pleased to make your acquaintance, m'sieur. I am Aimée Gaillain."

Dufresne kissed each girl's hand in turn. "Enchanted," he murmured, lingering over Aimée's slim fingers. He released her only when she gave an impatient tug. With a small smile, Dufresne addressed the priest. "If you will escort your fair charges to the end of the pier, we shall begin boarding as soon as all have arrived." He bowed, then returned to his duties without a backward glance.

Sensing trouble, Geneviève glanced at her sister.

Clearly piqued, Aimée shrugged. "Come, girls, let us watch to make sure these oafs don't drop our baggage into the ocean." Lifting her skirts, she flounced toward the activity near the gangplank.

The other three girls hurried after her, leaving Geneviève to follow on the arm of the priest. Oafs? From whence had her common-born little sister arrived at the notion that she was better than anyone else, particularly men who were doing her a service? Her assumption of Aimée's naïveté might be a bit over-hopeful. Father Mathieu would have his work cut out for him, keeping those four on a leash.

3

The sixty-foot, seven-ton barque Tristan used for transporting supplies upriver fought the current despite the best efforts of the oarsmen to set her course. It was going to be a long trip, especially if the women kept rocking the boat off-balance. He regretted his capitulation to Marc-Antoine.

For the last two hours he'd kept an eye out for alligators slumbering in the marshes alongshore. He could just imagine the uproar if one of his passengers spied one of the slippery monsters gliding along in the shallows.

Glancing over his shoulder, he caught the wide-eyed gaze of Mademoiselle Geneviève. Her lips trembled upward at the corners, though her face looked pinched. He hoped she wasn't going to succumb to the seasickness that often followed a sudden shift in motion after a long voyage.

Leaving the wheel to one of his mates, he

jumped over piles of cable and rigging and made his way to the stern, where the seven women and the priest sat holding on to their benches as if a typhoon might sweep them overboard at any moment.

"I trust you are still comfortable," he said, addressing the elder Mademoiselle Gaillain. He couldn't seem to avoid looking at her first. She was not as staggeringly lovely as her sister, but despite her pallor, the intelligence and humor in her expression drew his gaze.

She touched Aimée's rumpled golden head, which lolled against her shoulder. "Quite," she said, then laughed when her sister groaned and clutched her stomach. "At least, I am. Have we provisions aboard, or shall we haul to for the noon meal?"

"Can you really anticipate food so soon?" He glanced around at the other women, who all looked a bit green about the mouth. Father Mathieu knelt fanning one girl's face with a palm frond.

Mademoiselle Gaillain's chin went up a fraction. "Are you calling me a glutton?"

He saw that she was teasing and grinned. "If the slipper fits . . ."

She laughed. "I confess to a bit of queasiness at the outset, but I find myself enjoying the —" she paused, choosing her words carefully — "peculiar scenery."

Tristan followed her gaze to a pelican bobbing awkwardly in and out of the marshgrass that lined the scrubby shoreline. He tried to remember his first impression of this alien landscape. He'd been quite a young man then — or perhaps he'd grown up quickly in order to survive the hairraising events of mapping Bienville's colonial adventure.

He smiled. "You'll get used to it. And fish is our version of manna, so I hope you like it."

"I could eat just about anything, as long it doesn't have worms or smell like rot." She shuddered.

"No guarantees," he said, turning to brace his back against the rail. "The journey must have been difficult. Why choose to come to the other side of the world to find a husband?"

She stiffened and looked away, and he could have sworn terror had flashed in her eyes. "It is a . . . private family matter, sir," she finally said in a suffocated little voice.

He waited for a moment, but her lips remained firmly pressed together. Apparently the subject was closed. "Forgive me, mademoiselle, I must return to my duties. I will let one of the mates know that you desire something to eat."

But as he turned, she sighed and caught his wrist. "Wait. You are kind, and I thank you."

He stared at the dainty fingers which lay like flowers against his sun-darkened skin. "I haven't any drawing room manners. I don't mean to offend."

She quickly withdrew her hand. "I know." There was a long pause. After an awkward moment, the fine green eyes narrowed. "What is that place up there? Are we passing the fort already?"

He turned to follow her gaze to the top of a huge bluff, where the French flag flew next to a ten-foot wooden cross. "That is my plantation." He couldn't keep the pride from his voice. *Mine.* He'd bought the land from the Indians with the finest of Canadian furs — rich, well-watered, protected land, perfect for raising corn and sugar, just right for grazing cattle.

All the better that Bienville had ignored his advice, choosing to build the fort twenty-seven miles upriver. The Indians had never seen Tristan as a threat, and he'd settled with little fanfare on a five-mile square just outside the transient Mobile clan's winter quarters.

"Do you not live at Fort Louis? Why?"

45

He shrugged. "It's a long tale. In short, I prefer to provide for my own livelihood without interference from the Crown."

"Yet you fly the French flag. You are a strange man, Monsieur Lanier."

He chuckled. "Which is perhaps the truest reason for my solitude." He glanced at the younger girl, who had fallen into a fitful sleep against Mademoiselle Geneviève's shoulder. "Please let me know if your sister requires anything for her comfort. I shall send someone back with food."

He executed a curt bow and headed for his quarters. A woman would never understand his aversion to walls.

Geneviève stared at the sliver of salted fish in her hand and braced herself to put it in her mouth. Somehow she had expected the food to improve once they left the sea behind. Fish for breakfast. Fish for the noon meal. Fish for dinner. Manna indeed.

She leaned against the outer cabin wall, settled Aimée's head more comfortably in her lap, and nibbled at the dubious meal. The memory of fragrant aromas from Papa's bakery wafted across her palate, somehow covering the pungent mess in her mouth. Yeast, that inimitable substance of her childhood, had left an indelible impression that no amount of bad food could erase. Perhaps the jar of leaven she'd managed to secrete beneath her Bible had survived the journey.

The hope sustained her better than a hundred fine meals. If she could find a way to bake her pastries, she and Aimée would do well.

Swallowing misgivings, she peeked around the corner of the cabin, where Tristan Lanier stood with feet braced wide against the rocking lunge of the boat. When he turned suddenly and caught her staring, she ducked back out of sight, heart pounding. He didn't want a wife, she reminded herself. There was nothing to fear.

Fort Louis de la Louisiane
What I need is a wife, Julien Dufresne thought as he shepherded the last of the *Pélican* girls through the stockade gate and ordered it closed and locked. The spindly-legged cadet on guard, with a longing glance at the girls' well-padded backsides, saluted and moved to obey.

Julien drew his kerchief from the inside pocket of his jacket and mopped his face, cursing the heat, cursing the mud caked on the expensive Russia leather boots he'd had shipped from Paris last fall, and cursing the mosquitoes that found their way through three layers of clothing into his smallclothes. Most of all he cursed his nonexistent birthright — which was the reason he found himself in this godforsaken outpost, instead of comfortably ensconced in one of his father's salons.

He cheered himself by imagining the raw streets as they must one day appear. Bricked and lined with shops they would be, with clusters of brightly dressed women fluttering in doorways and carriages pulled by fine horses trundling under sunny skies. One of those carriages would be his, and one of the women would be carrying his child — a son born of legitimate union, blessed in the cathedral which he would endow.

One of the girls he had just safely delivered would be privileged to become his bride. Maintaining a legacy of education, refinement, and landed privilege required the finest of bloodlines, and he must begin as he meant to go on.

Several of the women had proved to be young and quite beautiful, which was frankly astonishing; one had to wonder what would motivate a gently bred female to voluntarily cross the ocean to this unsettled bog. Lack of virtue would be unacceptable in the wife of the son of the Comte de

Leméry — regardless on which side of the blanket he had been conceived.

One of those women would discover that she had made a most fortuitous decision in emigrating to the New World.

"Which canary did you swallow, Dufresne?"

Startled, he turned to find brick mason Jean Alexandre, a grin curling his thin-lipped mouth.

"I've no idea what you're talking about." Julien stuffed his kerchief back into his coat. "When are you fellows going to have enough bricks made to turn this quagmire into a decent thoroughfare?"

Alexandre shrugged. "Soon enough. Like most things, brick must dry before it is useful." There was a sour silence which Julien refused to fill. Finally Alexandre chuckled. "Come down off your high horse, Dufresne. You know we're all calculating which of the brides we can draw into the net."

"Twenty-five women to two hundred men." Julien passed Alexandre a sidelong look. "The odds aren't favorable for a mud-slinger with a face like a trowel."

The mason laughed outright. "This particular trowel-faced mud-slinger has been saving against just such a contingency. I may be able to afford considerably more than can a penniless rooster-crowned by-blow!"

Julien snarled under his breath and put a hand on his sword hilt, but Alexandre swung onto a side street, whistling. Fuming, Julien stared after him, but common sense cautioned him not to abandon his assignment. He could always deal with Alexandre at a later date.

He turned his steps once more in the direction of the L'Anglois home, located nearly a mile from the water's edge, whence he was to deliver his lovely freight. He observed the women from the rear, watching for reactions to their surroundings. The bare bones of a town were lines marked off with flagpoles bravely struggling to stay upright in the face of daily thunderstorms. Still, it would be hard for the uneducated eye to discern order in the muddy streets and thatched cottages built precariously upon stumps in an optimistic attempt to escape the incessant flooding.

At the largest of these homes — and the only one finished — the young soldiers leading the procession halted and turned. The taller of the two presented Dufresne with a smart salute.

The cottage door burst open, spitting out a stout little woman who bowled down the steps and pushed between the two soldiers as if they were a couple of wooden pins. "Oh dear, you are here!" She rolled to a breathless stop before the Gaillain sisters and grabbed a hand of each. "I am Madame L'Anglois, you precious ones! It has been my delight to arrange lodging for you until you are all, shall we say, situated."

The elder of the sisters gave Madame her friendly smile. "We are all grateful to have arrived safe and sound."

Madame L'Anglois made the rounds of the younger women, kissing cheeks, patting hands, and clucking like a biddy. "Come in, come in, and we shall manage a cup of tea, though it's that nasty Indian brew that isn't fit for man nor beast. But here, it's all we have, so I shan't apologize, though I'm sorry as can be."

Duty discharged, Julien called his men to order and bid the women adieu. He caught the eye of Mademoiselle Aimée and smiled, pleased when she blushed and looked away. Clearly he had established himself as a man of importance and authority.

"To the munitions house, boys," he said curtly. "Clean weapons and rearm, then report to mess." Laying a hand on his sword hilt, he executed a smart about-face and headed toward the fort without a backward look at the blonde beauty.

A bit of inattention would do her good.

Mobile village, twelve miles northeast of Fort Louis

The village was quiet this afternoon. Nika sat on the floor of her chickee with Chazeh's sweaty little head in her lap. He had been running a high fever since the day before, and she did not want him out in the sun. The others were all three miles away at Little Cedar creek; the women would be washing their few belongings — clothing, cooking utensils, and pots — while the children swam and splashed one another, practicing shallow dives off the natural bridge formed by a couple of felled water oaks. Chazeh's twin, Tonaw, had begged to go swimming with his cousin Undin, and Nika had gratefully agreed. It was hard enough to keep an active little boy cool and still without his much more aggressive brother wreaking havoc unsupervised.

Maybe she should have taken Chazeh to the creek after all. Its sandy bank was shaded by scrubby overhanging vegetation, and sometimes a waft of breeze penetrated the dense forest. She could have let him lie with his little brown feet in the icy water and giggle at the minnows nibbling his toes.

But Nika's sister-in-law Kumala, mother

of the irrepressible Undin, would ask questions. *Why are you wearing that hot dress on a day like today, Nika? Why don't you leave Chazeh with me for a few minutes and go swimming? What was Mitannu shouting about last night?*

The first two questions had a simple answer, but not one she wished to share with her friend. How Kumala and Mitannu could have come from the same family mystified Nika. Maybe it was simply the difference between male and female: Kumala with her wide smile and incessant talking, interested in everything and everyone, full of advice and recipes and gossip; Mitannu, suspicious of Nika, impatient with the boys and, as the chieftain's son, certain of his superiority over everyone else. He was the best hunter for miles around; thus he was always dressed in beautiful leather breechclout and leggings covered with Nika's fine beadwork, with expensive bells and shells woven into his long hair.

How could she have thought marrying him would rescue her from her dilemma? Yes, her father would have been angry. Perhaps would have beaten her. And she had dreaded disappointing her mother. But nothing could have been worse than almost five years of tiptoeing around Mitannu's temper. Five years of silence.

Chazeh coughed, a thin, rattling sound, and opened his eyes. "Mama, I'm thirsty."

"All right." She reached for a skin of water and trickled a little onto his lips. It was hot inside the chickee, and a fly buzzed with obnoxious busyness against the thatched wall.

Chazeh licked the water off his lips, sighed, and closed his eyes again.

Was his skin the faintest bit yellow? She brushed her thumb over his cheekbone, then his eye socket. The older he and his brother got, the more defined those bones grew. It was a wonder Mitannu hadn't noticed.

She flexed her aching shoulder. Maybe he *had* noticed.

If she had taken off her dress to swim, everyone would have seen, Kumala would have berated her brother when next she saw him, and his resultant anger would have been worse than last night. No. No more swimming until the bruise followed its colorful cycle of purple, black, green, and yellow.

She poured a little water into her hand and sprinkled it over her son's forehead, where the fever burned hottest, a sort of motherly baptism. The thought made her smile. Mitannu had refused to have the boys baptized when the priest named Father Al-Bair had visited in the spring. Mitannu didn't believe in the Frenchmen's crazy Jesus-God as his father did. Nika wanted to believe, but five years of praying to whatever God would listen had done little for her and her two babies.

So she had found another way, and soon she would have enough *sous* to leave for good. She wouldn't get very far now, on the coins hidden in her woman bag. Soon, though. She would miss Kumala and the other women, but she was going to take the boys away from here before it was too late.

Soon.

Tristan waited just inside the door as Marc-Antoine approached his superior officer. Bienville sat hunched, frowning, over a leather-bound book of lading lying open upon the rough table. The commander, though closer in age to Marc-Antoine, had once been Tristan's peer. But Tristan's resignation of his commission in the French army had resulted in the rather uncomfortable situation that Bienville hardly seemed to know how to treat Tristan anymore.

At the sound of Marc-Antoine's boots upon the wooden floor, Bienville looked up.

"Lanier. The women have arrived?"

Marc-Antoine nodded. "The last of them are climbing up the bluff. Don't you want to come out to welcome them?"

Bienville grimaced. "Of course. I was just —" He caught sight of Tristan. "Ah. The *other* Lanier. What brings you here? I wouldn't have thought you interested in French skirts. Your taste has always run to darker meat."

Tristan felt the hair rise on the back of his neck. "Your choice of phrasing, as always, Commander, is so refined." He met his brother's alarmed gaze with a shrug. "But, no, as you say, French skirts are not in my purview. I bring news from the upper river."

Bienville rose carefully, one hand pressed to his abdomen, indicating some injury. "And how would you know what's going on upriver?"

"As you well know, I maintain relationships with Sholani's people. My sources of information don't depend on kegs of ale."

Bienville scowled at Tristan for a moment. "If you say so." He fell back into his chair, grimacing.

"Is the stomach cyst still bothering you, sir?" Marc-Antoine took a worried step toward the commander.

Bienville stopped him with a raised hand.

"The pain comes and goes. I can stand it. What is important enough to bring you two in to interrupt me on the most auspicious day the colony has enjoyed in months?"

The arrogant swine. Tristan figured he should take his information back to his plantation and let Bienville fend for himself. But that would leave his own brother vulnerable as well — not to mention the women who had just arrived at the settlement. He reined in his impatience. "The British recently sent agents to the Koroa village and bought peace with them."

"*Bought* peace? The Koroa aren't stupid enough to believe the English will honor friendship sold at the price of a few beads and trinkets."

Tristan refrained from pointing out the irony of that statement. "It's more than trinkets. The Koroa are now armed with muskets and powder. If they can defend themselves against slave-takers and hunt meat for themselves, they'll become aggressive against our own Mobile and Alabama villages." He glanced at Marc-Antoine. *Jump in here anytime, brother.*

Marc-Antoine visibly gathered himself. "And, Commander, it seems the British have promised them more. More bread, more arms, and yes, more trinkets — if the

Koroa will break trade relations with us."

Bienville slammed a hand on the table. "They wouldn't dare."

"Yes. They would." Tristan no longer chafed under the hotheaded commander's authority, obliged to walk the thin line between obedience and truth. "The Koroa are just restless and bored enough to listen to those redcoat mercenaries. We have to do something."

Bienville's lip curled. "If you think I'll authorize emptying our warehouse and arsenal in some insane bribery competition —"

"No such thing." Tristan inclined his head toward his brother. "I suggest you use your biggest asset to create a peaceful coalition among the Koroa, the Choctaw, and the Chickasaw."

There was a moment of stunned silence before Bienville sputtered, "You think we can forge peace among three of the most contentious tribes in New France?"

Tristan nodded. "Send Marc-Antoine and let him take along a priest as a sign of good faith — but show strength with a small armed contingent."

Marc-Antoine was savvy enough to address his commander with respect. "What do you think, sir? We've got to find some way to control the influence of the British and keep them out of our territory."

Bienville rubbed his midsection. "I can't spare you. You're my best interpreter."

"Sir, you speak the languages almost as well as I do now." Marc-Antoine smiled. "You don't need an interpreter."

Tristan nodded. "Besides, I can't believe you'd expose those young women to attack and do nothing to prevent it." He knew he risked piquing Bienville's notorious stubborn streak, but the time for silence had passed.

"It could work." Bienville struggled to his feet again. "But for now, as you say, I must welcome our arrivals." Sweating with the obvious effort to hide his pain, he glowered at Tristan. "The two of you keep your brilliant plan to yourselves until I determine if I can spare enough men to accompany the expedition." He skewered Marc-Antoine with a look. "Is that clear?"

Bienville had conceded more than expected. Marc-Antoine responded with a salute, while Tristan simply nodded. He could depend on his brother's genius for good-natured common sense. The commander would come around — hopefully sooner than later.

4

The fort's tiny chapel, in which Élisabeth le Pinteaux was joined by rite of holy matrimony to locksmith Paul Loisel, reminded Geneviève of nothing so much as a chicken coop riding upon a set of stumps. Constructed of pine slats pegged together with wooden dowels, minimally protected from the weather by a soggy thatched roof, and subject to marauding mosquitoes and roaches through its uncovered doors and windows, the little room was barely big enough to hold the bridal couple and Father Henri, plus a handful of witnesses roosting upon overturned boxes like so many brooding hens.

Two days after their arrival at the fort, Geneviève sat in a place of honor near the front, along with Aimée and six other young women sufficiently recovered from the fever. She felt like the heroine of some macabre miracle play. A scant twenty-four hours ago, funeral rites for her friend Louise Lefevre had been conducted in this very building. Poor Louise had endured that miserable journey in hopes of becoming a bride, only to succumb to the fever yesterday morning. The funeral mass and burial had been conducted in such brisk, almost matter-of-fact fashion, by fat Father Henri, that Geneviève concluded that survival in this place must be more the exception than the norm.

Dear God, your purposes are so very strange. What if it had been me they'd hammered into that coffin and lowered into the marshy ground? What would have become of my sister?

Geneviève glanced at Aimée, seated to her left, hands clasped in her lap, feet tucked under the ragged hem of her dress. Her blue eyes were trained on the bridal couple, her lips moving in unison with every word of the priest's reading. Perhaps she imagined the day she would take a husband and become mistress of her own home.

Perhaps they *all* did. Geneviève felt the eyes of the male congregants burning into the back of her head. In fact, her every move seemed strange and awkward, since it was guaranteed to draw attention. It was a mortifying sensation.

61

Her glance cut to the other end of the pew. Françoise Dubonnier, self-appointed "governess superior," clearly entertained no such qualms. The lovely spinster's auburn hair, dressed with stacks of curls and ribbons arranged over a tall wire frame, blocked the view of the ceremony for anyone unfortunate enough to be seated behind her. A tiny, heart-shaped patch kissed the corner of her lips with seductive intent.

It was said that Françoise remained intimate friends with the King's ex-mistress, Madame de Montespan. Perhaps in Paris one could dress like a courtesan and maintain an image of decorum, but what about the contract all the women had signed before leaving France? More to the point, how had Françoise contrived to transport such finery all the way from Rochefort in the small quarters allotted aboard the *Pélican*? Geneviève herself owned only one other dress besides the one she wore.

"You have declared your consent before the Church," Father Henri intoned, drawing Geneviève's attention back to the ceremony. "May the Lord in his goodness strengthen your consent and fill you both with his blessings. What God has joined, men must not divide. Amen." The priest took bride and groom by the hand and turned them to face the congregation. "I present to you Madame and Monsieur Loisel. Go in peace, children."

As Geneviève rose with the other witnesses, emotion tightened her throat. She had traveled a long way in search of peace. Could it be found in this land of exile?

"If one more cabbage head refers to me as a '*Pélican* girl,' " Aimée said loudly as the congregation burst from the chapel and spilled onto the muddy drill ground, "I'm going to sprout feathers and peck his eyes out!" She paused to tweak the ivory lace fichu crisscrossed at her neckline, artfully exposing a more generous hint of cleavage.

"Shh! A little discretion!" Geneviève pulled her aside, frowning at the fichu.

Aimée sniffed as she restored herself to reluctant modesty. "Françoise says there are only three or four men of any substantial means in the entire settlement — and two of those aren't even here. They've gone off hunting or exploring or some such nonsense. She thinks we should wait until we've had a chance to meet them all before choosing a husband."

Geneviève chose to ignore her sister's budding hauteur, as anything that would prevent her from a hasty marriage must be a good thing. "How does Françoise know

63

which men are of substantial means?" She linked arms with Aimée and moved with the flow of celebrants toward the fort's main entrance. All had been invited to enjoy refreshments in the L'Anglois home.

"She knows who to ask questions of, and what questions to ask." Aimée glanced at the governess, who strolled along, a few feet ahead, in animated conversation with pudgy little Madame L'Anglois. "She says Commander Bienville is the finest catch of them all, and that he has not yet married because he wants a wife of noble blood."

Geneviève laughed. "Which lets you and me out of the running! Had you aspired to becoming the mistress of the entire settlement?" she added teasingly.

"I don't know why I should not!" Aimée flicked one of her golden ringlets behind her shoulder. "The commander is of a fine Canadian family and already owns what will become a sizable estate here — plus he has the ear of Monsieur Pontchartrain, who has the ear of the King himself. Françoise says his income is twelve hundred *livres* per year." She glanced at Geneviève, a defiant tilt to her small dimpled chin. "And he is quite handsome, in spite of those horrible tattoos."

"Not so loud!" Geneviève glanced around,

then whispered, "How do you know he has tattoos? Did Françoise tell you that too?"

"I saw it myself," Aimée said with relish. "I went out early this morning for . . . well, you know why. Anyway, I chanced to see the commander and some of his men coming from the direction of the river. I was back in the bushes, of course, so they didn't see me. They were quite loud, and I had . . . you know, finished, so I peeked out."

"What if they had seen you? You must never go without me again!"

"I was perfectly safe, so there!" Aimée snapped her fingers and grinned. "Commander Bienville has very broad shoulders. He had removed his tunic because they had been bathing — they were all dripping like fish — and I couldn't help staring at the pictures all over his back. Crazy jagged lines and a bird in flight under a crescent moon — I think. It might have been a monkey."

Geneviève didn't know whether to laugh or to strangle her hopelessly naïve little sister.

Before she had time to do either, Madame L'Anglois looked over her shoulder and caroled, "Ladies! Young ladies! I wish you to come this way! I have refreshments for everyone at my home."

Curious as to the nature of refreshments

in such a distant outpost, Geneviève allowed Aimée to pull her along willy-nilly in the wake of the hostess and found herself just behind the newly married couple. Élisabeth, tall and willowy in her gray kersey gown, a fistful of yellow wildflowers pinned at the waist, kept up a giddy spate of conversation with her red-faced bridegroom, trundling beside her like a wagon with a broken axle. Geneviève had been present at the betrothal agreement, when five eager couples had signed a series of documents joining their lives and estates. The legalities had been overseen by the three priests, Father Albert, Father Henri, and Father Mathieu, with Françoise keeping an eagle eye out for the women's protection and provision. Three of the prospective brides were illiterate; each document must be read aloud in its entirety before the young lady fixed a large *X* on the signature blank. Geneviève, who had learned her letters from Jean Cavalier, couldn't help being grateful that there was no danger of her or Aimée being taken advantage of.

"My mother would like to immigrate next spring. She will help with the children."

Geneviève blinked, jerked out of her thoughts. At first she had the crazy notion Paul Loisel's deep, shy voice had been directed to her, then realized that he was looking up at his open-mouthed bride.

"What children?" Élisabeth finally managed to stammer.

"The — the fruit of our union!" Loisel's square face was nearly as painfully red as his waistcoat. "I want an heir or two, and you will need girls to help in the house. I can't afford slaves, you know."

"Slaves?" Élisabeth's voice was a squeak of confusion. "I don't understand. What does this have to do with your mother?"

Geneviève quelled Aimée's giggle with a frown, but couldn't help listening.

Loisel gave his young wife a strained smile. "I came from Quebec with several other men, on the promise of rich estates with tobacco fields, fine houses, and a clutch of Indian slaves. The reality has been . . . less than promised." He sighed. "But Bienville convinced us that it was but a matter of time before women would flock to the New World from France. We would shortly be married, producing sons and daughters to people our estates. So we stayed, making the best of a difficult situation." He smiled, squeezing Élisabeth's hand. "And here you are. My lady, my *Pélican* girl."

Élisabeth gave him a blank look, swallowed, and kept walking.

"Cabbage head," Aimée muttered.

Tristan picked up one of Madame L'Anglois's sadly flat pastries and with a grimace put the whole thing into his mouth. It was the first Christian wedding he had attended since emigrating from Canada, and the jostling crowd made him long for the quiet solitude of his estate on the lower bluff.

The bland pastry made him miss Sholani. Her corn bread had been famous throughout the Indian villages from the northern Little Tomeh to the nearby Pascagoula, from whence he had plucked her as a sixteen-year-old virgin beauty. She had been gone for two years now, and he could get through most days without thinking of her. Sometimes, though, he felt her absence with a visceral ache.

"I'm surprised to see you still here, Lanier. You usually scuttle back to your little sand castle the moment business is concluded."

Tristan turned to find Nicolas de La Salle perusing the victual offerings at the other end of Madame L'Anglois's imported buffet. He could not understand why everyone was so surprised to find him lingering at the settlement. True, he had not stayed for more than a day since Sholani's death, but before that he had been Bienville's right-hand man. And would be still, had he not decided to trade his plot of swampy Louisiane ground and move closer to his wife's family.

Ignoring the master supply officer's sour comment, he allowed his gaze to sweep the bevy of young women fluttering amongst the men like parakeets. He would dearly love to have had a pencil and sheet of parchment in his hand and make a sketch. "Perhaps one of these ladies will be lucky enough to capture the hand of the settlement's most eligible bachelor — excepting Bienville himself, of course. Does the commissary see anything he likes?"

"My choice has long been made." La Salle's face settled into the habitual frown that had plowed a permanent line between his graying eyebrows. "Bienville agreed that, my comfort being critical to the smooth flow of commodities in and out of the settlement, the appropriate female should be set aside for me before the *Pélican* left France."

"How very obliging of him." Tristan hid his amusement by focusing on the dark crown of Geneviève Gaillain's head, which towered above the other women. She had unsuccessfully tamed her hair for the occasion into a loose knot from which dark curls escaped in every direction. It occurred to him that she bore an uncanny resemblance to the mermaid he had carved at the bowsprit of his barque. He glanced at La Salle. "Which one is yours?" Poor woman, traveling for months across the ocean blue, only to find herself strapped for life to Sourpuss La Salle.

"Her name is Jeanne de Berenhardt," La Salle replied. "She was chosen for me from the convent at Notre Dame, by the Grand Duchess d'Orleans of Tuscany herself."

Tristan followed La Salle's oddly pained gaze to the far corner of the crowded salon, where a statuesque young woman held court, dressed in a black silk skirt under a burnt orange coat-looking garment, belted with a black sash. Her boned corset was so stiff that when she dropped a dried plum on the floor, all she could do was stare at it in chagrin. Bending at the waist was clearly an impossible feat.

When no less than three men lunged to retrieve the escaped fruit, Tristan smiled. If La Salle remained less than impressed, there would appear to be a long line waiting to take his place. "Have your sons met their proposed step-mama?" Less than a month after their arrival in Louisiane, La Salle's first wife had died of a fever, leaving him with three young boys to rear alone. Tristan could only imagine the state of wildness poor Mademoiselle de Berenhardt would face when she took them in hand.

"I did not think it wise to introduce them to the lady so soon." A flash of fear — or perhaps guilt — humanized La Salle's hawkish visage. "Time enough for that after the betrothal contract is signed."

"Your reputation for clear thinking is well-founded." Grinning at La Salle's humorless grunt, Tristan turned to watch his brother dancing a rather clumsy jig with Aimée Gaillain.

If she had been lovely on the day of her arrival, pale-faced and limp with fever, today she was aglow, cheeks flushed from exertion and golden curls bouncing against her shoulders. She danced, hands fisted at her narrow waist to lift her skirts away from dainty flying feet.

The violinist, master of the house Robert L'Anglois, fiddled with more enthusiasm than skill, while a circle of guests clapped time. Though a noticeable air of inebriation pervaded the company, Tristan suspected his brother's giddy state could be attributed as much to his partner's blue eyes and bouncing bosom as the liberal lacing of liquor in the punch.

He stood against the wall and observed for a minute or so, reluctant to call attention to himself. Then he happened to catch the eye of Geneviève Gaillain, who had been watching her sister dance, her expression a mixture of pride and alarm. When he unthinkingly smiled, something he would almost call relief flooded her cheeks with color.

Do not approach her, he told himself sternly, even as his feet took him in a circuitous route to the other side of the crowded room. The L'Anglois family's house had been designed in typical box-shaped fashion, with one big front room and two small bedrooms behind, one of which doubled as the kitchen. It was one of the largest homes in the settlement, but the wedding crowd seemed about to burst the crooked knotty pine walls. Tristan compared it to his own cottage, constructed Canadian-style from shingled cedar. His furniture, simple and homemade, was designed for comfort and durability rather than beauty, but he wouldn't have traded it for Madame's fragile French furniture.

He hung back for a moment, just outside Geneviève's line of vision, watching her watch her sister. Her patent anxiety stirred something odd within him, something he could not name, but which drew him all the same. He had not seen her since handing her off his boat two days ago. She looked considerably more rested, the greenish eyes bright, her smile mischievous as he approached. He bowed, resisting the urge to kiss her hand.

"One would think that a wedding would be the last place to find the most confirmed bachelor in the territory," she said, laughing.

"Mademoiselle, I brave the gravest of dangers on the mere promise of food." He glanced at the refreshment table and gave an exaggerated grimace. "Though I confess, the reality doesn't quite measure up to expectation."

"If you are referring to the croissants," she leaned in to whisper, "I'm afraid I have to agree with you. Poor Madame L'Anglois is very kind, but she has no concept of the proper use of leavening."

"As do you?"

She shrugged. "My papa was a renowned pastry chef. He allowed me to assist before he was —" she bit her lip — "before he died."

Tristan waited for her to elaborate, but apparently the confidence was at an end. In spite of himself, curiosity bloomed. "And what was the secret of the leavening?"

She gave him another quick grin. "Ah, but if I told you, then it would no longer be a secret, eh?"

"Touché, mademoiselle." Amused, he laid a hand over his heart. "At least promise you'll give me a taste of the product of this secret. I've just bought two barrels of flour, and I'll pay you handsomely to turn some of it into real croissants."

"Now that is an intriguing offer. Unfortunately, my sister and I are guests of the L'Anglois family at present. I don't have access to my own kitchen." She tipped her head, thinking. "But if Madame will allow me to use her oven, perhaps we might come to some arrangement."

Briefly, ridiculously, he thought she might be hinting at a more permanent agreement, one which would involve the exchange of vows they had both just witnessed. Then common sense returned. There was nothing about him — exiled, bitter, old before his time — to attract the favor of any woman, let alone one such as this.

Then he realized that he had hesitated just a moment too long.

Her bright expression clouded with embarrassment, the beautiful full lips pressed together. "I am sorry, I didn't mean —"

"No — I mean, yes, that's what I meant!" Tristan wished wildly that he'd sailed with the morning tide; he'd be halfway home by now, instead of trading awkward half-sentences with this too-beautiful, secretive *Pélican* girl. "Please forgive me, I must speak to my brother!" With a jerky bow, he stalked toward Marc-Antoine and pulled him, protesting loudly, from the room. He could feel Geneviève Gaillain's puzzled green eyes following him all the way.

"Mademoiselle Gaillain, I would be honored if you would partner with me in the next dance."

Monsieur Dufresne gave Aimée an elegant bow, and she dipped a curtsey in return. She was pleased at his attention, though she must reserve judgment as to his prospects as a suitor until she had been introduced to the other eligible bachelors of the settlement. One could not be too careful.

The aide-major offered his arm and a self-possessed smile just as Monsieur L'Anglois broke into an unsteady passepied. When she placed her gloved hand upon his blue coat sleeve, he whisked her into the patterns of the dance. She couldn't resist a triumphant smile at Geneviève, who was fending off the awkward advances of three or four Canadian bumpkins. Monsieur Dufresne was a much better catch than any of them.

Now that the dreadful ennui of the fever had passed, and the sensation of walking upon a heaving landscape was merely an unpleasant memory, she thought she could make a sensible decision regarding matrimony. Dufresne had risen near the top of her list but, despite Geneviève's pessimistic assumptions, Commander Bienville — wild and tattooed though he might be — remained her first choice.

Above the tweedling of Monsieur L'Anglois's violin, she could hear Bienville's uninhibited laughter. As she and Monsieur Dufresne glided up and back, feet crossing and recrossing quickly, through the crowd she caught glimpses of the commander's dark head and broad shoulders. He seemed to dwarf every other man in the room. She could easily envision herself as the mistress of his estate, with large numbers of slaves to fetch and carry for her. It was said that Bienville bedded his female slaves . . .

The moment the thought crossed her mind, she choked on a wave of nausea. She shut her eyes against ghastly, suffocating images.

You are not that powerless girl, she told herself frantically. *You are young and beauti-*

ful. You are free, and you can choose.

"Ahem."

Wrenching her eyes open with a gasp, Aide-Major Dufresne's face came into focus. She couldn't tell if he was more amused or indignant at her obvious wool-gathering. He seemed to be clever at masking his true feelings.

"I'm sorry, monsieur, did you say something?"

"No, mademoiselle, but I am concerned for your sudden pallor. Are you feeling ill?" He took her hand and drew her toward a couple of spindly chairs against the wall — away from the commander and his retinue of officers. "Perhaps you would like to sit for a moment and rest?"

Biting her lip, she plied her fan to mask her discomfiture. "I am well, sir. But if you would procure me a cup of punch, I would be grateful."

"Of course." He turned and repaired to Madame's bounteous if boring refreshment table.

In truth, she had a bit of a headache, and the crush of bodies with all their odors and noise made it worse. How many evenings on board the *Pélican* had she longed for just such a party? It went to prove how seldom reality lived up to one's expectations.

The fan fell to her lap as the crowd shifted and her gaze picked out Marc-Antoine Lanier, who had asked her for a dance with gratifying swiftness upon her arrival. Now there was an interesting man, handsome and cheerful of countenance, well-spoken and clearly admiring of her beauty. Her first impulse had been to fix his obvious interest. But perhaps the wiser move would be to play him and Dufresne against the commander. Men were such competitive creatures.

Geneviève would be shocked to discover how much her little sister had learned about the ways of the world while aboard the *Pélican*. Indeed her childhood had ended, in many ways, when Papa had so foolishly defied the King, putting his religious beliefs ahead of protecting his wife and daughters. Aimée had no intention of allowing herself to be subject to the whims of any man, ever again.

5

Geneviève and Aimée shared the L'Anglois family's second bedroom with Madame's ten-year-old Indian slave, Raindrop. Her Apalacheee name had apparently gotten lost in translation when Robert L'Anglois purchased her from her family four years ago for the price of a cow, three knives, and a Turkish rug.

Raindrop seemed not to mind the new houseguests. Dressed in a shapeless gray homespun shift with legs and feet bare, she helped the sisters settle their few belongings, reverently touching Aimée's full-skirted dress with her pink mouth drawn into an *O* of admiration.

Two days after the Le Pinteaux-Loisel wedding, she was helping Geneviève stuff pine straw into blankets brought from Rochefort, all the while chattering in perfect French. Her dark eyes sparkled as she showed Geneviève how to treat the blankets with oil of lemon grass to discourage mosquitoes.

Geneviève found the little girl an amusing fount of information.

"Madame says you are going to get married and make babies for me to help care for." Raindrop wrinkled her nose. "I don't know why Madame has no babies herself, she's not *that* old. My mother had twelve, but the last two got the fever and died before they were a week old." She paused, frowning, both hands buried in a pile of pine straw. "That was after the black robes came to live in our village and brought the baptism. Perhaps baptism is not good for little babies."

"Perhaps." Geneviève had never before met a slave — or anyone who owned one, for that matter. She looked around to make sure Madame and Aimée were occupied in the other room. "Do your mother and father not try to bring you back home?" She had seen half-naked Indian men squatting here and there, smoking their funny clay pipes or tossing knives — apparently some game that involved gambling with tiny bells and seashells. There were no Indian families in the settlement, save three or four young slaves like Raindrop and a handful of women who served as housekeepers to the officers.

Raindrop's eyes widened. "Why would they do that? They love me very much and want me to learn from Madame! And if I am good, Monsieur sends a piglet to my father every Christmas."

Geneviève pursed her lips. It was a very strange world, where parents sold their children into slavery and priests rescued infants from hell by freezing them in cold water.

She finished the last seam of Aimée's pallet and bit off the thread. "Would you like to learn how to make bread, Raindrop?" As promised, on the morning after the wedding, Tristan Lanier had sent a barrel of flour to Madame's house with instructions for Geneviève to bake as many loaves as she had time for. He would retrieve them in two days' time before he pointed his barque toward home.

"Madame taught me already." Raindrop scrunched her button nose. "I don't like bread."

Geneviève laughed. "Perhaps my bread is a little different from Madame's."

"Raindrop!" Madame poked her head into the bedroom. "I want you to run and fetch the surgeon to the Loisels' house, and probably — yes, definitely bring Father Henri too. Tell them Madame Loisel is very ill.

Geneviève, I want you to come with me. Élisabeth is asking for you."

While Raindrop pattered from the room, Geneviève rose and put on her cap. Stomach knotted with worry, she followed Madame, picking her way around standing puddles of water in a vain effort to keep her feet dry. Madame's protests notwithstanding, rain seemed to be more the norm than the exception in Louisiane. Geneviève was beginning to feel rather froggish.

Whimsically imagining webs growing between her fingers and toes, she barely acknowledged Jean Alexandre's bashful greeting as he fell into step with her and Madame. But when he stepped squarely into a muddy patch, splashing her skirt, stockings, and shoes, she halted, unable to restrain a startled gasp. She stared in dismay as his large boots sucked clear of the mud one at a time, sending yet another double spray of goop her way.

"Sorry, mademoiselle!" The crimson-faced Alexandre seemed about to cast himself to his knees until Madame intervened, wagging a plump finger in his face.

"Monsieur Alexandre, you will please take yourself somewhere more useful. Mademoiselle Gaillain and I have no time at the moment for entertaining louts with feet the size of gunboats."

"But I only wanted to ask the favor of her company —"

"That is exactly what I mean!" Madame clapped her hands, then shooed him away like a mosquito. "If you want to be helpful, go ask Father Henri and Father Albert to pray." She took Geneviève by the arm and left the young mason to skulk away.

Geneviève struggled to keep up with her chaperone's balletic navigation of the muddy yard. "Really, Madame — gunboats? That seems excessively cruel."

"Pooh!" Madame waved a hand and skipped over a pool of water. "Jean Alexandre is like to propose to the first thing in skirts that crosses his path — no offense to you, my dear. His wife died nearly a year ago, and he has been like a lost lamb without her. You can do much better than him!"

Geneviève hardly thought it modest to agree. "He seems like a very nice man. And he couldn't have avoided that puddle without building a bridge!"

"Never mind. He will approach you in a much more seemly manner next time."

By this time, the two women had arrived at the Loisels' small cottage. Built of wooden timbers set directly into the ground, filled in with an oyster-shell-and-mud cement that the locals called tabby, it sat back several yards from the street.

Madame knocked upon the yellow pine door. "Paul! Élisabeth! I have sent for the surgeon, my dears, and I have brought your friend Geneviève to attend you."

There was a long moment of silence. "Perhaps we should knock again," Geneviève said. "Maybe they didn't hear you —"

But a set of slow, heavy footfalls preceded the reluctant opening of the door. The moment Paul Loisel's pale, red-eyed features appeared, Geneviève knew they had arrived too late.

"I am sorry, madame, mademoiselle," he said, voice raspy with restrained tears. "I — could not save her."

Geneviève reached for his large, shaking hands. "Ah, monsieur, I am so sorry." His marriage had been so very brief, but his joy had seemed intense.

He gripped her fingers. "Will you come in and attend her? I don't know what to do."

Geneviève and Madame followed Loisel into the house and found Élisabeth lying face-up on a pallet near the door, her hands folded neatly at her waist. Her simple white nightgown and cap, both trimmed with Alençon lace and almost transparent with perspiration, clung to the pitifully thin body. When Geneviève knelt beside her friend to close the staring eyes, she heard Loisel sigh behind her.

"How long ago, monsieur?" She brought up the coverlet to protect Élisabeth's modesty.

"I don't know. Madame? Shortly after you left . . ." His voice broke.

"I wouldn't have left," Madame said, "but I thought the surgeon should come" — she turned to Geneviève — "and I knew you'd done some nursing with the Sisters aboard ship. Both of them are still ill themselves."

"I did. But once yellow fever takes hold, it's almost sure to return." Geneviève looked at Loisel. "Élisabeth wanted very much to be married. You made her so happy." Propriety forbade touching him again, though she longed to comfort him.

He walked to the open window and leaned on the sill. "The fever came back so suddenly. No time to send for one of the priests . . . last rites . . . she's gone now, gone, and it's too late. I don't know how to pray."

"The Father already knows how you hurt," Geneviève said around the knot in her throat.

He looked over his shoulder, despair

clouding his eyes. "I told you, Father Henri never came. It's too late."

This was no time to argue over heaven, purgatory, and eternal damnation. "I meant your heavenly Father. Even Jesus wept when his friend Lazarus died."

Loisel frowned. "I don't know what good weeping will do."

Madame L'Anglois insinuated her pudgy little person between Geneviève and the widower. "Clearly there is nothing else for us to do here. We mustn't interfere in spiritual matters we know nothing about." She grimaced at Loisel. "Surgeon-Major Barraud will be here soon with Father Mathieu." She gave Geneviève a hand and pulled her to her feet. "Come on."

But just then a loud male voice, overlaid with a child's soprano and a third unidentifiable murmur, carried from the direction of the street. "I tol' you this is a waste of time," the speaker declared in slurred tones as heavy footsteps clomped across the wooden portico. "If she's got the fever again, all we can do is keep her comf'ble and wait it out."

"Monsieur!" came Raindrop's carrying little voice. "Wait! You're going to miss the —" A loud crash was followed by confused voices, a string of vigorous curses, and

86

Raindrop's giggles. "I'm sorry, Father, but he's so funny with his hat upside-down!"

Madame jerked open the door and gaped at the Indian child and lanky, black-robed Father Mathieu struggling to hoist a uniformed officer to his feet.

"Hey, Loisel!" bellowed the physician, a curly-haired fellow of some thirty or forty years — it was hard to tell, due to the black tricorn crammed down over his ears wrong side out. "Tell this black crow to let go! He shoved me down the stairs!" The officer attempted to dislodge his escorts.

Father Mathieu, red-faced with disgust, hauled Barraud to his feet. Raindrop ran past him up the steps and started to fling her arms around Madame, but the matron held her at a safe distance.

"Mercy, child, your hands are filthy! Wait here on the porch while I talk to Father Mathieu and the —" Madame paused, eyeing the swaying doctor — "Monsieur Barraud." She stepped back to allow the men to enter as Raindrop dropped cross-legged onto the wooden porch. "I'm afraid you're too late. Where is Father Henri?"

"With another family." The Jesuit took Loisel's hands. "When the child explained the situation, I came, thinking perhaps you wouldn't mind the offices of a stranger.

Where is your wife?"

Speechless, the poor man's red-rimmed eyes watered again.

"Élisabeth's body is here, Father." Geneviève glanced toward the still form at the back of the room. "She died just before Madame and I arrived."

Expression compassionate, Father Mathieu knelt by the body with a faint grunt of discomfort. Geneviève knew the heat and humidity had worsened the aches in his joints. He crossed himself and closed his eyes. "We beseech Thee, O Lord, in Thy mercy, to have pity on the soul of thy handmaid; do thou, who hast freed her from the perils of this mortal life, restore to her the portion of everlasting salvation. Through Christ our Lord, amen." Opening his eyes, he pulled a small brown vial from his pocket, uncorked it, and overturned it against a callused finger. He pressed his finger to Élisabeth's forehead, chin, and both cheeks.

As the sweet aroma of the oil overpowered the odors of illness and death, Loisel uttered a choked sob.

"Doubt there was anything else I could've done," the surgeon-major said, wandering over to peer at the deceased woman. He picked up her wrist, found no pulse, and dropped it. He gave Geneviève a charming if inebriated smile. "Would you like to get married, my dear? I have quite a neat little house next to the surgery."

She stared at him, robbed of words. "I beg your pardon?"

"I said —"

"I know what you *said*. I mean, have you taken leave of your senses? My friend has just died, and this is — this is hardly the appropriate occasion for a marriage proposal!"

Barraud shrugged. "No time like the present, I always say. The pig who's present gets the slops." He grinned. "I hope you'll keep me in mind. But you'd better hurry, because there aren't many officers still unattached." He turned to the priest, who had struggled to his feet. "Which reminds me, Father, it seems you and I'll be accompanying Captain Lanier to parlay with the upriver Indians. A man of medicine and a man of prayer — all eventualities covered, eh?"

Geneviève's outrage evaporated. Father Mathieu was leaving the settlement already? The priest was her friend, her protector. Why hadn't he told her? Did he not trust her? "Upriver? This is very sudden, Father. When will you go?"

"As soon as provisions can be pulled

together. We wait upon the arrival of the supply ship that was to follow the *Pélican*. She should arrive in a few weeks." Mathieu's smile for Geneviève was apologetic. "I'll be back before you know it."

"But, Father — !"

"I know you worry for your little sister, Ginette. Perhaps it will be best if neither of you makes any life-altering decisions while I am gone." A smile tugged at the priest's lips as his wry glance flicked to Barraud.

Geneviève couldn't help returning the smile. "Little danger on that score, Father. But . . . I hadn't realized you might take up a new mission so soon."

The priest cast a sympathetic look at the grieving widower. "Father Albert and Father Henri are capable of tending the flock here. You know our order's passion for evangelizing. Someone must go and tell the heathen the good news." He didn't meet her eyes.

Father Mathieu would not lie to her, but there was something he would not say in front of the others.

Barraud puffed out his chest. "Someone has to try to talk sense into the savages. The only law they understand is 'Blood must be avenged by blood.' Bienville says the British have been stirring the Indians in the north into raiding the southern villages."

Geneviève nodded, wondering why Barraud would be chosen for such an important diplomatic mission. If she hoped to make sense of the undercurrents rippling below the colony's surface, she had best begin to wade in a little deeper.

"Monsieur Barraud," she said, "perhaps there is something I could do to assist you in preparing Madame Loisel for burial?"

Mitannu had been gone for six days, during which time Chazeh recovered from his fever and Nika's bruised shoulder faded to a pale yellow. Camouflaging that with a judicious application of dye made from mashed and soaked sumac pods, she was able to join Kumala and the children for a swim in the creek.

Floating on her back in shallow water while the boys swam and splashed nearby, enjoying their squeals and shouts, she looked up at the soft clouds drifting overhead. Soon she would have to dress and return home to prepare the evening meal.

The water behind her rippled and sloshed, and a shadow fell across her face. She sat up, and as the water dripped from her ears, she realized the children had fallen into frightened silence. She turned.

Mitannu stood thigh-deep in the cold

water, his arms folded across his big bronze chest. He was still painted for hunting, and he smelled like a week without a bath. She made herself meet his eyes.

Contempt froze his expression. "I have been gone for six days, hunting for the food in your pot, and come back to find you floating like a dead fish in the creek."

She flinched, and Kumala, sitting on the bank nursing her baby, gasped. But at least he didn't hit her.

Stung, Nika reached for her pride. "The work is all done. The boys and I just wanted a short —"

"I don't want to hear excuses. You are the laziest woman in the village. I don't know why my father thought an Alabaman, especially of the Kaskaskian village, would be suitable for the chief's son." When she didn't answer, merely stared at him in resentment, he jerked his chin toward the shore, where a deer carcass lay on a litter. "Come and see the most valuable trophy I brought back." He wheeled and sloshed out of the creek, cuffing one of the boys across the back of the head on the way past. Tonaw laughed, but she wasn't at all sure the blow had been affectionate.

Nika slowly followed, avoiding Kumala's anxious eyes. There was nothing her friend could do to help. When she stepped out of the water, Chazeh grabbed her hand as if to follow. "Go play," she told him sharply, somehow sure that Mitannu had something unpleasant in mind. Chazeh reluctantly dropped her hand and plopped back down onto the bank. He was quickly absorbed in chasing minnows. Relieved, Nika swallowed her apprehension and walked toward her husband, who was kneeling at the litter, riffling through the hunting bag she had woven last winter. It was one of her most beautiful designs, the fibers and colors carefully chosen, the dyes pure and strong.

She stood watching him, her hands loosely linked in front. He was a handsome man, his hair and skin healthy and his profile clean and strong. It was the custom of the Mobile clan for the men to pluck their beards, so his angular chin always seemed to jut cruelly.

She searched herself for pride in his strength. All she felt was a knot in her stomach.

He found what he was looking for and tossed the bag aside, then rose with a fluid movement. In his fist was some kind of dead animal.

She blinked. Not an animal. A clutch of human scalps. She looked up at Mitannu.

The practice of scalp hunting was not unheard-of, though their clan did not often resort to it. The Mobile were a generally agrarian band, far enough south that the more warlike northern clans left them alone.

Mitannu shook the scalps at her like a dog with a bone. "For these, the French will pay in powder — great amounts of powder — ammunition for hunting." He gave her a slow grin. "Do you recognize the beading and feathers?"

Horror-stricken, she couldn't look away. Her head moved back and forth in negation, but of course she recognized the dressing of those hair locks.

Alabaman. Kaskaskian.

Tristan had managed to avoid Geneviève Gaillain for nearly a week, but it was time to return home. He had traded furs, hides, and corn for forged items like hooks, hinges, and knives; and he was bringing home a set of finely constructed cabinets, as well as a table and four chairs the town carpenter had made from timber harvested from his plantation. He had been up since sunrise, loading the barque for the trip downstream. Her shallow hold was full of the provisions he had purchased at Massacre Island, and the new acquisitions from Fort Louis had been crammed into the cabin topside. Fortunately, slipping downstream would take half the time it had required to struggle twenty-seven miles up from the mouth of the bay.

He dumped the last case of farm implements onto the rear deck and paused to wipe his sweaty chest with the shirt he had stripped off a couple of hours ago and left hanging in the cabin window like a flag of surrender to the heat. As he surveyed the crowded deck, his thoughts wheeled in self-disgust. Why had he blurted out that ridiculous request for homemade bread? Where in the name of King Louis's mistress was he going to put it? If he had kept the flour, he could have lived on it for months; as it was, he would be forced to store a quite unnecessary number of French loaves, which would undoubtedly spoil before it could all be eaten.

Perhaps he could give some of it to his Indian neighbors at the Mobile village, but they were going to think he had lost his mind. Or, worse, that he was trying to buy them off for some nefarious reason. He only prayed they wouldn't see through his thin excuses to the truth.

The Frenchwoman had bewitched him.

No, he hastened to correct himself, the

truth was that he had felt sorry for her. Sorry that she was going to have to marry one of the profane, woman-starved young cocked-hats that passed for soldiers here in Bienville's soggy little outpost. Sorry that some tragedy had brought her across an ocean to this alien world.

He spread his feet for balance and looked up at the top of the bluff, where the fort's timbered bastions marched on either side of the gate, its fleur-de-lis stirring in a desultory breeze. The whole fort was succumbing to rot, not two years after the raw timbers had been seated into place. Mildew claimed the outer face of every wall, and every board was spongy to the touch. July had been mercifully dry, at least for the three weeks in the middle of the month, but August promised to lay a pall of heat, moisture, and mosquitoes.

I tried to tell him.

But Bienville never listened to anything he didn't want to hear. He would simply thunder his arguments at greater volume until one had to give up or go deaf.

Desiring to present his best work, Tristan had first shown his initial drawings — carefully executed maps of the Alabama river system — to La Salle. Seated at a drafting table in his warehouse office on the island, the commissioner had pored over the parchments, clicking his tongue as he ran an ink-stained finger over each detail.

"The Indians are lying to Bienville. The settlement would better be located on the lower bluff." He adjusted his wig in that nervous way of his. "I suppose they would have their own reasons for wanting the fort higher up the river."

"I'm afraid you're right," Tristan sighed. "But I can't prove it."

"We'll just have to make a good case. He can't be *that* bullheaded."

But, as Tristan knew all too well, Bienville could and would insist on his own way. The fort had been built to Bienville's specifications at the upper location, while La Salle dug in like a particularly vicious flea under the commander's collar.

It had been a mistake, Tristan now realized, to press La Salle's support. So here he was, cramming supplies onto a too-small boat in preparation for another long season of isolation, while his only brother remained in service to the executor of his exile.

Consoling himself that he no longer had to listen to their sniping and conspiracies, Tristan jumped onto the warped pier that spanned the marsh below the bluff. Wearily he climbed the wooden steps that staggered up from the pier to the landing at the top of the bluff.

There he paused long enough to button his shirt and scrape the mud from his boots. Exile or no, he could pass for civilized when he tried. He almost removed the leather thong that tied his hair back at his nape, but opting for coolness over fashion, he set off at a brisk pace for the fort's main gate, set a scant quarter mile back from the landing.

It was odd to approach the stockade without bracing himself for disaster. The hole in his heart where Sholani had lived seemed to be shrinking to bearable size. Never would he forget her, nor could he forgive those who had taken her. But the hard-won return of sanity had brought with it a watchfulness that would surely protect him from the soft, insidious disease of affection.

At the gate, Tristan saluted a young cadet named Lafleur, who responded with an insolent stare as the gate swung open. Everyone here knew him as Marc-Antoine Lanier's brother and the commander's nemesis. He wasn't sure which gave him the most notoriety.

Whistling, he strode toward the dining hall adjacent to the warehouse, where he found his brother wolfing down a plate full of fried eggs mopped up with a chunk of bread. Marc-Antoine hailed him with a tankard of ale and gestured toward the bench opposite him. "Thought you would be miles downstream by this time, my brother."

"Soon." Tristan straddled the bench and accepted a tankard from a passing adjutant. He grinned as Marc-Antoine stuffed the remainder of the bread into his mouth and blissfully chewed. "I see Mademoiselle Gaillain has been sowing her talents abroad. I hope she hasn't sold off what she promised to me."

Marc-Antoine's eyes twinkled with mischief. "If I'd known she was for sale, I might have put in an earlier bid. Are you taking home a bride after all?"

"Just her bread. And keep your voice down." He looked around and found the handful of men there addressing their food with apparent absorption. "Where is she?" He lifted the tankard to his mouth.

"Who?" Marc-Antoine's expression was innocent.

Tristan cuffed him. "Don't be stupid."

Marc-Antoine laughed. "She's in the kitchen harassing Roy. He can't quite admit that a woman makes better bread than he does."

"It wouldn't take much." Tristan eyed the doorway into the kitchen. If he sought her out, she might assume too much. But he could hardly sit here all day, hoping for a glimpse of the woman. He should have arranged for someone to deliver the bread to his boat. He glanced at his brother, who was openly grinning. "What are your duties today?" he asked, summoning his dignity.

"Translating for some Chickasaw envoys who want to trade pelts for guns." The grin faded as Marc-Antoine shook his head. "The *Pélican* brought Bienville a letter from Pontchartrain, warning him His Majesty is set on protecting the Quebec fur trade. As you said, La Salle watches him like a hawk, but he insists a few pelts here and there can't hurt."

"I wouldn't worry about Bienville. He enjoys walking in quicksand."

Marc-Antoine leaned forward and lowered his voice. "He does. And if anybody understands his weaknesses, I do — but, Tristan, if anything happens to him, this colony will fall apart. Bienville is the only man capable of holding off the British, the Spanish, and the Indians, and keeping the religious from cutting each other's throats. Do you know he deliberately brought over this Jesuit Father Mathieu as chaplain, over Pontchartrain's objections? Father Henri is near apoplectic."

Tristan steepled his fingers against his chin in thought. "I talked with Father Mathieu on the trip upriver last week. He's a good man and seems to have no desire to take Father Henri's place."

"Then why choose him to accompany us into Indian territory on the peace mission?"

"Perhaps because he is neither fat, lame, nor speech deficient."

Marc-Antoine choked on his ale. "Could you be a little more forthright, my brother?"

Tristan shrugged. "You asked."

"I did indeed." Marc-Antoine pushed away from the table. "I just wish you were going with us. Nobody knows the river like you do, and another interpreter wouldn't go amiss."

"Marc-Antoine, I cannot —"

"I know, I know." Marc-Antoine stood up. "You have a garden to harvest and cows to milk. But if you change your mind . . ." He rapped the table with his knuckles. "Kiss the pretty bakery queen for me." He was gone, chuckling, before Tristan could untangle his tongue.

Tristan got to his feet just as a deafening clamor crashed from the kitchen, followed by a woman's shriek. He dropped the tankard and took off running.

Skidding into the kitchen, he found a young Indian wielding a meat cleaver scowling down at a cast-iron kettle lying on its side in front of the fireplace — the obvious source of the crashing noise. The Indian blew on the palm of his free hand as yellowish-white hominy spread in a thick, steaming puddle on the floor.

Geneviève, backed against the far wall, stared with patent horror at the string of scalps hanging at the brave's hip. The cook stood between the woman and the Indian, regarding the mess on the floor with an expression of immense disgust.

Tristan was relieved to see that, for the moment, no one was being murdered. "What's the trouble, Roy?"

"Grits pot fell over. Chief here decided to help himself and got in too big a hurry."

"Is he going to scalp us?" Geneviève's voice was high and breathless.

The cook shook his massive head. "Not if I give him something to eat." Using a wooden-handled pot hook, he lifted the kettle and set it back over the fire. He jerked a thumb toward the countertop. "You taking this bread off my hands, Lanier? Sooner it's gone, the better. Can't keep wandering cadets and savages out of my kitchen."

Tristan glanced at the rows of beautiful brown loaves. "Is that mine?"

Geneviève nodded.

As the Indian stalked toward Tristan, he returned the murderous obsidian stare. He didn't recognize the fellow, but the copper bells and yellow leather bands laced into his hair, as well as the design of his breechclout, were Mobilian.

He extended a civil greeting in the fellow's native tongue, then added, "If those are Alabama scalps, Bienville will buy them."

"It is as you say," the brave answered in his own language. He cast a contemptuous glance at Geneviève. "Crazy white woman." Dropping the cleaver onto a table, he snatched a loaf of bread and slipped out the back door.

Geneviève's light freckles stood out against her pale cheeks as she sagged against the wall. "I was going to give him some bread, but he grabbed the knife and shouted at me. And those horrible scalps . . ." She shuddered. "What is he doing with them?"

How to explain to this sheltered young woman the brutal realities of seizing a territory? Tristan remembered the first time he'd come upon a pile of scalped corpses left behind after the massacre of Irondequoit

Bay. He'd had nightmares for weeks. "Several months ago," he said, picking his words, "the Alabama ambushed a priest and a party of Mobilians who were guiding them up to the Little Tomeh. You've heard the term 'savage law'?" At her jerky nod, he spread his hands. "Bienville insists that we Frenchmen won't be respected as leaders if we don't repay such attacks in kind, so he offered to buy Alabama scalps from our allies."

She pushed away from the wall, her hands clenched the soft white fabric of her apron. "If we behave no differently than the savages, how can we call ourselves a Christian nation?" Accusation flared in the grayish-green eyes. "If we return cruelty for cruelty, massacre for massacre —"

"Lady," Roy interrupted, "life here ain't gonna be all sweet and clean like it was in that convent back in Paris." He ran the flat of his hand along the sideboard, swiping crumbs onto the floor. "Better get used to scalps and bugs and Indians and all kinds of ugly creatures, or you might as well sail back home on the next boat."

The girl's lips parted as she stared at the cook. Tristan halfway expected her to slap him — or to at least defend herself. He knew that many of the *Pélican* girls had escaped difficult if not impossible circumstances in France, else they never would have braved that long, harrowing voyage. He suspected the Gaillain sisters' lives had been harder than most.

Without thinking, he picked up the cleaver abandoned by the Indian and flung it end over end to stick in the table, quivering, right where Roy's middle finger had been three seconds earlier.

The cook leaped backward, stumbling into the puddle of hominy. His feet flew out from under him, and he landed on his rear.

"Some creatures are uglier than others," Tristan said, winking at Geneviève. "I'll take my bread now, if you please."

6

Julien Dufresne, seated at his desk in the outer office of the Le Moyne brothers' warehouse, leaned over his account book as he totaled the receipt column. He wished his father were here to witness the respect with which he had come to be regarded in the settlement. As the commander's accounting officer, second only to La Salle himself, he was privy to exclusive information regarding Bienville's dealings with the local savages, as well as the commander's profits from the sale of His Majesty's surplus supplies.

Interestingly, many of the supplies were not so surplus as Bienville claimed . . . and his profits had climbed to quite eyebrow-raising proportions of late. Not that Julien had any intention of spilling such golden information until the time was right. Besides, he could only admire such enterprising leadership.

For the moment, he was quite content to slip some of those profits into his own pocket and call it a fair exchange.

He looked up as the door opened and one of the savages Bienville was so fond of stalked in. Without a word the man flung a string of scalps onto the account book.

For a stunned moment Julien stared at the tails of long, coarse black hair, still attached to brownish skins curled like dark parchment at the edges. Each lock, he had been told, represented its owner's stolen soul, and Bienville had given clear instructions that only scalps of the warlike northern Alabama tribes were to be treated as bounty. His own scalp prickling, Julien gingerly picked up the leather thong that bound the scalps together and examined the arrangement of hair and decorations. These were definitely Alabama. He made himself count.

After recording the number in his account book, he wiped his pen and looked up at the scowling young Indian. Dressed in the familiar Mobilian breechclout and beads, he stood, arms folded over his sleek brown chest, bare feet spread in an aggressive stance. He smelled like an animal.

Julien had learned enough of the Mobilian tongue to transact business without resorting to a translator. "Ten *ecus* each.

Coins or powder?"

The Indian hesitated, then his mouth tightened. "Powder." He cupped his hand, then showed four fingers.

Julien shook his head once, vehemently, then cupped his own hand. "No, two."

"Three."

Julien pretended to think about it. "Very well. Three." In the account book he wrote *four handfuls powder, worth two hundred ecus.* He would sell the extra powder off the books and pocket fifty *ecus* from the transaction. "Name?"

"Mitannu."

He looked up at the Indian. He knew the name. He was the son of the chief, and the mate of a particularly lovely Mobilian woman, with whom Julien had attempted to strike a certain bargain. Because the man was a prolific and renowned hunter, rarely in the village, Julien had not crossed paths with him until today. He silently assessed the hawkish, alien features, the almond-shaped eyes and arched nose, comparing them to Nika's small twin sons, who were always dashing around underfoot when Julien was in the village conducting business with the chief.

Mitannu's posture shifted with suspicious aggression, and Julien transferred his attention back to the account book. After all, what difference did the parentage of a couple of Indian whelps make? Finishing the entry, he capped the pen, then rose and unlocked the warehouse door behind his desk.

An hour after the Indian left with the powder in a leather pouch tied at his waist, André Ardouin came in to purchase a smoked turkey. The ship's carpenter studied his receipt with suspicion. "Ten *ecus* is an exorbitant price for such a small smoked turkey."

Ardouin was one of a handful of colonists who could both read and write, so Julien was always careful not to cheat him. "The *Profond* is due to arrive any day now. Until it does . . ." Julien shrugged. "Supply and demand, my friend. Are you planning an entertainment?"

"My betrothed and her family will dine with me this evening. I want to demonstrate that I'm a man of sufficient income to support a growing family."

"Are you afraid the girl will withdraw her consent?" Julien asked slyly.

"The contract has been signed and notarized." Ardouin, who had converted from the humorless Reformist religion in order to secure one of His Majesty's Catholic brides, clearly resented being tweaked.

Julien smiled. "Isn't your bride-to-be related to the nun they call Sister Gris?"

"Yes — and Bienville has just named her midwife, an important post in light of the expected growth of our colony."

Which connection, Julien presumed, increased Ardouin's stature in the community and somewhat mitigated the lingering taint of Protestantism. But there was little sport in a verbal joust with an opponent who insisted on taking one quite literally.

Julien shrugged and rose. "Commander Bienville has bid his officers and several of the unattached ladies to dine with him this evening. Perhaps I may follow your lead and fix my own interest."

Ardouin nodded. "The commander grows impatient with the girls who are prolonging their decisions. They may find the support of the royal coffers withdrawn."

Julien stopped in the act of gathering his papers. "Who told you that?"

"My betrothed. The *Pélican* girls grew to know one another well during their confinement aboard ship — despite the fact that a few perceive themselves to be better connected. As if relatives in France could influence one's day-to-day life in a community as remote as ours." Ardouin's mouth tightened. "And as if a ship's carpenter weren't good enough."

"I see nothing wrong in taking time to choose one's life mate with care." Julien slid the papers into a drawer and locked it. "Bienville is impatient with everything that does not move to his liking. The Gaillain sisters have been invited to the gathering tonight. Do you find anything arrogant in the behavior of either?"

"They both seem to be sweet young women. My Catherine is a confidante of the elder." Ardouin paused. "Mademoiselle Geneviève has the more serious mind of the two, I would say, though I would not describe her as *arrogant*. In fact, she reminds me a great deal of my own sister back in La Rochelle." Ardouin blinked rapidly, then said hurriedly, "Although I'm certain Bienville would never have allowed . . ."

"Allowed?" Julien prompted when Ardouin seemed to find the rest of his sentence too shocking to utter aloud.

Ardouin looked away. "I abhor the spreading of gossip, Monsieur Aide-Major. Forgive me — I must retrieve my purchases in order for my cook to prepare dinner." After a clumsy bow, he exited in haste, clutching his receipt.

Julien released a soundless whistle. Ardouin had confirmed his suspicion that there was more to the Gaillain sisters than appeared. And was he implying some taint of Protestantism? Where there was secrecy, the persistent man could generally find money. Cheerfully he locked his desk and pocketed the key.

Julien Dufresne was nothing if not persistent.

All of life, Geneviève was beginning to suspect, consisted of slavery in one form or another.

She caught a glimpse of her unfamiliar self in the large gilt mirror hanging opposite the doorway into Commander Bienville's living room as she followed Madame and Monsieur L'Anglois inside. Grimacing, she resisted the urge to rub her aching scalp. Raindrop, who proved to be clever at dressing hair, had twisted the curly mass atop her head and jammed in a pair of large tortoise shell combs borrowed from her fashionable hostess. "Ooh, mademoiselle!" the little girl had chirped, bouncing on bare toes. "You look just like the princess in my book!"

Smiling at the thought, Geneviève glanced back at her sister. Aimée of the shining golden curls and rosebud mouth, gowned in the azure blue of her eyes, was the true illustration of fairytale royalty.

"Come, my dear." Madame reached back to pull Geneviève along. "The commander expects betrothals before the week is out." Her critical gaze flicked over Geneviève's Indian print robe, layered over a solid burgundy jupe and pinned beneath the bosom to its white-on-white embroidered stomacher.

Aware that the lace-edged chemise peeking above the stomacher drew attention to her décolletage, Geneviève laid a hand over the unaccustomed expanse of bare flesh. Madame had insisted upon loaning her a boned corset, which dug into her ribs with every breath. "We were told we might take our time to become acquainted with *all* our potential suitors," Geneviève said, torn between resentment and amusement. Madame seemed to take it as a personal affront that her charges were among the last of the *Pélican* brides to find husbands.

"I sympathize with your desire to contract the most favorable match possible, but Bienville's patience is at an end." Clearly Madame's was as well. She took Geneviève's wrist with a shake of her head that threatened to send her towering coiffure to ruins. "An ambitious lady displays all the wares at her —"

"Ginette!" Aimée leaned in to speak urgently in Geneviève's ear. "The gentleman over there . . . isn't that Monsieur Alexandre? — no, beside the buffet, behind Father Mathieu. What are you going to do?"

Geneviève turned to smile at the priest, but the glimpse of the balding sandy pate of the brickmaker behind him failed to raise even a spasm of discomposure. "Why, I shall warn him to avoid Madame's macaroons."

"Ginette! You know that's not what I —"

"Come, girls," Madame insisted. "I don't know why you dawdle so. You may talk to one another when you get home. Commander! Look, I have brought my two darling girls." She sailed forth into the mass of uniformed bodies crowding Bienville's salon, towing Geneviève and Aimée like nets behind a fishing boat.

Despite her light response to her sister's question, Geneviève's emotions scattered in all directions. What *would* she say to the man whose abrupt offer of marriage she had refused only yesterday? Alexandre had appeared in the guardhouse kitchen, where for the last week she had been experimenting with adding local grains to the dough, stretching the small amount of wheat flour available without ruining the texture beyond

114

recognition. Wheat had thus far refused to flourish in the moist, sandy coastal ground, and shipments of flour from France were unreliable at best. Chef Roy was so frustrated with the situation that he grudgingly gave Geneviève room to work around him. They had developed a prickly comradeship that only a woman who had trained with her father would be able to tolerate.

But Roy growled like a bear about the constant stream of besotted bachelors who trooped through his domain, hoping for a private word or at least a handout from the celebrated "Bread Girl." Geneviève had responded to most of the marriage offers she had received in the facetious spirit with which they had been extended. Poor Monsieur Alexandre, however, had been in obvious earnest.

Unfortunately, he took her gentle refusal for coyness.

That Bienville had invited him to this party, when he was not an officer, worried her. Had Alexandre appealed to the commander for her hand? How far would he go in coercing marriages?

"Dear one, you *must* smile," Madame whispered. "No man wishes for a bride with a countenance like stewed prunes."

In spite of her anxiety, Geneviève smiled

as the crowd around Bienville parted to allow the three women to curtsey in front of him. Rising, Geneviève looked up to catch the gleam of admiration in his black eyes.

"Good evening, Commander." Blushing, she looked at her sister.

Aimée dimpled and extended her white hand. "We are honored with your invitation, Commander."

Bienville transferred his attention to Aimée, took her hand, and carried it to his lips with a gallantry belied by his rough-and-ready reputation. He was clean-shaven for the occasion, with his curly dark hair hanging loose over the epaulets of his dark blue formal uniform. The bleached white linen tied about his throat had been cleverly knotted to resemble a waterfall, the ends tucked inside the coat's extravagant lapels. He somehow managed to look both wildly masculine and proper, and she couldn't help picturing the tattoos Aimée had described.

The sight of the commander's light attentions to her sister made Geneviève's thoughts flit again to Tristan Lanier, who had paid her for the bread and bade her adieu with a reminder to be careful of the Indian males wandering about the settlement. "They consider women to be little more than property," he warned. "Most would think nothing of carrying you off like some prize trinket." His dark eyes had been serious, the line of his jaw set.

As she thought of his quick-thinking response to the savage in the kitchen, Geneviève couldn't help wondering why he chose to live so far from the settlement. Clearly he held his brother, Bienville's clever young translator, in deep affection.

She glanced at Marc-Antoine Lanier, who stood on the other side of the room, entertaining a group of young soldiers with some apparently uproarious tale. He also managed to simultaneously flirt with Bienville's female slaves as they glided about the room in pursuance of their duties.

The three Indian women were dressed in simple belted shifts of soft gray cotton, their straight black hair confined in single plaits down the back, so similar in features that Geneviève thought they must be sisters or cousins. Their eyes remained downcast, rarely meeting the gaze of a guest, but Geneviève got the feeling the women were aware of conversation around them. She wondered how much French they knew.

Shaking her head, she admonished herself not to be fanciful. Just because her own conscience squirmed in constant discomfort didn't mean that everyone around her was guilty of espionage. Still, she knew she must guard her tongue. She could speak openly of her faith with no one but Aimée or Father Mathieu.

To her relief, the priest was seated to her right at dinner, a blessed buffer to Jean Alexandre on her left. The brickmaker's contributions to the conversation consisted of frequent references to the splendor of the home he had built on his large corner lot. He considered the location of this choice property, only four lots away from the influential L'Anglois family and one block from the marketplace and communal well, sufficient motivation for her to reconsider her rash refusal of his marriage proposal. By the introduction of the fish course, Geneviève was so weary of nodding with noncommittal politeness that she would have welcomed the intrusion of a cleaver-bearing savage or two.

Mercifully, Father Mathieu requested her attention with a gentle hand upon her forearm.

"Yes, Father?" She turned to him with an eagerness that brought a twinkle to his eyes.

"I was wondering how your bakery enterprise has progressed during the last week."

Geneviève sighed. "Lieutenant Roy has

118

been very kind to give me room to work, but I could do so much more in my own kitchen, with my own dishes and pans and oven." She could almost hear Madame's solution: marry one of these lonely, good-hearted Canadians, and a kitchen of your own comes with it.

Unfortunately, the husband who accompanied the kitchen would object to having a bakery run out of his home. And her first obligation would be to the husband. With a husband came household chores, a garden to tend, meals to prepare, children to *raise as good Catholics* . . .

Had she considered these things back in Rochefort, when Father Mathieu had first suggested she and Aimée take passage on the *Pélican*? Perhaps, in a cursory way — but uppermost on her mind had been escape. After all, what other choice had she had? She had signed the contract, promising to marry. She was bound to do so.

Father Mathieu was gazing at her quizzically.

She blinked. "In any case, the soldiers don't seem to mind eating my mistakes."

"Everywhere I go about the settlement, I hear of the lovely Mademoiselle Gaillain's crusty loaves." Father Mathieu smiled. "In fact, Monsieur Burelle has something of a business proposition for you. He asked me to inquire if you would entertain the idea of selling your bread through his shop."

"I think I haven't met Monsieur Burelle." She tried to remember the man.

"This is a terrible idea!" Alexandre leaned over Geneviève to address the priest. "No reputable woman would associate her name — or that of her husband — with commerce through a tavern!"

Geneviève felt the blood flush to the roots of her hair. This presumptuous *crétin,* with whom she had been acquainted for less than a week, dared to tell her what was proper?

The priest laid a gentle hand upon her wrist. "Your concern for Mademoiselle Gaillain's reputation is very kind," he said to Alexandre with a commendable absence of irony. "I'm sure she will take it under advisement."

One of the slave girls appeared at Geneviève's elbow with a dessert. She turned to smile up at the woman and caught a look of naked hatred in the dark eyes before they were shuttered by downcast lashes. "Enjoy, mademoiselle," the girl murmured as she moved to serve Father Mathieu.

Taken aback, Geneviève watched her move along the table from guest to guest. They all seemed oblivious to the ones serving, as if inanimate objects with movable arms, legs, hands, gave them what they wanted. No word of thanks, no smile of gratitude.

Of course the slave women would be resentful. But there had been a more active rage in the face of the one who had leaned over Geneviève's shoulder, as if the girl would like to have cut her throat. As she studied her graceful form, the shiny ebony plait swaying against the narrow back, the dainty ears and pink lips, it dawned on her how beautiful the servant was.

Her gaze moved to the commander at the end of the long table. Bienville was watching the servant girl as well, his expression possessive, masculine.

Suddenly Geneviève understood the girl's resentment. One of these Frenchwomen had come across the ocean to take her place, demoting her to a possession no more important than a milk cow or a broodmare. No surprise that a man with Bienville's power would take his pleasure from among the dusky beauties who surrounded him — especially with no white women available. After all, wasn't that the reason the King had summoned the *Pélican* girls in the first place? To keep the bloodlines of the new French colony pure?

Until now the implications had not dawned on her.

A flurry of motion in the doorway to the kitchen drew her attention, and a dark-skinned toddler darted around the legs of a male slave bringing in a tray of drinks. The little boy was dressed in a sleeveless tunic and breeches, his feet bare and the dark-brown hair chopped as if someone had set a bowl upon his head and cut around it. He ran to fling his arms around the legs of the woman who had just served Geneviève, giggling up at her. The woman laid a maternal hand atop his head, then peeled him off her leg, turned him back toward the kitchen, and swatted his bottom with a firm "Go play!" in French.

The child ducked away from her and ran toward Bienville, who scooped him up with one arm and planted a noisy kiss upon his round cheek. "Ho, Father Mathieu!" the commander called. "This little imp clearly needs a baptism. I would that you conduct it at the first opportunity." He made a production of sniffing the little boy's neck. "And some soap would not go amiss."

The child squirmed to get down. "No!" he shrieked. "No soap!"

Chuckling, Bienville let him go, and he darted back to the kitchen.

As if scales had dropped from her eyes, Geneviève watched the commander return to his flirtation with Aimée. His charisma like a powerful magnet drew the attention of every woman in the room. Forcing her gaze away, she finished her dessert, hardly tasting the delicious custard, grateful for Father Mathieu's willingness to engage Alexandre in conversation, which relieved her of the necessity of making small talk.

If Bienville took a wife from among the *Pélican* girls, what would happen to the women he called slaves and their children? How could a man keep a child whom he had fathered in the bonds of slavery?

More to the point, what if the man Geneviève chose as husband should elect to keep an Indian mistress? Would she have anything to say about it? A wife was in many ways little more than a servant. All her worldly goods transferred to her husband upon her marriage, and she would be pledged to obey him. Would she truly be any better off than she would be on her own?

By the time Bienville had moved his guests into the salon for drinks, Geneviève was considerably sobered. To her alarm, the commander sent Father Mathieu off to argue plans for the settlement's new chapel with the two seminary pastors, rotund

Father Henri and ascetic Father Albert, who dwelt in a rather Spartan cabin on the outskirts of town. He then drew Geneviève into a conversational circle comprising himself, Surgeon-Major Barraud, and the La Salle family.

Commissioner La Salle was a thin, dour gentleman of some forty years, fond of large, expensive wigs; with his new bride, Jeanne de Berenhardt, of course, she was well acquainted, as they had made the journey together aboard the *Pélican*.

"And I told the duchess — she and I were great friends, you know — that she mustn't keep giving me all her dresses, or she would end up quite naked!" Jeanne lifted her fan to titter behind it. "Oh, dear, I keep forgetting there are gentlemen in the company!" She glanced around to make sure everyone had heard and chosen to overlook her risqué comment. Satisfied, she snapped the fan shut. "But, there, my trunk was so full that it took *three* soldiers to carry it up from the boat!"

Poor La Salle, failing to find anything constructive to add to his wife's remark, cleared his throat and tugged at his cravat. Bienville winked at Geneviève and motioned for one of the male servants to refill his tankard.

"Speaking of heavy weights, Commander," she said, hoping to head off the new Madame La Salle's unfortunate proclivity for uncensored discourse, "I noticed what look like millstones piled near the river. I hope that means construction of a mill is soon to begin."

Bienville's expression blackened. He allowed his drink to be topped off, then dismissed the servant with a curt nod. "His Majesty has sent neither the rest of the materials nor an artisan with the skills to build it." He drank deeply and wiped his mouth. "Perhaps Mademoiselle would like to try her hand at convincing him to either loosen the royal purse strings or give me authority to raise the money myself."

Jeanne, oblivious to her husband's scowl, batted her lashes at the commander. "But surely, sir, as governor you must be the final authority on this side of the Atlantic!"

"Bienville has not been appointed governor," La Salle growled. "That position belongs to his brother Iberville, and they are both subject to the King's will through Minister Pontchartrain."

"I *am* governor in my brother's absence." Bienville's voice had softened to a dangerous rumble. "And you had best cease testing my authority, Monsieur La Salle, lest you find out just how far it goes." Without giving the commissary a chance to reply, he leveled a stare at the man's wife. "I am tired of all this bellyaching about fine Parisian flour, madame, when our native corn meal — which all but falls upon one's head when one walks down the street — makes perfectly good bread."

Jeanne squeaked, "But I wasn't the one who —"

"Indeed you weren't." Bienville rounded on Geneviève, folding his arms across his broad chest. "And I had all but forgotten the reason for this charming gathering. It has come to my attention, mademoiselle, that you have turned down not one, not two, but *three* legitimate offers of marriage since you arrived."

Geneviève could only stare at him.

"Is this true?" Bienville prompted.

"I — yes, sir, I suppose, but at least one of those —"

Bienville cut her off with a slash of his hand. "This coyness is ill becoming in one dependent upon the Crown for her very subsistence. I cannot afford to support a boatload of unmarried women indefinitely. Indeed you are taking food from the mouths of my soldiers."

Geneviève stood there in strangled humiliation. Surely it had not been necessary to call her out in such a public fashion. Where was the man who, not an hour ago, had so playfully and affectionately teased the Indian child?

To his credit, the commander looked away as if he knew he'd gone too far. He grimaced and rubbed a hand across his stomach. "Ah, I am plagued to death," he muttered, slanting Geneviève a sheepish grin. "I should have told the bishop to send only ugly girls — then I would not have my men fighting over you!"

"Please, Monsieur Commandant," Geneviève said, trying to still the tremor of her voice, "I mean no insult or disrespect. I have my little sister to care for, and . . . the offers I have so far received have been unacceptable."

Bienville glanced across the room, where Alexandre stood in conversation with a couple of carpenters and the steadily drinking surgeon, Barraud. "I fail to see the negative qualities of a brickmaker with an independent living and the only medical man in the settlement. Besides, your sister seems to be capable of settling her own affairs."

At that moment, Aimée danced past on the arm of Aide-Major Dufresne, Bienville's red-haired warehouse adjutant. Geneviève had thought her sister well on the way to capturing the heart of Marc-Antoine Lanier, but the handsome young lieutenant was nowhere in sight, and Aimée gave no indication that she missed him.

Geneviève bit her lip. "She is too young —"

"She is of marriageable age," Bienville said firmly. "It is my responsibility to grow this colony. I shall be generous and give you two more months to settle upon a husband." He gave her a curt bow and turned to signal a servant for another drink.

Geneviève could only stand there, her thoughts chasing one another like squirrels. She was not a coward, she reminded herself. She had survived much worse than marriage to a man she didn't love. She was safe and well fed and could even worship as she chose — as long as she kept her beliefs quiet.

But if all those things were true, the other half of her brain inquired, then why did she feel so abandoned?

Father Mathieu, glancing over his shoulder as he followed Marc-Antoine Lanier out onto Bienville's gallery, could tell that Geneviève was in trouble, but he could not for the moment come to her aid. Having finally managed this private interview, he must take the opportunity to investigate the man for whom he had sacrificed his life's work and reputation.

He fingered the rosary upon his chest. *God, preserve her. Help her. Help me. We only want your will, your glory, on earth as it is in heaven.* Crossing himself, he stepped out into the dark, moist evening.

Young Lanier waited, a broad shoulder propped against one of the yellow pine posts supporting the roof. He looked a bit raffish, long hair curling onto the frayed epaulets of his faded blue coat, a month's growth of beard shadowing lean cheeks, nose peeling from a recent sunburn. But at least he was clean, his cravat white as snow and fingernails neatly trimmed. The white lace of his shirtsleeves fell over strong, sun-browned hands that looked capable as well as clever.

Beyond the young man's personal habits of dress and hygiene, Mathieu liked the humor lurking around the firm mouth and a certain expression of self-irony around the dark eyes. Most telling, he had seen genuine affection between the Lanier brothers, as well as a rare mutual confidence.

He needed to be able to trust Marc-Antoine Lanier.

"Out with it, Father," the boy said on a deep chuckle. "Either you need money or I am derelict on confession. Whichever it is, please get it over with quickly so I can get on with enjoying the evening."

Mathieu laughed, tucking his hands inside opposite sleeves of his surplice. "I'm not privy to your confessional schedule, and I have no need of funds at present."

Lanier scratched his head. "Then I can't imagine what the Church wants with me. A less devout man than me you'd have trouble finding."

Mathieu hesitated. If someone else told him the tale he was about to relate, he would not have believed it. He began obliquely. "I was not specifically sent here by the Church. In fact I should be very surprised if the bishop were aware of my presence."

Lanier's dramatic eyebrows rose. "Ho. Then why *are* you here?"

"It is something of a personal quest, let us say, which involves your brother."

Lanier slowly straightened away from the post. "Is it so?"

Mathieu nodded, straining to see into the far shadowy corners of the gallery. Empty. Good. He stepped closer and lowered his voice to a murmur. "How much do you know about your parents, Marc-Antoine?"

Lanier shrugged. "As much as one can know about the two people who gave one birth. They are Canadians of Ville Marie, friends of the Le Moynes, which is how we were introduced to Bienville. My father is a cartographer, and he trained Tristan. Me, I've always been more interested in languages." His expression darkened somewhat with anxiety. "They are good people, Father, faithful Catholics."

"I'm sure they are." Mathieu weighed his words, not sure how much truth such a young man could withstand. "I bear a commission from one who takes an interest in your brother. An interest which will make a very rich man of him." When Lanier straightened, Mathieu put out a hand of caution. "It will also give him powerful enemies."

"My brother is afraid of no man."

Mathieu did not doubt the truth of those brash words. Still, he shook his head. "This . . . fortune comes with grave responsibility, my son. Should he accept, many lives besides his own will be altered forever, and he would have to return with me to France."

"I don't understand," said the boy. "Why did you not tell Tristan all this when he was here? Why did you not tell him *before* that, when he met the *Pélican* at Massacre Island?"

"I had been informed that Tristan was Bienville's lieutenant. Then upon our arrival, I saw that he is now clearly at odds with the commander — that he has exiled himself, far from his countrymen, unprotected against those who oppose the French Crown. So I decided to wait, watching to see what manner of man he has become." Mathieu spread his hands. "I confess to you, I can make no sense of his behavior. And so I ask you, his brother, to help me understand."

7

"Father, let us walk to the river." Without another word, Marc-Antoine Lanier turned and took the steps down from the gallery in one leap. He strode across the marshy yard and headed away from the relative civilization of the fort and town.

Mathieu was left to follow as best he might, splashing through a stretch of lowland swarming with insects, dodging piles of wood left to rot. By the time he arrived, breathing hard, at Lanier's chosen trysting place, his robe was wet to the knees.

Young Lanier waited, hands on hips, a faintly mocking smile on his lips. The only sound, besides the incessant drone of the mosquitoes, was the chugging of frogs and whir of crickets.

"Are you satisfied that we are alone?" Mathieu tucked his hands into his sleeves.

Lanier shrugged. "I don't want my brother's affairs to become public knowledge —

particularly if they touch upon the reputation of my parents."

He had been right to trust Marc-Antoine Lanier. "You were about to explain your brother's motives in cutting off his connection to Bienville. Does he no longer hold ambition for building the colony for France?"

"I'm not sure he ever had any such ambition. We were both young when we left Canada six years ago with Bienville. I was fourteen, Tristan barely twenty. We were in it mostly for the adventure — Bienville was the one with the ambition. The plan was to map the coastline of the gulf, to track the rivers that fed it, find a settlement site, and stake France's claim before Spain and England could get a toehold."

"You helped to build the fort?" For three weeks Mathieu had been asking indirect questions about the beginnings of the settlement. But this was his first opportunity to question one who had actually been present with the commander from the outset.

Lanier shook his head. "Bienville had discovered my affinity for languages, so on our first mapping trip up the river during the spring of 1698, he left me in an Alabama village. I was to become proficient by the time he came back for me."

"But it was my understanding that the Alabama are hostile to us Frenchmen."

"At the time, the Alabama were courting our favor, playing us against the English. They considered it a mark of prestige to have a white man living in their village. I was treated well." Lanier looked down for a moment, then continued his story. "By the time Tristan came back to get me, relationships with the Indian clans on the southern end of the river had deteriorated to a degree that Bienville claimed he needed an interpreter —"

"He *claimed*?"

Lanier's smile was shrewd. "Bienville has a way of feigning ignorance, which often dupes his opponents into revealing hidden motives. I had learned enough of several native languages to be helpful . . . so I returned. He would take me into a confab with some village chief, pretend not to understand a word, then listen to what they actually said as I fumbled to translate."

"Brilliant."

"He can be." Lanier's smile was rueful. "But when he's convinced he's right and you're wrong —" He reached down and broke off a cattail from the marshy riverbank grass. "The rift between him and Tristan began while I was gone. They had decided at first to locate the settlement down on the western bluff where the Mobile River opens into the bay. Tristan saw huge advantages in being near the deepwater port and the Massacre Island warehouse. But the Indian chiefs convinced Bienville that it would be better to settle up here, closer to their villages."

"That was five years ago, yes?"

Lanier nodded. "By the time Tristan brought me back, the fort was under construction and the town mapped out. Bienville parceled out land to those with the means to build on it, and probably would have allotted Tristan as much as any of the other officers." He shrugged. "My brother is a bit stubborn too. He refused to accept any land as a gift."

"Wouldn't that be considered insubordination?"

"Maybe — if Tristan hadn't been so valuable to Bienville. He lived in the barracks and did his job as far as he was able. Not long after, he took an Indian wife and went to live near the Mobile village. Bienville might have court-martialed him but for Le Sueur's intervention."

"But Le Sueur is now dead." And Tristan Lanier had a wife, a fact which Mathieu wouldn't have guessed from his reaction to

136

Geneviève.

"Yes." Lanier's young face was sober. "Le Sueur was a good man who helped keep Bienville somewhat grounded. Complicated relations with the court in France, the English starting to negotiate with the Indians to the east, plus the Spanish constantly asking for loans of provisions and munitions . . . Bienville walks a narrow bridge from crisis to crisis. No wonder he falls off occasionally."

"What caused the final break with your brother?"

The reed between Lanier's hands snapped. "I — I'm not sure I can speak of it, Father. You would had to have known Sholani to understand."

"Tristan's wife?"

Lanier looked away, but not before Mathieu saw the sheen of tears in his eyes. "Yes. She was — she made my brother so happy."

"What happened?"

"Two years ago, Bienville sent Tristan on another mapping expedition, across the river and heading north and west. While he was gone, a band of British-armed hostiles raided the Mobile village while their men were hunting and took some women and children as prisoners. Bienville wouldn't retaliate because nobody was killed, and he hoped to keep peace with the Alabama. I would have gone after Sholani myself, but I had been sent to Veracruz to buy supplies. Tristan got back and —" Lanier's hands mimed an explosion. "Everybody thought he was going to kill Bienville."

Mathieu crossed himself.

"But he wouldn't waste time," Lanier continued, grimfaced. "He tracked the Alabama up to the Little Tomeh village. They'd bought a few of the Mobile children, but said the women had been sold to English agents. So Tristan kept going. I guess he would've been crazy enough to go all the way into Carolina by himself —" He stopped and swallowed. "But he found her three miles away at an abandoned campfire."

"Dead." Mathieu had known it, but the word still fell from his lips like a lead weight.

"Yes. She'd been raped." Lanier's voice shook with quiet rage. "Tristan caught up with them that night and killed both men. He brought the other Mobile women back with him. That's when he resigned his commission and moved down to the lower bluff on the bay. To his credit, Bienville let him go. Now they circle around one another like wildcats, with me caught in the middle."

Mathieu had been blessed — sometimes,

he thought, cursed — with the spiritual gift of compassion. Tristan Lanier's grief and loss flayed him to the soul. He couldn't say whether fulfillment of his quest would bring relief or a greater burden, but he knew, deep within his spirit, that he must carry it out, come what may. He reached up to grip the cross upon his chest. "What makes Bienville think your brother will lead this new peace mission you propose?"

"Tristan isn't as detached as he'd like to appear. My father instilled in us the instinct to protect the weak. Now that these French-women have arrived, Tristan will do what-ever he can to keep them safe."

Mathieu bowed his head. Tristan Lanier seemed to be every bit the man he had hoped. Unfortunately, that also meant that he might not live to see another new year.

Holy Father in heaven, I wait upon your direction. Show me the way to go.

Seated upon one of the commander's ugly brocaded chairs, Aimée plied her fan, hop-ing that the deepened color of her cheeks from the heat in the small room would outweigh the unattractive (and uncomfort-able) damp patches under her arms.

She cast a glance up at Monsieur Du-fresne and found him, to her chagrin, absorbed in watching the doorway, where Father Mathieu had just followed Lieutenant Lanier into the room. She shut her fan with a snap and rapped him sharply across the knuckles. "Forgive me if I bore you, sir. Perhaps you'd like to yield your place to Sergeant Lefleur, so that you may seek the far more improving company of Father Mathieu." It was not an empty threat. Handsome young Lefleur had been casting languishing looks her way all night.

Dufresne rubbed his hand but gave her an indulgent smile. "You'd find that a waste of time, my dear. Lefleur lives on but a hundred livres per year and is in perpetual debt to the warehouse. I was merely wondering if we might slip away for a private conversation. One constantly feels the weight of your sister's disapproval. She is such a . . . severe young lady."

"I was sure you'd been watching her," Aimée said. "Geneviève can be quite beautiful, when she dresses correctly." She flirted her lashes, then lifted them coyly, as she had practiced in the mirror this afternoon. "I vow she makes me feel quite homely."

Dufresne raised her hand to his lips with a gallant flourish. "My dear, you are a rose among dandelions, everywhere you go. You will certainly have your pick of the eligible men in the settlement."

Aimée glanced at Bienville, in conversation with Father Mathieu. "Perhaps not all."

"The commander is . . . a hard man to understand. He stands to be governor of the colony, should his brother Iberville die, and in any case would be set for life with the choicest of estates. He has no need to marry for social or financial advantage." Dufresne shrugged. "But let us converse of more interesting things. I would like to know more of your family background. If I remember correctly, you and your sister joined the *Pélican* party from La Rochelle. Or was it Rochefort?"

"La Rochelle," she replied absently. "We met Father Mathieu there."

"But I had understood that the bishop chose the women from convents and orphanages in and around Paris, and they all traveled to Rochefort together. Captain Ducoudray says you all stayed in the Rochefort orphanage until the *Pélican* sailed to La Rochelle to pick up more supplies."

Alarm shot through her. "That's what I meant! We came from Rochefort first."

He smiled. "A natural mistake. Tell me your impression of Rochefort. It is, I believe, quite a smelly little city."

She eyed him warily. "I did not find it so."

"Well, perhaps not. Fish aren't known to smell so much." He reached inside his pocket and extracted a beautiful enameled snuff box. Dropping a pinch onto his wrist, he sniffed, then sneezed into his sleeve. "After all, the orphanage is quite ten miles from the oceanfront."

"Um . . ." She began to pleat her dress into a ruin of wrinkles.

"Come, *cherie,* it is not such a bad thing that you and your sister aren't like those shallow Parisian misses. Most men appreciate a woman who can comport herself in rather more rural circumstances, as long as she is cultured and devout."

She *must* deflect this disastrous turn in the conversation. "That is true. My papa took us to Paris once when the Comte needed him for a large court banquet. The girls we met there were as vain as peacocks, and could not even read or write their names!"

"The world is in a sad state, eh, mademoiselle?" Dufresne shook his head. "In what other disciplines did your esteemed papa instruct his beautiful daughters? I would venture to guess that you are conversant with all the classics from Plato to Horace."

She laughed at the very idea. "Oh, mon-

sieur, you are pleased to tweak me! I promise you, I am not like to bore you with
homilies and lectures of that sort. Geneviève is much more educated than I. Why,
she can quote large sections of the New
Testament!"

Dufresne looked impressed and somewhat
skeptical. "Mademoiselle, you astonish me.
I shall have to ask her to straighten me out
as to the Sermon on the Mount, as I'm
never quite certain whether one is to refrain
from coveting his neighbor's wife and
remove the splinter in his eye — or the other
way round!"

Aimée giggled, drawing the curious and
indulgent gazes of those who stood nearby.
"Monsieur l'Aide-Major, please don't tell
Geneviève I spilled her secret," she begged,
gaining control over her merriment. "She is
sensitive about being considered a big-
headed, overeducated woman."

He made a mime of buttoning his lip,
winked, and changed the subject. But Aimée
couldn't help noticing that during the ensuing conversation Dufresne's thoughtful gaze
frequently went to her sister.

She gritted her teeth. She would *not* allow
Geneviève to steal another beau from her.

Tristan hauled on the reins of the plow,

forcing his ox to halt midfield. He yanked at the kerchief loosely knotted about his throat, untying it and swiping it across his sweaty face. Why he had failed to bring a canteen of water with him he would never know. Well, perhaps he did know and didn't want to admit it. His thoughts these days always seemed to land where he had strictly forbidden them to go — twenty-seven miles north in Fort Louis.

Not since Sholani's death had he been so preoccupied, so . . . uncontrollably dreamy. He was reminded of days when his mother would find him perched in a maple tree drawing pictures of Jean-Baptiste Le Moyne's sister Catherine-Jeanne. Tall and strikingly lovely, socially as far above shy young Tristan Lanier as the stars in the heavens, Catherine had also possessed a kind heart. She never failed to greet him and give him her slow, curving smile when she passed in church.

Jogging the reins with a shout to the ox, he pushed the plow down the row of squash, a rueful smile tugging at his lips. The romanticized charcoal drawings inspired by Catherine Le Moyne would never hang upon the walls of Versailles, but they had at least convinced his father that he had sufficient talent to enter an apprenticeship with one of the greatest cartographers of the age, Charles Levasseur. Thus had begun his adventures with Levasseur, Iberville, and Le Sueur, and his deep friendship with the flamboyant young Bienville.

He sometimes wondered where life's road might have taken him had he chosen to stay in Canada, rather than joining the expedition to explore the Gulf of Mexico. A safer path, no doubt. But to have never loved Sholani? Never to have seen the ocean's roaring surf or stand in a field knowing that the land as far as his eye would reach belonged to him?

No, despite the pain of betrayal and grief so deep that it still sometimes clawed him awake at night, he would not go back.

One regret lingered . . . that he would have no son to come behind him, a hardy lad with whom to plot next year's garden, to teach the use of sexton and compass, to fill with stories passed down from his own father. The child he had created with Sholani had perished with her. Marc-Antoine would inherit this plantation, if he ever left off gadding about at Bienville's behest, so perhaps his sons would bear with the tales of crotchety old Uncle Tristan.

If that thought struck a minor chord of dissatisfaction, it was no more than he deserved. He should never have left her that day. She had begged to come with him, but he'd convinced her it would not be good for the baby. A pregnant woman, daily purging her breakfast, craving sleep every afternoon, would only slow him down. He'd wanted to discharge this one last long mapping mission for Bienville and get home, the quicker the better. Perhaps he had gotten too comfortable with the Indian way of ordering women about. Perhaps he'd grown a bit weary of the tears that seemed to lurk close to the surface and spill over whenever she was crossed. In the end he'd left her sobbing in their thatched cabin, shutting the door with just a bit too much force, striding off toward the river with a couple of soldiers assigned him by Bienville.

The last time he'd seen her alive, he had only kissed the top of her head and patted her awkwardly on the shoulder. *You are my heart,* he'd been thinking but could not say it.

The dull ache in his breast was threatening to turn into a knife wound, so it was a relief to espy a figure approaching over the eastern horizon. He squinted against the bright morning sun, and finally made out the dark head of one of his Pascagoula Indian neighbors. Bienville employed several of them as runners between Massacre Island and Fort Louis, paying them in ammunition, cloth, or whatever European sundry they might be in need of. It had been several days since a brave named Hatchet had passed through on his way to the fort, stopping only to accept a dipper of water from Tristan's well and promising to return with any word from Marc-Antoine, whom the Indians called Bright Tongue.

As the Indian got closer, Tristan saw that this fellow didn't have the sharp-boned face of the lugubrious Hatchet. He was on the short side, even for the small-statured Pascagoula, bowlegged but fleet, running over the soft ground that Tristan had struggled to clear all by himself in that season of blinding pain after Sholani was taken from him. The Indian easily loped toward him, raised an arm in greeting, and he recognized Deerfoot, a man who had taught Tristan much about hunting the dense coastal woods.

Leaving the ox standing with a handful of grass to occupy him, Tristan walked toward the Indian and when he got close enough hailed him in the Mobilian tongue.

"Tree-Stah!" called Deerfoot, giving his best approximation of Tristan's name. "Greetings on this beautiful day! You will have sunstroke if you stay out here with nothing on your head."

Tristan grinned, giving him a whack on the shoulder for greeting. Deerfoot had tried unsuccessfully on many occasions to talk Tristan out of his handsome tricorn. "I left my hat in the cabin to keep crazy Indians from stealing it. What brings you up from the island today?"

Deerfoot, part of a distant clan of Sholani's family, made his home at the east end of Massacre Island. He had a sweet wife and four little girls who adored "Uncle Tree-Stah" and delighted in decorating him with wildflower crowns and feeding him their mother's thick soup made of venison broth, crabmeat, and okra, with panfried corn bread to sop up the gravy. Very different from Geneviève Gaillain's delicate French loaves, to be sure, but tasty and filling.

"I'm on my way to the fort. Did you know that a supply ship has come from Martinique?"

"No! But that is good news. Can you wait for me to gather up a few things and come with you?"

Deerfoot tapped his chin in pretended reluctance. "I don't think you can keep up with me."

"And yet I beat you in the island footrace

not ten days ago." Tristan began to unhitch the ox.

Deerfoot jumped up onto the animal's broad, shaggy back. "I was nursing a twisted ankle that day. I am well now."

"Then you will have no excuse when I outrun you today." Tristan gave the ox a good-natured swat with his hand to get him moving and picked up the reins to lead him toward the barn.

"I've already run thirty-six miles this morning, but I'll be waiting for you at Burelle's tavern when you drag in." Deerfoot crossed his legs and leaned back on his elbows, lounging on the ox's muscular haunches as if he lay on a blanket next to his wife's cookfire. "What I don't understand, Tree-Stah, is why you hide out on this bluff, when you could live with us on the island, where there is at least an occasional game of dice — or up the river with your own people. Hatchet tells me the white women who came over the ocean are handsome to look at, even though they don't know how to cook a meal that will fill a man's belly."

Tristan could think of at least one Frenchwoman who was both handsome to look at and knew her way around an oven. It was a moot point anyway. Three weeks since her arrival, she was undoubtedly already married. He shrugged. "I like to be alone."

"You didn't like it so much in the days when my pretty cousin threw back her blanket for you. Sholani is dead for two years, my friend. It is unnatural for a young man to live out his days with nobody for company but a fat French cow." Deerfoot shoved the ox in the back of its square head with his foot.

Tristan scowled over his shoulder. "You gossip like an old woman, Deerfoot. Leave me alone, or I will send you on to the fort without so much as a drink of water, while I come in the boat."

Deerfoot snorted. "We will both go in the boat, otherwise you might never get there."

He fell silent as Tristan led the ox into the spacious corral he had built to keep the animal from wandering too far. Deerfoot slid to the ground and helped Tristan feed the chickens and find some scraps for the pig. The animals would forage for themselves until he returned in a day or two.

As he gathered items he would need for the trip, answering Deerfoot's lighthearted insults and closing down the cabin, he couldn't help anticipating what he would say to a certain green-eyed Frenchwoman when he saw her. Married. She would be married and possibly even with child. Someone else's child.

The dull ache of his heart was so familiar that he hardly noticed it was a different sort of pain, accompanied this time by a fizz of anticipation. He would at least see her and speak to her. He would congratulate her and offer to . . .

What? Draw her a map?

Rolling his eyes at his own ridiculous mental perambulations, he slid the bolt across his cabin door to keep out roaming wild animals and followed Deerfoot to the riverbank below the bluff. Maybe the Indian was right. Yes, a beautiful woman like Geneviève Gaillain would certainly be married by now, but perhaps one of the less attractive girls remained unclaimed. One who wouldn't mind coming to keep house for a sour, lonely former mapmaker with a hole the size of Canada in his heart.

8

It seemed to Geneviève, seated between her sister and Raindrop halfway back in the fort's tiny chapel, that every event of importance that occurred in the colony of Louisiane must be celebrated inside these rickety walls. If today's events — a burial, a wedding, and a baptism — were a harbinger of days to come, the walls were like to explode before the year was out.

It was the first Sunday of September, and the newly wedded Madame and Surgeon-Major Barraud, who had been chosen to serve as godparents for the infant to be baptized, were seated in a place of honor up front, on the only real pew in the chapel.

Father Henri, recently appointed as official pastor of the as yet unbuilt parish church, threaded his way through the dense congregation with a dignity that would have graced the cathedral of Versailles. Judging by the yellow tinge of his skin and a slight tremor of his hands, he was not fully recovered from the fever that had taken Levasseur.

The infant's parents, prosperous young locksmith Zacharie Canelle and his wife Céline, who had emigrated from Rochefort nearly a year ago, followed close on the priest's heels, beaming with pride in their screaming progeny. As the first white native-born Louisianan, or *créole,* their son would hold an important place in history, and the baptismal record book waited upon the vestry table for the signatures of parents, godparents, priest, and commander.

Geneviève smiled as Raindrop reverently kissed her little cross-shaped piquet necklace, mimicking Father Henri's dramatic salutation of the ebony crucifix upon his white surplice. Geneviève had tatted the ornament and given it to her in honor of her baptism last Sunday; as far as she knew, Raindrop had yet to take it off.

As Father Henri called the godparents forward to remove the baby's blanket and hold him naked, squirming and wailing as if he were under torture, over the baptismal bowl, Geneviève looked for Father Mathieu. She found him standing near the wall to her left, his sober black robe in stark contrast to the white seminary garb of perpetually irritated Father Albert, the third pastor of the community. Now that Mathieu had come to fill the post of chaplain to the soldiers, and with Father Henri named pastor outside the fort, Father Albert suffered from lack of sheep to guard. She had heard gossip about his reluctance to return to his mission among the Tunica west of the river, which he had abandoned two years ago after coming upon a couple of fellow missioners left with their heads bashed in by hostile Indians.

Geneviève increasingly felt her heart tugged toward the native peoples whom she encountered as she went about the settlement. Their vulnerability to the blandishment of white traders, intimidation by the military forces, and even manipulation in spiritual matters for political advantage had made some quite understandably suspicious. She had been working with Raindrop to learn a few words of the Mobilian tongue. So far she had learned enough to send the little girl into fits of giggles, but she was determined to keep trying.

Other than that, her days had been filled with helping Father Mathieu and the two nuns tend the sick in the community — most of them yellow fever victims — and the evenings trotting from one social engagement to another with Madame. Remembering Commander Bienville's blunt stricture, she felt obliged to entertain one awkward advance after the other from young Canadian soldiers and French artisan bachelors. She was not so naïve as to think one must be head-over-heels in love with one's husband, but it seemed only reasonable to hope for a compatible life partner. Remembering her mother's descent into grief and despair after her father's murder, she was almost afraid of that kind of all-consuming love.

She studied Barbe Savarit, standing beside her miraculously sober new husband, looking proud and nervous and excited all at once. Did she expect to be happy, tied to a man who spent every waking moment at Burelle's tavern, when he wasn't pulling rotten teeth or treating fever victims with what amounted to sugar water? At least Barbe had a home of her own to go to at the end of this day. And hopefully soon she would have a child of her own to pour herself into.

A muffled sob drew her gaze to Ysabeau Bonnet, who sat a few feet away on a packing box, dabbing at her eyes with a sodden handkerchief. Aboard the *Pélican,* Ysabeau and Aimée had become bosom friends, which meant that Geneviève had also come to know her quite well. Ysabeau was only fifteen, younger even than Aimée, but she had managed to snag the well-connected bachelor Levasseur. This coup had given her quite a lofty status among the women of the colony.

Now he was dead, and poor Ysabeau was inconsolable. The wealthy Levasseur had neglected to include her in his last-minute will, which meant that she must start all over in her search for a husband, with nothing to show for her cleverness and coquetry. The richest and most influential men — with the exception of Bienville, who occupied a level of desirability to which only the truly delusional aspired — had either already married or died from accident or the fever, leaving the same list of eager but penniless and unproven young men from whom Geneviève would have to choose.

The charming Marc-Antoine Lanier remained elusive; even on the rare occasions when he attended social functions, he seemed focused on putting out political fires for Bienville. One could not seriously count him as a matrimonial prospect, when he was to embark any day now on a dangerous mission into Indian country. Julien Dufresne seemed on the point of offering for Aimée, but Geneviève could not rid herself of a sense that the man's polished exterior overlaid some unpleasant secret. Maybe it was the chilly eyes that seemed vaguely familiar. She had more than once caught him watching her, as if he waited to catch her in a lie. She hoped Aimée hadn't been so foolish as to confide their family history to him.

Her sister chose that moment to whisper in her ear, "Ysabeau is getting really annoying. She's given herself the hiccups."

Geneviève frowned and put a finger over her lips, but had to cover a smile when a loud "hic" came from a few yards away.

Fortunately the baby's wail of indignation as the water ran into his ears covered Aimée's giggle. The priest proclaimed the infant baptized in the name of the Father, Son, and Holy Spirit, adjuring his parents and godparents to raise him in the Christian faith, setting an example of daily holy living.

Father Henri handed the baby back to his mother, nodding approval as she tucked him into his blanket and cuddled him close. "And we, gathered here today to witness this solemn rite, must not forget that we also are called to righteousness." His gaze passed over the congregation like a sword. "There must be no more adulterous cohabitation, particularly between master and female servant. Scripture tells us it is better to marry than to burn. Therefore, any man who has had carnal knowledge of a woman who is not his wife must either marry her or put her away and find a proper mate for her."

There was a collective gasp throughout the crowded room as Father Henri paused. He avoided the gaze of Bienville, who had cleared his throat several times until the sound escalated to a threatening growl.

The commander rose to his considerable height, arms folded across his chest. "Father Henri, this message — well intentioned as it may be — would surely be better imparted in private first. I would see you in my office immediately."

The priest's florid face seemed like to explode from the blood that rushed to his cheeks and forehead. Clearly he did not appreciate being summoned like a private caught in dereliction of duty. "Children, I adjure you all to go in peace," he said through pinched lips. "May you be blessed in accordance with your good deeds this day." He crossed himself and all but ran to the door.

Bienville's face was a thundercloud, but Geneviève lost sight of him as the crowd rushed to leave the chapel, separating her from Aimée and the L'Angloises as well. As she burst through the door, she found herself nose to chest with Marc-Antoine Lanier, who was trying to get in.

"Pardon me, mademoiselle," he said, setting her away from him, hands to shoulders. "Have you seen the commander?"

"Yes, but I'm not sure where he is now. He wanted to speak to Father Henri." She looked over her shoulder, but people swarmed past her as if she were a rock in a river.

Lanier smiled. "Then you'll be the first to hear the good news. One of Bienville's runners came just now with the news that the *Profond* has arrived at Massacre Island with supplies from Martinique. We'll be sending supply boats down to meet her this afternoon."

"That's wonderful!" Geneviève looked up at him, endeavoring to jerk her mind from the tense scene she had just witnessed.

Lanier studied her face. "What's the matter?"

She flushed. "Perhaps you should keep looking for the commander."

"Why? Has something else gone wrong?"

"I'm not sure. The wedding and baptism masses went well, but then Father Henri added a few comments regarding . . ." She bit her lip. "Oh, dear, you really should talk to Commander Bienville. He seemed very angry."

Lanier looked uneasy. "All right. I shall." With a quick bow, he turned to go, but stopped with a snap of his fingers, looking over his shoulder. "I almost forgot. My brother has returned as well. He asked after you and was most discomfited to hear that the lovely Mademoiselle Gaillain remains unmarried and unbetrothed."

Geneviève forced herself to meet his twinkling eyes. "I don't know why that information should disturb anyone save me."

"Perhaps he fears for his own safety." Chuckling, he turned once more and jogged across the drill field toward the headquarters building, which housed Bienville's quarters on one end and the officers' barracks on the other.

Geneviève stared after him, nonplussed. Perhaps Tristan Lanier wanted to buy more bread. She shook her head. Unlikely, as he had already bought enough to feed the entire French marine.

She felt a tug on her sleeve and looked down to find Raindrop dancing about on bare feet, twirling in giddy circles. "Come,

160

mademoiselle! Madame sent me to find you! I am to say there are boats coming from the Ile de Massacre! Perhaps we may buy stuffs to make you another dress which will make the handsome men want to marry you!" She grabbed Geneviève's hand and pulled her willy-nilly toward the gate of the fort.

Laughing, Geneviève picked up her skirt and ran. She had no money for dress material, but a distraction from the fluttering of her stomach would be welcome. Tristan Lanier had no need to concern himself about her state of matrimony or his own precious bachelordom. She would tell him so. Better yet, she would ignore him.

Maybe.

There was a huge crowd heading toward the wharf to greet the first transport boat from Massacre Island, but Dufresne managed to get out in front of everybody. There were advantages to being on the commander's staff.

As soon as the marine boys got the boat tied in and the gangway laid, Dufresne scrabbled down the twenty-foot bluff onto the sand and leaped onto the crowded deck. Captain Béranger, who had come up with the first load of cargo, hailed Dufresne with a shout. They had met on two previous occasions, as the *Profond,* a merchant frigate out of Martinique, plied back and forth with some regularity.

The bill of lading Béranger handed Dufresne listed lengths of choice Rouen cloth, broad Brittany linen, fine Bayeux thread, five hundred fifty pounds of steel, over three and a half tons of flat and square Biscay iron, and one cardboard crate of black Pontardement lace. The ladies were going to love the dressmaking supplies. Bienville would be pleased to have the steel. And there were also sundries that would enable Dufresne to pocket a little extra cash too.

Béranger had already turned to shout at a cadet about to drop a cask of fine wine, but he caught Julien's arm as he started to swing onto the gangplank. "Ho, there, boy, not so fast! I've a packet of letters you might deliver to the commander. Let me fetch them from my cabin."

Julien paused. "Ah. Very good, I'll wait."

The captain disappeared below decks as Julien stood whistling with his hands in his breeches pockets. He watched the activity onshore until Béranger came back carrying a battered leathern pouch fastened by a buckled strap. He handed it to Julien. "Make sure Bienville himself receives this. I think there's a communication for you too."

Julien nodded, but he waited until he had climbed the bluff, safely passed the crowd, and circled the fort alone before he unbuckled the pouch's strap. He leaned back against one of the palisade stakes, grimacing as it gave behind him. It wouldn't take much for an enemy to either burn down or breach the rotten red pine timbers. If the British ever found out how vulnerable was the French fort, they would be in serious trouble.

He extracted a handful of missives, most of them for Bienville, impressed with the seal of Minister of Marine Pontchartrain. One came directly from King Louis himself. Greatly tempted to open it and claim he'd found it that way, Julien in the end returned it to the bag. The Sun King had become a bloated, narcissistic windbag who let his counsel of ministers run the country. Doubtful he would have anything useful to say. Bienville would probably let him read the others, so there was little to be gained by courting reprimand.

But the last, as Béranger had indicated, was addressed in a spidery, agitated hand to Aide-Major Julien Dufresne. The seal was that of his noble father, Vital Hayot, Comte de Leméry. But as the comte had not written to him in the entire two years of his exile in Louisiane, and he knew his half brother Gilbert's haphazard, back-tilted hand, the letter inside must be from his stepmother. He couldn't imagine what would prompt the indolent comtess to put pen to paper. Curious and mildly irritated, Julien broke the letter's seal. The comtess rarely had anything positive to say to him.

"My dear boy, your father has tragically died," she wrote without preamble.

Tragically? How else, he wondered, did a person die? He examined his feelings for shock or dismay and found none. Still, this was big news. He kept reading.

Carefully, without touching the freshly cut end of the manchineel limb from which the dangerous sap still oozed, Nika stuck the plant cutting into a large gourd in her basket. "You must never let the sap touch your fingers, boys, or you will have terrible blisters."

Tonaw, kneeling beside her, looked at her wide-eyed. "Mother, have you —"

"Yes." She showed him a blotchy white scar between the first two fingers of her left hand. "It hurt so bad I cried for days."

"I'm not a baby," Tonaw said stoutly. "I don't cry."

"Yes, you're becoming quite a big boy." She smiled and ruffled his hair. "Still, don't touch it. It's poison — which is why your father uses it to coat the tips of his hunting arrows."

"Father said he would take us with him next time," Chazeh said with shy pride. He stood behind Tonaw, leaning over his brother's shoulder to watch Nika's demonstration of the proper way to collect manchineel for poison. "We are both good shots now."

"I'm better!" Tonaw, the competitive twin, gave Nika a grin. "Father says so."

Nika sighed and rose, since the gourd and the basket were now full. "You will both be great hunters — if you learn patience and humility as well." She hooked the basket over one arm, holding it against her hip, and laid a hand on each boy's shoulder. "Come, let us take our plants home and treat the arrows we made this morning. They will need to dry overnight if you are to use them tomorrow."

It was true, the boys were old enough to begin spending more time with Mitannu, learning to become men of courage and strength. There were things only a father could teach them. But everything in her rebelled at sending her sweet, playful little boys off to participate in the more gruesome activities of manhood — particularly in the company of her cruel, selfish mate. When it suited him, Mitannu could be reasonable. But she had also experienced his sudden fits of cold rage, which caused him to lash out at whoever happened to be standing the closest. Usually it was her — and her greatest fear was that one day Mitannu's unpredictable temper would bring irreparable harm to one of the children.

As she and the boys returned to the village through the woods, she let them run ahead, arguing excitedly about whose shot had brought down the squirrel they'd eaten for supper last night. Walking at a more sedate pace, she absently kicked at fallen pine cones and oak leaves, wishing for the thousandth time that there were some way to remake the choices that had brought her to this pass.

If she were a woman of courage herself, she would do something to change her circumstances, she thought, shifting the heavy basket to her other hip. She looked down at the fragrant leafy limbs clustered around and inside the gourd. A brave woman, who loved her sons more than life, would find a way.

9

On Monday afternoon Tristan met Marc-Antoine in officers' quarters, which was adjacent to headquarters and on the opposite end of the building from Bienville's quarters. Except for a handful of men dispatched to Massacre Island to assist in transferring the remainder of supplies from the *Profond,* the entire battalion was on the drill ground participating in daily parade exercises. Marc-Antoine found a pitcher of ale and a couple of tankards, then joined Tristan at one of the plain cypress tables stuffed into a corner, where one could find an unobstructed view of the door as well as a bit of privacy.

Tristan sipped his drink as his brother loosened the collar button of his uniform coat and sat back against the wall with a weary sigh. Marc-Antoine had arisen at dawn to attend Bienville's conclave with an envoy from the Spanish governor in Pensacola. It seemed the Spanish, who had over the past ten years developed into allies against the British, were once again in rather a financial pickle and in need of basic foodstuffs such as flour, corn, and salt. Marc-Antoine's task had been to negotiate a fair price.

Marc-Antoine took a deep drink from his own tankard, then set it down with a bang. "We might have been able to come to terms two hours ago, except La Salle sent his cockroach to make sure nobody made any profit."

Tristan raised his brows. "Cockroach?"

"Dufresne." Marc-Antoine made a face. "I swear the man is everywhere he's unwanted, which is . . . everywhere."

Tristan grinned. "You've a way with words, my brother. No wonder the Indians call you Bright Tongue."

"It's true." Marc-Antoine laughed. "I told you I'm tired. I'm looking forward to leaving the settlement. Six weeks without Bienville's contradictory orders! You should have heard him lighting into Father Henri yesterday afternoon."

"What about?"

"Mainly his diatribe about our men sleeping with their Indian servant women."

"Well . . . at one time Bienville was

concerned about that too. Isn't that why he sent for the *Pélican* girls?"

"Yes, but there still aren't enough white women to go around. Father Henri's solution is for the men to marry their concubines, to make them wives in the sight of the Holy Church."

"And what's wrong with that?" Tristan had married Sholani before taking her virginity, though she probably hadn't cared a *sou* whether the black robe said words over them or not. It had mattered to *him*.

Marc-Antoine's expression softened. "Nothing, as far as I'm concerned. But you and I both understood when we joined this expedition that the King is after establishing a French Catholic state here. Most Indian women won't truly convert, even to gain a white husband. Besides, Bienville is a pragmatist. These Canadians that we're talking about aren't like you, Tristan. If they're forced to marry one Indian woman or leave, they'll hightail it for the woods. Father Henri is all about morality, but Bienville wants to keep his men happy so they'll stay."

There was something inside him that rebelled at both viewpoints, though Tristan couldn't explain it to his brother. He and Marc-Antoine had been raised in a God-fearing home by parents who loved and respected one another, who demonstrated a partnership rare for the times in which they lived. He understood that marriage was a holy bond with a higher purpose than release for a man's lust. But it hadn't been just morality either, not for him and Sholani. They had been a family, despite the cultural differences that sometimes made them shout with laughter, sometimes reduced them to inarticulate frustration. He had wanted to hold his child with a fierceness that still on occasion caught him off guard.

He suspected his brother would either laugh and call him crazy — or, worse, look at him with pity. Marc-Antoine hadn't known their father like he had; after all, the boy had been only fourteen when they'd left home. He'd missed the quiet discussions about God and women and courage and patriotism Tristan shared with Antoine Lanier as they copied and colored maps commissioned by the wealthy peers of the province.

Marc-Antoine was the one to be pitied after all.

Tristan nodded. "There's no arguing with Bienville once he sets his mind, and the priest isn't going to change it by preaching at him." He paused. "Still, can Bienville make Father Henri stop encouraging the men to marry their mistresses?"

"I suppose not. But the commander will have more influence than any priest. He controls their wages and privileges, after all."

"And the priest controls eternal destiny."

Marc-Antoine shrugged. "Only for the superstitious ones."

"You think our faith is a superstition?" Maybe Tristan didn't know his brother after all.

Marc-Antoine chuckled. "I mainly don't see how making love to a woman who's perfectly willing is grounds to go to hell."

Tristan knew many men who shared Marc-Antoine's skepticism, but few were so bold as to express it out loud. "Damnation aside, Marc, there's the issue of procreation. You do agree that a man's children are his responsibility?"

"I suppose." Marc-Antoine looked away. "As far as I know, I have no children." Then he squinted at Tristan. "Have you not had a woman since . . ."

Tristan felt his face grow warm. "I dream of Sholani still. I can't — I don't want to — I'm too busy for it anyway." That sounded utterly stupid. He regretted opening the argument with his brother, who could always twist his words.

To his relief, Marc-Antoine overlooked the opportunity to twit him further. "Well, whatever has been keeping you so busy is going to have to wait. Bienville is ready to pull the trigger on this mission to the Koroa and Alabama, and I need you with me."

"Why? Your language skills are better than mine, and you're the one who lived with the Alabama."

"True, and true." Marc-Antoine smiled. "But the Koroa traditionally hate the Alabama. Getting them to agree to an alliance will take both of us. We can use the fact that your wife was native . . . and you know how the Indians love to have their portraits drawn." He paused, leaned over the table. "Tristan, you know how critical this mission is. We've almost waited too late. I hear rumblings that the British have gotten bolder. They've even sent Huguenot missionaries into a village or two, thinking nobody would catch on because they're French-speaking."

"Marc —"

"No, listen. I've seen your maps of the northern end of the river. You know the territory where we want to go, better than any other man in Bienville's company. With hurricane season closing in, we can't afford to lose time wandering around. We've lost so many good men this year . . . Tonti, Levasseur, Le Sueur . . . and the boys Pontchartrain sent to replace them are barely old enough to shave!" Marc-Antoine's expression was grim. "The Spanish are foundering too. If we don't turn this thing around, Fat Louis is going to abandon us altogether, and we'll be speaking English instead of French!"

They stared at one another for a long moment. Tristan knew that his brother spoke only the truth. He himself might be comfortably coexisting with both the Indians and the French settlement, but if Louis's colonial experiment failed and the English took control of the territory, his own plantation would be absorbed as well. And if there was one nation Tristan despised more than his own motherland, it was the British pigs who had bought his wife like an animal, raped her, and killed both her and his unborn baby.

He thought of his land — the soft earth turned up in spring, the smell of pine in his cabin, the abundance of fish in the icy creeks that spilled along the edges of the dense forest. His ox, his milk cow, and the chickens that provided food year round.

Then, before he could stop it, his all-too-vivid imagination conjured an image of the

173

Pélican's arrival, of that first young woman suspended in midair on a canvas sling, clinging to the rope in innocent assurance that all would be well in this new world. Her courage, her core of faith and strength had spoken to him in a language he hadn't known existed. And then to find those qualities housed in a package of physical beauty, intelligence, and humor . . . he might deny it to his brother, but he had been lost from the beginning.

Yesterday, when he'd arrived at the fort and asked after her, Marc-Antoine sealed his fate. Mademoiselle Gaillain was, miraculously, still unattached.

Castigating himself for a coward and a fool, he had gone out of his way to avoid her. What did he know about courting a gently bred young Frenchwoman? He hadn't even seen his own mother for seven years. It would take time to convince her that he was not a complete savage, that she might throw in her lot with him and expect a life at least as good as with any of the other Canadians in the settlement.

Now . . . now, Marc-Antoine asked him to embark on a journey that might take months, with no guarantee of returning alive. But if he didn't go, the colony would be in jeopardy of falling anyway . . . and around in circles he went again.

He laid his hands flat upon the table and stared at the scars across the knuckles.

"So." Marc-Antoine leaned forward, expression coaxing. "Are you coming with us?"

Despite her best intentions, during the past twenty-four hours, Geneviève had had little opportunity to ignore Tristan Lanier, as he seemed determined to avoid her first. She saw him disappear into the tavern in company with his brother, just as she was coming out of the dry goods store with Ysabeau.

"Geneviève! You are not attending!"

"I'm sorry, Ysabeau. What did you say?" Geneviève dragged her gaze from the open tavern door, from which issued a distinct roar of masculine frivolity, and fixed it belatedly upon Ysabeau's pouting face.

"I asked you," Ysabeau sighed, "if you think I should wear the yellow dress at my wedding, or would the rose go better with my complexion?"

"Wedding?" Geneviève, whose thoughts had been rather more occupied with the dark brown eyes of a certain lonely young planter, reminded herself not to be so selfish. "Are you really going through with this hasty match with Denis Lafleur? Father

Mathieu said —"

"Father Mathieu is an unromantic old raven! Just because Denis enjoys a game of cards every now and then, there was no cause to spoil my happiness by preaching me a private sermon."

"Ysabeau." Geneviève tried not to look as raven-like as the priest, though she couldn't help feeling troubled. "Only yesterday you were crying over Monsieur Levasseur all during Barbe's wedding. I just think you should be more careful —"

"Oh!" Ysabeau stamped her foot. "You are just jealous!" She whirled and dashed back into the store.

"Ysabeau, wait!" Geneviève started to follow, then shook her head. Papa used to say that the most effective school for fools was experience. Ysabeau was beyond listening anyway.

She glanced at the tavern. She had meant to ask Monsieur Burelle if he still had an interest in selling her bread.

But perhaps she should wait until the morning, when the tavern would be quieter, less busy with customers. She picked up her skirts and resolutely turned toward the L'Anglois home. If Monsieur Lanier wanted to see her, he could easily find her.

Tristan had secured one of the small second-floor rooms above the tavern, but he was beginning to wish he had opted instead for guest quarters in the guardhouse. Marc-Antoine had returned to duty, leaving him to mull over the decision whether to join the impending expedition. By eight o'clock that evening, Burelle's establishment was rollicking with off-duty soldiers in need of a drink, unmarried artisans with a few *sous* to gamble away, and officers who wanted to trade a few bawdy jokes and songs before either turning for home and spouse or retiring to quarters for the night. It was, for a man who had grown accustomed to absolute stillness and silence, a form of exquisite torture.

Resigning himself to a sleepless night, he accepted a tankard from Burelle's wife, left a coin on the bar, and made his way toward a rowdy group of men gathered around a faro table in a back corner, most of whom he knew. He had served with Boutin and Fautisse early in the beginnings of the settlement, as they built the fort and stockade. Another he recognized as Lafleur, a junior officer on Marc-Antoine's staff, and a fourth as brickmaker Jean Alexandre. Tristan picked up the names of the other two men as he leaned against the wall watching the game. Valentin Barraud, still dressed in his uniform and insignia of surgeon-major, received several risqué — and undoubtedly jealous — comments regarding his recent marriage, from a clearly inebriated young soldier named Connard.

The game proceeded, the bets getting wilder and losses deeper, until both Lafleur and Connard were out of chips and resorted to writing IOUs against future wages. Connard's narrow, clean-shaven face had become steadily pinker with heat and embarrassment, his brown hair wet and spiked from running his hand through it, until he looked like a baby possum that had fallen into a barrel of ale.

Lafleur looked with grim disbelief at the card given him by Alexandre, the dealer and banker, and muttered a curse under his breath.

Alexandre shrugged. "You're done, Lafleur. You've already lost three months' wages."

"Which I won't see for another year," Lafleur retorted. "What difference does one more month make?" He drew a scrap of paper from his coat pocket.

"No more paper bets," Alexandre said firmly. "If you're out of money, you can bet dry goods. Or ammunition. Or your wife." He sent a sneering glance down at Barraud, who lay under the table snoring.

"I don't have a wife," Lafleur said with an evil grin, "but I just got engaged today. Mademoiselle Bonnet should buy a substantial pile of chips, say two hundred livres. If I win, I get her back and you cancel my debts. If not —" He shrugged. "You keep her."

When Alexandre's eyes lit, Tristan knew he had to intervene. "Gentlemen, this is a bad idea."

Connard glared at Tristan. "Who are you to dictate our game?" He slammed a fist onto the table. "If I beat the bank, you forgive all my debt and I get the Bonnet girl." The whole settlement knew Connard had asked nearly every one of the unattached girls to marry him, with no takers. "If I lose, my brand-new hunting rifle is yours. It's worth at least a hundred livres."

Alexandre nodded. "Fine, but this is the last game." He looked at Boutin. "Are you in?"

Boutin looked alarmed. "I got a wife already."

"Fautisse?"

Fautisse gave a short, hard laugh. "I

wouldn't mind taking on the lovely Mademoiselle Bonnet." He shoved his entire pile of chips onto the queen. "But what if she refuses to honor the bet?"

Lafleur smirked. "Since when does a woman have any say in a man's business transactions?"

"I've been married for a month," Boutin said, "and already I know the answer to that question."

Hoots of laughter accompanied the soft whir of cards as Alexandre shuffled the deck and palmed it for the deal. After each player placed his chips on the layout, Alexandre turned over the top card and laid it face-up on the table to his right, then laid another to the left. The dealer's card on the right was a trey of hearts, matching Fautisse's bet. The punter's card on the left was also a trey.

Alexandre grimaced. "One for the other," he muttered as he realized the bank had neither gained nor lost.

The advantage shifted from player to player, until the last three remaining cards in the dealer's deck came up. Lafleur, confident in his luck, made a paroli final play, turning up a corner of his card to show that he intended to bet both his winnings and stake. In response, Connard doubled his money.

Fautisse dropped out in disgust. "I'm done."

Alexandre turned the last card and stared at the layout in disbelief. "Connard, you cheated."

Bankrupt, Lafleur jumped to his feet, overturning his chair.

"The only way to cheat in this game is to be the dealer," Connard chortled. "Pay me out, Alexandre."

Alexandre sat sullen for a moment. Tristan knew that the dealer, who staked the game and had the advantage of any split coup, generally went home with a hundred livres or two. It had to be galling to pay out such a large amount to smarmy young Connard. Finally Alexandre pinched his lips together and scraped in the chips, stacking them by denomination. He glanced up at Tristan. "Count with me, Lanier. I don't want any question of accuracy."

Tristan nodded. At the end, the bank was four hundred livres short. This was going to get ugly.

"Four hundred livres is the value of your gun, Connard, plus —" Alexandre glanced at Lafleur — "the value of Lafleur's affianced. You two work this out to your own satisfaction. I'm going home." He tucked

181

the deck of cards into his coat pocket, then began stacking the clay chips into their metal case.

Lafleur's eyes were blue slits of rage. "Connard, I don't know how you did that, but Ysabeau Bonnet won't settle for an ugly, perpetually broke, rotten tomato like you."

"It takes more than a pretty face to satisfy a lady." Connard, clearly unhappy to be looking up at the tall sergeant, swayed to his feet. "It won't take her long to realize her good fortune in escaping a man who sires at least a dozen half-Indian papooses a month."

"Says the man who smells so bad the squaws won't even stay in the same room with him." Lafleur laughed. "First thing tomorrow morning I'll propose to Edmé Oüanet. Almost as pretty as Ysabeau, and she can read and write."

Fautisse lurched to his feet, fists bunched, knocking Tristan hard against the wall. "I've been courting her, Lafleur! Keep your hands off!"

"Then may the best man win!" Lafleur swept a mocking bow.

Before he could rise, Fautisse swung and hit him under the chin. Lafleur shook his head, recovered, and made a return swing.

Shouts of "Fight! Fight!" went up all over

the tavern. Tristan found himself in a maelstrom of fists, elbows, knees, and broken chairs. As he tried to extricate himself, ducking and protecting his face and midsection, from the corner of his eye he saw Alexandre shove his faro supplies into a canvas knapsack, drop to hands and knees, and crawl along the wall toward the door. Not the method Tristan would have chosen, but perhaps the safest course for a man who wanted to avoid a night in the brig. Bienville had small tolerance for fighting amongst the ranks.

Indeed it was less than ten minutes by Tristan's reckoning before the blast of a musket, presumably fired at the ceiling, penetrated the din. He was very glad he was not asleep in the bed directly above the bar.

The noise and confusion faded, and the crowd parted to admit an officer wielding a smoking musket in one hand and a drawn sword in the other. Through the smoke Tristan recognized his little brother.

"What is the meaning of this?" roared Marc-Antoine. He had apparently been abed, as he was sketchily dressed in breeches and a linen shirt, halfway buttoned and tails flapping, and had bothered with neither waistcoat nor shoes. The dark hair flowing freely about his shoulders and a two-day growth of beard added to the look of a particularly enraged pirate. Then his eyes widened. "Tristan? What are you doing here?"

"I assure you it's not by choice." Tristan grabbed Connard and Fautisse each by the collar and hauled them forward. "Here are two of your culprits, and the third is sliding along the wall over there." He inclined his head toward Lafleur, who was attempting to slip out the door unnoticed.

"Don't let him get away!" Marc-Antoine snapped at the uniformed guard loitering nearest the door, then turned his attention back to the sulking and bloody miscreants wriggling in Tristan's grasp. "You started this? Never mind, we'll sort it out at headquarters. Where's Burelle?"

"Here, sir." The tavern owner pushed through the crowd.

"Shut this place down. Everybody go home, to the barracks, or face arrest." He scowled, brandishing the musket. "Not you, Lafleur! You're coming with me."

In five minutes or less, the tavern was clear of patrons. Burelle set to work righting chairs, shaking his head over a broken table, and picking up dented pewterware. Tristan, lending a hand to the tavern-keep, saw a side of his happy-go-lucky brother that seemed to have developed in his absence: the decisive, clear-thinking officer with a natural gift for leadership. Marc-Antoine sheathed his sword but continued to grasp the musket as he searched the deserted room, making sure no troublemakers lurked in shadowy corners. When he came upon the surgeon-major, still slumbering peacefully beneath the card table, he poked the man with a bare toe. Barraud failed to respond. Marc-Antoine cracked a smile visible to no one but Tristan and let him be. The three miscreants slouched near the bar, Connard bracing a set of cracked ribs and Lafleur mopping at a bloody nose.

Marc-Antoine pronounced himself satisfied that the situation was under control and ordered the troublemakers to move out ahead of him. He turned at the door. "Tris, will you come? I'll want a sober witness."

Tristan fished in his pocket for a couple of sous, which he flipped onto the bar as he passed. "I'll be back later, Burelle."

The march across the dark parade ground was accomplished in short order, Marc-Antoine being in no mood to sympathize with cracked ribs or broken noses. At the guardhouse, Marc-Antoine produced a key and shoved his prisoners inside with no ceremony.

"I deed the surgeod," Lafleur protested.

"You'll have to wait until he sobers up." Marc-Antoine slammed the door and locked it again. "Come on, Tristan. Bienville will want a report."

By the time the two of them crossed the short distance between guardhouse and headquarters, Marc-Antoine had buttoned his shirt, but it still flapped loose over his breeches. Tristan wondered what time it was. The moon was a silver boat floating over the stockade, and nothing but the whir of an owl and the clanking of Marc-Antoine's sword broke the silence.

Tristan stood back as his brother rapped on the door to Bienville's quarters. At an impatient "Come," they entered to find the commander seated at his desk, fully dressed except for tricorn and coat. Bienville laid down his quill and addressed Marc-Antoine. "Situation under control?"

"Yes, sir."

Bienville scowled at Tristan. "What's he doing here?"

"Witness."

Bienville's lip curled. "Witness or participant?"

Tristan's hands bunched. "Do I look like I've been in a brawl?"

Bienville had the grace to look away. "It's

186

been a long, frustrating day." He gestured for Marc-Antoine and Tristan to pull over chairs. "Sit down and tell me what the uproar was all about."

They did so, Marc-Antoine finishing, "Fautisse, Connard, and Lafleur are in the guardhouse."

"Anybody hurt?"

"Bloody knuckles, broken ribs and noses, the usual. Burelle's place took some damage."

Bienville grunted. "What started it?"

Marc-Antoine looked at Tristan. "Not sure. That's why I brought my brother."

Bienville's thick brows drew together. "All right then. Let's have it."

Tristan briefly described his approach to the faro game and his sense that trouble could be brewing, inferred from the toxic blend of undisciplined and inebriated personalities at the table. "And then the money and credit ran out for Connard and Lafleur. The bets turned to women."

Bienville slid a hand over his face. "I knew this was going to happen. Any woman in particular?"

Tristan tried to remember. "A girl named Ysabeau Bonnet and another one . . . Oüanet maybe?"

"Last week it was the Gaillain sisters and

187

Françoise Dubonnier. I warned them this has got to stop. Choosing a husband shouldn't take this long." Bienville's smile turned grim. "Maybe I should line them up and draw lots, like they used to do in the Bible."

Marc-Antoine sat up straight. "Sir! You can't —"

"I'm joking, Lanier." Bienville barked a laugh. "After all, that's what started this contretemps, eh? I've been too patient with these double-minded women." He snatched a piece of parchment and jabbed his quill into the open inkpot. He scratched furiously for a minute, sanded the ink and blew it clean. "Make sure La Salle gets this before breakfast. The remaining single women have one month to choose husbands. At the end of that time, I'll host a ball to announce the betrothals of any women still holding out. On that date, financial support from the Crown ends." He handed the paper to Marc-Antoine. "If you want the younger Gaillain girl, you'd better speak up now. You leave for Alabama territory in less than forty-eight hours."

Marc-Antoine shook his head. "She's pretty, but I don't need the headache. She's too fond of her own face."

"Fine. Then get your gear together and

prepare your contingent. Wait, one more thing." Bienville stroked the quill through his fingers and looked at Tristan. "Is it true you're willing to go with them?"

"Yes." Until that moment, he hadn't been sure of his answer. Perhaps his brother's heretofore unsuspected maturity had tipped the balance.

"That's good. I'm . . . glad you're here. Can you keep your mouth shut?"

"You know I'm not a talker."

"No, you're a thinker and a doer." Bienville gave a one-sided smile. "I've missed your input, and I'm sorry I didn't listen to you on more than one occasion. But your country needs you this time."

10

During the heat of the afternoon, the women of Louisiane had developed the habit of meeting in small groups in someone's home for tea and conversation — a short break from backbreaking labor in kitchens, in gardens, or over washboards at the creek. Those with infants or small children would put them down for a nap on pallets on the floor, then settle themselves on the gallery outside, hoping to stir a breeze with fans woven from palmetto fronds. Skirts would be hiked to the outrageous vicinity of the knees, stockings and shoes kicked off, and stomachers unlaced at the bosom. There was a tacit agreement for mutual nonjudgment, even amongst the most prudish of the matrons. It was simply too hot for more than minimum clothing.

Today there was much to discuss, particularly among the unmarried women. Françoise Dubonnier, self-appointed spokeswoman for the *Pélican* girls, had drawn together Geneviève and Aimée, Ysabeau and Edmé, and Noël Dumesnil — the so-called "holdouts" — for a meeting on the gallery of the Brossard cabin, home of recently wed Thérèse Brochon. Thérèse had outdone herself as hostess, producing a silver plate of delicate rice cakes dusted with confectioner's sugar her besotted new husband had purchased on the black market from Julien Dufresne. She served sassafras tea in delicate Limoges cups, given her by her mother and coddled all the way from Rouen. Geneviève guessed there was not a woman in the group who would not have given her right pinky for one of those cups — or who would have admitted it.

The Brossards owned two straight chairs and a rocker, which Pierre had paid for by bricking the foundation of carpenter Claude Fautisse's cabin. The fact that Fautisse — who had been courting Edmé — was presently incarcerated in the guardhouse because he had fought two men in defense of her honor had been the topic of considerable conversation already. Edmé sat fanning herself in the rocker, endeavoring to look modestly flustered at such notoriety, but achieving a pronounced simper at best.

Poor Ysabeau — Geneviève noticed that

"poor" seemed to have become a permanent part of Ysabeau's name — had no such romantic embarrassment to sigh over. She had lost one fiancé to yellow fever, and the second had gambled her away over a faro board, earning his own fare to the guardhouse. The third man to claim her, Ensign René Connard, was also currently under arrest.

Ysabeau sat on the floor of the gallery, hugging her knees and sniffling into a yellow lawn handkerchief. "I want to go home," she said over and over, making Geneviève wish she could stuff the handkerchief in the girl's mouth.

Geneviève herself perched barefoot on one of the broad rails of the gallery with her skirt lifted to her knees, perhaps not a particularly ladylike posture, but more apt to catch a chance breeze. She had passed on the sassafras tea, preferring to occupy her hands with her tatting.

"You cannot go home, Ysabeau," Françoise said with far more patience than Geneviève felt. "We all agreed to come for our own reasons and, for most of us, circumstances in France were worse than they are here anyway. If you can't find a suitable mate here, where the men outnumber us ten to one, what hope do you have of contracting a husband at all?"

"I don't know," Ysabeau wailed, "but I wanted to marry Denis Lafleur! He is so good-looking, and he even has a pretty name!"

"Do you really want to marry a man who would gamble you away on the turn of a card?" Aimée frowned. "As if you were a possession like a horse or a pig, for heaven's sake? Have you no pride?" When Ysabeau promptly burst into fresh tears, Aimée lifted her hands. "Ysabeau, you know there was no betrothal contract with Monsieur Lafleur, no matter what he told you."

"Perhaps Monsieur Connard will turn out to be the best husband in New France," Noël said. A shy, plain girl with stick-straight brown hair, hazel eyes, and freckles sprinkled across a blunt nose, she was the only one who had received no marriage offers at all as of yet. She tended to hide in corners at social functions, and would turn an unattractive orange if unexpectedly addressed. "You are so pretty — just think, you have had six offers already."

Ysabeau gave Noël a tremulous smile of gratitude, but her answer was cut off when their governess swept to her full, statuesque height.

"Girls, this is getting us nowhere," Françoise said. "What concerns me most is Monsieur le Commandant's highhanded attempt to strong-arm us into making hasty decisions about this serious and delicate matter. If we do not choose mates by a certain time, he says he'll cut off the financial support of the Crown." She paused, hands on hips, and looked around at her companions. "I for one don't plan to stand for this — this — interference!"

Geneviève suspected that some of Françoise's dudgeon could be attributed to the commander's failure to be reeled in by her less-than-subtle lures.

Aimée bounced to her feet. "I agree! It is not fair that he removes himself from the list of eligible bachelors, when he has perhaps the greatest income and property in the entire settlement! And then to send the next greatest catch off on some ridiculous Indian mission — !"

"I don't know, Aimée," Thérèse said, looking over her shoulder as if she expected a savage to come bounding out of the forest at any moment. "I shouldn't like to be carried off and made to wear those shapeless tunics the Indian women wear."

"They don't wear them because they're Indians, ninny, they wear them because they are slaves." Edmé wrinkled her forehead.

"At least I think so."

"Do you think the Indians are people in the same sense that we are?" Noël asked. "The King does not want us to intermarry with them because they are heathen."

Geneviève had heard enough. She slid off the rail onto the soft ground below the gallery and stood with her hands clenched behind her back, trying to gain control of her temper. The King had sent dragoons into her home in the name of God. He had beheaded her father in the name of God — when everyone knew Louis kept more than one mistress and had more illegitimate children than legitimate. Despite that contract she had been forced to sign, she was not going to marry the next Catholic bachelor who offered, just because Bienville said she must.

God in heaven, I came here by faith. I came because Father Mathieu made a way, and I trust him. Help me see your will in this muddle. Help me take care of my sister . . .

The other girls were staring at her. She took a breath and let it out. "Noël, of course the Indians are people. Their language is different, their skin is darker, but don't you think those women are just as afraid of change as you are? Still, they've lived here

195

longer, which means we can learn from them."

Edmé looked skeptical. "Would you marry an Indian man, Geneviève?"

"I don't know." Geneviève looked away. "There's little chance one would ask me." She thought of the man with the string of human scalps she had encountered in Roy's kitchen — the day Tristan Lanier bought her bread. She remembered Tristan's intervention between her and the Indian, the genuine alarm in his eyes, the measured way he had spoken to the man in that harsh, alien language. She had not understood the words, but clearly they had been discussing the scalps — in a businesslike tone, as if they had been animal pelts brought in for sale.

In a wash of clarity, she was in Pont-de-Montvert, on the day the Abbé of Chaila was assassinated. Three dragoons in full regalia had come for her father — young men like these boy soldiers who stood guard here with Bienville. They were laughing at her mother, who had flung herself to her knees begging for mercy, flirting with Aimée and promising to come back for her, even as they dragged her father from the kitchen through the bakery shop. Two of the young men had her father by the arms, and the other walked behind them, prodding their prisoner with his sword.

Standing at the top of the stairs, listening to her mother scream, she knew she must do something. She went for her father's rifle leaning in the corner beneath the stairs, then found his powder horn and shot in a small cupboard. Jean Cavalier had thought it amusing to take her hunting on Sunday afternoons; he had shown her how to prime and load it, how to aim and brace herself for the kickback. They had killed rabbits in the wooded hills beyond the village, bringing them back for her mother's stew pot, and she had thought little of it — until she stalked those young dragoons headed for the green, where their officers waited to deal with traitors and heretics who had dared to "reform" the King's religion and murder the Abbé. Cavalier was elsewhere now, and she was on her own.

Who had murdered the Abbé? Geneviève wouldn't be surprised if it were Cavalier himself. But it was not her gentle father, who rose every morning when the sky was still dark, to read the Scripture and kneel for half an hour in prayer. Father, who spent his days creating beautiful and mouthwatering pastries for the loyalist elites in the neighboring village of Fraissinet-de-Lozère.

The laughing young dragoons did not suspect they were followed by the chef's older daughter. The pastry shop was at the edge of the village, and it was a long, circuitous walk along the road to the green. With the gun under her arm, Geneviève cut through the candlemaker's yard, ducked under some laundry hanging in the summer breeze, then ran parallel to the main road until she darted to the right and came out a hundred yards ahead of the dragoons. Panting, she planted herself in the middle of the road, raised the gun and waited. She could hear them coming, heard the cursing when one of them tripped on the rut that always washed out in front of Monsieur Malbècq's pigsty. Her heart thundered like a millstone rolling downhill. It had not occurred to her at the time that she could only shoot one of them with the musket, and that the other two were certain to take reprisal. She only meant to stop them from taking her father away.

By the time they rounded the bend that followed the boundary of Madame Babin's property, her resolve was steeled.

Her father saw her first. "Ginette!" he groaned. "No! Go home!"

The dragoons halted for a moment, no doubt nonplused by the sight of the crazy girl in flour-dusted cap and apron, aiming a gun at them. The one with the sword stopped scraping pig slop from his boots and burst out laughing. He came around in front of her father and his companions, playfully thrusting the sword at her. "Come here, little one, and I will teach you the duel of love."

She shot him first.

And that was how she came to be aboard the *Pélican.*

"We'll take two pirogues." Marc-Antoine stood behind Tristan, who was seated at a table in officers' quarters. He leaned over Tristan's shoulder to unroll the map and flatten it on the table. "The Alabama villages begin about three hundred miles upriver, the first one on the Koasati bluff. We hope to make an average of ten miles a day, which should put us back here within a couple of months."

Tristan followed his brother's finger as it traced the river bends on a map he himself had drawn during that last fateful mapping expedition nearly two years ago. He had traveled with the parchments, a bottle of ink, several quills, and his sextant packed in a cleverly designed map case his father had given him the day he left with Iberville.

Father had made it himself out of a pine log cut in half, then hollowed out and lined with cedar. It had been flattened slightly on top and bottom so that it could function as a seat, and was finished with leather hinges and a hand-worked iron hasp.

The chest was under his bed at home. He didn't remember giving the maps to Marc-Antoine, but he supposed he must have done so sometime before the discovery of Sholani's disappearance.

He blinked away memories and looked up at his brother. "Who's going with us?"

"Barraud, Guillory, Saucier, and Father Mathieu. Bienville's plan is to take enough arms and manpower to provide force, with the priest along to give an impression of good will." Marc-Antoine's smile was sour. "God only knows why Barraud will be along. The man is useless as a surgeon and a soldier."

Tristan nodded, remembering last night's tavern scene. "Has Bienville provided gifts for the Indians?"

"Shirts and blankets for the chiefs, strings of beads, bells, a few pairs of red stockings. We don't want to overload the pirogues." Marc-Antoine paused. "What do you think?"

"Sounds about right."

200

Marc-Antoine's expression was peculiar. Something besides trinkets and clothing was clearly on his mind. It was not like his gregarious brother to hold back his thoughts.

"What is it?" Tristan braced himself.

There was a long pause during which sounds of the garrison filtered in through the open window: someone firing a musket in the distance, the clanging of iron from the forge, muffled conversation and laughter as a party of soldiers passed. Marc-Antoine finally shrugged and looked away. "Nothing." He took a breath. "Tris, how well do you know Father Mathieu?"

Tristan blinked. "But little. We spoke a bit on the trip up from the island when he and the women first came. Why?"

"He's a good man. You should spend some time with him." Marc-Antoine looked a bit anxious, the kind of expression he'd had when they were children and he knew a secret he couldn't tell.

What business could the priest possibly have with his little brother? Marc-Antoine would be the last man alive to profess any religious bent. And there had been nothing particularly mysterious about Father Mathieu that Tristan could discern.

Tristan smiled. "We'll be traveling together

for several weeks. I'm sure we'll get acquainted."

"Yes." Marc-Antoine looked relieved. He picked up the map and rolled it up. "That's true."

Tristan pushed his chair back and rose. "If we're leaving at daylight, I need to give Deerfoot some instructions about feeding my animals and closing up the cabin. He's waiting for me at Burelle's." He cuffed his brother with rough affection. "Maybe I'll buy Father Mathieu a pint as well."

He exited the headquarters building, rolling that peculiar, understated conversation with Marc-Antoine around in his head. Tristan had had little interaction with priests of any sort, so he had paid scant attention to the newest black robe, as the Indians termed the Jesuit missionaries.

He understood Bienville's use of priests as one peg — military force and bribery being the other two — in the tent of political commerce. The Indians were a deeply spiritual people who accepted the concept of Father God, and generally respected the authority of his earthly representatives. However, the village medicine man, quite understandably, sometimes came to resent the priest's power — with potentially violent results — and Tristan had learned to be cautious when traveling into Indian territory with a Jesuit or seminarian in tow. Father Mathieu being an unknown quantity, Tristan was doubly curious about the motives of Geneviève's mentor.

He crossed the drill ground without incident, then passed through the chapel without encountering Father Mathieu or either of the other two priests presently living in the settlement. As he went out the secondary entrance at the back of the fort, however, he nearly crashed head-on into Geneviève herself.

"Mademoiselle! I'm so sorry!" He caught her by the shoulders and set her away from him, scanning her face for signs of injury or distress. "If you're in such a hurry, perhaps I could hoist you over my shoulder again and take you there faster."

Her expression lit in a most gratifying way, chasing away the stormy expression in the sea-colored eyes. "I assure you I'm quite capable of arriving at my destination on my own two feet. But if you're going to the tavern you may walk with me."

"As it happens, that's exactly where I'm bound." He bowed and offered an arm. "I'll be honored to accompany you, if you'll promise to slow down enough for a man of my advanced years to keep up with you."

Laughing, she laid her hand lightly upon his forearm. She seemed glad of his support, since the road contained more bumps and ruts and puddles than straightaways. She was quiet for several paces, then looked up at him. "Thank you for not asking questions."

He studied her upturned face. She was a bit freckled and sunburnt across the nose, due, no doubt, to her cap hanging by its strings down her back. But she looked healthier than most of the other Frenchwomen he'd seen about the settlement, many of whom were still recovering from the fever. He was glad to see that her cheeks had filled out, and her simple blue dress no longer hung on a skin-and-bones frame. She was still far from plump, but she possessed delightful curves in all the right places.

To have a woman walking beside him, clinging to his arm, the top of her head reaching just above his shoulder, fed his masculinity in a manner he'd almost forgotten how much he enjoyed. When her lips curved and a dimple appeared in her cheek, he realized he'd been staring without answering.

"I didn't mean that you shouldn't talk to me at all," she said with a hint of laughter in her voice.

"I told you before that I'm no beau," he said ruefully. "Forgive my lack of conversation. But I can't help wondering why you're in such a hurry to reach the tavern."

She bit her lip. "I have . . . business with Monsieur Burelle."

"Ah. Then your wonderful bread is for sale to the public."

She blushed. "Yes. It became necessary to find a way to support myself and my sister. It seems the commander has laid down an ultimatum. Either get married or face starvation."

The realization that his brother was correct, that she had not contracted a betrothal, lit his veins like a fuse attached to a bomb. Desperately he tried to douse the flame. "Forgive me, mademoiselle, but you agreed to this arrangement, yes? Are you surprised that Bienville grows impatient?"

"Not . . . precisely surprised." The profile she presented to him was sweetly elegant, the beautiful full lips a bit pinched. "It's just that the situation here was very much misrepresented to all of us." She stopped, swept out a hand to indicate the muddy, broken street, the rudely timbered cabins with their thatched roofs and unglassed windows. Chickens and pigs ran free, leaving their waste. Rotting tree stumps had been left like decaying teeth, and mosquitoes, flies, and gnats swarmed everywhere. "If this were all, I could say to myself, well, at least you are better off here than you were in France. But I find that I cannot bring myself to unite with any of the men who have thus far proposed marriage." She looked up into his face. "I am a realist. I don't expect poetry and romance from men who are scratching out a living in this difficult place. But I can't help looking for a God-fearing man of honesty and integrity and moral strength. Where are those men, Monsieur Lanier?"

I am that man. The words trembled on his tongue. "You are right to insist on such qualities," he said instead, somehow holding her gaze. "My brother and I are about to set out on a very dangerous mission. If we return, and you are not —"

He stopped, knowing that he had all but set off the explosion inside his heart when her feelings were a complete mystery. This was no simple, passionate Indian girl to woo with beaded necklaces and wildflowers.

To his astonishment, her eyes filled and her lips began to tremble. "Monsieur Lanier —"

"Tristan. My name is Tristan." He wanted to hear her say it.

"Tristan," she whispered. Her gaze fell, and he felt as if a gift had been taken away. "I don't know what will happen tomorrow, much less in a matter of months. We could all die of yellow fever next week." She swallowed. "But if you should return, and I am still here, I . . . oh, dear, I don't know what you were going to say." Snatching her hand away from his arm, she whirled and took off toward the tavern once more.

He caught up in one stride, recklessly caught her wrist and stepped in front of her. "Yes you do. You know exactly what I mean, because I see my heart in your eyes. Look at me, Geneviève. Let me see."

"This is wrong. I can't do this."

"What do you mean?" He laid his palm against her cheek, tucking his thumb under her chin to lift her face. So soft. So fragile. He felt like he held a wild bird.

Her face crumpled, eyes squeezed tight. "I'm not what you think I am."

He couldn't help laughing. "What do you think I think you are?" They stood in the center of the town, out in the open where anyone could see, but somehow he didn't care. He felt like uttering a war whoop.

Then she did look at him, in her eyes the passion he'd suspected in full view, but overlaid by temper and fear. "You think I'm a convent-raised flower of French semi-nobility. Tristan, my father was a baker. I've never even seen a convent. I can't tell you the rest because I — because I can't." The tears spilled over and ran warm into his palm. "So please don't ask me."

"Why not? Do you not want to marry at all?"

The word was out there now. Insanity. He didn't want to marry again. But he wanted this woman with his whole heart. And he was a man who paid for what he took.

Geneviève dragged in a breath as if she had been punched in the stomach. "Oh, dear God."

He knew that was a prayer rather than a curse. "Answer me, Geneviève."

"I don't know." She stared at him, the tears still running. She sniffed childishly, making him smile. "You said you don't want a European wife. Why are you doing this?"

"I don't know." He shrugged.

They stared at one another, moments ticking by, until her lips curved upward at the corners and he found himself smiling too.

"This is ridiculous," she said.

"Yes. So let's be ridiculous together. Neither of us particularly wants to get married at all, so we might as well marry each other and save trouble for everyone concerned."

Her smile faltered. "I told you —"

"Yes, yes." He rolled his eyes. "I will be getting a very bad bargain, and I shall be sorry if I settle for an unreligious common-woman who makes the best bread on three continents." Absently he turned his hand and stroked his knuckles across her pink cheek. "But as I am a man who craves adventure, all that somehow doesn't worry me. Besides, chances are great that after tonight you may never see me again, making this whole argument pointless."

"Tristan! Don't say that!" She gripped his forearm. "You must come back — I insist!" She laughed at herself, blushing.

He found himself grinning, completely intoxicated as he had not been for a long time. "I don't take orders from a woman who is not my wife. Therefore if you wish to have any control over my survival during this mission, there are certain legalities which must be observed." He caught her hand and tugged her willy-nilly back toward the fort. "I didn't see any of those useless priests in the chapel, so they are probably at home on the rue du Séminaire. I'm sure Father Mathieu is preparing for the journey with us, and he seems like the least contrary of the three, so we'll ask him to take care of the formalities."

"But, Tristan, *now?*"

He looked back to find her trotting behind him, holding her skirts above the muddy ground, her face a comedy of shock, excitement, and sheer bewilderment. Having made up his mind, Tristan couldn't wait to hold her in his arms, to kiss those sweet lips, to —

He cut off his galloping thoughts. One step at a time. He needed to find Marc-Antoine as well as the priest, because he could not get married without his brother. And Geneviève would want her sister, useless though she might be.

"Now or never," he said firmly.

For her wedding Geneviève wore the dress she'd worn to Commander Bienville's dinner, except she refused the corset and left her hair in its usual simple plait down the back. She had been inclined to leave on the comfortable blue everyday dress she'd worn all day, but Madame insisted one only got married once. She thought wryly of Pierre Brossard, who had reputedly married and buried three wives, then made Thérèse Brochon number four.

Still, she felt Tristan deserved some concession to celebration on the part of his bride, however confused and taken aback she might be. As she followed Madame and Aimée toward the chapel, she listened with one ear to Raindrop's chatter, and almost dispassionately assessed her own feelings. Her skin felt electrified, every nerve atingle, her heart beating as if it would leap out of her throat. Life after childhood had thus far brought circumstances which wrought fear, rage, and heartache, but she could not remember feeling anything close to this . . . delirium.

Tristan Lanier had chosen *her*.

Oh, there was so much she didn't know about him. She was crazy to fling herself into matrimony on so little information. But the things she did know reassured her that her instincts had not failed. He was a man of principle, strong enough to stand up against the force of Bienville's personality. He had established his own property and quietly worked it alone, when weaker men seemed to either cave in or explode in rage at the commander's vacillating and some-times ill-judged policies. Tristan's brother respected and admired him, and little Raindrop, who had emerged as quite a clever judge of character, clearly worshiped him.

And then there was Father Mathieu,

whose opinion she trusted implicitly. When she and Tristan had finally run the priest to ground in the brickyard, he had been all but incredulous at their request that he perform their marriage ceremony. But after a moment's thought, he'd smiled broadly and wrung Tristan's hand. Then he'd caught Geneviève in a fierce hug. "My dear one, this is such a very good thing, and I hadn't hoped —" Clearing his throat, he set her away from him briskly. "Yes, I approve, and yes, I'll marry you. Give me half an hour to go home and brush off the dust. I'll meet you in the chapel."

Tristan had left her to locate his brother, while she went to Madame's to collect Raindrop, Madame and Monsieur L'Anglois, and Aimée. Now here they were at the gallery steps outside the chapel, and she was about to become a married woman. She would be Madame Lanier, who could bake and sell bread if she wanted to.

Aimée dropped back to wait for her as she reached the gallery and caught her hand to speak urgently in her ear, "They say he lived with the Pascagoula and married an Indian woman, you know that, don't you? He's as much a savage as any of them."

Geneviève tried not to let her sister rattle her. "*They* say lots of things that are neither true nor kind. Monsieur Lanier — Tristan — is a man of substance and good sense. We shall deal well together."

"Have you told him about —"

"No," Geneviève answered sharply. "I will talk to him about it tonight."

"Oh, that will make scintillating pillow talk." Aimée made a small derisive noise. "By the way, *cherie,* I am a wanted felon in France. You will never be able to go back —"

"Aimée!" Stung by her sister's hateful words and tone, Geneviève stepped back. "What is the matter with you?" She could almost swear she saw jealousy in the blue eyes just before Aimée lowered her gaze.

"I only want you to be careful," Aimée muttered, turning away. "Never mind, let's go in. They'll be waiting for us." She slipped into the chapel, leaving Geneviève to stare after her, hands pressed against her knotted stomach.

After a moment, she inhaled a deep breath and forced herself to enter the chapel. Her gaze went immediately to Father Mathieu, dressed in formal cassock, standing behind the altar with the prayer book open. Madame was fluttering about, moving furniture and adjusting the altar cloth for no apparent reason, while Raindrop stood, hands behind her back, examining an ivory crucifix which held a place of prominence on a beautiful mahogany side table. Aimée had sidled up to Marc-Antoine Lanier, who leaned against a wall like a prisoner of war.

Then she found him, her bridegroom. Standing in front of the altar, moccasins braced wide and arms folded, Tristan filled her vision as if there were no one else in the bare, shabby little room. He was a tall man, and the open-collared white shirt broadened his shoulders, drawing her eye to the strong column of his neck. His beard and mustache had been recently trimmed, but his hair fell in ragged curls to his shoulders, and there were those slashing, piratical eyebrows. . . . She might have turned to run but for the look of sheer terror in his eyes.

She couldn't help smiling. To her delight, his expression lightened, his posture relaxed, and she went to him like a compass needle drawn north. For the first time since her father's murder, she felt as if the morrow might bring happiness.

Watching her friends take husbands had not prepared her for the surreal experience of standing beside Tristan Lanier, listening to Father Mathieu read those solemn charges, promising to love and obey this man until death claimed him or her. As she took the communion bread from his big callused hand, she noted again the scars across his knuckles and wondered what had caused them. She had scars of her own that were going to be very hard to explain. Perhaps her husband would not see them. She had only a vague idea of what to expect in the marriage bed, but it was too late to ask Madame. The bread stuck in her throat as she swallowed it, and the knot of anxiety that had left her midsection began to twist again.

Then she took the heavy silver cup and shivered to find it still warm from Tristan's mouth. She suddenly had a glimpse of why Christ had compared the church to a bride accepting the sustenance and protection of her bridegroom. It was indeed a profound mystery that the Messiah would join himself in intimate communion with sin-stricken human flesh and blood. She drank, closing her eyes, letting the same wine that her husband had tasted flow over her tongue, bitter and sweet as a blood sacrifice. Was it too much to hope that her life with Tristan would bring that kind of love to them both?

She handed the cup back to Father Mathieu, blushing as he set it aside and took her hand and Tristan's to clasp them together between his palms. "May the Lord in his goodness strengthen your consent and fill you both with his blessings. What God has joined, men must not divide. Amen." The priest smiled broadly. "It's done, my children. Your time together will be brief tonight, so I recommend beginning your celebration without further delay." Chuckling, he clapped Tristan's shoulder and kissed Geneviève's cheek, then stepped away.

The small congregation of witnesses, released from solemnity, stood and rushed forward. Aimée still pouted, Madame was openly crying, and Marc-Antoine seemed perplexed. He leaned in to mutter into Tristan's ear, but Geneviève was right there and couldn't help overhearing.

"Had you thought where you and your bride will spend the night, my uncharacteristically impetuous brother? The barracks is off-limits, as is officers' quarters. Are you really going to consummate your marriage in a room above a public tavern?"

Looking exceedingly uncomfortable, Tristan glanced at Geneviève, who looked away, pretending to be deaf. He clicked his tongue against his teeth for a moment, then gave his brother a sheepish grin. "Do you have any suggestions?"

Marc-Antoine grinned back, clearly

pleased to have the upper hand for once. "As a matter of fact, I do."

11

Thunder grumbled over the river as Tristan assisted his clearly petrified new wife up the steps to the gallery of Charles Levasseur's vacant cabin. At some level he was saddened by his old friend's absence, but he could only be glad that Marc-Antoine had arranged for the cabin to be made available for him and Geneviève. He could imagine Bienville's ire at being informed that one of his precious *Pélican* brides had been stolen out from under his nose by "Monsieur Nothing," as Bienville liked to call Tristan. But once the marriage was consummated, there would be nothing he could do about it.

Tristan had every intention of claiming his bride in every sense of the word before he left for Alabama territory. He had weighed all the consequences and prepared for all eventualities. If he should die while on the trip, Geneviève would be well cared for, and should he have the blessed good fortune to sire another child, so much the better.

He smiled, thinking of Marc-Antoine's incredulous reaction to the information that his presence was required as witness to his brother's last-minute nuptials.

"I wanted you to marry!" he had shouted, flinging his hands in the air as he was wont to do when excited. "In fact, the whole thing is entirely my idea! But to do it less than twelve hours before we depart for a two-month journey — this is insanity. And I can't believe Geneviève Gaillain would consent —" Marc-Antoine stopped, frowning. "What have you done to her? Is she drunk?"

Tristan burst out laughing. "I don't think so. But if she is, I don't care. I want her, Marc-Antoine." Sobering, he sank into a chair in Marc-Antoine's room, and repeated softly, "I want her."

Marc-Antoine stared at him for a moment, then finally shook his head. "All right, then, I suppose we'd best write your will. You'll want to leave her cared for, in case neither of us comes back."

Now Tristan stopped with a hand on Levasseur's front door and looked at Geneviève. His wife. Lips pressed together tightly,

219

she was staring at her hands linked together across her stomach.

"I'm sorry I can't take you to your own house tonight. Tomorrow you'll go back to the L'Anglois family, stay there until I come back, and then I'll take you to my — our cabin down at the Mobile bluff." He waited for her to answer, but all he got was a flash of her eyes and a quick nod before she looked at her hands again. He sighed. "Geneviève, please, look at me."

Her long eyelashes fluttered, then lifted. He could imagine what was going on in her head. The blue-green eyes were glassy.

He touched her face. "It isn't too late to change your mind. According to the church, an unconsummated marriage can be annulled."

"No!" Blood fired into her pale cheeks. "I mean, I won't change my mind." Her chin lifted, and she gave him a trembling smile. "This is my choice too, Tristan."

Oddly encouraged, he bent to kiss her cheek. But she turned her face under his hand, and her lips met his, cool and innocent, then parted on a gasp, and he was all undone, pulled into teaching his wife how to kiss on his deceased friend's front gallery.

Somehow he got them inside the door,

shut it behind them, and located Levasseur's bedroom. He would forever be grateful to interfering Madame L'Anglois, for sometime during the simple supper they had enjoyed at the tavern, the hostess had come in and fluffed the mattress, covered it with a new blanket, and left a fragrant pile of Geneviève's personal belongings on a small table in the corner.

Much later, while rain sluiced down upon the thatched roof, he paused to cup her face and make sure one more time before he was beyond the bounds of control. "I don't want to . . . hurt you," he whispered. Then swallowed, incurably honest. "Sometimes, I think, it —"

"I don't care," she whispered back. "I trust you."

After that, he made her his wife in truth as well as words.

Sometime in the middle of the night, he woke and loved her again, overwhelmed that this beautiful woman had given herself to him. The rain had stopped, and the moon through the window shone carelessly upon his bride, allowing him to study the porcelain whiteness of her skin, so fair against his own swarthiness. He didn't know how he was going to leave her in just a few short hours.

He found himself praying for her, something that had never occurred to him when he slept with Sholani. Truthfully, it had been a very long time since he'd felt the presence of his Creator, but there was something about Geneviève that reached a deep spiritual well within him. He knew that he would never be the same after this night.

When he lay still again, with her curled against him, he stroked her back, smiling at her deep, contented sigh.

Suddenly his fingers paused upon a ridge of raised flesh striped across her shoulder blades. He moved his hand down and found another, then a third thicker than the first two. "Geneviève."

"Yes," she said drowsily. "It's me."

He moved away from her, turning her so that the moonlight fell upon her back. He wanted to retch. "Who did this?"

She lay very still, her face turned away from him. After a long moment she said, "It doesn't matter."

"It does matter. I will kill him. *Who did this?*"

Moving one muscle at a time, she sat up, drawing the blanket up to cover herself. She hung her head so that her long, beautiful curly hair, which he had released from its braid, rippled about her face, shielding her expression even in the bright moonlight. "I don't know his name."

She had been a virgin. Nothing made sense. What could she have done to earn a whipping that would leave such violent scars? He couldn't force her to tell him anything, but perhaps, if he were patient, in time she would trust him with the truth.

So he bent to plant kisses along the scars until she threw her arms around his neck and pulled him back down to the bed.

"I don't want you to go," she said.

"I know." He laughed softly. "It seemed like a good idea at the time. But my brother is right. If we don't intervene, the British will continue to stir one Indian clan against the other until they destroy each other. And that will leave us vulnerable to invasion from the east. I don't understand why Louis doesn't send more troops here, but —"

"Would he do that? I thought this was a peaceful settlement."

Her question struck him as odd, but he supposed women weren't taught to understand the colonization process. "Marc-Antoine is in a better position to know the plans of Bienville, Pontchartrain, and — by extension — the King himself. But generally speaking, there must be military support and protection for a settlement to prosper." He sighed, twining a lock of her hair round his finger. "The difficulty comes in balancing friendly overtures to the natives and response to aggression."

"That sounds very . . . complicated. What good will your presence on this trip do?"

"I'll be along mainly as a guide. Marc-Antoine is very good at his job as a diplomat and translator, and your Father Mathieu seems to be a man of reason. But the others will need to be watched carefully, lest misunderstandings arise and conflicts escalate. If we can diplomatically convince the more warlike Indians to ally themselves and stop the slave trafficking, our troop deficits won't be so dangerous."

She was silent for a moment. "Why do you think the Crown has been so reluctant to provide support for us here?"

Her anxious tone tugged at his heart, making him long to reassure her. "*Cherie,* there is nothing to worry about." He kissed her softly, and then more urgently. "I will come back to you, and we will live on our little plantation away from all this political maneuvering. You can meet my friend Deerfoot and his family and bake all the bread and cakes you want."

"Deerfoot?"

"One of Bienville's runners. When we first

arrived at the Mobile River, we were all stationed at Massacre Island until Iberville could determine where the fort and settlement should be built. The Pascagoula clan there were friendly to us. Deerfoot in particular helped me with the native languages, and we often went fishing together. My wife, Sholani, was his relative." He stopped. He had told himself not to mention Sholani. Not tonight, when his union with Geneviève was still so fragile and new.

But she put her hand on his chest, over his thumping heart. "I'm so sorry you lost her."

Some piece of his broken spirit fell back into place. "I remember the good times so that I can survive the bad times." His fingers traced the ridges on her back. "Perhaps you can do that too."

Her voice cooled a little. "Perhaps."

He was silent. She didn't want to name her enemies, but neither would she forget them. Because he understood that, and because they had so little time, he comforted them both by holding her close until her breathing became regular and she relaxed in his arms.

He didn't sleep after that, as his thoughts revolved in an endless cycle of awestruck wonder at his good fortune in finding two such women in one lifetime, of mental preparation for the coming negotiations, of bone-chilling fear for the real possibility of disaster.

God, he prayed at last, just as the first rays of dawn chased away the moonlight, *since I have to leave her, would you watch over her until I return? Would you grant me wisdom and courage for the task ahead? And would you help me to understand your purposes as Father Mathieu seems to do?*

He didn't know what else to ask. So he rose and dressed, then stood looking at Geneviève for several precious moments. He didn't dare kiss her for fear that he wouldn't leave at all, so he backed away, closed the bedroom door behind him, and quietly left the cabin.

He had few illusions that a God as big and inscrutable as the one the Catholic Church championed had any interest in a ragged Canadian mapmaker. But with the welfare of Geneviève Gaillain unexpectedly in his hands, he wasn't willing to take any chances.

From Levasseur's cabin he walked the short distance to the riverfront, where he was to meet Marc-Antoine and the others at daybreak. He found Father Mathieu, dressed in his usual black robe cinched at the waist with a plain hempen cord, the bald spot at the top of his head covered by a black cap, and sturdy leather sandals on his feet, rocking on his heels at the top of the bluff. The priest hailed Tristan with twinkling eyes, then pointed down at the landing below, where Marc-Antoine supervised the loading of two pirogues commandeered for the trip. Crates of clothing and household items set aside as gifts for the Indian chiefs had been wrapped in waterproofed tarps, as had packs of dried foodstuffs that the personnel would eat when hunting and fishing proved unsuccessful.

Trying to look nonchalant, Tristan scrambled down the sandy bluff, which the rain had left soggy and soft, and landed with a thump of boots at the bottom.

Marc-Antoine, standing amidships of the near pirogue, looked around and whistled between his teeth, grinning. "Good morning, brother. You're here bright and early. How fares your lovely bride?"

"Asleep and likely to stay that way until we're well upriver."

"Worn out, poor girl, I daresay." He ducked, laughing, as Tristan picked up a canvas bag of sugar and flung it at him.

"Jealousy is unattractive in an officer," Tristan said mildly. He looked around at the sound of voices on the bluff above, and frowned. "What's Dufresne doing here?"

"Don't know." Marc-Antoine squinted into the half light over Tristan's shoulder. "Let's go see." Leaving the packing to a couple of young cadets in the second pirogue, he leaped lightly onto the beach.

The two of them climbed the bluff, Marc-Antoine making it to the top just ahead of Tristan. He vaulted up the last few feet and caught his brother just as Dufresne pulled a roll of parchment out of his coat and opened it with an obnoxious flourish in Marc-Antoine's face.

Dufresne eyed Tristan, his lips curled as if he'd just eaten a bad persimmon. "I want to check your supplies against this manifest from La Salle," he said with his nasal Continental drawl. "Where are they?"

Marc-Antoine jerked a thumb over his shoulder. "Already in the boats. La Salle checked it himself last night, so I know he didn't send you. Give me that." He tweaked the parchment out of Dufresne's grasp and scanned it. "This is somebody's shopping list. La Salle wouldn't tell you what we took, so you came to see for yourself." He grinned at Dufresne. "Didn't you?"

Dufresne bristled. "What if I did? I'm detached to Bienville, not La Salle, and it's my job to keep the commander informed."

"And yourself in the process." Marc-Antoine flicked the parchment at Dufresne, who grabbed it, startled. "Take your scaly self back to headquarters and spy on someone else. I've got work to do." He turned to Father Mathieu. "Are all your goods onboard, Father?"

"Yes, I —"

"Wait." Dufresne interrupted the priest with a chopping motion of the parchment. "Father Mathieu, you take too much upon yourself. Father Henri says you have superseded his authority on many occasions of late, and he insists that you back off. Is it true that you performed a marriage ceremony yesterday without his permission?"

Father Mathieu glanced at Tristan. "I did perform the wedding of Monsieur Lanier and Mademoiselle Gaillain. But I don't see that Brother Henri has any say in the duties I take on as chaplain."

Dufresne's complexion rivaled the color of his hair. "But as Father Henri is pastor of the Louisiane parish, duly commissioned by the bishop, protocol requires that you request permission from him before ministering to civilians."

Tristan stepped between the aide-major and the priest. "Dufresne, you are ridiculous. What possible difference could it make to you who performed my wedding ceremony?"

"It — I — it is the principle of the thing!" Dufresne blustered. "Ridiculous, am I? That wedding was illegal, and you have ruined that young woman. Who will want her, now that —"

Tristan's fist connected with Dufresne's jaw, sending him flailing backward to tumble, cursing, head-over-heels down the bluff. Tristan leaned over the edge of the bluff to watch, shaking out his bruised knuckles, while Marc-Antoine shouted with laughter.

Father Mathieu gave a sigh of irritation before following Dufresne at a safer, more decorous pace. "Tristan," he called over his shoulder, "please collect yourself while I check on the poor fellow."

"Yes, Tristan," his brother mocked, "you have exploded all over the lot of us. What demon has prompted you to such violence? Oh, wait, I know — it is lack of sleep. Nothing a good nap won't put to rights."

Ignoring him, Tristan watched Dufresne crash to a halt against one of the boats and lie there dazed until one of the cadets reached to give him a hand to his feet. The aide-major stood there with mud streaking his hair and face, one epaulet dangling off his shoulder, holes ripped in both knees of his fancy breeches, mouth opening and closing like a river bass.

Satisfied, Tristan turned and gave his brother a sour smile. "I've been wanting to do that."

Geneviève woke up when a mannerless rooster announced daylight. She opened her eyes and stretched, yawning, then sat up, looking around for Tristan. The only remaining evidence of his presence was the mussed bedding and the fact that her clothing lay in an untidy heap on the floor just inside the bedroom door. She pressed the heels of her hands to her temples as floods of sensation washed from her toes to the roots of her hair and back again.

Married. Taken as a woman. Abandoned.

Her elbows went to her updrawn knees, and her hands slid to cover her face. She hunched, trembling, afraid to move lest she retch. Dear Lord, what had she done?

Several ragged breaths later, she began to calm, and the nausea faded. Another deep breath, slower this time, and she took her hands from her eyes. Clenching them against her abdomen, she looked around the room. She was in Charles Levasseur's cabin, one of the larger houses in the settlement. The thatching of the roof had rotted in places, allowing last night's heavy rain to penetrate and leave wet patches on the floor. Fortunately, the ceiling above the bed remained intact, else she and Tristan would have had a miserable wedding night.

She closed her eyes as if that would shut out the overpowering intimacies of the past hours, but her husband's scent remained all around her, in the bedding, no doubt in her own hair and skin. He might be a hundred miles away and she would still be able to feel the brush of his beard against her face, the tenderness of his lips on hers, the strength of his back when she flattened her palms against it.

This would never do. He was gone. He had left while she slept, without kissing her, without saying goodbye, as if she were a courtesan that he had bought for the night. There was every possibility he would never return. So she must piece herself back together. She must go on as if her world had not once more turned on its head, as if she had not deliberately removed any chance of marrying a safe young Canadian soldier and producing little Catholic babies to be raised in accordance with the True Church of Louis XIV.

Bienville was going to have her arrested, if she didn't get out of bed, get dressed, and preempt him.

So she did that. Ten minutes later she picked up the comb that someone — presumably Madame L'Anglois — had left on the corner table and started combing the snarls out of her hair. When she had finally managed to tame it in a braid, she made her way slowly, with wobbly knees, through the cabin's front room and out onto the gallery.

The sudden glare of sunlight had her squinting and shielding her eyes with her hand, but as her eyes adjusted, she saw that a woman sat on the front steps of the house across the street. Ysabeau Bonnet, she realized, recognizing the faded yellow dress and red-gold curls. She looked a bit dejected, chin in hand, elbow resting on her knee, but at least she didn't seem to be openly crying.

Geneviève sighed. She had no time to waste. But she should at least stop to speak to the girl. "Ysabeau?" she called as she crossed the street. "Are you all right?"

Ysabeau sat up. "Geneviève? What were you doing in Monsieur Levasseur's cabin?"

"It's a long story. I'll tell you later." Restraining a wince, Geneviève sat down on the step above Ysabeau and hugged her knees. "Why are you out here alone so early in the morning? Where are the Lemays?"

"Monsieur Lemay has gone to the powderworks. I came out to feed the chickens because the boys are arguing over some stupid toy, and Angela is in bed, claiming she's having labor pains. She's been having them every morning for the last week. I think she's faking, since they always seem to miraculously clear up by lunch." Ysabeau clenched her small fists as she glanced at Geneviève. "I've had all I can stand of this family. I'm going to marry Monsieur Connard today."

"Ysette, please don't do anything rash." The irony of her plea took Geneviève to the bounds of self-control, but with a supreme effort she managed to keep a straight face. "Have you even spoken to Monsieur Connard for more than five minutes?"

"He came to see me as soon as they released him from the guardhouse yesterday. He is — he is quite good-looking, if one squints a bit. And he wagered a *hundred livres* for me, Geneviève! That's a lot of money — isn't it?" She looked uncertain, but before Geneviève could answer, she stood up, smacking her hands together. "Anyway, he is as good as any of these

234

backwoods Canadians, so I should take him before he changes his mind." She jumped to the ground and marched off in the direction of the fort.

"Ysabeau! Please don't do this!" Geneviève went after her, but since the girl refused to even look at her again, she gave up and stopped at the corner of the street. She watched Ysabeau disappear behind the house at the end of the next block. There was no one to whom she could go for counsel. Father Mathieu was gone with Tristan —

A singularly unproductive thought. Plans. She must make plans. Tristan had agreed she should support herself with her bread-baking, so perhaps she should talk to Monsieur Burelle about that.

Squaring her shoulders, she set off for the tavern. Tristan was gone, but there was hope for a secure life here, for herself and Aimée. He had himself encouraged her to remember the good times in order to survive the bad times.

She thought about the note Cavalier had placed in her Bible, just before he left her with Father Mathieu. Worried that she might find herself in as precarious a situation as the one she'd escaped, he'd warned her to be very careful to whom she revealed her faith. Cavalier only asked her to make what observations she could, put them in a short letter, and send them through an Indian woman named Nika to the Huguenot pastor in Carolina.

Geneviève had of course eagerly agreed. After all, Cavalier had saved her life, and she owed him everything.

But her perspective was so different since she had come to Louisiane, lived here among its inhabitants, *married* Tristan Lanier. Her bitterness and fear — the rage she had felt toward the King and all he stood for — all that had blurred into the daily rhythms of making a new home. When Tristan began to explain last night the complicated political inter-workings among French, British, and Indian powers, she had almost stopped him. The less she knew, the less she must be obliged to divulge to Cavalier.

Thoughts aboil, she was almost at the end of the block when an ear-splitting scream issued from an open window behind her. She stopped in her tracks. Ysabeau had said the little boys, aged three and five if she remembered correctly, were at home by themselves except for their mother, who was about to give birth any day now. Should she go directly for help? Surgeon-Major Barraud, even if he weren't a useless drunk, was already on his way upriver with Father Mathieu and the Lanier brothers. Sister Marie Grissot had been named midwife. She was a sweet woman, but notably slow and easily flustered.

Reluctantly Geneviève turned around and headed up the brick pathway to the Lemays' two-story house. It was small and rough compared to Continental standards, but it was one of the largest and most luxurious in the settlement. Powdermaker Xavier Lemay possessed a skill critical to both military and civilian life, and he was evidently well compensated.

She mounted the steps to the gallery and hesitated at the front door, which stood open. Two little boys with curly dark hair and big brown eyes perched at the foot of the stairs, the younger one with his thumb in his mouth and the elder glaring at her truculently, both grubby fists clutching a wooden toy trailing a string.

"Good morning," she said, trying to sound cheerful. "Is that your mama upstairs? She seems to be having some difficulty."

"Mama's havin' the baby," the little one said around his thumb.

"No she ain't, stupid," said the older one.

"Ysabeau said it wouldn't be for another few days."

Another scream pierced the air, perhaps amplified by the uncarpeted hardwood floor and stairs. Both children looked frightened.

"Let me check on your mama, boys. No, stay here. I'll be right back." She hiked her skirt to leap lightly over them and hurried up the stairs. At the landing she stopped to listen and followed the gasps of pain coming from one of the two bedrooms. "Angela? I'm coming. Are you having the —" Unable to finish, she halted in the doorway to suck in a breath, then rushed to the bed, where poor Angela, blown up to whale-like proportions, writhed in pain with her bedgown wadded about her waist. Geneviève took the woman's hand and winced at the strength of that vise-like grip. "How long have you been like this?"

"The pains have been coming — off and on — all night," Angela gasped between her teeth. "Ysabeau — so hateful, I can't stand it anymore. Geneviève, please get Sister Gris. She'll know what to do — she delivered the Canelles' baby."

"Yes, of course. Can I do anything for you before I go?"

"Where are Serge and Émile?"

238

"Downstairs playing. I'll watch out for them."

"Thank you." Angela's head twisted back and forth on the bolster. "Could I have some water? I'm so thirsty."

Geneviève ran back down the stairs, giving the little boys a reassuring pat on the head as she passed, and ducked into the kitchen. Fortunately she found a pitcher of clean water on a table and poured a little into a pewter cup. She took it upstairs to the uncomfortable young mother, then dashed back down the stairs.

She stopped long enough to reassure the boys that she would be right back, that they should stay in the salon and play quietly. Then she hurried outside, down the gallery steps, and along the rue de Ruessavel toward the nursing sisters' little house on the next block. She knocked on the front door, shouting, "Sister Gris!" Without waiting for an answer, she opened it and found Dames Grissot and Linant blinking at her over a breakfast of eggs and hominy. Both were in habits without veils.

"Geneviève!" Sister Linant set down her tea cup with a thump. "What's the matter, child?"

Geneviève addressed Sister Gris. "It's Angela — she's having her baby, and it doesn't look good. She's been in pain for more than a day — I told her I'd come for you. Please, Sister —"

"Of course." Sister Gris rose, pushing away from the table. She looked at her friend. "Forgive me for leaving you with the dishes."

"Go ahead, don't worry. But, Marie, you need your wimple."

"Oh, yes." Distracted, Sister Gris put her hand to her wiry gray locks. "I'll be right back," she said to Geneviève and hurried through the doorway into the second room. Within a few minutes she returned, wearing the distinctive gray headgear of her order, albeit slightly askew, and she and Geneviève were on their way back to the Lemay house.

Geneviève could hear Angela's screaming groans from two blocks away. The two little boys must be terrified. *Dear Father in heaven, help us know what to do.*

She and Sister Gris looked at one another, then simultaneously started running. The nun, gasping for breath, tried gamely to keep up with Geneviève's lighter step and reached the Lemays' front door not far behind. Geneviève grabbed her arm and all but pulled her up the stairs, then left the nun to care for Angela while she hurried back to the ground floor. She looked all over

240

the house, but the two little boys had vanished.

"Oh, no. What now?" she muttered, walking out to the front gallery. Where could they have gone? Anxiously she looked up and down the street. *If I were a frightened little boy, where would I go?*

Levasseur's cabin across the street caught her eye. Was she going to blush in shame every time she looked at the place for the rest of her life? There was no shame, she reminded herself, in a bride having marital relations with her lawful wedded husband.

Her eyes widened, and she put her hand to her flat stomach. What if she had become *enceinte* during that short night with Tristan? Could it happen that fast? What if she were left to bear a child alone and raise it on whatever she could make, baking for Monsieur Burelle?

Geneviève! she scolded herself. *Don't ask for trouble. You must find those children!* Pulling in her careening emotions, she tried to think.

The little boys she'd known in France had been fond of climbing, fighting, and hiding. Here in the middle of the settlement, the biggest trees had been cut down for lumber, even had the boys been tall enough to climb them. Frowning, she went back inside.

Maybe she had missed something.

She looked at the empty staircase again, wincing in sympathy as another guttural groan found its way down the stairs. She walked over and sat down on the next-to-bottom step where Serge and Émile had been playing with the wooden spinning toy earlier. As Angela's cries faded to whimpering, she heard something else, possibly a faint giggle . . . from *below*? She stood up and peeked around the banister, which Xavier had sanded and polished to a buttery smoothness. The space beneath the stairs had been walled in to form a closet with a small door. Smiling, she pulled the latch.

And there they were, huddled side-by-side in the dark like a couple of puppies, Émile with his thumb in his mouth and Serge scowling like a pirate.

Serge scooted backward. "We ain't coming out."

But Émile started crying. "I want Mama."

"Shut up, you little baby." Serge gave his brother a patronizing look. "Mama don't want us no more, now that she's getting a new one. We got to take care of ourself."

Geneviève's already bruised heart broke in two. She sat down in the closet doorway and propped her elbows on her knees. "Your mama was very worried when she couldn't find you. As soon as the baby comes, I'm to bring you in to meet him." She fixed Serge with a stern look. "You mustn't frighten your brother. Did your mama stop loving you when he came into the family?"

Serge's feathery brows came together as he considered her question. "I guess not." He shrugged.

"Of *course* she didn't." Geneviève leaned forward and touched her nose to his. "Your little brother will need you two big boys to watch out for him. That's a big responsibility."

"Mama said it might be a *girl.*" Oceans of scorn dripped from the word.

She laughed and sat back. "Then she'll need you even more. Come, let me fix you something to eat."

The thumb popped out of Émile's mouth. "Eat?"

"Yes, my little rooster. What would you like for lunch?" She got to her feet, then reached for Émile's hand.

Within a short space of time, she had settled the little boys in their cubby with bowls of gruel and left them to run up the stairs to check on Angela and Sister Gris.

The scene she walked in on was one of chaos and sweat and blood and noise.

Angela sat up against the beautiful carved headboard of her bed, groaning, knees apart, straining to deliver a child who seemed to be as reluctant to enter the room as Geneviève, who gripped the doorframe with both hands, thinking that all she had to do was retrace her steps, walk out the front door, and pretend she'd never heard Angela Lemay's cries for help.

You are no coward, she reminded herself, embarrassed that she could even think of running away. Straightening her spine, she let go of the doorframe. "Sister Gris, how may I help?"

The nun looked over her shoulder. Wimple askew, her round face nearly as red and wet with perspiration as her patient's, she leaned over Angela, holding her hand. "Come get her other hand. This baby has been too long in the birth canal. We have to make him come, or she's going to —"

"Yes of course." Geneviève darted to the other side of the bed. "Angela, take my hand. I'll help you."

But her friend had slumped against the stained bolster behind her back. Tipping her head back, she let out a sobbing moan that seemed to come from her toes. "I can't. I'm too tired."

"You have to. You want this baby, don't you?"

"Of course I do. But he's — just like Xavier. Stubborn." A weak giggle told Geneviève that the fight was not yet over.

She gripped Angela's hand hard and exchanged glances with Sister Gris. "Then you've got to push again. Wait till the pain comes again, then —"

"Pain? Why, this is —" She lurched off the backboard and shrieked, *"— nothing!"*

Geneviève felt the bones of her hand crunch together, and the next few minutes seemed to last for days as Angela pushed and panted and screamed and pushed again, until at last a little darkcrowned head appeared. She and Sister Gris assisted as best they could, though Geneviève felt that it was little enough. The pain of birth — God had said it must be so. The Bible predicted that a woman's desire would be for her husband, and the product of their union must result in agony as well as ecstasy.

She had seen and experienced that paradoxical truth this very day.

Our God, we are only women. Help us trust you to keep us in what you give us to bear.

12

He was probably going to have to kill her too.

As he waited for Geneviève Gaillain to meet him at the gate, Julien took his stepmother's letter from the pocket inside his coat and read it again. He had long since memorized it, probably should have burned it, but there was something about the weight of it in his hand, the curl of the words on the page, that steadied and focused the anger that now fueled his every waking thought.

Of course I knew about the other boy, for what man of your father's virility has not had one or more indiscretions? But because he — the boy, not your father — went off to live in the Canadian wilderness with his mother, and one never heard another word of him, praise to the Almighty, I deemed it prudent to withhold his existence from dear Gilbert, and I presume he — your father, not the boy — wouldn't have any reason to mention him — the boy, not your father — to you or your mother.

"The boy," of course, was Tristan Lanier, and it had taken the countess half a scrawling page to clarify the fact that his father had managed to sire not one, but two, illegitimate sons presently living in the wilds of America. Furthermore, her reason for suddenly divulging this shocking information was due to his father's inexplicable decision to legitimize his eldest son and confer on him all due rights of inheritance — to the exclusion of the other two. The letter had rambled on for another page or two before coming to the point: Anne Chevalier, Comtess de Leméry, expected Julien to politely murder his half brother, as well as Father Mathieu, the priest who had journeyed to Louisiane to inform him of his good fortune.

Several implications had occurred to him in succession that day, when he had opened and read that fateful letter. First was the bare fact of a third contender for his father's name and fortune. Having grown up knowing that he was a bastard, Julien had more or less come to terms with the idea that he would never receive the privileges of legitimacy. His father might be negligent and somewhat arrogant toward his younger son, but Julien had never wanted for any physical necessity. He had been educated, groomed for gainful employment, and taught manners appropriate, as the comtess acknowledged, for his station.

Discovering that he was not the comte's only love child put to death any notion that his father had ever loved his mother. She had been merely a mistress — one of two, probably many. And she hadn't even been the first.

Tristan Lanier was his brother. *Tristan Lanier is your brother.*

He said it aloud. "Tristan Lanier is your brother." The words still tasted metallic on his tongue.

Standing here in the sun waiting for Lanier's wife, he knew a burst of rage so hot he thought his head might explode. A man who loved his child so little that he would send him and the mother across the ocean to live with another man — that kind of man was his own sire.

The latent pride that Julien had always kept well hidden, pride that he was the son of the *noble* Comte de Leméry, died a violent death in that moment.

Pride gave way to resolve. There weren't many things Julien knew how to do better than revenge. He had never murdered anyone, but as he searched himself, he knew that he could do it. Brothers from the beginning of time had done what they must in order to survive. Cain had served well, and what thanks had he received? Rejection. *Abel's sacrifice is better.* Julien understood perfectly why the insult required blood.

The thought of killing the priest gave him pause. But he understood that if the priest lived, it would be more difficult to hide what he had done. Father Mathieu would ask questions, and questions would inevitably lead to one who would profit from Lanier's death. Two accidental deaths in this wild and dangerous land would not be so remarkable. Yes, it would have to be done.

Of course, once he had taken care of Lanier, there would be Gilbert himself, and possibly his mother.

He opened his hand and smoothed the letter, which he had crumpled in his distress. He read it once more, biting his lip. Anne Chevalier was a twit, but like most women, understood self-preservation. What did she mean, precisely, by a "proper reward"? He would want more than money — at least a title and some of the de Leméry lands. Gilbert was easy to persuade.

Shoving the letter back into his uniform coat, he began to pace along the stockade. He must find a way to do the thing without it being traced to himself. Perhaps he should start with Geneviève. If he'd known his half brother was going to wed the girl before departing for Indian territory, he would have found a way to prevent it. But it had never occurred to him that Tristan Lanier would overcome his antipathy for white society and choose a Frenchwoman as his bride. In fact, in a twist of diabolical irony, by the looks of it, Lanier had fathered a couple of illegitimate Indian whelps of his own and foisted them on the unsuspecting son of the Mobile chief.

He'd watched Lanier carefully every time he appeared at Fort Louis. There had been no sign of attachment to any of the *Pélican* girls, let alone the standoffish Geneviève Gaillain. So while Julien had turned his back for less than a day, Lanier took the woman to wife and bedded her without anyone else the wiser.

Bienville was, of course, apoplectic that one of his expensive *Pélican* brides had married the renegade Lanier, leaving one less family with which to convince the king of the settlement's growth and prosperity. As soon as word reached him, the commandant had convened a tribunal of officers to interrogate the woman. Julien had sat amongst them, outwardly icy, watching Geneviève's white face flush as Bienville did his best to undo what Father Mathieu had done — and humiliate her in the process.

Bienville's main objection was that the marriage had taken place outside the authority of Father Albert or Father Henri, a fact which Henri himself loudly decried. Ironically, in other circumstances Bienville might have stood in support of the Jesuit Father Mathieu, with whom he was politically aligned. However, there was nothing anyone could do about a signed and witnessed marriage contract. Vows had been — according to the crimson-faced bride — duly consummated, and she refused to consider annulment.

In the end, Bienville had to let her go, coldly informing her that the financial support of the Crown had come to an end for her. She must scrape together a living for herself as best she might.

With a dignity that would have befitted the Queen herself, Geneviève had given the commander a brief curtsey and quitted headquarters without a word or a glance for anyone else in the room.

Julien could only admire her composure, though the marriage created one more obstacle in his bid for his late father's fortune. If Geneviève should be with child, Julien's claims upon the de Leméry dynasty became even more distant, and the route he must take to bring himself back in line became that much more complex.

He paused in his endless perambulations as he tried, not for the first time, to untangle Father Mathieu's role in the family drama. If the priest were functioning as legal as well as spiritual counselor to the comte, logically he would have been apprised of Julien's existence, which did not seem to be the case. After reading the comtess's letter, Julien had almost confronted Father Mathieu. Erring on the side of caution, however, he had simply watched the priest's eyes for recognition or signs of a hidden agenda. In vain.

"Good morning, Monsieur l'Aide-Major. I am sorry to have kept you waiting."

Julien turned to find his companion for the day picking her way through the muddy trampled grass around the stockade entrance. He sketched a bow, extending his arm to assist her around a puddle. "No apology necessary, mademoiselle."

Geneviève's request that he accompany her to the Mobile village in search of cooking instruction had struck him as fortuitous as well as strange. Any one of the layabouts infesting Burelle's tavern would have served, but during his last visit to the L'Anglois's home to court her so-lovely younger sister, Geneviève had steered the conversation to Indian corn bread. Before he could blink, he had been conscripted to escort her to the Mobile village on the first clear day.

He surreptitiously studied her. She was dressed in a simple but neat ensemble he had not seen before, and he recognized the blue Rouen cloth imported on the *Profond*. He had checked the inventory himself and handed it to La Salle with only a few minor adjustments. Details being his bread and butter, Julien noted her modest décolletage and loose-fitting sleeves. Not so modest was the gored skirt, which cleared the ground by at least three inches and gave one a generous view of slender ankles above a pair of deerskin moccasins. Lanier was going to find his wife in need of a stern beating when he returned.

But as Lanier wasn't likely to return, perhaps some other man would have to assume that chore. Hiding a smile, Julien shifted his gaze to his companion's uncovered dark curls. She had adopted the role of married woman, going about without a cap, though she would have been wiser to keep the sun off that fair skin.

She seemed unaware of his regard, keeping her attention on the uneven ground. "I'm grateful you were willing to give up your valuable free time to come with me. I feared that without introduction the Indians might not allow me to enter the village."

His eyebrows rose. "Mademoiselle, you should never leave the settlement without escort. The Indians aren't the only danger you would face."

"I wish you to address me as 'madame,' if you please. I am a married woman." For all their bluntness, the words were spoken with composure.

"Pardon, madem — madame." He smiled. "It is difficult to think of one so youthful as yourself as a matron."

"Yet you court my sister, who is two years my junior." The clear, green-gray eyes flicked his way. "Perhaps you should withdraw your suit until she grows up."

"Touché." He smirked at her. "We shall agree that you are quite on the edge of the grave and must be addressed as such."

"Indeed." Her lips quivered on a suppressed smile. "And as one whose advanced age and marital state informs her responsibility for protecting a younger sibling, sir, I claim the right to propose a few questions regarding your background."

"Ask away, my dear, though I claim no equal responsibility for answers."

She laughed. "Well, that's honest at least! The problem is, information is difficult to come by. No one seems to know much about where you came from."

"Straight from the head of Zeus, I swear." He lifted a hand. "Though society is reluctant to believe in my supernatural parentage. Careful — that branch is rotten."

She leaped lightly over the fallen limb, and he suddenly appreciated the wisdom in her decision to resort to native footwear. Many of the women had taken to going about barefoot when their fragile Paris-made shoes disintegrated in the damp, sandy coastal terrain. They had passed from the cleared settlement area to enter the forest, through which a hard-packed and crooked Indian trail led to the Mobile village some eight miles distant. The dense trees blocked the sunlight, so that they walked in a dappled half-light, accompanied by the rustling and twitter of birds and small animals. Geneviève betrayed no discomfiture; rather, the tension in her hand upon his arm relaxed.

It occurred to him that he was every bit as curious about her as she seemed to be about him, and that he had made little headway in discovering what the ex-Protestant shipbuilder suspected. That must be corrected.

They chatted of inconsequential things as they walked on at a brisk pace, until Dufresne deemed that she had relaxed sufficiently to have let down her guard. "It seems you have much in common with my friend Ardouin. He speaks highly of you."

Her expression closed at the abrupt change in subject. "Catherine's husband?"

"Yes. He says you remind him of his sister."

"I don't know what you mean. I barely know the man."

"Frankly, I'm not sure what he meant either. Ardouin is a very sober fellow, raised by Protestant parents. He converted to the true religion so that he would be allowed to marry your friend Catherine. Most commendable."

"Indeed." She glanced at him, then up at the canopy of branches overhead. The leaves had begun to turn colors and drop off, creating a pleasant crunch underfoot as they walked. "How much farther to the village?"

"Another hour's walk. Are you tired? We

could rest for a few minutes."

"No, it is merely that I'm anxious to arrive." She picked up her pace, all but tugging on his arm to drag him along. "One never knows what the weather will do in this climate."

"True." He kept his tone neutral. "I can understand, I suppose, why Ardouin recanted his so-called religion, in favor of that of our King. But I should have admired him even more had he stood fast in his beliefs. So many are like the trees, swayed this way and that by every wind." His expansive gesture encompassed their surroundings.

She was silent so long he thought she wasn't going to answer. He looked at her and found her lips buttoned tightly together. After a moment, she said stiffly, "I'm sure Monsieur Ardouin had his reasons for recanting. One must give grace where it is due."

"Well, in the end, one religion is much like another, in my opinion. The Indians worship a god who is in the trees and the wind itself. Who is to say that they are wrong?"

"Monsieur l'Aide-Major, you'd best have a care who hears you propose such blasphemous questions." There was an intensity beneath her light tone that told him he had hit a nerve.

"Madame, am I to understand that you sympathize with our dark-skinned brethren?"

"You can understand whatever you wish, it is neither here nor there to me." She gave him a penetrating look. "Surely you don't believe the Creator of the trees and the wind could be held captive in his creation."

"It's an interesting supposition." He shrugged. "When we first began clearing the land for the settlement, the Indians spoke of the idols of five gods who dwelt on Bottle Creek Island just north of here. The natives considered these idols a form of holy protection. Bienville convinced some lesser Mobilian headsmen to take him there, to see for himself. While Bienville approached the idols, the Indians cowered on the beach, begging him not to touch them lest he be struck dead. What he found were five plaster figures — a man, a woman, a child, a bear, and an owl — apparently left by the Spanish in an earlier exploration. Our intrepid commander, of course, swept them right up and had them transported to Massacre Island."

Geneviève's eyes sparkled. "Indeed! And yet he was not struck dead!"

Julien shook his head. "Miraculously not

— and so our Indian friends were even more impressed with French courage and superior authority. Iberville later took the idols back to France, where he demonstrated at court that our simple Indians would be easy to sway to our support."

"This seems to me further proof that Almighty God doesn't dwell in man-made icons, as the Church would have us believe."

Julien studied Geneviève and found her expression thoughtful, her mouth wry. She seemed unaware that she had just uttered a much more sacrilegious remark than any which he had proffered. He did not call attention to the slip but filed it away for further speculation.

"Of course you are right, madame." He couldn't quite put his finger on why he found the inner workings of this insignificant woman's mind so fascinating. That she had married his half brother, whom he knew to be rough-mannered and ill-dressed, irreligious and often antisocial, strengthened Julien's conviction that some ulterior motive drove her actions.

Could it be that the priest had taken Geneviève into his confidence? Maybe she was even the priest's handpicked choice as Tristan Lanier's bride.

"Monsieur?" Geneviève's clear voice

broke into Julien's ruminations. "I see light ahead. Are we coming to the end of the forest?"

He blinked. "I believe it is so. Forgive my inattention." He smiled at her. "We've arrived much sooner than I'd anticipated. Perhaps we'll find food at the end of our journey. Come, let us walk a little faster."

No sooner were the words out of his mouth than a peculiar buzzing sound ripped past his head. He reached up to touch his stinging ear, then stared at his hand, incredulous. His trembling fingers were smeared with blood.

Aimée, hauling a heavy wooden bucket, trudged along the muddy trail which bore the rather grandiose name "rue de Sérigny." She shifted the bucket to the other hand and thought resentfully of the bruises that would no doubt mar the fair skin of her legs later today. *Why* must she be the one sent to fetch water, when Raindrop could just as well have gone after she finished her own chores? And heaven forefend that Madame actually carry anything heavier than a thimble herself!

She consoled herself by singing a little song her mother had taught her as a child, wishing for the hundredth time that she could have Mama here to advise her as to which of her two blue ribbons most closely mimicked the color of her eyes. But Mama had pined herself into the grave over Papa, and Aimée had been forced to leave their home and get on the boat in La Rochelle, just because Ginette and that beastly Jean Cavalier said she must.

She had thought things would be better once they reached dry land. New France, they called it — Louisiane, in honor of the Sun King. But there was nothing "new" about this moldy, dingy, waterlogged swamp. Bugs and snakes and pestilence everywhere, and she had not felt completely clean since the day she got off the *Pélican* fifty-four endless days ago.

Worse still, she had assumed that the handsomest of the purportedly brave and resourceful young Canadians, desperate for women to grace their homes, would kneel at her feet and offer her the life of luxury that was her due. But not one suitable gentleman had offered her marriage, and she was one of two *Pélican* brides who remained unwed. Well, three, if one counted the unfortunate Ysabeau Bonnet. Nearly a week ago, Edmé Oüanet had married Denis Lafleur, and even homely Noël Dumesnil had accepted a sudden and inexplicable offer from Claude Fautisse. They were to say their vows later this afternoon, when Father Henri returned from baptizing a couple of Indian babies.

Everyone knew that Françoise Dubonnier was holding out for Commander Bienville, though Aimée could have told her that Bienville was as likely to get married as he was to fly to the moon. After all, why should he buy a cow when he could get free milk whenever he liked? But that was neither here nor there. Françoise would listen to no one.

She looked up at the sky, trying to gauge the likelihood of rain. Blue morning skies could turn to howling storms by afternoon, and one had best be prepared to duck into the closest building at a moment's notice. The weak September sun flirted from behind a bank of innocent, puffy white clouds, giving no indication of their intent.

Which put her in mind of her deceitful sister, who had disappeared that very morning with Aimée's only hope of advantageous matrimony, leaving her hostage to Madame's endless nagging to be "useful." She kicked at a chicken that had wandered into the road and watched it run away squawking and flapping. Wouldn't it be just like Ginette to dissuade Julien from his determined courtship? She couldn't understand why he'd agreed to escort Ginette to the Indian village on his day of leave, instead of squiring Aimée about on a fashionable promenade.

In fact, Geneviève herself had turned into quite a queer sort of person, ever since she had married that backwoods Canadian, Tristan Lanier. The day after the wedding, she had actually delivered the Lemay baby all by herself — Sister Gris had been there as well, but one could hardly count *her* as any useful help — and then later defied the commander's attempt to annul her marriage, despite the fact that Monsieur Lanier was for all intents and purposes a traitor to the French Crown. Julien said it was so, and he must be believed.

As she entered the marketplace, Aimée could see the community well located in the center of the square. Two women stood there waiting their turns to draw water, while a third leaned into the well almost to the waist. Aimée recognized Noël Dumesnil by the wilted brown hair trailing from the back of her cap and Jeanne de Berenhardt's Amazonian height, but it was impossible to identify the woman hanging over into the well.

What on earth was she doing? Had she

dropped something down the well and decided to fish for it? Who would be so foolish as to —

Then in an instant she knew who it was. She had seen that petticoat many times on board the *Pélican.*

Ysabeau had had little to do with Aimée of late. There had been a couple of skirmishes early on, genteel catfights over the handsomest, richest, and most courtly of the unattached men. However, Ysabeau's engagement to the highly respected Levasseur, a coup of the first order, soon set her in a completely different social circle. By the time Levasseur succumbed to the fever, leaving Ysabeau abruptly free, Aimée was satisfied with the flattering attentions of Aide-Major Dufresne. Her friend's desperate and pathetic engagement to the handsome and raffish Denis Lafleur, who promptly traded her off in a card game, left Aimée with no choice but to treat Ysabeau with smug pity.

Mama used to always tell her that "pride goes before a fall," which was apparently somewhere in the Bible. Ysabeau's misadventures certainly proved it. The girl had been proud as a peacock.

Now here she was in the middle of town in broad daylight, barefoot as a yard dog and dressed in nothing but her shift and petticoat, with her head inside the well. It was entirely too much.

Aimée dropped the bucket in the dirt and marched over to join Noël and Jeanne. "What on earth is she doing?" She could hear Ysabeau's high, sweet voice echoing from the well like the keening of the wind on a winter night in the Cévennes. "Is she *singing*?"

"I — I d-don't know," Noël stuttered. "It s-sounds like it."

"How long has she been there?"

Even the stately Jeanne looked worried. "At least an hour . . . maybe more. Noël and I tried to get her to come out, but she just ignores us."

"This is unacceptable! She must go home and put on her dress."

Noël wrung her hands. "Do you suppose she's ill? Maybe she has the fever too."

Aimée snorted. "She was perfectly healthy at mass yesterday morning. Where is her husband? Monsieur Connard is responsible for her now."

"I don't know him," said Jeanne. "I think he is a soldier. Perhaps he is on duty."

Aimée looked at Noël, who shrugged. She stamped her foot. "You two are no help at all!" She would just have to take care of it herself.

She reached Ysabeau in three quick strides. It was worse than she'd feared. Not only was Ysabeau en déshabillé below the waist, her lacy shift was covered only by a loosely fastened corset, leaving her back and shoulders almost completely bare. Her beautiful mane of red-gold curls hung loose against the slimy brick walls of the well, her arms dangling like pale ropes. She was looking down into the darkness as if into an oracle.

Aimée planted her hands on the rim of the well. "Ysabeau! Stand up this minute! You are getting your hair wet and dirty. What will Commander Bienville think of this behavior?" She waited, but Ysabeau only continued to sing in that thin, unearthly soprano, words that Aimée finally recognized as the nursery song she herself had been singing on the way to the market.

Shivers prickled her arms and crept up the nape of her neck into her scalp as Ysabeau warbled into the well,

Fishing for mussels,
I no longer want to go, Mommy,
Fishing for mussels,
I no longer want to go.

The boys from Marennes,
They left me, Mommy,
The boys from Marennes,
They left me.

I shouldn't have believed
All their fine vows, Mommy,
I shouldn't have believed
All their fine vows.

Boys are fickle
Like rain and wind, Mommy,
Boys are fickle
Like rain and wind.

Girls are faithful
Like gold and silver, Mommy,
Girls are faithful
Like gold and silver.

Shaking off her momentary paralysis,
Aimée seized Ysabeau by the waist and
pulled. At first Ysabeau was limp as a sack
of flour. But she stiffened, her voice escalating into a shriek, as Aimée pulled her
backward, scraping her bosom and chin
against the bricks. Ysabeau began to buck
and flail her arms.

"Ysabeau! I'm trying to help you!" Aimée
dodged Ysabeau's elbows. "Let me take you

home, there's a good girl. Where's your —
where is René? He will miss you, and you
can't stay out here in public with nothing
— Stop it!" Aimée looked around to find
both Noël and Jeanne gawking at her like a
couple of ninnies. "Jeanne, go get her
husband! Or get one of the guards! Hurry!"

Jeanne recovered and hurried away in the
direction of the fort, clearly relieved to have
something useful to do.

"Noël! Come help me. She's going to hurt
herself. Ow!" Ysabeau had just elbowed her
in the eye socket. Freshly indignant, Aimée
gave one more tug and went reeling backward to land on her rump with an undigni-
fied *"oof,"* Ysabeau in her lap. Shoving the
girl off into the dirt, Aimée scrambled to
her feet, shaking with righteous indignation.

Noël crept closer. "I'm so sorry, Ysabeau
— I don't know how to help. Are you all
right?"

"Is *she* all right?" Aimée rounded on
Noël. "I'm the one with a black eye!" When
Noël backed away, bleating another apology, Aimée made a disgusted noise and
glared down at Ysabeau. She was sobbing
like a child, fists knotted against her eyes.
Her dirty hair streamed over her shoulders
and bosom, curling past her waist. "What is
the matter with you, Ysette? You cannot

come out of doors dressed like a strumpet."

Ysabeau peeked through her fingers. Her swollen eyes were red, and her nose was running. "No one wants me," she said dully. "Papa says I must get on the boat in the morning."

Ignoring her throbbing eye, Aimée knelt beside Ysabeau and took her by the shoulders. "Your papa is in France. Did you have a bad dream?"

Ysabeau picked at her fingernails. "There isn't enough money for all of us. The baby is dead. Dresses and shoes cost too much. I must go to New France and find a husband."

"What are you talking about? You married René Connard nearly a week ago!" Aimée shook Ysabeau hard. "Wake up, you stupid goose!"

"Fishing for mussels I no longer want to go, Mommy," Ysabeau sang sweetly, "fishing for mussels I no longer want to go." She folded her legs crisscross and began to play with her hair.

Aimée stared at the girl, listening to the heartbreaking rhyme that used to make her think of her own mama. Something had happened to send Ysabeau into an interior place that no one else could reach. In the docile acceptance of the same winds of fate which had blown her from home to an alien wilderness, from man to man to man, she had succumbed to some illusion of childhood, and there was no saying if or when she might emerge.

Terror shook her for a moment. She released Ysabeau's shoulders and instinctively looked around for Geneviève to tell her what to do. But Ginette was married now and had moved in over the tavern so that she could bake bread for the Burelles. For the first time in her life, Aimée was responsible for her own decisions.

There was only mousy Noël, wringing her hands, staring wide-eyed at Ysabeau.

Then she saw a group of men and women coming toward the marketplace, led by Françoise Dubonnier, who carried a folded length of gray cloth over one arm, with Father Henri limping just behind her. Jeanne and her husband, Nicolas de La Salle, trooped along in the rear in company with a couple of uniformed soldiers. Conspicuously missing was René Connard. Could Connard himself be at the root of Ysabeau's madness?

Aimée's aggravation abruptly turned to pity. She put a protective arm around Ysabeau. "Françoise! Make these men go away. Where is Monsieur Connard?" She glared at the priest, whose florid face was purple with disapproval as he inspected Ysabeau's state of undress. He might be a holy father, but he had no right to stare so. "Ysabeau, be quiet," she pleaded in a whisper. "What if they arrest you?"

Ysabeau continued to sing, twisting a lock of red-gold hair round her finger.

To Aimée's relief, Françoise knelt in front of Ysabeau, shielding her from the eyes of the men. "How long has she been like this?" she asked quietly, wrapping the length of fabric she carried around the girl's shoulders.

"I found her leaning headfirst into the well, when I came to get water about thirty minutes ago." Aimée didn't particularly like the bossy Françoise, but she had her uses. "What happened to her husband? What did he do to her?"

"He seems to have disappeared." Françoise bit her lip. "The commander sent me to escort her in for questioning, and Father Henri insisted on coming." She glanced over her shoulder.

"Questioning her is pointless. She thinks she's back in France, about to board the *Pélican*. And she mentioned a dead baby!"

"Oh dear." Françoise took Ysabeau's face

in her hands and attempted to catch her gaze.

But Ysabeau's vacant gray eyes followed the flight of a bird that chased overhead.

"I could take her home with me. I'm sure Madame wouldn't mind." She didn't know any such thing, but what else was she to do? Ysabeau and René had been living with Paul Loisel until René could afford to build a house of their own. Ysabeau could hardly live alone with the widower, and Françoise had moved in with the La Salles, who were otherwise overcrowded with children.

Françoise looked doubtful. "I wish Father Mathieu were here to advise us. I suppose we'd best take her to the commander first. He'll know what to do."

"I hardly think that wise." Father Henri, who had limped close enough to overhear their quiet conversation, stood with his arms folded, looking disapproving. "Bienville is a notorious womanizer who cannot be trusted with young unmarried women."

"Ysabeau *is* married," Aimée said, "and — and the commander gave a direct order. Besides, Françoise and I will be with her." She glanced at Jeanne and her stodgy husband. "As will the La Salles, I'm sure."

Father Henri looked affronted at her defiance but stepped aside when the soldiers responded to Aimée's beckoning. The two young men hoisted Ysabeau to her feet, the younger one reddening when she smiled up at him and clung to his arm.

"My papa said I should watch out for sailors, especially the handsome ones. I'm to remain a maiden until I get to Louisiane." She flirted her long eyelashes. "But perhaps we could dance under the stars after we get under way. Papa will never know."

Father Henri looked scandalized, but Aimée took his arm and pulled him in the direction of the fort. "Come, gentlemen," she said over her shoulder to the soldiers. "The commander will be waiting for us. Françoise, watch out for her, I beg you. She mustn't be left alone again." Without giving anyone else a chance to argue, she towed the priest out of earshot of Ysabeau's babbling.

But inside her head, the nursery song filtered like an evil wraith. *Girls are faithful like gold and silver, Mommy, boys are fickle like rain and wind.*

13

As Geneviève examined Dufresne's bleed-ing ear, two small Indian boys, as like as puppies from the same litter, stepped into the clearing. One of them held a miniature longbow and had a quiver of arrows strapped to his back. The other, carrying a dead pheasant, leaned over to jabber in his brother's ear, pointing first to Dufresne, then in the direction from which they had come. The boy with the bow looked fright-ened and turned as if to run.

"Wait!" Geneviève called. "We need help!" She doubted they understood French, but they seemed to interpret her frantic gesture.

They turned back to regard her with big, scared brown eyes. The hair of both was chopped off at the eyebrows and hung in ragged brown clumps about their naked shoulders. Both boys wore breechclouts made of woven palm fronds but not a stitch more. Their skin was dark teak from exposure to the sun, but lacked the olive tint Geneviève had noted in the native peoples with whom she had previously come in contact. She put them at no more than six years of age, probably less.

"Let them go," Dufresne growled, hand to his ear. "I'll tell the chief who did this, and they'll be sorely punished."

The boy with the bird stepped forward, motioning to his cowering companion to stay put. His little cleft chin was elevated, his posture proud. "Madame and monsieur, my brother sorry. Shoot for turkey. He miss."

"Accidents happen," Geneviève said, trying not to laugh. Dufresne wouldn't consider this a funny situation. "I am Geneviève. What is your name?"

"I am Tonaw." Tonaw flung a hand backward and whacked the other boy on the chest. "My brother is Chazeh."

Chazeh nodded without speaking, and Geneviève got the feeling Tonaw did most of the talking for the two of them. She thought of Émile and Serge and smiled. "You speak French very well."

"My mother is good French lady. She teach."

"Their mother is the woman we are going to see." Dufresne walked around the little boys with barely a glance, gesturing for Geneviève to follow. Clearly he was tired of wasting time in conversation with children. "Nika is the best cook in the village. Her mother-in-law is a gifted medicine woman too, and I'm hoping she will do something about the notch in my ear."

"Yes, of course, I'm sorry." Geneviève followed Dufresne, but paused to look over her shoulder. "Boys, will you come with us?"

Chazeh shook his head, looking frightened, while Tonaw shot a resentful glare at the French officer's back. "Yes, but mademoiselle, please do not tell that Chazeh shot the rooster-head. She mistake him for turkey and put him in the stew pot!"

She couldn't help a shout of laughter. "I promise," she said, laying a finger over her lips. The mischievous dimple in the boy's brown cheek put her in mind of someone, but unable to put an exact face or name with the image, she shrugged it off and beckoned the children to walk with her in Dufresne's wake.

In less than fifteen minutes, they reached the first hogans of the Mobile village. The two little boys ran ahead toward a one-room cottage thatched with palm fronds on a wooden pole frame. The slatted floor had been cleverly tied a foot or so off the ground, no doubt in deference to the nearby creek's tendency to overflow its banks. Near the cottage was a small lattice-type enclosure made of river cane, in which a few chickens scratched and squawked, with a fat pig lolling in a muddy trough nearby.

In response to the boys' shouts of greeting, a pretty young Indian woman appeared at the cottage's open doorway. She answered in their own language, shooing them away on some errand, then lifted her hand to shield her eyes as Geneviève and Dufresne approached. She seemed to recognize the aide-major, but her expression was cautious as she looked past him at Geneviève.

Geneviève raised a hand in greeting as Dufresne turned and waited, scowling, until she caught up to him. She supposed she could hardly blame him for his bad temper. His wounded ear, still dripping blood onto the shoulder of his uniform, probably stung like fire.

"Nika, I have brought a friend to visit," he said in French, drawing Geneviève's hand through his arm. "This is Mademoiselle Gaillain — I mean Madame Lanier — newly come here from France. She would like to learn about cooking with native plants and herbs. I told her you're the best cook in the village."

"You are — Lanier, you say?" The young woman had shot a startled glance at Geneviève, then quickly schooled her expression into a smile. "The elusive Captain Marc-Antoine Lanier married at last?"

Geneviève shook her head. "No, his brother, Tristan."

"Ah." Nika's smile neither grew nor dimmed, and Geneviève couldn't tell what she made of the distinction.

She did her best to present a friendly mien. "My husband has gone as part of a peace contingent sent to the Alabama territory. I decided to occupy my time in learning to feed him." Of course there was every chance that Tristan wouldn't come back, but speaking that aloud wouldn't help anything.

"The Alabama will not be easy to persuade, madame. A warlike people they are."

"Please, call me Geneviève — or better yet, Ginette, as my friends do." She impulsively held out her hands, sensing that the Indian woman might become a truer friend than the women of her own race. "I know my husband is on a dangerous mission. But I trust his life to God."

Dufresne rolled his eyes. "You ladies will get along much better without me. I have business with the chief. Nika, is Mitannu in the village today?"

"He is with his father." The Indian woman looked as if she wanted to question him, but with a quick glance at Geneviève, she stepped back. "Come inside, madame. You are welcome."

"Madame, I'll come for you —" Dufresne pulled a pocket watch from inside his coat and consulted it — "in three hours. I want to be back inside the fort well before dark."

Geneviève addressed Nika. "Have you that much time to spare?"

"Of course." Nika smiled and waved a dismissive gesture at Dufresne. "You are correct, sir. You are not needed."

Dufresne bowed an ironical farewell, turned smartly on his high-heeled boots, and strode off toward the largest hogan in the village.

As Nika welcomed her into her home, Geneviève wondered what Dufresne's business could be, then found herself caught up in studying the native cottage. Simple, clean, and neat, she decided. The thatched roof seemed to be well-made, for the floors, walls, and bedding — which had been rolled up and tied in bundles in one corner — were all dry and fragrant. Simple braided mats lay scattered over the raised floor, and Nika gestured for Geneviève to seat herself on one as she herself collapsed upon another.

"Your home is lovely," Geneviève said politely, not quite sure how to start a conversation with one whose life was so entirely foreign to her own. "This is the first Indian house I have been in."

Nika looked pleased. "Thank you. But it makes me laugh to be called an Indian. I believe our territories were mistakenly assumed to be the near eastern continent by your first explorers. Our clans and nations are as diverse, with regard to language and cultural habits, as are your own in Europe. It would be as if I lumped you and your countrymen with the Chinese."

Geneviève laughed. "I see how that would be insulting. I'm sorry."

Nika waved away the apology. "I find it funny." Her smile faltered. "My husband, however, is not so easily amused. If you meet Mitannu, please do not call him anything other than Mobilian — or his name."

"I'll remember."

"Thank you." Nika tilted her head so that her heavy black hair swung over her shoulder. "You are the first Frenchwoman to visit the village. Are you not afraid I will kill you and eat you for dinner?"

Geneviève laughed again. "That never occurred to me. I think the other ladies aren't afraid of you, so much as stumped by the language barrier. I'm surprised at how good your French is. Your boys speak well too. Well, Tonaw does," she added, remembering Chazeh's taciturnity.

"I had a good teacher." Nika looked away. "I am Kaskaskian, of the Alabama people that your husband visits. Many years ago there was a young Frenchman who lived among us. We exchanged languages."

"But aren't the Alabama at war with the Mobile and other southern tribes? I hear stories of attacks and slave trading . . ."

"At the time of my marriage, there was an alliance, and I was given as a seal of peaceful intent." Nika turned her hands palm up. "Alliances are broken all the time."

Days had gone by since Geneviève thought of the war at home. As she looked into Nika's troubled eyes, she saw the face of her childhood friend, Nicolette — Catholic Nicolette, who had loved Papa's pastries and who had stopped talking to her when the bishop came for a visit.

"Yes," she sighed. "Alliances can be broken." She began to understand why Jean Cavalier had told her to find and trust Nika. The woman's loyalties must be with her own clan, and the Alabama were known to favor the British over the French. Still she must be very careful. As careful as Nika herself. She smiled and opened her hands. "But I came to learn anything you have time to teach me about cooking with native fruits, grains, vegetables, meat, seafood . . . I'm realizing more each day that the way things were done in France won't necessarily translate here."

"It is true." Nika grimaced. "The Frenchmen come here and complain about the lack of flour for bread, the toughness of the meat, the bland vegetables. There are ways to compensate, but as I said, the women will not come here to learn." She shook her head with a smile. "Until today. Come. We will start with what to do with *uche* — corn. Such a useful grain."

Nika took her out the back of the cottage, where the boys were playing some noisy game that involved crouching and leaping at one another, growling and wrestling in the dirt like young bear cubs. Smiling at their play, Geneviève stood there a moment looking around, shielding her eyes with her hand. Behind the cottage, which stood on a slight rise, lay a small garden plot, where browning cornstalks and other, smaller plants withered in the harsh autumn sun. It was obviously well tended, clear of weeds and planted in neat rows. A few chickens scratched and pecked near a thatched hen-house; behind it a blanket was suspended by its four corners atop a frame made of hickory poles. A well-worn path led from the main house down to a creek. In the distance, the roofs of other hogans appeared among the trees. It all looked domestic and remarkably civilized.

Geneviève discovered Nika to be a wonderful teacher. With humor and patience, the Indian woman explained and demonstrated the use of mortar and pestle, as well as a set of beautiful handmade baskets specialized for fanning and sifting the softened corn kernels.

"See? Easy as can be." Nika's dark eyes sparkled as she plunged her hand into a basket full of hominy, which she claimed could be used as cereal or bread, or even a thickener for meat and vegetable dishes. "Now we do it again . . . and again . . . and again." With the gourd she scooped up more corn kernels and poured them into the mortar. "Would you like to take a turn with the pestle?"

"Of course." Geneviève took the pole and set to work. She discovered the corn kernels had a tendency to slide away from the pounding of the pestle, and it took her a few moments to get the hang of keeping them centered in the bottom of the bowl. A primitive method of grinding grain, this, but there was a certain satisfaction in mashing the soft kernels and turning them into a substance that would feed a hungry family.

As a child, she used to love to accompany her father to the mill on the outskirts of the village, riding in the mule-drawn wagon for miles over craggy, sloping hills, following one of the streams that rushed from the top of the mountain to the valley below. In sight of the beautiful three-story stone mill, they would halt at the river's edge for several moments to watch the water sluice over the paddle wheels, the roar drowning out every other sound for miles. After crossing the stone bridge and leaving the mule tethered outside the mill, they would clomp down the stairs to the ground floor, where Papa would inspect bag after bag of flour. "You must choose only the best ingredients, little cabbage," he would tell her, touching her nose and leaving a dusting of flour that made her giggle and sneeze. "Good bread needs fine flour and strong yeast."

They would return to the village and store the sacks of flour in the kitchen loft, then make loaf after fragrant loaf for customers who happily paid well for Monsieur Gaillain's famous crusty bread.

Until the summer Jean Cavalier came to be Papa's apprentice. Fiery, handsome young Jean, warrior for the cross, had changed them all. Geneviève, barely fourteen years old, had of course been in love with him and believed every word he preached. Papa saw truth in him and swayed Mama. But martyrdom? None of them had seen it coming.

No one guessed that neighbors who bought bread from Papa on a Friday would be cheering for the dragoons on Monday.

"Mademoiselle! Ginette! Come, you will have powder if you grind it anymore!"

Geneviève looked up blindly to find Nika's face close, her strong hands on the pestle, halting Geneviève's fierce jabs of the pole into the mortar. "I'm . . . sorry," she said, loosening her grip and backing away in embarrassment. "I'm very sorry, Nika. But I have to talk to you about a message I must send to — to someone outside the French territory. I'm told you can do this."

In all her short life, Aimée had rarely seen such a pigsty as Commander Bienville's office. During the dinner she and Geneviève had attended a month ago, she had been able to inspect only the commander's public rooms, and they had been neat and well cared for — due in large part, no doubt, to the work of his Indian servant women. Geneviève seemed to think those women were more than housekeepers and cooks, but then her sister tended to cynicism. Aimée preferred to think the best of people until proven otherwise.

But if the state of his office was anything to judge by, Bienville seemed to live rather a double life. There were papers and parchments everywhere. Maps, letters, bills of lading, receipts — those were the things she could see — and who knew what else was in the towering stack teetering on the edge of that gigantic teak desk. She saw a blowgun decorated with colorful feathers leaning against the wall in a corner, next to a long saber-ended musket and an oddly shaped piece of stiff hide, which she assumed was a shield of some sort. A pair of large muddy boots had been tossed into another corner, along with a shapeless tricorn hat. On the floor next to the desk was a wooden tray containing a decanter of some thick brown liquid, an empty tankard, and the smelly half-eaten carcass of a roasted hare.

The mess seemed not to bother Bienville, for he shoved a pile of ledgers out of his chair onto the floor and sat down, propping his elbows upon the leather journal in front of him. He was in uniform as usual, but his neck cloth was rumpled and loosely tied, and he needed a shave. Dark circles ringed his fine black eyes, and pain pinched his eyebrows together over that magnificent nose. Still, he was a handsome rascal. Aimée couldn't help thinking of the exotic tattoos she'd once seen etched upon his broad dark back and densely muscled arms. It was too bad he was such an uncivilized lout.

After fat Father Henri took the only other chair in the room, the remaining company — Aimée, Françoise, Ysabeau, Jeanne, and her husband, La Salle — arranged themselves awkwardly about the office, waiting to be told what to do. Aimée stayed close to Ysabeau, both to make sure the impromptu cloak stayed about her shoulders and to keep the girl out of Father Henri's line of vision. The man frankly made her skin crawl.

Before Bienville could so much as open his mouth, Father Henri and La Salle spoke simultaneously.

"Commander, you should know —"

"Commander, it is my opinion —"

The two men looked at one another indignantly as Bienville held up a large, elegantly manicured hand. "Gentlemen, this is my meeting, and I will ask the questions." He looked at Françoise, who stood, shoulders back and spine straight, close to the door. "Mademoiselle, I grow weary of your charges cutting up my peace. What have you to say about this latest scandal?" He frowned at Ysabeau, who sat studying her fingers tented in front of her nose. She looked fairly cross-eyed.

Françoise, clearly uncowed by Bienville's disapproval, clenched her hands at her waist. "I say that you have much to answer for, that you allow your men to *gamble* over this poor girl, and then treat her to the humiliation of marriage to a *defector*! How dare you blame a fragile, gently bred young lady for the sins of the roughnecks you call soldiers of the King? When I write to the Duchess to apprise her of the sad state of affairs here in the colony — that nearly every promise made to us before we boarded that wretched tub *Pélican* has been broken ten times over —"

"How dare you threaten me!" Bienville lurched to his feet, wincing at the sudden movement and grabbing his midsection. "I'm well aware that tattling letters have gone out from here already, spewing such lies that it's a wonder the ships that carried them didn't go up in flames." He rounded on the priest, who sat gobbling in inarticulate outrage. "And that a supposedly holy father would contribute poison to the tales — I only regret the day I requested the bishop to send a shepherd for our flock, as he has seen fit rather to send a wolf in a sheep's garment!"

Françoise's gasp popped her mouth and aristocratically sleepy eyes wide open. Father Henri fell back in his chair, crimson of face, huffing and puffing. Ysabeau started to cry.

Aimée could tell that the confrontation had escalated well beyond Ysabeau's public misdemeanor. She took her friend in her arms, shushing her as best she could, while listening for the next juicy explosion of political accusation. She had picked up from Julien Dufresne's chance remarks that unspoken jealousy and competition for royal favor and financial reward had riven the parties of the colony asunder. But this overt vitriol was as entertaining as a play. Perhaps now she would gain a sense for where she should place her own loyalties.

She would once have placed her bets on Françoise, but Bienville seemed a formidable opponent. His rage loomed like clouds preceding a thunderstorm.

To this point, La Salle had hovered in the background near the door, arms folded over his shallow chest. Now he stepped toward Françoise, positioning himself and his silent young wife, who clung to his elbow, in clear alliance with the governess. "Father Henri, it would seem that the commander is not to be trusted with the King's mail." His tone was soft, controlled, and sarcastic. "I wonder if he also knows the number and sex of the sheep Madame La Salle and I have requested to be brought on the next ship from Havana."

Bienville planted one palm flat on the desk and leaned over it to fix La Salle with dangerous eyes. "I have read no one's mail, sir, and if you charge me with such, you are a liar. Your resentment of my authority is no secret, as you have bragged of your intent to play sneak-thief to anyone who would listen."

Françoise took a deep breath and released it slowly. "Monsieur le Commandant, I beg you to reserve these personal contretemps for a later date. These children need to be settled as quickly as possible, wouldn't you agree?" She glanced at Ysabeau, then ruefully met Aimée's eyes.

Though Aimée would prefer not to have been lumped in the "children" category, she appreciated the governess's diplomacy.

Bienville reddened. "I suppose," he growled, looking at Aimée with little favor. "What have you to say for yourself, mademoiselle?"

"Sir, I'm not sure what triggered Ysabeau's behavior, but it does seem to have something to do with Monsieur Connard. Your men claim that he has disappeared from the fort and the settlement without warning. Is this true?"

Bienville maneuvered himself upright again. "I . . . cannot vouch for his exact location at the moment." He picked up a chunk of stone, carved in the shape of an ugly bird, which served as a paperweight on one of the piles on his desk. "When is the last time Madame Connard saw him?"

Aimée looked down at Ysabeau, who had fallen asleep like a child on her shoulder. She didn't look like Madame anybody. "I honestly don't know, sir. When I found her at the well, she was leaning into it, singing a nursery song. She seems to have retreated to some time before leaving France."

"What do you mean?" Bienville dropped the paperweight with a *thunk*. "Has she forgotten everything that happened since?"

"I'm not sure." Aimée would have given anything for her older sister's wisdom. "She spoke of her father as if he were in the next room, and flirted with the soldiers like a — like a very young girl." Which was precisely what she was — a very damaged young girl. Aimée struggled to explain the inexplicable. "I don't understand it myself. I only know she is not the same Ysabeau she was the last time I saw her."

Bienville frowned at Françoise. "What do you propose we do with her? She cannot walk about the settlement in her . . . undergarments!"

"She is her husband's responsibility, and therefore yours, as the man's superior officer." Françoise's expression was implacable.

Bienville looked horrified. "But you were paid to watch over these young ladies!"

"Yes, and my duties as well as my wages end with their marriage."

"Perhaps, Commander," La Salle said silkily, "you would like to rethink your insistence on maintaining the salaries of your layabout Canadians, in order to provide funds for a caretaker for the girl."

Bienville rounded on him. "I'll have you court-martialed for your insolence —"

"As I am neither your subordinate nor your inferior, you'll do nothing of the sort. I answer directly to Pontchartrain." La Salle extracted a tin of snuff from a small pocket in his waistcoat and removed a pinch, which he laid upon his wrist and inhaled. After sneezing, he regarded Bienville, blinking like a lizard in a sunny patch of garden.

Visibly gaining control of his temper, the commander tried a more moderate tack with Françoise. "Perhaps, then, mademoiselle, I might solicit one more favor for the Crown before you completely release your charges." His charming, raffish smile made a sly appearance.

A tinge of pink stained Françoise's high cheekbones. "What — what is it?"

Bienville grinned, clearly considering himself the victor in this battle of wills. "The most logical caretaker would be the nursing sisters, and I'm sure they'd agree to help, if you'd use your influence —"

"Out of the question," La Salle interjected. "Mademoiselle Dubonnier is cousin to my wife. She will not add to the insult you have paid us by taking your part in this conflict."

Father Henri heaved himself out of his chair and onto his feet. "Besides, the Sisters are servants of the church and are not to be at your beck and call. This situation has developed, sir, out of your own hasty, self-serving policies."

"Is it so?" Bienville asked grimly. "I beg you to inform me of those policies so that I might properly repent."

Father Henri failed to perceive the underlying threat. "Shall we start with failure to supervise your rowdy and ill-behaved men? And you have ignored the needs of sick soldiers. My parishioners are starving, because the food His Majesty sent to feed them has been sold to the Spanish to line your pockets — while the meager supplies left over are sold to the settlers at exorbitant prices." Father Henri's face grew redder and sweatier by the moment.

"I defy you to prove any of that." Bienville's voice grew softer, and Aimée would have bolted to the other side of the room, had she been in Father Henri's sandals. "Quite to the contrary, I have swiftly punished any of my soldiers who step out of line. And La Salle will testify that I allotted money to you, to distribute among the soldiers only last week! What did you do with it?"

"Do not change the subject in an attempt to deflect your own guilt onto my head!" Father Henri wagged an accusatory finger.

La Salle didn't seem to be any more intimidated than the priest. He gave Bienville a sour smile. "And proof of your price-gouging tactics will be discovered when Pontchartrain sends someone to audit the books and the contents of the warehouses."

A flash of alarm reflected in the commander's eyes. "I've not had word of an auditor arriving, other than my brother Iberville. I have expected him for some time now."

La Salle shrugged. "Even your brother will not be able to help you when Pontchartrain sees the report from Dufresne's ledgers. Perhaps you thought he was your partner in crime, Bienville, but he has gotten cocky of late — and, therefore, a bit sloppy. You may both find yourselves recalled before the year is out."

Aimée sat up at that, jolting Ysabeau's head off her shoulder. Julien Dufresne could not be in trouble — could he? Did that have anything to do with his trip to the Indian village with Geneviève?

She would have a thing or two to say to her sister when she got back to the settlement.

"I want to send a message to . . . family who have settled in the British Carolinas." Geneviève stumbled over the lie, telling herself that the Huguenots with whom she needed to communicate were spiritual brothers and sisters, if not by blood. Nika would not understand that, so there was no point in trying to explain.

Nika, kneeling in front of a small cookfire, tending the bread frying in a shallow cast-iron pan, looked up at Geneviève. Her expression was bland. "I can get it there, but how will the messenger find them?"

"Will you not take it yourself?"

Nika shook her head. "How could I leave my boys long enough to deliver a letter some eight hundred miles away? I am part of a system of runners operating throughout the Spanish, English, and French territories. We are not political, and no questions are asked at either end." Holding the pan by its handle, she briskly flipped the bread to reveal a beautiful brown crust, then set it back on the grate over the fire. "Do not fear. Your message will arrive safely."

Geneviève bit her lip. She had no choice but to trust Nika and her couriers. She slid her hand into the interior pocket of her skirt. Her feelings about sending this message were more than mixed. Though its contents were little more than an acknowledgment of her arrival in the colony, writing to the King's enemy could still be construed as treason.

But she had promised Cavalier.

She slowly slipped the letter out of her pocket and proffered it to Nika with a trembling hand. "This must go to a man in Charlestown, named Elie Prioleau. He is a . . . pastor, a very holy man, well respected. He will handsomely reward whoever brings him this letter."

Nika looked at her for a moment before setting the sizzling frying pan aside. She took the paper from Geneviève's hand, carefully folded it, and tucked it inside the bodice of her dress. "I will make sure it gets to him. Do you expect him to answer right away?"

Geneviève looked away. "I don't know. Probably not." Had she been foolish to choose to come to New France instead of finding a way to get to the Carolinas herself? But to come among a people who served the British king, even though they worshiped as her family had worshiped . . .

But if she had not come to Fort Louis, she would never have met Tristan Lanier. Never to have known his laughter, his burning dark eyes, the kiss that had all but drowned her. His awkward, courtly bow, his scarred hands that had touched her so gently in the darkness.

Nika gave her another searching look, then nodded. "All right then. I will let you know if anything comes back."

With that she had to be satisfied.

14

Geneviève had no idea what to do about Aimée's rage, demonstrated in the way she politely did the opposite of everything Geneviève asked her to do in Monsieur Burelle's kitchen. The sisters were practicing making *popelins* for Madame L'Anglois's ball, which was to mark the end of the social season as well as Commander Bienville's support of the so-called *Pélican* brides. If the cream-filled pastry puffs lived up to her father's training, Geneviève's talent as a *pâtissière* would be set.

As she had explained to her sister, the soft balls of paste must be handled gently, lest they collapse into flat, chewy disks. Aimée smiled sweetly and dropped a pan full of them upside-down on the floor. "Oh, dear," she said, blinking dry blue eyes. "I'm so sorry."

Speechless, Geneviève stared at the bottom of the tray.

In one of her earliest memories, she sat with her little sister at Papa's broad kitchen table, making patty-pan tarts and singing the nursery songs their mother had taught them as babies. "Sing it again!" Aimée would lisp, puffing up a cloud of flour as she clapped her little dimpled hands. "Sing it again, Ginette!"

So Geneviève would start over once more on Aimée's favorite — the one about fishing for mussels in Marennes. Mama had learned it as a girl growing up on the seacoast, where she had met Papa when he came to apprentice with the great chef Massialot. Aimée would try to sing along, warbling the rhyming word at the end of every other line and making up the parts she didn't know. When Geneviève grew tired of the repetition and moved on to another song, Aimée would poke out her bottom lip. "Papa, Ginette is mean!" And Papa would give Geneviève that disappointed look that made her sigh and go back again to the mussels of Marennes.

Aimée must never be made to cry. As a baby she had been fragile and almost died, though as a little girl she seemed to Geneviève to be healthy as the mule that pulled Papa's wagon back and forth from the flour mill.

But today, when she dropped that tray and spoilt a pound of white milled flour, along with half the morning's work, Geneviève knew a strong urge to box her sister's ears. She clutched the starched apron Madame Burelle had made for her in honor of the opening of the bakery, slowly releasing her breath until she could speak evenly. "Pick them up, Aimée, and scrub the floor. You have cost me and the Burelles a day's wages."

Aimée's mouth trembled, but the resentment in the clear blue eyes was startling in its intensity. "I hate you, Geneviève." She fell to her knees, sobbing aloud. Turning the tray over, she began to plop the blobs of dough onto it higgledy-piggledy.

"Why?" Geneviève released the apron to spread her hands. "What have I done but feed you and clothe you and treat you as my beloved sister?"

Aimée looked up, a log of dough squashed in each hand, tears now streaming pitifully down her flushed cheeks. "What have you *done*? You know it's your fault that Julien hasn't yet made an offer for me!" Giving a pitiful little hiccup, she tossed the dough onto the tray. "He was about to do so when you made him escort you to that horrid Indian village. He hasn't been the same since then — forever looking over his shoulder, watching to make sure we aren't watched."

So that was it. Geneviève knelt and picked up the rest of the ruined dough from the floor, set the tray aside, and took her sister's trembling hands. "Listen. My dear, I've made no secret of the fact that I think you can do better than Monsieur Dufresne. I just don't trust him."

"But why? He has beautiful manners and dresses well, and he's one of Commander Bienville's intimates. I know Julien loves me, for he tells me so at every opportunity!"

"You mustn't be so forward as to address him by his Christian name, Aimée. And he shouldn't be speaking to you intimately unless you are betrothed. It isn't seemly."

Aimée snatched her hands away. "You don't understand! Besides, you are one to call the kettle black! Ysabeau said she looked through the Lemays' window and saw you kissing Monsieur Lanier outdoors in broad daylight."

"At least we were married —" Geneviève pinched her lips together. "But that is much beside the point! The reason I asked Monsieur Dufresne to escort me to the Mobile village that day was to discover more about his parentage and gain a sense of his inten-

301

tions toward you."

Aimée's expression clouded further. "And I have told you your interference is unnecessary. If Commander Bienville trusts him as an officer and Father Henri considers him a good Christian, I don't see what objections *you* can hold! Are you afraid he'll run away to Pensacola like Monsieur Connard, leaving me addled like poor Ysabeau? I assure you, Julien — oh, Monsieur Dufresne, if you must — is not like to do so! As to his parentage, he is the son of a nobleman, in line to inherit property and title, so that we may return to France once he has made his fortune here in the colony." Aimée paused, her eyes widening. "You have begun to regret your own marriage, and so you think to interfere with mine. That must be it!" She scrambled to her feet, smearing tears from her face. "I tried to respect you as my older sister, and to help you with this stupid bakery, but no more. I will see Julien when and where I wish, so there!"

Geneviève rose as well. "You will do no such thing!"

"Oh, yes, I will! I shall do precisely as I wish. Madame likes Julien, and she is my guardian now. I'll tell her you don't need me further, and she will see that I have all I need until I marry." Aimée dropped an impertinent curtsey. "I don't need you anymore, big sister. Good day." She sashayed from the kitchen without a backward glance.

Geneviève stared after her sister. *Oh, Aimée.* Her hand went to her heart, feeling it thud in dull rhythm. Betrayal, she had discovered, felt like another sort of mourning. One could survive it, though each time faith got a little weaker and revived a little more slowly.

She picked up the tray and started to empty its contents into a waste bin. But though the bread could not be sold, it would make flatbread that could be given to hungry traveling soldiers. She would not be guilty of wastefulness. With a sigh she stuck the tray into the brick oven Burelle had commissioned to her specifications and turned to open the larder where her barrels of flour were stored.

As she worked, she listened to the sounds of life stirring overhead in the family rooms, the extra guestroom, and the tavern common room. The five Burelle children would be starting their morning chores, while the lady of the house flurried about, flapping her apron and tucking loose strands of graying hair back under her cap. Monsieur Burelle himself had gone to the market with a list of dry goods needed to restock the pantry.

Relaxing into the rhythm of her task, Geneviève began to hum and pray. Several hours passed. Despite the extra work, she found it almost a relief not to tiptoe around her sister's mercurial moods. She had done all she could to give Aimée a chance at safety and happiness, and though Madame L'Anglois might be a flibbertigibbet, she had a good heart. *God, grant my sister eyes to see the truth.*

How ironic that as the gap between herself and Aimée had widened, her friendship with Nika had developed into something approaching sisterhood. Because she couldn't talk about her faith or her family with other women of the settlement, Geneviève found herself seeking out the Mobile woman. Using her curiosity about Indian food preparation techniques as an excuse to visit twice more during the past week, she had ignored Dufresne's strictures about traveling unescorted and walked to the village, taking only Raindrop as a companion.

When the subject of religion naturally arose, she was delighted to discover that Nika had done quite a bit of thinking about the French Jesus-God. The Indian woman had heard many Bible stories from priests who had visited her childhood village, as well as Father Albert, who had apparently in previous years spent some time with the Mobile people. When Geneviève kindly corrected some of her rather peculiar misunderstandings, created no doubt by the language barrier, Nika had no trouble accepting the concept of God-Become-Man, atonement for sin by perfect substitution, and resurrection from the dead.

The day of Nika's conversion came as a blinding ray of light in a very dark time for Geneviève. Later they sat poring together over Geneviève's precious Huguenot Bible on the creek bank near the Mobile village, while the children wrestled about in the icy water nearby.

After reading the story of Jesus's conversation with the woman at the well, Nika looked up with a pucker between her perfect dark eyebrows. "Jesus behaves just like a Frenchman."

Geneviève laughed. "Why do you say that?"

"He asks the woman for a drink, then confuses her with many words. At last she understands that he loves her, but when she becomes happy, he goes away." There was great sadness in the perceptive dark eyes.

Geneviève nodded, remembering the way

she had felt waking up to find Tristan gone. "I know what you mean, I think," she said slowly. Had something similar happened to Nika? "But remember that Jesus is more than a man. He had to go away in order to save everyone. And he comes back to live here." She pressed her fist to her heart. "When I am lonely or sad, he fills the emptiness."

"It is so." Nika looked away, watching her boys splash one another. "I thought Chazeh was going to die, but I prayed, and God healed him. Perhaps he will one day answer my other prayers."

"I'm sure he will. But, Nika —" Geneviève hesitated, not sure if the truth would be wise. "Sometimes his answer is no."

Nika's eyes filled, but she blinked the tears away, clearly embarrassed. "I know this in my heart. But I must keep asking anyway."

"Can you tell me what you ask, so that I may pray too?"

"No! Some things must not be spoken aloud."

Remembering Nika's genuine alarm, Geneviève had to respect her reticence. After all, she had secrets of her own.

She folded the dough under her hands and pushed her fist hard into its center. *God, keep my husband safe. Perhaps he left me out of love for me. Maybe he will come back in due time.*

And maybe she was every bit as delusional as Aimée. She should be grateful that her monthly flow had begun during the night, proving that Tristan had not left her behind with a child.

"Geneviève? Why are you weeping into the bread dough?"

She looked up with a start to find one of the Burelle daughters standing in the kitchen doorway, regarding her with a puzzled frown. "It's nothing, Yolande." She forced a smile. "Just the smoke from the oven, making my eyes water."

"You aren't going to burn the bread, are you?" Yolande was a miniature version of her mother, anxiously passing from one crisis to another.

"No, it's fine." Geneviève dusted her hands together over the dough, removing the loose flour, then wiped them on a hank of cheesecloth lying on the counter. She peeked into the oven to make sure. "Did you need me for something?"

"There's an Indian man outside asking for you. Papa told me to come find you." Yolande looked worried. "I wish he'd go away. I'm scared of Indians."

"Be a good girl and tell him I'll be right

out." An Indian man? Geneviève couldn't think who it would be, but she removed her apron and hung it on a hook behind the door. She entered the tavern and found Monsieur Burelle sweeping a perfectly clean floor.

He stopped and smiled at her as she crossed toward the front door. "How goes the *popelin* business?"

Well he would ask. Since she used his kitchen and sold her product out of the tavern, they had agreed on a 50 percent split of profits. Madame's *popelin* commission was a business boon.

She paused and sighed. "Rather a bumpy start, but once Aimée quit and went home, things got back on track." When his eyebrows rose, she shook her head. "I'll tell you about it later. Yolande says I have a visitor outside."

Burelle went back to his sweeping. "One of those smelly Indians, she says. Don't let the bread burn."

Tempted to mention that the Indians were no smellier than the unwashed Frenchmen she encountered in the tavern every day, she made a face and replied, "I won't," on the way out the door.

They had traveled slowly, making barely ten

miles a day during the last twelve days. Mathieu knew he must soon speak to Tristan. Each day of delay increased the risk that circumstances would prevent him from unburdening himself.

By now he was certain that Tristan was just the man to whom the comte had hoped to leave his wealth and title. He was not quite so certain, however, that Tristan would wish to accept either one.

The rhythmic splash of paddles in the river accompanied the procession of his mental arguments. Surgeon-Major Barraud sat in the front of the second large pirogue, with Tristan paddling behind and Mathieu balanced amongst their supplies in the middle. Ahead of them in the lead boat were Marc-Antoine and the two cadets, Saucier and Guillory. At first Mathieu had taken a set of oars with the intention of helping. But half a day of Tristan's gentle but firm corrections convinced him that he had best leave the rowing to the experienced seamen.

Thereafter he spent his time jotting notes and drawing pictures in a small journal he had brought along, in an attempt to describe the riverbanks, the water, the sky, the fish, the flora and fauna that made up this new world. Mathieu was not a gifted artist, but he was good with words. He didn't know for whom he was recording his experiences, but something told him the information would someday become valuable. At the end of each day, when the six adventurers tied the boats up at the riverbank and disembarked to camp for the night, he had fallen into the habit of reading aloud from his journal. Often one or the other of the men would add a comment or sing a song that he added into the narrative. The journal had grown into quite a history.

The book now lay open in his lap, and he put down the pen, lifting his face to the pleasant breeze. Despite the autumn sun that beat down on his bare head and cooked his poor peeling nose, it was much cooler here on the water than when they camped ashore at night.

"Do you see the deer over there, Father?"

Mathieu looked over his shoulder to find Tristan pointing to the northeast shoreline. After peering a few moments, he distinguished a buck with a large rack of antlers, then a doe and two fawns, camouflaged by the golden-brown foliage and underbrush that lined the river.

"Beautiful," he breathed, wishing for the hundredth time that he had been gifted to capture on canvas the natural wonders he'd seen since arriving in the New World. He'd been delighted to discover that gift in Tristan. The young cartographer had brought along ink and blank parchment, along with a set of old maps, stored in a beautiful velvet-lined cedar box. Tristan had been tweaking the maps as they traveled, but in the late evenings around the campfire, Mathieu talked him into producing more creative images.

Tristan must have read his mind. "Take the oars, and I'll draw it for you." He traded the oars for Mathieu's journal and pen, but capped the quill in favor of a stub of charcoal he drew from his pocket.

As Mathieu awkwardly plied the oars, struggling to keep time with Barraud's lazy, competent pulls, Tristan produced in several quick strokes a fine sketch of the deer in their autumn habitat, with the water rippling below the bluff in the foreground.

"Thank you!" Mathieu took the drawing, returning the oars, and sat admiring it for several minutes. "You have quite a talent," he said, turning to straddle the seat, but careful not to capsize the boat. "Who taught you?"

Tristan shrugged, switching the oar to the port side. "My father taught me the art of perspective, how to judge distance, how to look for details. Making the leap from maps to pictures was not so difficult. He wouldn't allow me to draw for fun until I had put in the bread-and-butter work for paying customers."

"Have you tried oils?"

"A bit." Tristan's cheeks turned ruddy. "I don't think they're very good."

Mathieu was silent for a moment. If Tristan accepted the legacy he was about to be offered, he could afford to study with any of the masters currently working in Paris. Finally he said gently, "You underestimate yourself, my young friend. Your father was perhaps a good man, but I think he didn't encourage your artistic bent."

"My father was a *very* good man!" Tristan scowled. "He wanted me to be able to support myself and my family, which is why he discouraged frivolous drawing — and he was right to do so."

"Yes, yes, of course." Mathieu smiled to smooth over the unintentional offense. "But now that you are an adult, wouldn't you like to see what you could do with this extraordinary gift? Perhaps take a trip to France and see the wonders of Versailles?"

Tristan looked at him as if he had lost his mind. "My home is here. My *wife* is here. Why would I want to see a noisy, crowded place like Paris?"

"Take Geneviève with you." He had been thinking this through. Geneviève was wanted for murder in the Cévennes, but the Comtess de Leméry would never be connected with the young girl who had harbored Jean Cavalier and shot a dragoon in the streets of Pont-de-Montvert.

"Father, you are strange today." Tristan shook his head. "In fact, I suspect there's something you aren't telling me. My brother has asked me some odd questions, and I know you watch me when you think I'm not looking. Perhaps you'd best come out with it."

Mathieu glanced toward the front of the boat, where Barraud was singing a drinking song in time with the motion of the oars, lazily doing his part to keep the pirogue moving upriver in the wake of the other boat. Mathieu closed the journal and swung his leg across the seat to face Tristan. "Yes. It is time. You see, I know your father, and his name is not Antoine Lanier." He braced himself for an explosion.

Tristan just looked at him, a sort of pitying inspection that seemed to strip away layers of divinity and penetrate to the mansoul of Mathieu Benoît. It was the sort of look he imagined Jesus might have given to Nicodemus, he of the priestly garments and childish questions.

"Did you hear me?" He had not expected this nonresponse.

"I heard you." Tristan leaned into the oars, setting muscles to bunching along his arms and shoulders. His expression changed not a whit. "I'm waiting for you to tell me why it matters."

Geneviève recognized the Indian's homely face, but if she'd heard his name, she couldn't remember it. She crossed the gallery, taking her time, assessing the friendly expression, the lazy way he propped himself against the post that supported the roof, the European shirt and breeches. Strands of gray streaked his long black hair, which was tied back from his forehead with a strip of faded pink calico cloth.

She stopped a few feet away from him. "I understand you asked to speak to me? I'm Geneviève Lanier."

The Indian straightened and smiled, transforming his face to something almost beautiful. "Yes. I see now."

He'd spoken French, but the words didn't make one bit of sense. Perhaps he had misunderstood her. "Did you have me confused with —"

"I am not confused. Tree-Stah is the crazy

one, to leave such a pretty lady alone in this wolf pack."

"Tree-Stah?" Geneviève looked around, hoping Monsieur Burelle was within earshot. The Indian man's French was good, if simple in syntax, and he didn't seem inclined to hurt her, but she didn't know what to make of his familiar way of addressing her.

"Your . . . husband, I think is the word? He tells me to look after his Jon-a-Vev."

Husband. Tree-Stah was Tristan. Jon-a-Vev must be . . . *me.* "He . . . when did he tell you that?" Why would Tristan ask a man she'd never even heard of, especially an Indian, to look after her? Who was this man?

"The day he marries you, he comes to the tavern and says he must travel upriver to be the peacemaker. I am left to feed his animals and guard his woman." The broad smile gentled to twinkling dark eyes. "I am Deerfoot, of the Pascagoula clan. My family lives on the Massacre Island. Your commander pays me to run messages. Tree-Stah is my good friend who also marries my cousin."

Geneviève felt her mouth form an *O*. A relative of Sholani, Tristan's friend.

Deerfoot made a face. "I see he has told you little. This is a very smart, but also stupid man you have married."

315

Indeed. *What other surprises has he left me, I wonder?* "Please, will you come inside with me? I am baking today, and I don't want to burn . . ." She looked over her shoulder at the tavern's door, left open to catch any wayward breeze that might chance by. Remembering Burelle's "smelly Indian" comment, she wondered if he might object to her bringing an Indian man through the front.

Again, Deerfoot demonstrated his perceptiveness. "Burelle doesn't mind me," he said with a smile. "Commander Byah-Vee-Yah allows me free run of the place."

And what if Burelle *did* mind? She would not treat Tristan's friend like a dog. She smiled. "I could probably find you a loaf of bread, if you're hungry. Come with me." She turned to reenter the tavern and was relieved to find that Burelle had disappeared, making explanations unnecessary. When she looked over her shoulder to make sure that Deerfoot followed, she was startled to find him close on her heels. "Oh!" She hit the doorfacing hard.

"I am very quiet," he said with a grin. "I teach Tree-Stah how to track and hunt in the woods."

"I'm sure you did," she said, ruefully rubbing her bruised shoulder. "Come in. You can sit on that stool in the corner while I work."

After tying on her apron, she removed the tray of golden pastry puffs from the oven and set them on a trivet to cool. The room instantly smelled of warm bread and sugar. She skimmed the cream from a pitcher of milk, knowing Deerfoot was eyeing the pastry tray. "Would you like to try one?" she asked with a smile.

His eyes lit. "Yes!"

"Then help yourself." She poured the cream into a clean bowl, added a teaspoon of sugar and a ground vanilla bean, and began to apply the whisk. The cream developed bubbles and froth, then thickened into a beautiful, snowy fluff.

Deerfoot slid off the stool and inspected the pastry tray. "Tree-Stah has married a gifted woman this time." With nimble dark fingers, he selected the biggest puff and popped the entire thing into his mouth. His eyes closed in ecstasy. "You will please teach my woman how to make this bread."

Geneviève showed him the whisk with its thick coating of whipped cream. "Wait until you taste it with the cream in the middle."

"Poor Tree-Stah." The Indian shook his head. "He will return to find his Jon-a-Vev in great demand. You will be so busy making these little cakes you will have no time for him."

Knowing he was teasing, she laughed. For some reason she felt free to broach a question she had been burning to ask. "What was Sholani like? Did you know her well?"

"I did. She was pretty — in a different way than you. Not so tall, maybe. She was dark like the earth, but her spirit was lighter than an ocean breeze. She brought joy to my friend Tree-Stah when he was so angry with Byah-Vee-Yah that he no longer wanted to live among his own people."

Geneviève nodded. She knew that kind of frustration and anger. Only her love for her sister and the deep awareness of God's love for her had kept her from succumbing to hopelessness. "He wouldn't tell me how she died," she blurted. "Was it so terrible?"

Deerfoot's countenance darkened. "As terrible as death can be."

Death could be very terrible indeed. But she wanted to know the man to whom she had given herself. "Tell me."

15

Ten days later, as he scrambled in the lead up the Koasati bluff, Tristan flexed his scarred hands, remembering the day many years ago when Marc-Antoine had burst into their father's drafting studio, smelling of fish, spring air, and wet dog. Tristan, seated at the drafting table opposite the door, where he was occupied in copying a map of Lake Huron's western shore, grabbed for his parchment before it could fly away with the sudden gust of wind. His ink pot fell over, ruining the map.

Marc-Antoine, of course, paid no attention to Tristan's growl of frustration. "Tris! Did you know Iberville is looking for a language expert for the southern expedition?"

Mopping up ink as he avoided his father's kindling gaze, Tristan shrugged. "No. Why would I care?"

"You are good with languages! Your Latin

is as good as your French — and you've even learned that barbaric English tongue!"

"Moderate your tones, if you please." Father got up to take the stained parchment from Tristan with two fingers and set it aside for cleaning. "Where have you been today, to get so filthy and smelly? Your mother will have a fit of vapors."

Marc-Antoine waved a hand. "At the docks. Tristan, it's your patriotic duty to join the marine. Bienville says they must have a full crew, or the expedition will be canceled. You should go talk to him now! He's still at the tavern."

Tristan met his father's eyes. Jean-Baptiste Le Moyne, the young Sieur de Bienville, had always had a knack for dragging his friends into adventure. Mad to prove himself the equal of his older, more celebrated brothers, he had joined the French marine when barely out of short coats, following his older brothers off to help wrest the great lakes of Illinois away from the Huron Indians. When King Louis XIV decided to extend his influence along the great rivers that bisected the American continent, the Le Moynes were chosen to lead the establishment of forts and settlements along the Mississippi and on down to the gulf coast. Bienville had apparently been chosen to visit all the local gathering places and recruit necessary manpower.

Father scowled as he provided Tristan with a new parchment. "Bienville is a stupid young warmonger, and his brothers aren't much better. You will stay away from him, Marc-Antoine, or I shall cut off your allowance."

Tristan could have predicted his brother's reaction.

"Why?" Marc-Antoine rounded on his father. "Bienville is only providing opportunity for advancement and fortune for men who would otherwise be stuck here in this frozen wasteland for years on end! *You* are afraid to leave, and so must be everyone else."

Father's face went white as the parchment in his hand, and then flushed with fury. "*What* did you say to me?"

Marc-Antoine's extravagant eyebrows, so like their mother's and Tristan's own, met above his nose like the wings of an angry hawk. "I'm tired of playing at life like a child! I'm capable of choosing my own friends and making my own destiny. And that is exactly what I plan to do — beginning right now!"

Tristan pushed back his chair. "Marc, be careful."

"Careful never got anybody anywhere." Passion vibrated in every line of Marc-Antoine's tall, gangly body. "If *you* won't go with Iberville, then I will." He glowered at his father. "And there's nothing you can do to stop me!"

Tristan's hands stung with phantom pain as he recalled the lengths to which his father had gone in the attempt to keep Marc-Antoine from leaving home at the age of fourteen. In the end they had both gone — Marc-Antoine in wild-eyed resentment and Tristan with a promise to watch after the young prodigal. Only, unlike the protagonist of Christ's story, the two of them had received neither inheritance nor tearful goodbye. Furthermore, far from coming to his senses in a foreign pigpen, the younger brother had discovered fame and fortune with the Le Moyne brothers and never spared a backward glance.

Tristan, the elder, had met his own destiny in the beautiful dark eyes of Sholani — who bound him to this wild land as surely as his father's whip had driven him from home.

But — *not* his father, as Father Mathieu had just informed him. Deep in his spirit, he'd known it all along, had recognized a fundamental distance in his relationship with Antoine Lanier, compared to the blistering rage and unspoken pride that had pulsed in nearly equivalent measures toward Marc-Antoine.

Was the dead Comte de Leméry his father in truth? A man he had never met, certainly never loved. A man who, far from loving his mother, had sold her, for the price of silence, to a Canadian mapmaker.

Turning to give a hand up to the men behind him, Tristan pondered whether he should speak of his doubts to his brother. Would his parentage matter to Marc-Antoine? He suspected not. And, as he had said to the priest, it mattered little with regard to his life here in New France. Nothing fundamental had changed.

His brother came over the edge of the bluff, rolled, and landed lightly on his feet, then helped Tristan assist the panting priest. When Mathieu was safely out of the way, the surgeon, followed by Saucier and Guillory, climbed onto the landing. They all took a moment to brush sandy clay off their hands and knees, somber now that they had arrived at their destination. It had been ten days since Tristan's conversation with Father Mathieu, over three weeks since they had first set out on this journey. Since it was almost dark, the plan was to make camp for the night, then approach the Alabama village in the morning. None of them could predict how the natives might receive them, but experience had taught Tristan that the Indians would be less threatened, and therefore more receptive to gestures of friendship, during the early hours of the day.

"What's the matter, Tris?" Marc-Antoine pulled him aside, his expression quizzical. "I remember this place from my trip back four years ago, and it was a good camping spot because of the spring on the other side of those trees. You look uneasy."

Tristan shrugged off his brother's worry with a smile. "No, just tired of fish for breakfast, lunch, and dinner. I'll take my bow and see if I can get a rabbit or a deer before the sun goes down."

Marc-Antoine nodded, clearly not convinced. "Good idea. We'll set up camp, build a fire. It will be good to sleep on dry ground."

Bow in hand, Tristan set off along the stream trickling through the woods. Dusk was falling, and he knew he wasn't likely to find much in the way of game, but he needed the time alone. He was going to have to talk to Marc-Antoine about the priest's crazy tale, get his take on it. He needed his brother to laugh and tell him not to be soaking in fairy tales. They *were* brothers, in the most important sense of the word, and nothing could change that.

Shaking off his turbulent thoughts, he continued deeper into the woods, walking without a sound in the manner Deerfoot had taught him. Before long he heard the distant gabbling of a flock of turkeys. Slipping closer, he saw a broad-bottomed tom with brilliant comb and wattle. Drawing an arrow from his quiver, he nocked it against the string and aimed at the nearest fowl.

A second later the turkey was dead, the arrow having clipped it through the eyes and gone to rest in the trunk of a pine tree. As the other birds in the flock flapped awkwardly and noisily away into the forest, Tristan retrieved his arrow, wiped its soiled head on a patch of moss, and returned it to the quiver. Picking the bird up by its feet, he swung back toward camp. He was perhaps a mile away when he stopped at a loud cracking sound perhaps thirty yards away. Something much heavier than any forest animal had stepped on a limb. Heart thudding, he listened to the stillness.

He was alone and outside shouting distance of the rest of his party. Utterly foolish to have left on his own. He backed toward the closest tree, an ancient oak with a broad scarred trunk and mossy gnarled roots.

Almost he thought he had imagined the noise, but then he heard a muffled but unmistakable sneeze. He slowly lowered the turkey to the ground, then reached over his shoulder for an arrow. Just as he got it nocked, three Indian braves in Alabama dress melted out of the forest with their own bows armed and aimed. He was surrounded.

The hair on the back of his neck rose. The dark faces were inscrutable, the mouths clipped into tight lines, the eyes narrowed. They were young, perhaps still in their teens, each sporting a single combat feather in the light headdresses woven into their long, black hair. Come upon like this, apart from the village, they must be considered hostile. If he shot first, he could kill one, even as the other two sent arrows into his own heart. If he yielded, they would take him prisoner and torture him before murdering and scalping him.

Frozen with fear, he prayed for wisdom.

Nika ran through the darkening forest alone, but sometimes when she listened, the pounding of her heart sounded like someone running near her. Out of habit, she looked over her shoulder, though she was confident she was not being followed. Mitannu had left to go hunting yesterday, and her sister-in-law, Kumala, was busy tanning hides for winter use. Nika had told Kumala that she wanted to visit an old friend who now lived in the village of the Apalachee, so that if she and the boys were missed, no one would come looking for them.

When they had first left the Mobile village, Chazeh and Tonaw ran ahead of her. No matter how many times she had cautioned the boys to silence, they were too young to remember for more than a few minutes at a time. She hadn't been able to tell them that this hunting game was deadly real. Frightening them would have done no good, and might even have slowed them down.

The three of them had walked along the Mobile River toward the Apalachee village, skirting it for safety's sake, then headed due north through the forest west of the winding Alabama River. Though paying someone to paddle her and the boys upriver would have been less tiring, the detour cut off several hours of travel. By the time they reached the Little Tomeh in late afternoon, both boys were whining about food, so she had gone directly to Azalea's hogan.

Nika and Azalea had grown up together in the Kaskaskian village of the Alabama nation, a loose confederation of clans located near the juncture of the Coosa and Tallapoosa Rivers, which together flowed south, forming the Alabama River. The two girls had been close friends until the young Frenchman called Bright Tongue came to live in their village. Nika's father chose her to tutor their guest in the Alabama language, and that was that. Azalea had warned her that the beautiful white boy would not stay, but Nika didn't want to hear it. She had swallowed his sweet words whole, eagerly fed him kisses in return, and soon the seeds of two little boys grew in her belly.

Such grief and such joy she had known since those two were placed at her breast. She would sacrifice anything to keep them safe. Leaving them with Azalea had been the hardest thing she had ever done, even harder than leaving her home to follow Mitannu, the Mobile headman's eldest son, all the way to the mouth of the big river, where it gushed into the bay that opened like a blessing into the wide waters. She had seen the great gulf once, and it was just like Bright Tongue described it — though even he could not do justice to the vastness, the power, the crashing *noise* of it. She had begged Mitannu to take her back to the Mobile village, and he had laughed at her

— not kindly, as the Frenchman would, when he teased her about her funny way of saying his name. *Mah-Kah-Twah.*

"Mah-Kah-Twah." She said it aloud again, savoring his name on her tongue as she had once felt his lips upon hers.

Suddenly she stopped running to cast her arms around an oak tree in her path, pressing her forehead hard into its wooden skin so that the harsh reality might banish the foolish dreams that caught her off-guard more and more often in these unhappy days under Mitannu's domination. For now, the boys were safe with Azalea, and no one would think to look for them there. Mitannu didn't want them anyway, for she suspected he knew they weren't his. She was going to deliver this one last letter into the British stronghold in Carolina, accept payment for it, and then return for her children. She would take them to live with her mother's people in Kaskaskia, far away from Mitannu. Her father might beat her, but he wouldn't turn her and the children away.

And most importantly, she would be far from Bright Tongue, who didn't want her or the boys either. If he had, he would have stayed. He would have demanded the right to take her from her father's hogan. But he had not. She had awakened one morning to find him gone, vanished with his older brother, leaving her to mourn like a widow. How could a man who loved her walk away? Even a very young man who spoke another language?

She relaxed her arms, turned to brace her back against the tree, and felt in her pocket for the paper Ginette had given her. It had been folded many times and sealed with a blob of greenish wax. She fingered it, wondering what message was worth risking so many lives for. Ginette said the Huguenot priest would pay well for it. She hoped so, for it would take money to safely transport those two little boys such a long distance. And her father would more readily accept her if she could offer to pay for their food and shelter. Perhaps there would be enough to buy a hog, a milk cow, or even a horse, livestock valuable to the northern Alabama culture.

Her fingernail slipped under the edge of the wax, loosening it just a bit. What if it came off? Bright Tongue had been teaching her to read French just before he left the Tuskegee village. She might be able to decipher the note, and perhaps she might sell the intelligence elsewhere. On the other hand, removal of the seal might decrease the letter's value to its recipient.

She smoothed it back down and lifted her skirt to tuck the paper back into the pocket tied around her waist inside her dress. After all, she doubted that a nice Frenchwoman like Ginette would have anything to say that would be of any real interest.

Unmoving, Tristan watched the eyes of the closest Indian flicker toward the turkey at his feet. The boy's nostrils flared.

Tristan waited until his heartbeat receded from his ears and settled back in his chest. He must not display weakness. He stood with the bowstring taut at his cheek and ready to fire.

The brave with the Roman nose lowered his arrow to aim at the ground. "You shoot turkey?" he asked in the Koasati dialect.

Tristan nodded. "Yes. You hungry?" It dawned on him that the young men were painfully thin, their ribs prominent above the pale leather breechclouts. What had happened to the game near their village?

"Hungry," the brave repeated, dropping his bow with a sweeping gesture that commanded his companions to follow suit.

Tristan lowered his own weapon, full of wonder at this turn of events. "Koasati?" When the brave gave him a wary nod, he bent down to pick up the stiff turkey and offered it to the Indians. "I come with French warriors and black robe, to make peace with your people."

"Peace," the young man grunted, stumbling over the word as if it were foreign to his tongue. He brought one fist to his chest in a theatrical and oddly *young* gesture. "Our chief sends us to greet the French brothers from the south river. We welcome them to our village to smoke the calumet of peace."

Tristan wondered what the Indians would do if he fainted from relief. He gestured once more with the turkey. "First we eat. Then I will go with you."

The Koasati spokesman took it, shaking the bird's tail into a gigantic, brilliant fan, which he somberly admired. "Our brothers have found food where there has been none for many days. It is a sign of the French God's favor. We are honored to eat with you."

Peace, Tristan thought. Perhaps God was listening after all.

When she came upon Mitannu and his men, Nika was about to slide down a steep bluff covered in vines, briars, ferns, and pine striplings. At the bottom of the bluff burbled a spring that became a rushing little icy-fingered creek she and her cousins had swum in when she was a girl. She had been running without stopping for two hours, and she was mortally thirsty. Besides, it was time to stop for the night. The outermost Alabama village should be nearby, if she remembered correctly. It had been years since she had traveled this route herself, though she had sent her runners this way every so often.

She had knelt to choose a safe footing, when movement among the trees on the other side of the creek caught her eye. Instantly she flattened herself, melting into the brush. Heart pounding, she lifted her head just enough to peer down into the bowl of the creek.

It hadn't been her imagination. Even with his face painted in the alien clay-reds and ocher-yellows of the Koasati tribe, his hair twisted into the topknot favored by northern hunters, she would know her husband's guttural voice among ten thousand others.

She pressed her cheek against the ground, almost glad of the briars driving into her skin, because the pain kept her from blacking out. He had followed her after all. Hunting had been a pretext to make her relax her guard. And if he had followed her, then he also knew where the boys were. What if he had taken them? What if he had hidden them somewhere, where she wouldn't be able to find them? He was just spiteful enough to have done so.

Eyes squeezed shut, she crammed her fist against her mouth to keep from groaning aloud. *Think. Nika, think.* She could not. Thought burned in a flaming burst of fear. Then something Ginette had once said came to her. *When my father was murdered, all I could do was pray. And God came to visit me in my anguish. Just like he did for men and women of the Bible. He came.*

God?

It was a weak, tentative plea. She didn't even know how to ask for help. But he could see her. Yes, and he saw Mitannu. Her little boys too. Had she been a bad wife in trying to keep them safe? But she had to ask.

Please show me what to do.

Bit by bit her shivers stopped. The fear was still there, a knife at her throat, but as she gained control of her body, she opened her eyes, slowly turned her head, and looked over the rim of the bluff.

What she saw almost made her smile. Mitannu and five braves, all adorned in Koasati war regalia, knelt in the creek shallows, noisily slurping the water like dogs.

I am but a woman, fearful and weak, she

told herself, *one against six proven warriors. But with God I am all my children need. After all, he gave them to me, and he has kept me hidden thus far.*

Her heart lightened. What she must do now was stay out of sight, follow Mitannu, and see if he led her to where he had hidden the boys. Surely she would think of what to do next.

She relaxed. But just as she did so, Mitannu abruptly raised his head, water dripping from his yellow-and-red-striped chin. His narrowed gaze pointed right at her.

"Who's there?" he demanded.

16

Dark had fallen by the time Tristan cleaned the turkey, roasted it, and shared the meat with his French companions as well as the three young Koasati braves. It was a big bird, but it didn't go as far as he'd hoped.

Still, the young natives seemed almost friendly as they licked the grease from their fingers, and patted their lean stomachs with satisfaction. The leader with the Roman nose, who called himself something unpronounceable that translated to "Fights With Bears," got to his feet with fluid grace and addressed Tristan. "You will come with us. My father wishes to meet the leader of the French brothers."

Tristan exchanged alarmed glances with Marc-Antoine. What the Indians wanted was a hostage.

"We will all come," Marc-Antoine said, "first thing in the morning."

"My father will not be pleased if I disobey." The boy's chin was set on stubborn lines. "One of you must come now."

"Marc-Antoine, I will go with them." Father Mathieu rose. "I will be honored to meet the headman." The priest had eaten his share of the meal quietly, watching the gestures and body language of the young Indian men and listening to Marc-Antoine's and Tristan's part in the conversation. Clearly he had picked up on the gist of the present dilemma.

"No!" Tristan stepped between Mathieu and the Indians, though he doubted Fights With Bears understood the priest's words. He spoke in rapid French. "Father, you mustn't go alone. They speak peace now, but the northern tribes have been known to murder our priests on a whim. Besides, they want our leader — and that would be me." He eyed his brother, warning him silently to back down.

But Marc-Antoine of course would have none of that. He too was on his feet. "This is my responsibility, Tristan. The chief will respect my uniform."

"He might, but more likely he would take it as a sign of aggression. There's been no indication of hostility so far," he added, discounting his less than friendly initial encounter with the natives, "but if something should go wrong tonight, you must stay alive to carry word back to Mobile. Do you think Bienville will be pleased if his best officer and translator is murdered?"

Marc-Antoine flushed. "I don't care what Bienville thinks —"

"Yes you do." Tristan mutely sought the priest's support. "For whatever reason, maybe simply because they met me first, they think I'm in charge here. Marc, there was a reason you insisted I come along." He softened his tone, praying his brother would give in. "Diplomacy is my gift. Now let me use it."

Marc-Antoine's jaw worked for a moment, then he gave a rough chuckle. "Oh, all right. You could talk the squirrels out of the trees, I swear. But please, come back to me with your scalp intact, or your bride will be relieving me of mine!"

Weak-kneed with relief, Tristan grinned. "You don't know how true that is." As he bent to pick up his musket, bow, and quiver, which lay near Mathieu's feet, he murmured, "Father, please don't mention our earlier conversation to anyone until I return. I haven't decided what I want to do about it."

The priest gave a reluctant nod. "Be careful. Much rides upon your safe return."

"I will." As he turned to leave with the three Koasati boys, he looked over his shoulder. His brother stood feet planted wide apart, arms crossed in clear mutiny. But he was safe, thank God.

Tristan had yet to break his promise to their father.

Julien had quite made up his mind.

In fact, he had planned on the morrow to apply to the commander for permission to declare himself to Mademoiselle Aimée Gaillain and ask for her hand in marriage. Circumstances being what they were, however, he feared it might be several days before he became free to do so.

In short, he had been assigned to guard duty, a task for which he was eminently overqualified. But Bienville was adamant. Only a senior officer could be trusted to make sure mad Ysabeau Bonnet remained inside the guardhouse, and that all male visitors be kept out.

He shifted his chair, propped on two legs against the gallery wall, into a more comfortable angle, wishing the Bonnet girl to perdition — where she was bound to go anyway, her crimes being of such a diabolical nature that even lazy Father Henri wasn't likely to accept a bribe in return for absolution. He could hear her through the high barred window now, singing like a drunken siren. *Go to sleep, Colas, my little brother, go to sleep, you will have your milk.*

That she had dropped the Lemay infant into the well was beyond doubt. No one was sure if she had killed him first.

Julien shook his head and sighed. A nastier web of machinations he had yet to see. The grieving parents — perhaps instigated by Father Henri or La Salle — blamed Bienville for the child's death, claiming that he had starved from lack of milk. Though Bienville sympathized and agreed to restrain poor Ysabeau, lest in her madness she commit further atrocities, he refused to accept responsibility for the tragedy.

Personally, Julien thought the girl should be hanged or shot at dawn, and thus released from her misery. Even if she were cleared of infanticide, no man in full retention of his senses was likely to take her on in marriage — or any other relationship, for that matter.

In any case, he had more pressing concerns. He would give much to know how his plans were proceeding in the northern Alabama woods. Mitannu had been most receptive to the suggestion of annihilating the man who had cuckolded him and foisted two bastards upon him. That the savage was also likely to murder his wife and the two boys was an unfortunate side consequence. Nika was a beautiful woman, as well as a useful agent, and Julien had once considered taking her for his mistress. Had she been willing, events might now be proceeding in an entirely different manner. One must, however, cede small pleasures for the greater good.

The greater good, specifically of Julien Dufresne, meant that in colonial matters, the French Crown must yield to the English one. Since it was only a matter of time before England overcame Louis's feeble attempts to claim this shifting bog known as Louisiane, Julien had no qualms about benefiting from Queen Anne's inevitable conquest over the southern Indian tribes — as evidenced by the Alabaman resistance to Julien's covert trade lures. By that time, if all went according to plan, he should be safely ensconced in his ancestral home in the Cévennes.

But first he would need to make sure Tristan Lanier did not survive to supersede him.

So deep in his thoughts was he that he did not hear Aimée's approach until she was all but upon him. The front legs of his chair hit the porch with a thump as he leaped to his feet. "Aimée! Mademoiselle!" Caught off-guard, he struggled to make out her features in the gloaming. Her pale face gleamed like alabaster in the moonlight, the blue of her dress a ghostly shade. She really was a little objet d'art. "Is something amiss?"

"No, why should you think so?" She stepped closer to the edge of the gallery, but her voice was so soft that he had to strain to hear her. "I only came to make sure Ysette is comfortable . . . and to see if you had dined as well. I brought you some blackberry tartlets." She showed him the basket over her arm. "I made them."

"Did you? How kind." He looked for a chaperone behind her and found none. The slight tremor of her voice told him she knew how improper this meeting was. He relaxed. Mademoiselle Aimée was a minx. He took his time descending the shallow steps from the gallery to the ground.

"Here." She shoved the basket toward him. "I must go back to —"

"I wish you would stay and keep me company," he murmured, taking the basket with one hand and her warm fingers with the other. "It is so lonely out here with only crazy Ysabeau singing to me."

That was a mistake. Aimée stopped looking at him to focus on the open window behind him. "Do you think she really did it?"

"At this point, I wouldn't be surprised at anything. That fool René Connard has gone over to the Spanish, and they refuse to deport him. He knows enough about artillery development to be somewhat useful to them, and now those of us to whom he owes money are out of luck." Stifling his irritation, Julien made the effort to focus on his little sweetheart. "But look how my luck has turned just now! The most beautiful woman in New France has come to bring me a treat. What must I do to convince you to stay and share it with me?"

"You mustn't tease me." She pulled her fingers coyly from his. "I'm not the most beautiful woman in New France."

"No, you are the most beautiful lady in all of Europe and the Americas." He slid his arm around her waist and drew her close. She smelled of lavender and sandalwood, and she was so petite that her curls brushed his chin. "I hope you came to share more than a pastry."

"I don't know what you —"

He kissed her, sure that she would belong to him soon.

But he wasn't particularly surprised when she puckered her lips and pulled away. "You must not!"

He supposed the real fear in her voice was to be expected. "I know I mustn't, but I can hardly help myself, you are so very lovely." He dropped the wretched basket on the ground and seized her hard in both arms. "I was going to ask the Commander for you on the morrow, but I'm not sure I can wait that long."

"You were? I mean, you are? Oh Julien!" She beamed at him. "Then Ginette will have nothing more to say, and you will build us a house, and we shall have half a dozen beautiful children!"

He ignored the blithe reference to imaginary children. "Why do you think your sister is so adamantly opposed to our marriage?"

A tiny frown drew together her perfect brows. "It isn't like her to be spiteful, but she thinks you have been spying on her. I told her you don't care one bit about her silly religion. The King is nowhere near to sending dragoons here to arrest dissenters as they did my papa. One church is as good as another, as long as the proprieties are observed. Don't you agree?"

"Of course I do, *cherie,* as I told Ginette the day we walked to the village together.

But she insists that her God is a rigid, color-less Reformer who loathes our beautiful Madonnas and the music of the Mass, and anything else reeking, as she says, of ritual and tradition."

Aimée chewed her lip. "That doesn't sound like Ginette . . ."

"She doesn't want to hurt you, my dear. I had hoped that by getting her alone that day, I could sway her from these foolish and dangerous notions." He sighed. "But I'm afraid she remains quite adamant."

"It's all the fault of that wretched Jean Cavalier! Ginette has always harbored a sort of hero-worship for him." She pressed the back of her hand to her mouth. "Oh, Julien, you won't tell anyone, will you? I'm so angry with her, but I truly wouldn't want her to be in trouble!"

Jean Cavalier? The Black Camisard who had been leading His Majesty's dragoons in a merry dance in the south of France? This was even more than Julien had hoped.

He half closed his eyes to hide his excite-ment. "No, never. Of course I wish only to protect you and your foolish sister." Julien drew Aimée to the gallery steps and tucked her close to his side with an arm around her tiny waist. "Is there . . . anything in writ-ing that would incriminate her?"

Aimée was silent for a moment. "No, I don't — oh wait! There is her Bible. Cavalier gave it to Papa — and Ginette managed to retrieve it before we left the Cévennes. I see her reading it every so often, and there's what looks like a note in it . . . that she always hides when she sees me coming. I think it could be a note from Cavalier himself." She clutched Julien's coat. "Oh, Julien! Do you think they would — arrest her, if it were found in her possession?"

"I'm certain of it." Julien kept his voice as somber as a gallows. "*Cherie,* you must help your sister. You must retrieve that note and give it to me for safe-keeping."

"But I don't think I could —"

"My darling, if you love Ginette, you'll do whatever you must to protect her from herself."

Aimée continued to gnaw at her lip in silence. Finally she said slowly, "I suppose . . . I suppose I could try."

Julien squeezed her waist. "I know you can do it."

The stentorian snores emanating from the other side of the campfire fairly shook the ground beneath Mathieu's knees as he prayed, making him long for some cotton wadding with which to plug his ears.

Surgeon-Major Barraud's skills as a physician might be in question, but there was no doubt of his ability to imbibe copious amounts of corn liquor and maintain his grip on this mortal coil. Saucier and Guillory were sound asleep as well, full of roasted turkey and flatbread.

Tristan had gone into the Koasati village, leaving his younger brother in somewhat sullen command of the remaining peace party. Marc-Antoine had rolled himself into a defensive knot as far from the others as he could get, and still feel the warmth of the fire. He had a good heart, no doubt, and seemed to be no more selfish than most men, but he was not going to be pleased when Mathieu took his best friend and mentor away for good.

But, dear God, King Louis needed men of wisdom, intellect, and integrity surrounding him in court. Otherwise, the factions that corroded the nation from the inside must continue to work their diabolical schemes, until there would be no one left to withstand the King's hedonistic spiral into destruction.

In thoughts from the visions of the night, when deep sleep falleth on men, fear came upon me, and trembling, which made all my bones to shake. Still on his knees, Mathieu reeled, Job's words piercing his anguished spirit, as he strove to hear God's voice above the clamor of his own weariness. *A spirit passed before my face. The hair of my flesh stood up. There was silence, and I heard a voice saying, Shall mortal man be more just than God? shall a man be more pure than his maker?*

He opened his eyes and could swear the same spirit crossed his vision. Terrified, he flattened himself against the ground. Was it too much to ask that France be rescued from the consequences of human weakness? Was there no patriot strong enough to halt the inexorable march of the Church's corrupting influence?

He raised his head in shocked denial. *Me? Never me, Father —*

The shadow of his imagination became a solid form, hellishly distorted behind the campfire. Another followed, arm raised to brandish a flashing knife, and a third embellished with a trembling cockscomb of turkey feathers. The first two silently swooped upon the Frenchmen sleeping on the opposite side of the fire — Guillory and Saucier never moved, though their snores abruptly ceased.

Frozen in horror, Mathieu knew that Barraud and Marc-Antoine Lanier would be next. He could save them, if he moved, if he shouted, if he did *something.*

Just as the third attacker raised his knife to drive it into Barraud's sleeping form, Mathieu screamed. The sleeper jerked, rolled into the fire, and sat up with a startled grunt. His attacker moved behind him, grabbed him by the hair, jerked his head backward, and swiftly lowered the blade in his hand.

That was all he saw before a wrenching, scalding pain exploded in his head.

It was over before Nika could do more than gasp in horror. When she had earlier come upon Mitannu and his men, a pheasant had flown out of the underbrush, diverting her husband's attention from her hiding place above the creek. It had been easy to follow the disguised Mobilians as they slipped through the forest. Towering in helpless fear, she had watched them butcher all five Frenchmen, including the priest. He had screamed like a wildcat just before Mitannu, who carried a musket, had shot him.

Murdered him, the man of God, with deliberate, cold violence, then melted away into the forest with his men.

The magnitude of her husband's savagery sank in. Her body went into an earthquake of fear as she crouched inside a dense copse of shrubs on a rise not five yards from the scene of carnage. Nausea rose, but she held it back lest the noise bring the attackers down on her. She didn't know where or how far they'd gone or if they would return. All she knew was a terror that overcame all earlier determination to go forward with courage.

She didn't know how long she cowered there on hands and knees, arms wrapped around her head, before a faint groan penetrated her stupor of fear. She cringed into a smaller ball. What if Mitannu had returned?

Then she heard it again and realized it was a moan of pain, coming from the campsite below.

Someone was still alive down there.

She lowered her arms and lifted her head, her body still rigid. The forest around her was quiet, even the wildlife still, perhaps in sympathy with the death scene below. She waited, listening for any sense that Mitannu might be watching nearby. Then she realized that he would not do that. He was so arrogant that he would assume he had completed his work.

Moving like a woman thrice her age, she crawled through the brush, wincing at every rustle of leaves under her hands and knees. Closer, she became aware of the labored breathing of whoever lay wounded near the smoldering fire. Close enough to see the outline of the still figure, she waited another count of one hundred, tried to decide who it was. Not the priest in his black robe and white collar; she recognized his body, fallen where he had been praying on his knees before the attack. This man, sprawled on his back, was tall, much taller than the priest, dressed in buckskin breeches and boots, and a white full-sleeved shirt marred at the shoulder by a large dark-brown stain.

Blood. Much blood. Too much blood for the man to be alive, yet his chest continued to rise and fall in shallow gasps, the intermittent groan escaping into the night. How was this possible?

She crept closer, eyes darting side to side in fear of the return of the enemy.

All was quiet. She ventured close enough to distinguish the man's features by the light of the small fire. He was young, his hair dark and curly, unmarred by gray, his fine beard neatly trimmed. His eyebrows slanted wickedly above deep eye sockets and high cheekbones.

She fell to her knees beside him. *"Mah-Kah-Twah!"* she whispered.

17

Tristan could hardly keep his eyes open, and his entire chest stung as if a hundred wasps had attacked in the night. Yawning, he staggered through the forest, down the gradual slope from the Koasati village situated about a mile from the riverbank where the rest of his party had camped for the night.

The Indians had feasted him, dancing madly to drums and feathered reed instruments, the headmen dressed head to toe in animal skins topped by skeletal horned masks. The dance of the young men became wilder even than their elders, who with whips and rods flagellated each boy as he passed until the blood ran. *Run, young warrior! Dance with courage as did our heroes of old! Dance and sing to prove your strength!*

Tristan had seen the ritual before and found it bizarre — but less so than some of the religious ceremonies of his own people.

His mind went inexorably to the welts on the soft, fragrant skin of his wife's back. He would find the man who did that to her and make him pay. It was certain.

His hosts wound down the peace celebration sometime toward morning, retiring to their thatched wattle-and-daub houses to sleep off the excesses of food, tobacco, and alcohol. Tristan, mercifully left to his own devices, had rolled himself in a borrowed blanket beside a dying fire to doze for a couple of hours until daylight. Nobody stirred when he rose, gathered his belongings, and headed for camp.

Ruefully he rubbed his burning skin through the buckskin shirt. Allowing the headman to tattoo a series of snakes from shoulder to shoulder across his chest had seemed like a good idea at the time. Bienville and Iberville both had endured similar rituals in early congresses with Indians of the lower Mississippi region. He didn't remember either of his superiors mentioning the significant pain that accompanied the deposit of charcoal under the skin with fish bones.

Presumably the sting would eventually go away as the lacerated skin healed. At least it was keeping him awake and on his feet.

By the time the trees began to thin near

the juncture of the Coosa and Tallapoosa Rivers, dawn had brought enough light that he could see several yards ahead. It occurred to him that he should be able to hear morning noises from the campsite. But all was still, except for the twitter of birds awakening and small animals rustling in the pines and oaks overhead and in the underbrush. His companions had apparently drunk deep and slept heavily.

He stopped, frowning. His brother was the rare soldier who refused to consume hard liquor when on duty. He at least should have nursed the fire back to life by now.

Not a wisp of smoke drifted from camp.

Tristan began to run. Ignoring the pain across his chest, blood throbbing through his veins, he zigzagged around trees, his shoulder hitting one hard enough to stagger him. Regaining his balance, he threw himself forward.

He reached the camp. Stopped in an agony of despair. The buzzards had already arrived.

The first soft fingers of morning were seeping through the thatching above her bed when Geneviève wearily rose and dressed in the Indian print robe that Tristan had admired the day of their wedding. As she brushed and replaited her hair and washed her face, she tried to forget the vivid nightmare that had awakened her hours earlier.

It was not the first time she had dreamed of the savage who had invaded the kitchen in the fort, on the day Tristan had bought her bread. But this time the Indian had not been content to skulk off with a loaf of bread and a handful of hominy. He had flung his knife at Tristan's head and wrapped the string of scalps around Father Mathieu's neck, choking him. Once she dragged herself awake, heart pounding and face buried in the pillow, she'd lain curled on her side, feverishly praying — oddly enough, not for Tristan but for Mathieu. She had never been so glad to find that a dream was just that — a creation of her own anxiety.

As she hurried down the stairs to the kitchen, she prayed for Tristan's and Nika's safe travel and for successful delivery of her message. But once she arrived in her domain, there was so much to do, with nobody to help her, that all other anxiety fled. Aimée's mutiny hurt in so many ways. Her sister might be a petulant assistant, oftentimes slow to obey, but at least Geneviève didn't have to explain in detail how she wanted things done. Their father had been a patient teacher, and their mother a thorough housekeeper. Aimée might not *like* housework or baking, but at least she knew how.

Then yesterday had ruined everything.

As she lit a piece of kindling and laid it under the firewood in the fireplace to catch, Geneviève wondered if there was anything she could have done to avert Aimée's unreasonable jealousy over her trip to the Mobile village with Dufresne. The whole thing was maddening. Why would she, a woman married to Tristan Lanier, try to seduce — or let herself be seduced by, for that matter — a red-haired game-cock like Julien Dufresne?

"Madame, you are banging the pots loud enough to awaken the entire town!"

Geneviève turned to find all three Burelle girls, still dressed in their night rail, standing in the kitchen doorway. Laure and Yolande each held a hand of four-year-old Fleurance, who somehow managed to pout and yawn at the same time.

"I'm sorry to have woken you." Geneviève smiled. "I will have your eggs ready in just a bit. Would you like one of the blackberry tartlets I made last night? I think there were three left."

Laure and Yolande looked at each other, big-eyed. Yolande started to speak, but Laure shook her head in warning. "We promised not to tell," she whispered.

"Tell what?" Fleurance demanded.

"Hush, Fleurette." Laure squeezed her little sister's dimpled hand.

"Oops," said Yolande.

Geneviève couldn't help laughing. "Girls, it's all right if you ate the tartlets. We can have toast for breakfast."

Fleurance started to weep. "I didn't get a tartlet! I want one!"

"None of us got one," Yolande blurted. "Aimée took them all."

Geneviève put her hands on her hips. "*Aimée* took them? When?" She had been at the Lemays' house with Sister Gris, attending the still grief-stricken Angela and her little boys.

"We're not telling," said the conscientious and stubborn Laure.

Yolande had less scruples. "After supper. Mama said it was scandalous for her to take them to the guardhouse without a chaperone, but Mademoiselle Aimée paid for them, so Papa took the money and told Mama to mind her own business." She wrinkled her freckled nose. "What does 'scandalous' mean?"

Laure reached around Fleurance to yank Yolande's braid. "It means 'mind your own business.'"

"Ow!"

"Girls, please, your papa is right. You mustn't tattle." Geneviève was too worried to laugh. "Laure, help me slice the bread for toast. Yolande, you and Fleurette find your mama and see if she needs help making the beds." She clapped her hands. "Come, hurry!"

Breakfast and chores provided just enough distraction to keep the little girls from asking too many unanswerable questions, and soon Geneviève herself nearly managed to stop fretting about her sister's more-than-strange behavior. As she prayed and baked and cleaned and prayed some more, it occurred to her that she had been trying to manage Aimée almost as if she were her mother instead of her sister.

Had her own mother been this anxious when the handsome and reckless young Jean Cavalier came to be Papa's apprentice in the bakery? There had been no real danger of Geneviève committing any serious indiscretions with him, for Jean was good in the same way that the early saints had been good. He was eager to spend time with Geneviève — as he was with her entire family, for they were to him a part of the body of Christ. Geneviève had been miserably aware that her adoration of Jean had been reciprocated by the affection of a teacher for one of his disciples.

As a result of Jean's eventual leadership of the militant Black Camisard party in the violent civil wars of the Cévennes, Papa had been the martyr, but the whole family had suffered. Geneviève suspected that something had happened to Aimée during that time, something so terrible she couldn't speak of it except in the nightmares that still shook her awake a year later. Something so terrible that she couldn't tell Geneviève, who loved her more than life.

At least . . . at least they were safe from persecution here in the colony of Louisiane. Yes, safe, unless the oh-so-accommodating Julien Dufresne found a way to exploit their vulnerability.

After tucking the last loaf of bread into its waxed paper wrapping, Geneviève took off her apron and hung it on the hook behind the kitchen door. Her work was finished for the morning. She went to her bedroom in the attic above the tavern and stood for a moment, irresolute. The little room was small and rather Spartan, but it suited her needs for the moment. There was a narrow bedframe pushed against the interior wall, with just enough room left over for her trunk, a tiny oaken desk, and a matching wooden ladder-back chair. Her chamber pot was stowed under the bed, with a small white pitcher and basin for washing up perched on one corner of the desk.

She continued to keep her Bible hidden away beneath her winter undergarments in the trunk. Personal reading of the Bible was looked upon as freakish in the Catholic society of the colony, but she tried to pull it out for a refreshing read at least once a week. Perhaps it was time to do so now, since she found herself in such a quagmire of uncertainty. Looking over her shoulder to make sure she had not been followed by one of the curious little Burelle girls, she dropped to her knees before the trunk.

She drew the key, suspended on its fine silver chain, from beneath her bodice and opened the padlock that fastened the trunk. Lifting the lid, she searched for and found the thick unwieldy book inside a pile of woolen ruffles. It had been one of Papa's most prized possessions, purchased with some of his first profits from the bakery, and protected like the jewels of the queen's crown. She held the Bible in her lap, enjoying its weight and the smell of the leather cover, exquisitely decorated with a silver filigree Huguenot cross. She lightly touched her finger to each of the eight points of its four arms, reciting the Beatitudes they represented.

Blessed are the poor in spirit: for theirs is the kingdom of heaven. Blessed are they that mourn: for they shall be comforted. Blessed are the meek: for they shall inherit the earth. Blessed are they which do hunger and thirst after righteousness: for they shall be filled. Blessed are the merciful: for they shall obtain mercy. Blessed are the pure in heart: for they shall see God. Blessed are the peacemakers: for they shall be called the children of God. Blessed are they which are persecuted for righteousness' sake: for theirs is the kingdom of heaven.

Papa had taken ownership in the kingdom of heaven. Perhaps the whole family had. Certainly she felt kinship with those who had endured the dragonnades. But it was peculiar to find herself safely away from that persecution and peering back at it dimly as if it had happened in a dream.

With her thumb she rubbed one of the four fleur-de-lis which joined the arms of the cross. France, the mother country, overshadowed her life, even here in Louisiane — but it also seemed, in truth, a

distant reality. She no longer felt the con-
suming rage toward the King who had
burned her home and murdered her father
— only sorrow.

Still, she would never go back there. *Never.*

Except for worry about the safety of her
children, Nika would have had no qualms
about attending Bright Tongue. But if Mitannu lingered near the ambush scene and
should hear the Frenchman's feverish rav-
ing, the hollowed-out bluff under which she
had taken shelter would provide little protection, no matter how much camouflage
she pulled across the opening.

Quaking with fear lest her husband's men
should return and discover her, she had first
cleaned the nasty hole in the unconscious
Bright Tongue's upper shoulder — the bullet had gone clean through and exited out
the back — with water from her gourd. In
other circumstances she would have made a
fire and cauterized the wound and packed it
with softened pine resin as Mitannu's
mother had taught her — but the danger of
attracting unwanted attention made that
impossible. Instead she ripped a strip of
fabric from the tail of his shirt, wrapped it
under his arm, and tied it round the shoulder. She would just have to hope that it

would not fester and rot.

As a married woman, one of her main chores had been dressing the carcasses Mitannu brought home from his hunting trips. Some of those had been eight-point bucks weighing as much as a hundred and sixty pounds. Still, dragging her former lover's dead weight to safety took all her strength and determination. She had forgotten how tall and muscular was his body — or maybe he'd grown since leaving the Kaskaskian village five years ago as a lanky teenager. In any case, once he regained consciousness, he thrashed about so that she was hard pressed to keep those long legs and arms out of sight.

"Mah-Kah-Twah," she whispered, kneeling above him, pressing with all her might into his good shoulder. "You must lie still. You will reopen the wound."

He mumbled something unintelligible in French, twisting his head back and forth, and tried to jerk out from under her.

"No," she pleaded, switching to French, "listen, I will lie beside you, but you must be quiet. Please, beloved, lie still."

Instantly he quieted. His eyes opened. They were glassy, too bright, the pupils contracted. "Nika?"

What had she said? "I'm here," she whispered. She drew back, but he caught her arm with his good hand.

"Don't go." His voice was hoarse, urgent.

"I won't, but be quiet and don't move. He might come back for you." She checked the opening of their shelter. The camouflage was still in place.

Following her gaze, he lowered his voice. "Who? What happened? Why are you here?"

She picked through those questions. "I am traveling to visit my family."

He tried to rise on his elbow to peer at her, but his color drained on a gasp of pain, and he lay back again, eyes closed. After catching his breath, he looked at her, his expression more lucid. "Your family in Kaskaskia?" When she nodded, looking away, he touched her face. "Were you with the Indians who attacked us? The Koasati?"

Almost she shouted at him, but remembering just in time, she whispered, "No! Of course not. And they weren't Koasati. They were Mobilians, in disguise."

He frowned. "How do you know that?"

"They were — the leader, the one with the gun — that was Mitannu . . . my husband."

They stared at one another for a long moment, worlds of unspoken emotion between them. They had been all but children when they had loved one another. Nika for one had felt the weight of adult responsibility for so long that she could barely remember that young girl. However, she had not forgotten the magnetism of Bright Tongue's personality, the candor and fearlessness in his gaze. And this new maturity that had settled into the bones of his face, the way he looked beneath her words for nuances of meaning, drew her damaged heart like the tongue going to a sore tooth.

"I would have gone back for you." He said it as if the words were dragged from him.

"I waited for a month, and you did not come. I was afraid to wait longer."

"Nika, I was a young fool. When I saw you in the Mobile village, I thought you had followed me. I strutted like a cockerel and bragged to Tristan that I had won the princess. And then I saw that you belonged to the Indian and — and had his children." He sighed and looked away. "You have beautiful children, Nika. I'm glad you've been happy."

Tears blinded her, and her throat clogged with bitterness. She wished there were anyplace else she could go. But no, she must face him, *lie* with him here, bear the consequences of their childish folly. "I saw your brother in the village often. I never saw you."

His expression clouded. "I have some pride. Besides, my religion forbids me to covet another man's wife. How could I come there and watch you serving him?"

You blind fool, I would have left him for you! the soft side of her heart screamed. But the reasoning part of her mind reminded her that to have left Mitannu for the white man would literally have brought war to them all.

As, in the end, had come to pass anyway. But how in the world had Mitannu found her out? She had never let on, by word or expression, that she still loved Mah-Kah-Twah. She had been faithful in action if not in her secret heart.

Suddenly, utter weariness and despair claimed her mind, her face, her body. She laid her head down on her forearm as the storm built into silent, soul-shaking sobs.

To his credit, Mah-Kah-Twah made no attempt to stop her. Or perhaps he was in too much pain to speak.

When her grief had spent itself, she heaved a broken breath and said in a small voice, "I'm sorry. I'm worried for my sons."

"Where are they?"

"I hope they're with my friend in the Apalachee village. Unless Mitannu took them."

"You should go and find out. I can manage." He hesitated. "How many bodies did you find at the campsite?"

"Three. The priest and two soldiers."

"Two soldiers? There should have been a third — two ensigns and a medical major. Describe the uniforms," he demanded.

She tried to think. "Plain gray breeches, blue coats, plain buttons." She shuddered. "Their throats were cut, but they didn't seem to be important men."

"Then Barraud must have gotten away," he muttered. "My brother had gone into the Koasati village for the night but would have come back by now. Unless they murdered him too." He grew restless again, jostling her as he struggled onto his elbows. He panted for a moment, caught his breath, and with his good hand felt for the bandage she had contrived around his wound. "I don't understand why the Koasati would attack, when they had been friendly the night before. They shared meat with us and promised to smoke peace with Tristan."

"Didn't you hear me? They weren't Koasati! They were Mitannu's men." She shoved his good shoulder, none too gently. "Lie down before you start the bleeding again."

He ignored her, scowling. "This is a bullet

367

wound. Did you see his gun? What kind was it?"

"I don't know! A gun is a gun. Our troubles started when you people brought those terrible weapons into our villages."

"Oh, no, you all were doing just fine before we got here, killing each other with arrows and tomahawks and bludgeons." He gave her a fulminating look. "It matters whether these savages were armed by the French or the British. Tristan and the priest and I came all this way to try turning the Alabama away from the English, and to get them to band together with the Choctaw, the Chickasaw, and the Mobile. You've got to stop raiding each other's villages, stop taking slaves and selling them to the British. If you don't, your nations will slowly implode, and we'll all be left as subjects of Queen Anne."

She pressed her lips together. "Would that be so much worse than being slaves of King Louis? Your people do not respect him. Your officers rob the royal warehouses to sell goods to our chiefs, and I know at least one who sells information to the British!" She stopped on a gasp, horrified at her lapse in discretion.

Mah-Kah-Twah swiftly caught the back of

her head in his hand, his fingers plowing roughly into her hair. "*What* did you say?"

18

Geneviève tried to think when she and Aimée had last been in a room together for purely social reasons. Oh, there had been the occasion nearly three weeks ago now, the same day she'd discovered Aimée's purchase of her blackberry tartlets. To give them to Julien Dufresne, whom Aimée knew Geneviève couldn't bear, as a lover's gift of sorts . . . that had been a most egregious disloyalty.

She'd best not think of it, if she expected to endure the evening.

Tonight half the settlement seemed to have been invited to Madame L'Anglois's harvest celebration — the official ending of the season before winter's chilly fingers began to clutch the colony. The socialite had had good Monsieur L'Anglois working from dawn to dusk, cleaning out his barn so that there would be room for young couples to dance while their elders refreshed themselves with an assortment of Geneviève's pumpkin pies and cream pastries, washed down with a punch made from the juice of watermelon and wild berries, mixed with the last of the wines from the warehouse.

It was a merry scene indeed, the military men of the crowd freed from a month of intensified guard duty. Word had come from the south that British warships had been sighted off the coast of Massacre Island, hovering like dogs below a treed opossum. They were gone now, and no one knew precisely what they had gained by skulking in the Gulf for six days, but despite the jocularity of the men, the women continued to fret.

Even Geneviève, who was helping Madame keep the refreshment table filled and tidied, couldn't help listening to the officers discuss Bienville's plans to dispatch soldiers to the Island. Usually she could dismiss the flutterings of the other women as a waste of energy, but the serious undertone of the men's conversation carried weight. Tristan's safety was never far from her thoughts. Also, she couldn't help worrying about her message sent through Nika. If it fell into the wrong hands, it could be considered treason.

"Madame Lanier, you are looking lovely

tonight. Could I trouble you for more punch?"

Startled from her guilty thoughts, she turned. "Commander!" Regaining her grip on the punch ladle, she freshened Bienville's drink. "Thank you. You are very kind." She knew she looked well, for she had taken particular pains with her hair and had freshened her stomacher with new ribbons for the occasion.

She felt her cheeks warm as Bienville's black eyes flicked over her. "Lanier will find himself a most fortunate man when he returns. I pray that he and his brother will bring us a report of a successful mission within a week or two."

Mistrusting his conciliatory tone, Geneviève returned his regard, absently wiping the lip of the ladle with the corner of her apron. "Have you decided to forgive him of the sin of marrying me then?"

His lips quirked. "Madame Bakery Queen, you have surely learned by now that my anger is generally short-lived — particularly with regard to men who serve the interests of the French Crown as best they know how." He sighed. "The Lanier brothers have been two of my closest allies, as well as a source of keen aggravation. Please disregard my insulting questions the day after your so-hasty marriage. I was surprised that I wasn't invited to witness the ceremony, that's all."

Though she doubted that was the sole reason for that intrusive interrogation, she shrugged. "We shan't speak of it again."

He nodded. "However, there's another bone I must pick. You'll have to believe that I choose my words with fear and trembling." He hesitated, glanced away.

She caught her breath. Had he found out about the message?

Then she realized Bienville was focused on Aimée, who was dancing a reel with her back to Julien Dufresne but giving the young redhead a sparkling look over her shoulder.

Geneviève sighed. "What has she done now?"

Bienville chuckled. "You should rather ask, what has she *not* done? If she doesn't hurry up and choose a husband, I shall soon find my officers involved in an elimination round of pistols at dawn."

Geneviève blinked. "I — I thought she had already become engaged to Aide-Major Dufresne."

"Then she hasn't told you?" He gave her an odd look. "Dufresne informed me he offered for her nearly three weeks ago, but she has been playing the tease."

"That sounds like Aimée. But my sister and I have been somewhat distanced lately. Frankly I haven't encouraged her to settle on the aide-major, so I'm glad to hear she has not."

"Pray tell, what is your objection to the son of one of the wealthiest and highest-placed peers in France?" Bienville stared down at her, frowning. "I've found him nothing but diligent in his duties and sensible of the privileges he enjoys as one of my officers. Mademoiselle Aimée is a pretty thing, I grant you, but she should thank God on her knees that Dufresne has shown her favor."

Geneviève wondered what he would think if she informed the commander that her sister had once aspired to the post of mistress of the entire colony.

"It isn't false pride that makes me discourage the match." Geneviève struggled to find words that would not unduly offend the commander. "I agree, Monsieur Dufresne could be considered a fine catch. But — but, Commander, I don't believe he has been entirely forthcoming with me or my sister, and his motives for pursuing her don't seem quite —" Oh dear, he was looking down his nose at her, in clear irritation.

"I mean, I just think there may be something other than real affection —"

"Please do not try to tell me you are one of these ridiculous females who cling to romantic notions of true love between a woman in need of a husband and the man who generously meets that need." His lip curled. "Was that the way of it between you and my Know-Nothing erstwhile lieutenant? Secret meetings in the still of the night? Poetry, songs, and sweet *nothings* exchanged through open windows?"

Geneviève wrapped her arms about her middle, feeling as though she had been punched without warning. Bienville looked away, a faint stiffness of shame in his expression, but she would not let him off this time. "What did Tristan do to you, sir, that you treat him with such contempt? As you said only a moment ago, he is a good man who would give his life for you! Yet you seem to find it difficult to speak a civil word in his behalf."

Bienville pressed his fine lips together. He did not reply for several moments, and the lilting strains of a Purcell minuet from Monsieur L'Anglois's violin filled the silence.

Finally he gave her a curt bow. "Please forgive my reluctance to resurrect old wrongs, Madame. I assure you I meant no insult to you or your sister. Just remember that she must choose a husband tonight — or I will be forced to choose for her." Turning on his heel, he cut through the center of the dance floor and disappeared behind a crowd of men in the open doorway of the barn.

Geneviève stared after the commander, every iota of charity to which she had clung evaporated. She was very glad Aimée had not managed to attract his arrogant regard, for if she had been forced to entertain him as her brother-in-law, she would surely have murdered him within a fortnight. Turning her back on the refreshment table, she yanked her fan from her apron pocket and attempted to cool all trace of upset from her face.

"Madame Lanier, you are like to create a tropical surge in the punch bowl if you persist in such violent fanning." Julien Dufresne's sardonic baritone behind her preceded his appearance. "Perhaps you will consent to share that welcome breeze with the rest of the room. It is fiendishly hot in here."

She snapped the sticks of the fan together and jammed it back into her pocket. She was in no frame of mind to joust with this weasel. "Please excuse me. Madame L'Anglois seems to have need of me."

He snagged her arm before she could walk away. "Ah, you must have mistaken her for someone else, as I just passed her on the way to the, er, privy."

Would this miserable evening never end? "What do you want, Monsieur Dufresne?" she said between her teeth.

He sighed in feigned injury, his pale eyes glinting. "Why, my dear, such shortness of temper. Could it be that you are increasing? I've heard it said that such an interesting condition often makes shrews of the most gentle-natured of women." Surveying her figure with blatant insolence, he shook his head. "I only wished to exchange courtesies, Madame. After all, you and I are like to be the closest of relatives ere too long. We had best learn to get along."

Increasing? She wished fervently that Tristan were here to pitch the impudent wretch headfirst into the punch bowl. She had heard about the scene that took place between the two men on the riverfront landing the morning after her wedding. It had afforded her many a private giggle every time she recalled it.

Now, even the mental image of Dufresne dancing a jig with watermelon juice dripping from his red curls enabled her to conjure a smile. "I have heard no wedding banns read, sir, but I shall be sure to let you know when I do."

Fleeting uncertainty crossed his expression as he glanced over his shoulder at Aimée, who was dancing opposite Denis Lafleur. "Bienville has said I may announce the betrothal tonight," he said loudly. "It is his wish that I wed your sister."

"Perhaps he should have informed her first. She appears to be ignorant of this stunning news."

At that moment the tune ended, and Aimée curtseyed before the laughing Lafleur, who grasped her fingers and brought them to his lips. She blushed like a rose, peeping up at him from behind her lacy fan.

Dufresne's teeth clicked together hard. He swiftly gained control of himself, pulling out a fresh, snowy handkerchief to blot his beaded forehead. "Aimée cannot help the packs of dogs who follow her like a —" He smiled. "Like the beautiful woman she is. When we are wed, she will have reason to contain her smiles for her husband."

Cold fingers traced the back of Geneviève's neck. There was a very specific threat beneath those words. "What do you mean?"

Dufresne flicked the handkerchief against the sleeve of his uniform coat. "I think you understand me. His Majesty the King may perhaps not be the best model of marital fidelity, but he has been very clear about the fate of his subjects who dare to stray from the Holy Roman Church." He gave her a malicious glance and went back to dusting his sleeve. *Whick. Whick.* "He takes a very dim view of spiritual unfaithfulness."

Her mind took the leap. He knew. Aimée had betrayed her, betrayed them both.

They had been three days making their way — painful, limping mile by mile — in a southwesterly direction from the outskirts of the Koasati village back to the Apalachee. Nika, weary and sick at heart, anxious for Bright Tongue and anxious for the safety of her children, had refused to linger where they were, despite her companion's wish to wait for his brother to find them. They had wasted half a day arguing, Nika insistent that it was dangerous to expose themselves to the enemy, who were more likely to remain in the area than was Tristan Lanier.

In the end, Mah-Kah-Twah sent her on a roundabout course back to the scene of the attack to look for signs of disturbance. "We can't leave the bodies there, especially the priest. They should be decently buried. Can you do that, Nika? Will you do it for me?"

Unable to resist the pleading dark eyes, shadowed with pain because of her husband's cruelty, she had reluctantly nodded. "Though I think it is a waste of time. We should go to my family in the Kaskaskia. You would be safe there, and our medicine men would heal you." Besides, she still had a message to deliver.

Apparently satisfied that she would obey him, he lay back. "Good. And look for any papers left on the dead. The priest has a book — a journal he kept, with drawings and such. I want it."

She couldn't see what good a few religious pictures would be, but she agreed and left him in a restless sleep.

By the time she arrived at the dead campsite, the bodies had begun to decompose, and the stench was terrible. The Alabama way of burning their dead was much cleaner and more efficient. But she had promised, so she waited nearly an hour to make sure she was alone in the forest and then began the work of digging a grave for the priest. She chose a soft, sandy area, far enough from the water to be safe from floods, and went to work with an improvised shovel made from a trencher she found in one of the soldier's packs.

It was nearly dark before the grave was prepared, and she was so tired she longed to simply lie down in it and go to sleep. But the thought of her children and the injured Frenchman made her grimly search the black robe's stiff body before rolling it into the shallow grave. There were no papers on the body, but when she riffled through a leather satchel nearby, she found the book that Mah-Kah-Twah had mentioned. It was about the size of a man's hand, leather-bound with fine parchment pages that made a crinkling sound when she flipped them. The writing was small and crabbed, blotted with ink here and there. Every few pages she found delightful charcoal drawings of animal and plant life of the forest and the river. Fascinated, she wanted to sit and look at them, but she had already been too long away from Mah-Kah-Twah. They would look at them together on the morrow.

She put the book back into the satchel, then slung it onto her back and took a last look around the campsite. She had done her best, and with that she would have to be satisfied.

Please, God, my boys . . .

Now, she stumbled through the woods with Mah-Kah-Twah leaning heavily upon her, his good arm draped across her shoulders. His fever had soared again once they started traveling, but he refused to stop longer than a few minutes at a time, to take a sip of water from her canteen. She thanked God that she had begun to recognize trail markings that were less than a mile outside the Apalachee village. The Frenchman would not have made it a step further.

That was how she made herself think of him now. *The Frenchman.* Not *my lover,* not *my children's father,* not even *my enemy* — all those terms were too personal. Even the sound of his name on her tongue — the name the Kaskaskians had given him, as well as his French name — turned him from the silent, pitiful wraith who depended upon her for sustenance and bodily support, into the handsome, virile, laughing young man who had stolen her maiden heart.

Azalea had warned her, and it was so. Her childhood friend was not going to be happy to see this particular Frenchman again.

But she could not leave him in the woods to die. And he would die without her.

One of her weary feet caught on a hidden vine, and she staggered. Her companion's weak body overset her balance, and they both went down, she to her knees and he falling on his side with a groan of pain.

"Mah-Kah-Twah!" she cried, reaching for him too late.

"It's — I'm all right," he said between his teeth. "I just need — water."

She touched his face, and indeed his lips were dry and cracked. His skin had taken on a chalky pallor, his eyes sunken and the cheekbones prominent as knife blades above his fine beard. She uncorked the canteen, glad she had refilled it at the last stream they crossed. Slipping her hand beneath his head and holding the gourd to his lips, she let him sip slowly, careful to see that he didn't choke.

"Thank you." He turned his head and opened his eyes to scan the canopy of trees overhead. He looked puzzled. "It's getting dark already."

"Yes, we've been traveling all day." She gently laid his head down and corked the canteen. "We're slowing down, but I don't want you to fall again. Maybe we should camp for the night and go into the village in the morning." His confusion worried her.

"I know you want to see your boys. You go ahead. I'll get up in a minute and follow you."

She shook her head. "Don't be stupid. You can't move by yourself."

"Nika." He swallowed, met her eyes. "Why

383

did you do this? Why did you come for me?"

Over the last four days she had repeatedly asked herself that question. She shrugged and looked away. "If you do not know, then you don't deserve to know."

"Then it's true."

She didn't answer.

"I've been a monumental fool."

"That is also true." She couldn't keep her lips from quirking.

His chuckle broke her heart because it was so beloved.

But, God, I will not do the wrong thing. I am not free. I am Mitannu's woman. "When you left me," she said, "I walked into the river, meaning never to come back. But my friend Azalea found me drifting there and pulled me back to shore."

"Nika! Why would you do such a thing?"

She sighed. "I was ashamed. The women of my village are not promiscuous."

He caught her hand and kissed her palm. "I hadn't told anyone. No one would have known."

She snatched her hand away. Was there no end to this man's stupidity? "Mah-Kah-Twah, in a few months everyone would have known."

"What — what do you mean?" He sat up, clutching his wounded shoulder. "Nika, what do you mean?"

"My father sent for Mitannu. Our mothers are cousins and had talked of the marriage since we were children. He agreed to marry me and take me to the Mobile village." She lifted her hands and faced him. "I had no choice."

If she had picked up a musket and shot him herself, he couldn't have looked more stunned. "How old are your boys?"

"They will be five in November."

"Sweet Mary, mother of Jesus."

Geneviève's head was splitting. The ball had been going for three hours now and she still had no idea what to do about Julien Dufresne's blatant blackmail.

As she accepted a cup of weakened punch from Paul Loisel, who had danced more often upon her toes than the floor of the barn, her mind skittered from one possibility to the other.

If she were on her own, she might have spiked Dufresne's guns by openly proclaiming her Reformed faith and bearing the consequences. True enough, this was a Catholic colony, where her beliefs were against the law, but few indeed seemed aware that there was a religious civil war going on in the mother country. Even sour

Father Henri would probably be reluctant to sentence to death one of the few women in the fledgling colony.

But what if Aimée were punished for her sister's illegal religion?

"I saw Burelle's kitchen when I was setting the locks on the tavern door, mademoiselle — I mean, madame." Loisel quaffed his punch, then wiped his mouth on his sleeve. "You would find my new brick chimney draws much more evenly than his." He looked at her hopefully. "Perhaps you'd like to come and inspect it on the morrow to give it your opinion."

"Give my opinion?" Geneviève blinked at the locksmith, only vaguely aware of the subject under discussion. "I'm sure it's — lovely." Dufresne might be a decent husband for Aimée, as long as he got what he wanted. But the moment he was thwarted, he was the sort of man to make her pay in a hundred painful ways.

"Lovely?" Loisel scratched his bearded chin. "I suppose a professional baker like you would prefer real bricks to wattle. Élisabeth never got a chance to use it," he added sadly. "She died so soon after the wedding."

Geneviève opened her mouth, but could not think what to say. How had they come to be talking about chimneys and bricks and

Loisel's deceased wife, all in one breath?

He flushed bright red. "Please forgive me, mademois— madame! Alexandre warned me not to address you so soon, and he said above all I must not mention my first wife."

Wildly she realized several things at once. Loisel had been courting her, and he either did not know or didn't care that she had recently married — but then he seemed to understand that she must be addressed as a married woman.

She inhaled deeply and slowly, using the time to regain her wits. "Monsieur Loisel," she said as gently as she could, "you must feel free to speak to me of Élisabeth any time you wish — after all, she was my good friend, and I miss her too." Perhaps more than he did, it seemed. "But Monsieur Alexandre is mistaken. You must not address me as anything other than a friend — ever. Surely you know that I wed Tristan Lanier nearly a month ago."

A mulish expression crept into his confusion. "Well, but everyone knows Lanier is ineligible to wed one of His Majesty's brides. He is expatriate. Many men would not want you after — Well, but I'm not one for such quibbling. Besides, we all know Lanier is not likely to return from the expedition to the savages." He straightened proudly. "I only wish you to consider my suit before others you may receive. I would make you very happy."

Geneviève could see that she wasn't going to win this particular argument. It did not matter anyway. If Tristan never returned, it would take more than a fine house and a smokeless chimney to make her happy. "I shall consider what you have said," she said and curtseyed to Loisel. "Please excuse me. I must speak to Commissioner La Salle."

Her plan had developed over the last fortnight, heading toward this gathering when she knew that all the players would be in the same room. Tonight or never. Bienville's ultimatum had made it imperative.

She made her way through the press, aiming for the scrivener and his wife.

Her father had impressed upon her that a liar would always eventually catch himself, forgetting some detail, plowing deeper and deeper until the lie turned into a trap. She had observed Dufresne's secretive behavior, his self-centered interaction with others, his half-truths, his tendency to disappear into dark corners and emerge with no warning. Even his sideways manner of carrying himself proclaimed the habitual sneak.

The day of their trip to the Indian village she became convinced the man maintained some hold over Bienville himself — and possibly the Mobilian chieftains. If there were a connection between the two, it would be in Dufresne's management of the warehouse and its supplies. While she and Nika had discussed corn and cooking techniques, Dufresne had met with Mitannu, Nika's husband and the son of the chief. During the return to the settlement, Dufresne had seemed almost giddy. Of course he had not let down his guard enough to give her details. But clearly he was pleased to have settled some advantageous business arrangement.

"Pardon me," she mumbled as she bumped someone's elbow while she edged through the crowd by the open barn door, the sole source of fresh air. Peripherally she could see the fire of Dufresne's red hair as he headed toward the corner where her sister held court with Françoise Dubonnier. She hesitated. How much damage could he do in the next few minutes while she engaged La Salle?

Suddenly the crowd pushed against her, shoving her backward into the barn, as if a bull had charged into the building. Women screamed against the roar of men's voices, and Geneviève staggered and would have fallen except for the press of bodies about her. She couldn't see over the tall men between her and the door, but silence fell like a cloak.

Then labored breathing and a grunt of pain as a body hit the ground. And gasps from those near the door.

Geneviève shouldered her way through the crowd, toward the source of excitement. Something told her she must get there to help. Finally she broke free.

Surgeon-Major Barraud lay crumpled on the floor, and she would have assumed him to be drunken, as he was wont to be on a Saturday evening — but for the dirty and bloody state of his uniform. He lay on his side with his right arm cradled against his body. Eyes closed, skin ashen, his breath came in shallow gasps.

Geneviève was the first to react. She fell to her knees. "He's hurt. Someone bring clean water and towels." She looked around at the gaping, petrified ring of faces and snapped, "Hurry!" She turned back to Barraud and gently touched his face, afraid to move him. "Monsieur Barraud, where are you hurt? What happened?"

"Must see —" he paused for a gasp of air and licked dry lips — "must see the commander. They said he would be here."

She looked over her shoulder and found

Paul Loisel standing by gawking. "You heard him! Find Commander Bienville immediately." She leaned over Barraud to examine his injured limb. If she hadn't already been sick with dread, the state of his uniform would have completed her discomfiture. His entire right side was soaked with blood from collar to the wrist, the sleeve packed into a deep cut at the shoulder. She looked around for the closest uniform and found, improbably, Denis Lefleur. He was squatting close, waiting for her command. Relieved, she met his eyes. "We'll need to move him to the infirmary. Find Madame and ask for a blanket to make a stretcher."

Lafleur grunted agreement and rose.

She turned back to the injured man. "The commander is coming. Can you tell me what happened? Where is the rest of the party?"

Barraud had begun to shiver, great racking shudders that seemed to magnify his pain. He groaned and curled tighter into himself. "Dead. They're all dead — Indians —" He fainted. His body relaxed and rolled face up, revealing a gaping cut at least three inches deep into his shoulder.

Dead? *Tristan* was dead? Father Mathieu too?

Numb, she looked up as Bienville shoved through the crowd. They stared at one another, the horror on his face reflecting her own.

Not Tristan. It could not be true.

"Please, Azalea, you cannot turn us away!" Nika was ashamed to find herself reduced to begging shelter from her oldest friend, but what choice did she have? Mah-Kah-Twah could go no farther in his weakened condition, and where else could she be certain of her children's safety?

She and the Frenchman had made the last difficult mile into the Apalachee village, arriving in the still hours of the night. Nika had scratched upon the door of Azalea's husband's hogan, fortunately rousing only the light-sleeping Azalea, who had ducked outside without protest. But discovering Nika was accompanied by a feverish and weak Frenchman — *the* Frenchman who had selfishly caused her friend's need for the doubtful protection of the brutish Mitannu — she had folded her arms and refused to let them in.

Even in the moonless darkness, Azalea's frozen disapproval was palpable. "You will bring murder and rape upon us all. I could understand your weakness for the white boy when you were a child, but to bring him here now — you, a married woman, whose husband will rightly pursue you and punish your unfaithfulness!"

"I have not been unfaithful!" Nika bent her head, hot tears breaking past the barrier of her self-control. Perhaps her marriage had been an unfaithfulness in itself — a wicked attempt to cover up one sin by committing another. But Bright Tongue had deserted her, her frightened young heart had insisted. What if her baby should suffer the taint of her promiscuity? How could she have foreseen Mitannu's brutality? How could she have known what pain awaited her with Mah-Kah-Twah's sudden reappearance?

"Don't — don't turn the children away because of me." Mah-Kah-Twah's hoarse whisper penetrated Azalea's cold silence. He had slumped against the side of the hogan, a boneless form in the dark. "Nika has done nothing wrong. If you'll give us shelter for the rest of the night, I'll be on my way at dawn."

"Where will you go?" Azalea asked. Her voice dripped suspicion. "What will I do if Mitannu follows you here?"

"He might," Mah-Kah-Twah admitted. "But he doesn't know Nika was with me.

You can tell him I passed through two days ago. That I'm already back at the fort."

The slurred weakness of his voice frightened Nika. "You'll never make it that far by yourself. I'm going with you."

"No . . ."

Nika, falling to her knees beside him, knew with despair that he had fainted again. She looked up, searching for her friend's face in the stygian darkness. "Please, Azalea. Please help us."

There was a long silence during which Nika prayed — a halting, desperate supplication that barely formed words.

At last Azalea moved away from the door of the hogan. "If he brings harm to my family, I will kill him myself."

19

Dawn sent a pale prism of light filtering through the narrow window in the infirmary's exterior wall as Geneviève woke sitting straight up in the ladder-back chair Lefleur had brought in for her last night. Bienville had decided not to send for Sister Gris, who had been in sickbed herself for several days, and curtly assigned Geneviève the role of nurse. Requesting that she let him know if Barraud awoke with further information, the commandant and his officers had since been holed up in his office, putting together a plan to deal with this new crisis.

Geneviève had been attending the surgeon-major alone for the last four hours, with a young cadet stationed outside the guardhouse to relieve her at intervals and to run for any supplies she required.

Barraud continued to breathe with labored irregularity, stirring every so often out of a feverish stupor into muscle spasms and unintelligible muttering. Geneviève had changed the dressing of his wound every couple of hours. Upon uncovering it for the first time, she had turned away at the stench of rotting flesh, certain that she would be sick. But she gathered her willpower and, with Cadet Foussé holding the surgeon down, cut away the blackened wad of damp pine resin with which Barraud had packed his own wound.

Despairing of his recovery, she had sent Foussé to Sister Gris for her recommendation of herbs with which to redress it. The ensuing hours passed in an endless cycle of checking the surgeon's thready pulse, turning his pillow, washing the festering wound, and praying for some miracle to save the men Barraud had abandoned in the Alabama woods.

Tristan, she thought, sitting rigid in the half-light of dawn. *My husband. My heart. How can it be that you left me so soon?*

It wasn't possible to think of his vital flesh gone to dust. Surely God had not done this violence to her again. Surely Barraud was mistaken.

She reached out to place a finger at his neck again. He still lived.

Awaken, you wretched drunkard. Wake up and tell me my husband lives.

The wretched drunkard twitched and emitted a dense snore. Geneviève released him and put her hand in her lap. She heard music in her head and, unthinking, began to hum along.

Girls are faithful like gold and silver, Mommy, boys are fickle like rain and wind.

She lifted her head, which had drooped until her chin rested on her chest. That was a real voice, a thin, eerie soprano coming from the other side of the building. Ysabeau. She'd forgotten all about the poor girl, contained for her own safety in a guard-house cell meagerly furnished with a bed, a washbasin, and a chamber pot.

She got up, glancing at Barraud, who lay still as death. She wouldn't be away from him for long. She crossed to the open infirmary door and leaned out. The guard-house cells were contained on the other side of a thick wall strengthened on the outside by forged iron bars and accessed through a steel door. Surely it would be locked.

But she crossed the breezeway between the two sides of the building anyway and rattled the latch of the guardhouse door. It lifted easily in her hand, so she pushed the heavy door inward and slipped inside. There were three unoccupied cells, with Ysabeau in the fourth corner cell. She sat on the floor beside the cot, wearing nothing but her shift and corset, twisting her hair and singing.

Geneviève walked up to the bars of the cell. Compassion instantly seared her, flooding her eyes with tears. She sank to the floor, the cold iron bars sliding through her palms, until she was knee to knee with the prisoner. She thought of the way the women at the party last night had whispered about Ysabeau, mercilessly, as if she had voluntarily cast herself into madness and refused to come back. Having stared into that abyss herself, Geneviève knew it wasn't that simple. Madness rooted itself in a garden of fear, growing to tangle about one like prison chains. Only by God's grace had she found the strength to escape.

She began to hum with Ysabeau. She didn't know all the words, but the tune was familiar, a song that her mother had sung while she sewed, cleaned, and tended the family garden. Beautiful, sad Mama, who had grieved herself into the grave when Papa was gone.

In the middle of the last verse, Ysabeau stopped singing. "He took my clothes away."

"What?" Geneviève blinked away tears. "Who?"

"René. He was fickle too. He wed me and he left me. He said he would never come back. Because I wouldn't do what he wanted."

Geneviève could hardly bear the despair in Ysabeau's eyes. *Tristan left me too. But not like this, never like this.* "Ysabeau, no one can take your clothes. It's not right that you — you uncover yourself like this. I'll give you my other dress. I don't need it."

Ysabeau sighed and leaned her head on her hand. "Aimée tried to give me her dress too. But I want mine. I want the yellow one he tore when I said no."

"He tore your dress?" Geneviève thought she might go mad herself from outrage. Why had Bienville not chased René Connard all the way to Pensacola and brought him back to be flogged? "Did you tell the commander this?"

Ysabeau shook her head sadly. "A wife should not say no. They would lock me up in the guardhouse."

Geneviève wondered if Ysabeau knew where she was.

Before she could ask, Ysabeau continued, "I heard Aimée agree to marry Monsieur Dufresne. I don't think she should. He's a fickle boy too. He came in to visit me after she left." She scowled. "I do not like Monsieur Dufresne."

Neither do I, thought Geneviève. "He

399

won't bother you again," she said. "You may come to live with me and work in the bakery. And I'll make you another yellow dress." She had no idea where she would get the fabric. Neither did she know how to free Ysabeau from the guardhouse, but when she explained about Connard and Dufresne —

"There is someone drowning in the hall," Ysabeau said, wrapping her arms around her knees. "We're all drowning."

Geneviève looked over her shoulder at the open door. "There's no one —"

But a gurgling, raspy voice could indeed be heard faintly from the direction of the infirmary. Barraud had awakened. She'd forgotten all about him.

She scrambled to her feet. "I shall come back later," she promised Ysabeau. Without waiting for an answer, she dashed across the hallway into the infirmary.

She found the surgeon attempting to sit up, wild-eyed, clutching at the bandage over his shoulder. It was already seeping greenish blood. Frightened, Geneviève pushed him down on his back again. "You mustn't, sir! Lie still, I beg you."

"Tell Bienville — the Koasati attacked —" Barraud gasped for breath, closing his eyes — "middle of the night," he mumbled. "I knew we shouldn't have —"

The broken report ended as Barraud fainted again.

Geneviève stared at him, one hand on his good shoulder, the other over her own pounding heart. She felt an insane urge to shake him until his teeth rattled. "Oh, no. No no no. Wake up! What happened to Tristan?"

"I fear your husband is dead, Mademoiselle. I mean, Madame." Julien Dufresne sauntered up from behind her to stand looking down at the surgeon, hands clasped behind his back. He looked concerned, as if he had just discovered a scuff on one of his shiny boots. "Those treacherous Indians." He shook his head. "Barraud is right. We shouldn't have trusted them."

Tristan tied the pirogue off at the landing below Fort Louis, where a couple of young cadets waited to help him and his Indian companions ashore. He leaped onto the sandy beach without aid and stopped to stretch aching shoulder and chest muscles, relieved to have the long downriver journey behind him. Bienville would not be happy with his report, but Tristan was anxious to deliver it. In fact, he hadn't even spared the time to bury the massacred members of his party.

All three Koasati boys he had met in the woods had been eager to accompany Tristan back to the French settlement. The chief had been reluctant to allow both his sons, Fights With Bears and Turtle Boy, to travel so far together, but he seemed to understand the necessity of sending representatives to demonstrate the good will of the clan. In the end, he decided to let them go, along with their tall, lanky cousin, Little Frog.

While Tristan had waited in unbearable impatience to be gone, the chief outfitted the youths in traditional ceremonial costume of fine deer-leather breechclouts and leggings, with heavy woven necklaces made of dyed river reeds clanking against their scarred chests and tufts of feathers tied into the formal topknots of their hair. He then carefully painted red-and-yellow streaks across the boys' cheekbones, speaking to them of courage and pride and brotherhood. They must represent the Koasati village of the Alabama nation well. And they must bring back presents to prove they had earned the respect of the French King.

Duly noted, thought Tristan, shifting from one foot to the other. Presents.

He had already given a set of stockings to

each of the three boys, plus a blanket and a musket for the chief. He wondered what had become of the rest of the goods the contingent had brought upriver.

At the massacre site he had scared away the buzzards with a couple of musket shots and then assessed the scene. Two puddles of blood, one near the fire and one at some distance, indicated that Marc-Antoine and Barraud had either escaped or been taken prisoner by the attackers. The one farthest away seemed to have been dragged off into the woods, where Tristan lost the trail in a sudden rainstorm. The other trail of blood disappeared at the river. One of the pirogues was missing, so presumably either Marc-Antoine or Barraud had gotten away in it.

By the time Tristan retraced his steps to the camp, heavy rain had obliterated all traces of the fight. But it appeared that the two soldiers, Guillory and Saucier, had died quickly, their throats cut, while the priest had been shot in the head from behind. As he had inspected the evidence of the massacre, a blind rage nearly tore him apart. First Sholani, now this. His brother, murdered by —

There he stopped, for he couldn't say who had done it. He couldn't help glancing back toward the village he had left that morning.

The Koasati had been receptive to his offer of peace and friendship; it didn't seem likely that they would have perpetrated this unholy murder.

In the end, all he could do was take the story of what he had found back to the Koasati chief and watch for reaction. And he could swear that what he saw in the face of the chief was genuine shock and sorrow — and worry, lest the French blame him for the massacre and retaliate.

Hence the chief's willingness to send three valuable young braves down to Louisiane with assurances of alliance.

Fights With Bears, followed by Little Frog and Turtle Boy, leaped lightly from the boat onto the pier, showing little physical effects of the journey. Rainstorms had dogged them off and on as they pulled the oars through the swift southward current of the Alabama river, sluicing over rapids here and there, and then tying up to make a fire, cook a couple of large fish, and sleep on the riverbank at night.

Tristan had found the young Koasati to be amusing and energetic companions, apt to pull pranks on one another, but always willing to take a turn at the oars and to share camp chores. Each carried a spear, as well as a fine ash bow and a quiver of well-made arrows, with which they competed to show off their hunting and fishing skills.

Under other circumstances he might have enjoyed the adventure and appreciated the boys' obvious excitement at being so far away from home and out from under their chief's gimlet eye. But before Tristan could even kiss his wife, he had a difficult encounter with Bienville ahead of him.

Bracing himself at the top of the bluff, he turned and shrilled down a whistle that brought the young Indians, who had stopped to gape at the imposing stockade around the fort, running effortlessly up to join him.

"Big guns!" marveled Little Frog, pointing to a cannon poking its snub nose from a corner bastion. "Boom!" He mimicked falling backward, slyly whacking his elder cousin in the chest.

Fights With Bears dodged neatly, catching up to Tristan. "My father will be glad to hear of this powerful protection. He says we may retreat here, if the Kaskaskian devils attack us. He has talked of moving the village south."

Tristan wondered if Bienville had any notion what hopes and assumptions he had fostered in his Indian allies along the river. How were they expected to feed several hundred extra hungry mouths on the meager amount of supplies they were allotted by the Crown, when the colonists were having such bad luck with the production of food crops?

At the fort's main gate, a young sentry he didn't recognize stepped in front of him, gun across his chest. Tristan stopped, gesturing for the Koasati youths to stay behind him. They obeyed, sobering, as if they understood the gravity of their presence in the settlement. Tristan hoped they did.

The sentry's eyes widened as if he recognized Tristan. "C-Captain Lanier?" he stammered. "Y-you're supposed to be dead!"

Tristan's heart slammed into his throat. "I'm Tristan Lanier, the captain's brother. You knew about the massacre?"

"Yes, sir." The cadet swallowed, his Adam's apple bobbing. "Surgeon-Major Barraud got here last night, but he died this morning. He said everybody else in the party was dead." The boy looked Tristan up and down. "You aren't dead!"

And neither was Marc-Antoine, please, God. Tristan smiled grimly in spite of his weariness and anxiety. "I certainly am not. Where's the commander?"

The cadet lowered his bayonet and

shrugged. "I don't know, sir. Probably at headquarters with the other officers. They've been making plans to go after the Koasati."

Tristan could feel the tension jerk behind him as the Indian boys heard the reference to Koasati. He hoped they didn't understand its context. "That won't be necessary," he said. "Let us through. I must present my report."

"Yes, sir." The boy saluted, despite Tristan's present lack of military rank or uniform, then moved back to his post in the guard tower.

Tristan beckoned Fights With Bears, Turtle Boy, and Little Frog to follow and headed for headquarters. He could feel the stares of the soldiers drilling in the quad following him all the way across the green. Ignoring them, he took the shallow steps onto the gallery two at a time and banged on the doorframe with the side of his fist. As he waited, he could hear voices from inside, loud with strain and tension. One was Bienville's familiar growl, another La Salle's nasal drawl, and two others he couldn't immediately identify.

After a long minute, he heard boots thunking against the wooden floor.

"Didn't you understand the commander's order that we aren't to be disturbed?" Châteaugué, Bienville's younger brother, appeared in the doorway scowling. His eyes widened. "Lanier! Thought you were dead."

"So I heard. Let me in."

Châteaugué's gaze flicked to the Indians behind Tristan.

"They're with me. Now let me in so I can bring a report."

Châteaugué stepped back, plowing a murderous stare into the young natives. "Commander's office."

Tristan nodded and headed for the office, the three boys on his heels and Châteaugué bringing up the rear. Without bothering to knock, he strode into Bienville's office. He found the commander seated at his desk, with La Salle and Dufresne ranged at two corners and Châteaugué's empty chair across. All three officers gaped at him with varying degrees of shock.

"I know. I'm supposed to be dead," Tristan said, heading off the inevitable. "Sentry said Barraud made it back. What about my brother?"

By now Bienville was on his feet. "No. And Barraud's dead. What happened? You look unscathed." His expression was almost accusatory, as if Tristan's escape made him culpable in the attack.

And perhaps he was. How could he say

for sure? He looked away from his old friend's gaze. "Could we sit down? I'd be grateful for a drink, and for these men too." He gestured toward his companions, who had lingered close to the door, shifting from one foot to the other. "Fights With Bears, Turtle Boy, and Little Frog."

Châteaugué moved toward a side table supplied with a pitcher of ale and a clutch of tankards.

Dropping into his chair, Bienville regarded the Indians with suspicion. "They're Koasati. Have you lost your mind?"

Handing Tristan a tankard, Châteaugué kicked the empty chair into the center of the room and gestured for Tristan to take it. "I'll stand." He walked toward the door, where the Indian boys were crouched against the wall. Folding his arms, he stood amongst them, disapproval in every line of his body.

Tristan sat, assessing the potential threat in La Salle and Dufresne's presence. So far both had remained watchful, silent, as if waiting for an opportunity to object. La Salle was always at odds with the commander, Dufresne a boot-licking toady. Châteaugué, of course, would back his brother.

He met Bienville's frowning gaze. "I don't

believe the Koasati are responsible for the attack. I spent that night in their village and smoked peace with the chief. I was awake most of the night. I would have heard the attackers leave or return if they had been Koasati."

Dufresne leaned forward. "I heard Barraud's description of the attackers before he died. Cockscomb headdresses, red-and-yellow paint streaks on cheeks and chin —" He gave the Indian boys a murderous look. "Do you deny the similarity in their costume?"

"No, but listen. These boys could have killed me the day of the attack when I came across them hunting. They didn't. In fact, we shared a meal together, all of us, and they invited me to return with them. Why would they wait until night to attack?"

"Perhaps to lull you into false security," Dufresne said, looking to La Salle for corroboration. "The Alabama clans have hated us for years. They've invited in the British and traded slaves from the southern tribes in return for arms."

La Salle grunted agreement. "Don't forget they've killed our missionaries too. Which is why Father Albert is so reluctant to leave the fort and start a mission there."

Dufresne pressed the point. "We mustn't

410

tolerate such outrage." He shoved his chair back, stood, and sent Turtle Boy a contemptuous look. "We've got to retaliate, show them who is strongest."

Tristan leaped to his feet. "Bienville, if you execute payback to the wrong clan, you'll start a war you won't be able to end. Listen to me — make certain of the facts before you act."

Bienville pinched the bridge of his nose. "The war is already begun! Lanier, they murdered your brother, not to mention another of our priests!"

That just might be true, though Tristan prayed not. If Marc-Antoine lay dead, somewhere in the Alabama forest, he knew not how he would survive. Still, his gut told him the Koasati were innocent. Somehow he had to prove it.

"Let me take Deerfoot and these three boys, plus another man of your choosing. Give us two weeks, and we'll discover who's really behind the massacre. If we haven't returned by then, launch your attack and I'll stay out of the way."

"Or what?" snarled La Salle. "You'll go renegade and join your precious Indians against your own people?"

Tristan fought to keep Bienville's fractured attention. "Commander, my wife is here! I may be disgusted with the lot of you, but I'm no traitor." More calmly he added, "You know that's true, no matter what happened between us."

Bienville stared at him, indecision in every line of his body. But there was also a flicker of guilt. "The irony is inescapable. You blamed me when I didn't pursue Sholani's captors."

Tristan nodded. "Fair enough — but this is different." He pressed for compromise. "I know you don't want all-out war with the Indians, not with the British hoping we'll annihilate ourselves in the process. Listen, keep one of the boys hostage here, as a sign of good faith." He glanced back at Fights With Bears. "His father is the Koasati chief."

Fights With Bears surged to his feet. Though he didn't understand French, he clearly sensed the conflict in the room. Proudly he hit his chest with a fisted hand. "The Koasati are afraid of nothing," he said, addressing Tristan. "My father bids me follow you into battle."

Tristan held Bienville's gaze. The commander had a fair command of the Alabama tongues himself. Surely the Indian boy's courageous words must sway him to common sense.

412

Châteaugué grabbed Fights With Bears' arm. "You cannot trust this savage, Bienville! If we wait to go on the offense, they may bring the violence to us here, gathering up all the other clans along the way." He glared at Tristan. "Lanier *is* a traitor, and don't forget he's trained to negotiate with words. You ought not trust him either."

Julien had been so sure that he'd killed the proverbial two birds with one stone. Lanier's escape now made everything so much more complicated.

Bienville had assigned him the task of inspecting the powder magazine and delegating the inventory of weapons in the event that the garrison went on the defensive. What the commander had *not* agreed to was calling out an immediate detachment to march north and attack the Alabama nation. Apparently Lanier was to be granted his two weeks to obtain proof of the Koasatis' inculpability in the murder of three of His Majesty's men and a priest. Bienville might be an erratic and gullible fool, but no one could deny his loyalty to old allies. Any other garrison commander would have had Lanier hanged as a traitor, rather than allowing him to keep one of the largest tracts of land in His Majesty's southern colony.

At least there was incontrovertible evidence that Father Mathieu had perished, and with him documentation of Lanier's legitimation and claim to their father's title. Now all he had to do was secure his rival's demise — again — and the gates to the de Leméry fortune would once more swing open before him.

As though it were a symbol of that latent fortune, he pulled open the heavy iron-bound door to the powder magazine. Before him marched row upon row, ceiling high, of dry powder kegs. It was a goodly store and would provide plenty of ammunition in case of siege or attack — but should Bienville decide to fling their small garrison into Anglo-Indian war, it would be depleted soon enough. And if some natural disaster such as fire or flood destroyed the magazine . . .

Julien allowed himself a secret smile. There was no limit to what the commander would pay the one who possessed the resources to replace it.

For two days Geneviève had barely had time to mourn Father Mathieu. She had taken it upon herself to provide meals for Ysabeau Bonnet, still incarcerated in the guardhouse — and in the process to make sure the various young cadets assigned to prevent her escape did not sneak in to "comfort" the girl with their unwanted caresses. The commander, having now much more pressing concerns than the madwoman in his prison, seemed not to care whether Geneviève fed her or not.

Under the circumstances, she hadn't the temerity to approach him with her suspicions regarding Ysabeau's treatment at the hands of his men. But she found to her surprise that her agreement to tend the now deceased Surgeon-Major Barraud had purchased a certain amount of favor in the eyes of the commandant. And so when she requested permission of the sentry guarding the fort's principal gate to exit into town, the cadet gave her a hasty, wide-eyed salute accompanied by an inexplicably sly grin and let her pass.

The slate-colored clouds blocking the sun today seemed to reflect her morose spirits. As one in a stupor, she walked past the vacant corner home of deceased hero Henri de Tonti. So many good men gone, killed by fever or violence. Hardly anybody in this place lived to quiet old age.

Not Élisabeth le Pinteaux. Not Angela Lemay's baby. Not Father Mathieu. Not Tristan's good friend Charles Levasseur, in whose home they had spent their wedding night. And she must face reality — perhaps not even Tristan.

She hesitated, turned the corner, and faced Levasseur's still vacant house, catty-corner from the home of the Lemay family, with whom she had become quite friendly. Serge and Émile would now run for her when they saw her, and she loved to scoop them up in both arms, reveling in their musky little-boy smell of dust and sweat and fresh air. Angela of course still bitterly mourned the loss of her baby. The simple proximity of coincidental facts — the baby's death at the same time that Ysabeau's hold on reality snapped — had convinced the young mother to lay blame at the only door available.

Geneviève had done everything in her power to prevent two tragedies creating a third. Continuing her slow walk toward the seminary burial grounds, she gave a heavy sigh. Finally she felt prepared to pay her formal respects to Father Mathieu. It occurred to her that Jean Cavalier would want to know of his friend's martyrdom. Somehow she would have to get another message to the Carolina pastor. The familiar ache of dread gnawed at her stomach. No matter how much she owed Jean, the underhanded way she had to communicate with him continued to trouble her.

Shaking off fruitless worry, she picked up her pace. She still had a list of chores to complete in the kitchen at Burelle's before she could lay her aching head upon her pillow for the night. Halfway down the street, she heard a sharp whistle behind her.

"Hey, Madame! I am in the market for someone to bake me a boatload of bread. I will pay well, should you know someone who can oblige me."

She stopped. That almost sounded like . . .

Heart leaping, she turned. And there he was, leaning against one of the posts holding up Levasseur's porch, sunburnt, bareheaded, and coatless, grinning at her utter astonishment. With a shriek she ran for him, oblivious to public decorum, heedless of the scandalous amount of shin bared as she picked up her skirt to free her stride.

Tristan caught her halfway up the steps and swung her off the ground, hauling her hard into his embrace, staggering backward with her until they bounced against the front of the house and rolled inside the open doorway. He kicked the door shut and leaned back against it, holding her so tightly that she could feel the hammering of his heart against hers.

"I missed you," he said, and kissed her.

Eagerly she responded, fearless this time. Drunk on sensation, she knew not how much time had passed before he loosened his grip enough to allow her feet to touch the floor. With her arms looped around his neck, she tipped her head back to see his face. "What's the matter?" Her lips felt numb.

"Nothing." His expression was quizzical. "I just wanted to make sure I'm not —"

"You aren't hurting me," she said fiercely. "I'm as strong as you are."

He laughed and drew his thumb across her lips and cheek. "You look like you've been rubbing noses with a bear."

She smiled and tugged his beard. "No doubt I have." She sobered. "I was afraid you were —"

"Dead, I know. Seems to have been the popular belief." The smile faded as he searched her face. "I'm so sorry about Father Mathieu. I know how much you loved him."

"Yes." She laid her head on his chest to mask the sorrow that knifed through her joy. "I — I still cannot believe it's true. I feel as if he ought to swing through the door at any moment with a child by the hand, asking for cake batter or beignets." She paused and made herself say the words. "And your brother —"

"He is *not* dead."

The grit in his voice grieved her more than Mathieu's death. "Tristan, wishing will not make it so."

"Bienville says Barraud was out of his mind with fever. He thought I was dead too, remember?"

"Yes, but —"

"Geneviève, I studied the campsite. Marc-Antoine's body wasn't there. It looked like someone dragged him off into the woods and then went back to cover the trail. Carefully and cleverly done, but if you knew what to look for, it was obvious. The Indians who perpetrated the raid wouldn't have bothered. They left the other three bodies where they fell."

She stared up at him, perplexed. "Who would have done such a thing?"

"I don't know, but my brother isn't dead. I just know it." He laid his cheek against the top of her head. "And there's one other thing I know right now — my wife will be in my arms until I leave again tomorrow."

20

Tristan had not slept so soundly nor so long since he was a young teenager, worn out from a day of hunting the woods or fishing the streams of Ville Marie, and full of his mother's fish stew and baguettes. He awoke to the crackling lightning and echoing thunderclaps of a storm outside Levasseur's cabin. Unable to tell what time it was — he was voraciously hungry, so it must be near noon — he sat up, stretching the kinks out of his achy body and wondering where his wife had got to.

Vaguely he remembered her leaving the bed some hours ago, kissing him and giggling when he tried to drag her back down again. Too sleepy to chase her, he'd let her go, telling himself he'd make it up to her later. Now he tried to remember exactly what she'd said. Something about bread . . .

His stomach gave a loud rumble at the very thought.

He rolled out of bed, found the washbasin and pitcher Geneviève had thoughtfully refilled for him, and dressed. Juggling lingering worry about Marc-Antoine and hopefulness brought with a full night's rest, he left the cabin and dodged through the storm to Burelle's.

He stopped on the tavern's gallery to shake the water out of his hair and sluice down his buckskins, thinking wryly it would likely be hours before he dried out completely. As he entered the common room, he raised a hand to Burelle. The tavernkeep was behind the bar, polishing tankards and carrying on a lively argument with Father Henri, who perched on a stool like a fat white goose in a lily pond.

"She's in the kitchen," Burelle called with a wink.

Tristan laughed at the priest's disapproving stare and made a straight path for the kitchen.

He stopped in the doorway. Geneviève, flushed from the heat, was using a flat, tray-like implement attached to a long wooden pole to remove a couple of fragrant loaves from the big arched brick oven. She carried the loaves to the other side of the room, slid them off onto the counter, and set aside the pole, then covered the loaves with squares of flannel. After flouring her hands, she opened one end of the kneading trough and took out two hunks of raw dough, shaped them, set them out to rise beside two already fully risen loaves, then crossed to shake a bit of flour onto the oven floor.

When she bent, floury hands on her hips, to stare into the oven, he couldn't resist stepping behind her to lay his hands on hers. He leaned over to see what she was looking at.

With a startled shriek, she jerked upright, nearly knocking him cold with the back of her head.

"Ow!" He jumped back, too late to protect his chin.

"Tristan! What are you doing here?" She grabbed the back of her head, leaving a speckling of flour over her hair. "You scared me!"

"I'm sorry." He gingerly shifted his aching jaw. "Really sorry. I was hungry, but I may not be able to chew for a couple of days." He glanced at the blackening flour at the bottom of the oven. "What are you doing?"

"Checking the temperature before I put in more loaves to bake." She turned to gently deposit the two risen loaves on the tray of the pole implement, then carried them back to the oven and slid them in.

"I'm not used to having company."

"So I see." But she was so beautiful, flour-dusted hair and temper notwithstanding, and the room smelled so heavenly, that he forgave her instantly. He eyed the steam coming from the flannel-covered bread. "Could a man who is about to go on a fortnight's journey talk you out of a slice of manna?"

Her eyes softened. "I'm making this for you to take with you, but I saved you some crepes from breakfast this morning. Come sit here and talk to me while I work." She moved a stool up to the counter, took down a plate and a fork from the shelves above, and began to whip about the kitchen like a small whirlwind.

Before long he was seated on the stool, thanking God above for a woman who knew how to make the lightest and sweetest crepes he'd ever put in his mouth, filled with preserved apples and whipped cream, and served with crisp bacon. As he ate, he told her about his conversations with Father Mathieu, beginning with the pictures in the journal.

"I wish I'd picked it up and brought it with me," he said, shaking his head. "Not only for the drawings, but you would have enjoyed the stories he wrote down. I didn't know a priest could be such an entertaining companion."

"He saved my life," she said, leaning in to check the bread in the oven. "Aimée and I wouldn't have had a place on the *Pélican* if it hadn't been for his intervention."

Tristan waited, hoping she would elaborate. He had kissed every one of her scars last night, but resisted the urge to push her for explanations. After all, there were things in his own life he found difficult to divulge. Still . . . one of them must open up first.

He remembered the day he had impulsively asked her to wed him, her initial resistance. *I'm not what you think I am.* She'd claimed never to have seen a convent. *I can't tell you the rest because —*

And she had left the sentence unfinished, leaving him to imagine all the terrors which could befall a very young, very beautiful daughter of a common baker. A whip laid upon the delicate skin of her back, surely intended to humiliate as well as injure.

"Geneviève, I am a bastard," he said.

She jerked upright and whirled to stare at him.

He braced himself. Perhaps she would come to see that it wasn't his fault. "My mother was seduced by a nobleman, who arranged for her to marry a mapmaker

424

about to emigrate to Canada. Antoine Lanier raised me as his own, and I never knew until your Father Mathieu informed me that this nobleman had changed his mind and decided to legitimate me. They want me to return to France and take up the title and estate, to snatch it away from a half brother I never knew I had."

He blurted it all out in one long rush, because he was afraid he otherwise would never have the courage to tell her. He didn't want to go to France. He wanted neither title nor estate. All he wanted was his plantation and his wife — and possibly four or five sons, and maybe a little daughter as beautiful as her mother.

He waited, looking at his hands, one of which gripped the fork, still speared with a cooling stack of crepes, and the other clenched into a fist upon the table.

She came to him, dusting the flour from her hands before catching his face between them and kissing his forehead. "You must do it, Tristan," she said with her lips close to his ear. Her voice was fierce and full of tears. "France needs men like you in Versailles, to advise the King in making wise and good decisions for *all* his people."

He pulled her into his lap and held her close, smelling the yeast and sugar and browned flour that was uniquely Geneviève. "I cannot decide until I have found my brother," he said into the top of her head. "You must pray for the good God to guide my steps and sharpen my eyes, so that I may come back to you quickly. You must pray that war will not tear us apart."

"I will pray." Her voice broke. "But you know that God in his goodness is not always kind."

She had married an aristocrat.

Geneviève said it to herself again so that she wouldn't forget as she prepared to send Tristan off on this second, even more deadly mission. If he survived, and God willing he would, his responsibility became taking his place as a peer of the court of Louis XIV.

As she walked in the rain across the market square green, she asked herself why Father Mathieu had allowed — nay, encouraged her to marry Tristan, knowing that she could never return to France. The moment she did, she would be subject to arrest as a murderess of one of the King's dragoons.

She shuddered, overcome by a wave of despair so great she wondered if she might join Ysabeau on her journey to madness.

God, have I displeased you by holding my faith in secret? Am I a coward for running from prosecution for my crime? How will I survive if Tristan goes away?

Somehow she knew she would. But the sweetness and color that had unexpectedly alit upon her life like a butterfly was just that fragile. She could hold on to it, hold on to Tristan with all the cunning at her disposal. But if she truly loved him, how could she be so selfish as to keep him from his destiny as God's instrument of change?

The weight of what she must surrender pressed her forward. *What you must do, do quickly.* First she must purchase fabric and thread with which to patch Tristan's clothes, as his lengthy journey had left him all but in rags. No time to sew him a new shirt herself, but perhaps she could buy one with the money in the little pouch in which she kept her bakery earnings. Jingling the coins for reassurance, she straightened her spine.

She was no traitor, no matter what the French legal system said.

The dry-goods shop seemed to be more crowded than usual this afternoon. Geneviève could hear the rumble of loud voices even before she reached the corner where the shop sat cheek-by-jowl with the locksmith's. As she approached the entrance, the door burst open and a uniformed soldier backed out, hauling a woman by the arm.

The woman screamed, the soldier moved, and Geneviève recognized Ysabeau.

"Leave her alone!" She rushed toward the two. "What's going on?"

Foussé, the young soldier who had helped her tend Barraud, gave her a harassed look as he tried to hold on to the wriggling and screeching Ysabeau while backing into the street. "Out of the way, Madame! I have orders to arrest this madwoman."

"But why is she here? Who let her out of the guardhouse?" Abandoning her errand, Geneviève followed the soldier's awkward progress with his prisoner away from the dry goods. "Ysette, stop struggling or you will injure yourself!"

Foussé glanced over his shoulder. "All I know is, someone reported a disturbance here, and I was sent to settle it."

"Please, Foussé — You do remember me, don't you? — Please, take her into Burelle's for a moment so I can talk to her. Let's at least get out of the rain!"

The soldier growled something rude, but apparently saw sense in her suggestion. In less than five minutes they had reached the tavern porch. Unfortunately, the altercation had drawn a crowd. Madame Burelle was not going to like this at all.

Foussé let go of Ysabeau's arm and aimed

his bayonet at the gawking onlookers. "Get out of here, the lot of you! Official business! Go home!"

Everyone obeyed, grumbling, except Françoise Dubonnier, who happened to be near the back of the crowd. They gradually peeled away, leaving her standing arms akimbo, heedless of rain, mud, and leveled bayonets. Expression horrified, she addressed Geneviève. "What's the meaning of this nonsense? Are you hurt?"

"No, of course not — I'm just trying to help Ysabeau." Geneviève gripped her trembling hands together. "Someone let her out of the guardhouse."

Geneviève, Françoise, and Foussé all looked at Ysabeau, who burst into tears. "I didn't mean to! It was an accident!"

"Stop sniveling, Ysabeau," Françoise snapped. She picked up her skirts and marched up the porch steps. "And you — put down that gun, before I take it away from you and use it to search your head for brains!"

Ysabeau dried up and dropped down cross-legged on the porch, while poor Foussé executed a disorderly parade rest.

Françoise's normally immaculate appearance was rather the worse for wet feathers hanging limply about her coiffure and mud splashed up to her knees, but her haughty expression would have cowed the queen herself. "I'm waiting for an explanation," she said, staring down at Foussé.

"They — they said it's my fault she escaped," he stammered. "Aide-Major Dufresne came to relieve me last night. He says he found her cell open and her missing. He didn't want to get me in trouble, so he looked for her all night. Turns out she was sleeping on the gallery of the dry-goods store when Rivard came to open up." He caught his breath and met Geneviève's eyes, looking desperate. "You know how hard it is to talk sense into her, Madame. She wouldn't go away, kept saying she just wanted a yellow dress."

"I promised her one," Geneviève remembered with a pang. "But I forgot it when the surgeon-major died and Tristan came back. I'm so sorry, Ysette," she said, kneeling to take the girl's hand. "Let's go back to the guardhouse where you're safe, and I'll bring you a new dress. Foussé won't hurt you."

"Could I have another cream puff?" She looked up at the young soldier, red lips pouting. "Please?"

He was already shaking his head, but Geneviève said hastily, "Yes, of course — there were some left yesterday afternoon.

Let me get one before we leave."

But she had barely gotten to her feet when another disturbance arose from the direction of the river. This time, the noise traveled up the rue de Bienville, becoming louder and louder until it suddenly burst past the two Juchereau establishments that flanked the east side of the square.

Tristan was at the head of the group marching toward them. He carried something over his shoulder — no, some*one*. It looked like one of the Indian boys he had introduced to her this morning after she offered to bring them breakfast.

Something was terribly wrong. The body Tristan carried appeared to be lifeless. And the other native boy seemed barely able to walk, stumbling along with his arms wrapped about his midsection and his head bowed to his chest.

Geneviève forgot Ysabeau, forgot Foussé, forgot everything except her husband. Tristan's face was a study in tragedy.

"What is it?" she cried, running toward him. "What has happened now?"

He stopped, bending to let the body of the young Indian slide from his shoulder to the ground. They stared at one another over the inert body. He shook his head, hands raised, empty, shaking. "I found Little Frog on the pirogue, dead. Foam about his mouth, curled up as though — as though in agony. Fights With Bears says his cousin wouldn't eat the gruel you brought this morning, because he had already eaten the — the pastries you left earlier." He stared at her. "How is this, Geneviève? Explain this to me!"

She shook her head. "I don't understand. I didn't go down to the river until you took me with you."

Tristan turned to speak to the tall young Koasati with the Roman nose, a brief command in the guttural Alabama tongue.

The boy looked at her then, and the hatred in his almond eyes should have burned her to cinders. She flinched as his brown hand opened to reveal a squashed mass of cream and cake which might once have been one of her delicate cream puffs.

She looked at Tristan. "I don't understand," she repeated. "How did he get that? Is it poisoned?"

Tristan glanced down at the younger Indian, lifeless at his feet. "I would say so. Fights With Bears and I went to buy a couple of replacement oars and some rope, leaving Little Frog to watch the boat. When we came back, he was lying on the foredeck, dead."

Geneviève felt numb. "This makes no sense at all. Maybe he was bitten by a snake."

"Perhaps he was." Grief suffused his face. "I found this in the basket with the one pastry left uneaten." He reached into his shirt to withdraw a small scrap of paper and flicked it at her.

Startled, she grabbed it. It was a piece of the waxed paper she used to protect her pastries, covered with what looked like her own handwriting. *A surprise for you, my darling. Eat these and think of me.*

"Of course I made the pastries, but I did not write that note!" Geneviève sat in a chair in the center of Bienville's office, her hands knotted in her lap. Her face was the color of the waxed paper Dufresne had produced as evidence of her crime.

Treason.

The rest of them encircled her like wolves baiting a trapped doe, but Tristan stood back against the wall, searching her face for anything that would tell him the truth. Despite her secrecies, he had thought he knew her. Had thought he could trust her with his life.

In fact, he still held out hope that there was some mistake. It was at his request that she had been granted this interview before Bienville put her in the guardhouse along with her simple-minded accomplice, Ysabeau Bonnet.

It went without saying that he didn't trust Dufresne, but he couldn't deny the corroboration of so much outside evidence. The poison had been found in her bedroom above the tavern, a little vial that matched the jar of yeast-starter she had brought from France. Her sister, brought in by Bienville, identified it, reluctantly. Aimée now sat in a corner of the office, shivering like a kitten in a cold bath.

"Where would I get poison?" Geneviève said with tears in her eyes. "I don't know anything about poison! I'm a *pastry chef*!"

Dufresne cleared his throat before Bienville could respond. The commander, seated at his desk, nodded, giving him silent leave to speak.

The red-haired warehouse clerk spread his hands. "My dear, everyone knows you spend hours with Nika in the Mobile village. Those little boys of hers are always hunting with poison arrows — they make it from the manchineel plant, which is common in the woods around their camp. Don't you remember the arrow that went past my ear the first day you went with me?" Smiling, he touched a recently healed notch in the top of his left ear.

Geneviève's face paled even more. "We were grinding corn that day!"

"Perhaps." Dufresne shrugged. "Perhaps not. Commander, you might be interested to know that one reason I went to see the Mobile chief that day was to warn him he's been harboring a British spy since his son took the lovely Nika to wife. Her periodic absences from the village have been noted and watched. She seems a most dangerous companion for our secretive Mademoiselle Gaillain, who practices the Reformed religion and, worse, is an intimate of their notorious commander Jean Cavalier."

Bienville sat up. "Can you prove this?"

"As it happens, I can." Dufresne reached inside his uniform coat and withdrew a closely written and crossed paper.

Aimée emitted a strangled squeak.

Bienville's attention snapped to her. "Do you recognize this document, Mademoiselle Gaillain?"

"No!" Aimée's pink cheeks flamed.

Dufresne gave her a tender look. "There is no need to lie for your sister, *cherie.* You know this letter from Cavalier was hidden in her Reformist Bible."

Feeling ill, Tristan snatched the page from

435

Dufresne's hand. It was addressed to Geneviève. He skimmed it, down to the scrawled signature: "Cavalier."

Instructions to write to him when she reached New France. A plea to live quietly but faithfully, eyes and ears open. What did that mean?

It meant Geneviève Gaillain was a fugitive, running from His Catholic Majesty's dragoons. She had every reason to hate both the Sun King and his Papist government. He could see it on her face: her terror, her betrayal.

But he loved her in spite of everything and longed to protect her. He could feel her raised scars on the pads of his fingers, against his lips.

"Bienville," he said, forcing calm into his voice, "these are serious charges. But Little Frog's death, whoever caused it, makes it even more critical that I journey north with the other two boys to reassure the Koasati of our friendship, make restitution for the loss of their young warrior, and enlist their help in punishing the perpetrator of the massacre of our men. I beg you not to decide my wife's fate until I return." He looked around at Bienville's officers, crowding the office, all staring at him with a variety of anxious, angry, and skeptical expres-

436

sions. "And in the absence of my brother, I offer my counsel — that you band together, put aside revenge, and prepare yourselves for the onslaught of enemies from the north and the east. Deerfoot tells me that he sees signs of violent weather closing in as well. You'd do well to prepare to move the entire settlement to higher ground — I invite you to make use of my plantation on the south bluff."

He waited, knowing that Bienville could have Geneviève executed on the spot. Such was his power.

Bienville stirred, always uncomfortable with interpersonal, relational questions. He was a man of action, at home commanding ships or making business deals. He slapped his hands upon the desk and pushed himself to his feet. "All right, Lanier. Lock her in the guardhouse for now. I'll make sure she's treated well until you return." He speared Tristan with a penetrating look. "I hope you understand that all past debts are hereby paid in full."

Tristan nodded and reached a hand to Geneviève. "Come with me," he said gently.

"How could you possibly believe I would p-poison you?" Shivering, soaked to the skin from the rain, Geneviève followed Tristan across the drill green. He held her by the hand, but he was so silent that she may as well have been chained and boxed in a prison wagon. It had started. Everything she had dreaded since her father's arrest had come to pass, compounded by her love for this man.

"I can't believe it," he said without looking at her. "But you are so-called Reformist, are you not?"

She'd thought her broken heart could feel no more pain. "Do you know what that means?" She jerked her hand from his. "It means I am of a people persecuted for centuries for obeying Scripture and for refusing ritual worship. It means I am under the rule of God rather than any man, be he king or archbishop or dragoon. It means I must forgive you because Christ first forgave me. Tristan, I love you!"

When he turned, she saw the clashing emotions in his eyes. "Do I know what it means? I don't care about theological debates or parsing Bible verses to shore up political loyalties. I know you've suffered for those things. But I also know that your Jean Cavalier is in bed with those British dogs — enslaving the Indian nations to gain control of French and Spanish territories. The woman I loved was a victim of that abomination." He closed his eyes. *"You* forgive *me?"*

They stood in the beating rain on the deserted green, together but oceans apart.

At last Geneviève summoned the strength to move. Nothing worse could befall her, now that the truth was revealed. "Come, let me tell you how it happened." She turned and dragged herself up the guardhouse steps, Tristan's slow footfalls behind her.

She went into the open cell next to Ysabeau, who lay fast asleep on the floor, curled like a kitten on a blanket Geneviève had brought her several days ago. Water dripped from Geneviève's dress, forming a puddle as she sat on the cell's military cot and waited for Tristan to follow.

He sat beside her and stared at a broad crack between the boards of the flooring.

"You are Canadian," she began, "so you don't know the traditions of the Cévennes, the mountains where I grew up."

"I am Canadian," he said evenly, "but that doesn't make me ignorant. I know the King tolerated the Huguenots for some time, allowing them to settle in a place where they would cause little damage." He shot her a glance. "Which worked until the rise of Black Camisards like Cavalier."

"I know Jean. He didn't do half what he's

accused of. He was in our home the day the Abbé of Chaila was assassinated."

"Your family hid him?"

"Yes." Geneviève swallowed tears. "Someone told. By the time the dragoons came, Jean was no longer there, so they took my papa instead. I followed them with Papa's — the gun was so heavy without Jean there to help me — but I was angry and frightened. I knew what they were going to do, and it wasn't right! So when the soldier said he would — I knew he meant it, and the gun went off. I can't remember the rest of the day, except they said I killed him and they cut off Papa's head and burned the village. They would have executed me too, but for Jean. He got me out of the prison in Fraissinet-de-Lozère and took me to Father Mathieu."

"Father Mathieu was no Reformist! He was a Jesuit!"

"Yes." She nodded. "But he is — was, I mean, sympathetic to the doctrinal questions of Reformed believers. He didn't approve of the persecution, and he was even friends with Cavalier. They knew of the *Pélican* and persuaded me to take Aimée and go. I didn't want to run, but Jean said he could help other Reformists get out of France if I saw that there would be tolerance in the new colony. You saw the letter. I was to keep quiet about my beliefs and get a message through to the Huguenots in Carolina, reporting on the political and religious climate of Louisiane."

"Then you did come as a spy." His voice was heavy, his expression pained.

She sat up, straightening her spine. "I came first of all to protect my little sister from execution as a traitor. She had nothing to do with my crime. That I could also repay the man who risked his life for mine — it is an honor."

For a long moment, Tristan sat looking at the wet floor, elbows on his knees, fingers plowed into his hair. Finally he heaved a sigh. "Geneviève, you are a good woman, but what you've done is a serious thing. It won't be easy to make Bienville understand the provocation." He looked at her then. "For now, I must go. The death of Little Frog makes the situation even more complicated, and I have to know what happened to Marc-Antoine." He rose, drawing the key from his pocket, and looked at her soberly for a moment, then bent to kiss her cheek. "You will be safe here until I return. God be with us both."

21

Aimée sat in her corner chair in Commander Bienville's dirty, cluttered office, half listening to the men argue over their next course of action. Probably they had forgotten her. *Why* could men not talk about their problems, as women did, until they worked them out peacefully? They must always be producing a gun or a knife, or setting fire to something, as if the violence would not inevitably cause some man on the other side to react with bigger guns and longer swords and hotter fires.

A spasm of worry for her sister disturbed the carefully constructed unconcern that was her only protection from the sort of insanity that had swamped Ysabeau. She had tried to tell Ginette to leave behind her Bible and all else that stank of their old life in Pont-de-Montvert. But Geneviève was always the hardheaded one. Just like Papa, she must always stick to principles, no matter the consequences to everyone around them. And look where that had gotten Papa. Now they had hauled her off to the guard-house.

Ginette should have been more careful. If she'd already burned the letter from Cavalier, Aimée could have gone back to Julien and truthfully said there was nothing to worry about. But he had made her swear to bring it to him. So while Ginette was in the Burelle kitchen baking, she had slipped upstairs and unlocked the identical trunk with her own little key and extracted Cavalier's note from the Bible. It was too bad Julien had been obliged to produce it as proof of the poison.

It was a little odd that Ginette had done that, but perhaps there had been some mistake. Ginette always landed on her feet. She would be fine.

All Aimée wanted was a little house with a garden, clean floors, and a picture or two on the walls, and maybe a baby to rock. The husband that would come with such a scenario was truly a necessary evil — but if one must have a husband, preferable that he be easily manipulated like Monsieur Dufresne . . . Julien, as he liked to be called.

She considered him, over there arguing with the commander about what should happen to her sister. Julien was so heroic, insisting that Geneviève be given a chance to recant, when Aimée could have told him that Ginette would recant when the Pope gave up the palace in Rome and moved to an Indian camp in Quebec.

Drying her eyes, she rose and tucked her handkerchief into her sleeve. She glided over to address Bienville. "Please, Monsieur le Commandant, will you excuse me now? I should like to go home and compose myself before our afternoon ladies' soiree. Madame L'Anglois will expect me to entertain with a song or two, and I must practice."

Bienville scowled at her. "There will be no soirees this afternoon or anytime in the near future. You may go home and say the rosary in memory of the soldiers who will be leaving the fort to protect you."

Aimée blinked. "There's no need to be rude —"

"I'll escort her home, Commander, with your permission," Julien said, taking her hand and drawing it through his arm. "You can see that my betrothed is too innocent to fully comprehend the seriousness of our circumstances."

Betrothed? That had a lovely sound. She bestowed a smile upon Julien.

Bienville grunted. "By all means, take her

out of my sight. But make sure she understands that no further Huguenotish lean-
ings will be tolerated in the colony. Good
day, mademoiselle."

Aimée clung to Julien's arm and allowed
him to lead her from the office. She could
hear Bienville's gruff voice in sharp altercation with Commissioner La Salle, a most
disagreeable man if ever she had met one.
She didn't know how Françoise tolerated
dwelling in the same house with him, with
only her cousin Jeanne there to provide civil
discourse over breakfast. Presumably Bienville would cave in at some point and
request Françoise's hand in marriage. In
Aimée's opinion, they were the only two
people in the entire colony strong enough
to deal together, without devouring one
another whole.

Outside the office she came upon Françoise and Father Henri.

Aimée dropped Julien's arm. "Oh, Françoise, that beastly commander accused my
sister of treason! I can never hold my head
up again!" She allowed Françoise to fold
her in comforting arms.

"Never mind, I'm sure it's all a terrible
mistake. We will insist that Geneviève be
treated well." Françoise held her away,

445

hands on her shoulders. "Isn't that so, Father?"

"Oh." The priest harrumphed. "Of course. Yes, of course."

Françoise's gaze lit on the open office door. "Commander! I wish to speak to you, if you please!"

"I'm afraid he's very busy with state business, mademoiselle," Julien said.

"Which is why I must have his attention right now." Françoise marched to the office door.

Aimée held her breath. To her surprise, Bienville appeared, La Salle on his heels like a cur following an alpha wolf.

"What is it now, Mademoiselle Dubonnier?" Bienville rubbed his belly, eyebrows hooked together. "I don't have time for visiting the Indian school this afternoon. I have repeatedly told you —"

"Yes, yes, I know." Françoise waved away his objections. "I only wanted to ask if anyone has located this Nika woman, to ask about her part in this farce. I'm sure Aide-Major Dufresne has good intentions —" she looked at Julien as though she doubted any such thing — "but appearances can be so deceiving."

"I was just asking the same thing," put in La Salle, adjusting his ill-fitting wig. "We have jumped to so many illogical conclusions in the last four years that it's a wonder we aren't drowning in them. We must question this woman Nika. Where is she?"

Looking harassed, Bienville gave Julien a pointed stare.

Julien cleared his throat. "She — ah, she has not been located, sir. She seems to have escaped from the village along with her two children." He tugged at his immaculate neckcloth. "I will apprise you first thing when she returns."

Bienville folded his arms across his broad chest. "There's your answer, mademoiselle. Now will you please allow me —"

"One more thing," Françoise interrupted smoothly. "I'm sure you are aware that Monsieur l'Aide-Major has every reason to wish Geneviève Lanier discredited. She has noted his tendency to, shall we say, get creative with the warehouse books and has, at Monsieur La Salle's request, observed and noted certain illicit transactions occurring about the warehouse. I know for a fact that she can prove that Monsieur Burelle has bought and resold stolen goods with Monsieur Dufresne's full knowledge and assistance."

Aimée had no notion what Françoise's words meant, but they sounded awful, and she could tell by his heightened color that Julien was getting angrier and angrier by the minute.

Bienville had listened, mouth clamped shut, but he put up a hand to forestall Julien's response. "I've had enough unsolicited interference for one afternoon, Mademoiselle Dubonnier," he said evenly. "Dufresne's father is of a higher rank than your own, and a significant investor in our colonial enterprise. It will take more than the word of a British spy — and a whining accountant — to convince me to distrust him." He sighed. "Now you will oblige me by occupying your fertile imagination with something less critical to our survival. Good day, mademoiselle." He backed into his office, shoved La Salle out, and slammed the door.

Aimée, wide-eyed, met Françoise's shocked gaze. "Oh dear," she said.

Bienville, Julien was convinced, sat fully in his pocket. His jubilation only slightly doused by the driving rain, he assisted Aimée Gaillain's descent of the headquarters gallery steps, resigned to the fact that her mincing steps would turn the short walk from headquarters to the chapel into a thirty-minute funeral procession.

The commander had no idea that Vital Hayot, the Comte de Leméry, had gone to his eternal reward, leaving the feckless Gilbert holding the reins of the estate in his incompetent grasp. All Julien had to do was wait for the Brits to land at Massacre Island, and he would be forever shut of this miserable, waterlogged colony and its illiterate bourgeois inhabitants. Of course, should he be able to bring about his original plan to do away with the seemingly un-killable Tristan Lanier, he might change his mind and make use of the title after all.

One must keep one's options open, after all.

He began to listen to Aimée's artless prattle. The girl occasionally had something interesting to say, and she might be useful in his pursuit of fame and fortune. Besides, as his future wife and mother of his heirs, one could argue that she held a minor stake in the game.

". . . so I was all taken aback when you told the commander about Geneviève's Bible. That was very bad of you, I vow."

He gave her an amused look. "Sometimes one must do something a little bad for a very good reason. You do understand that your sister has been breaking the law for quite some time, do you not?"

"Y-yes, I suppose." She looked away. "Though owning a Bible does not seem such a terrible crime. She wasn't hurting anyone."

"I know, *cherie,* but think. First it's reading an illegal Bible. Then it's helping spies to hide in one's house. Then it's actually spying for the enemy. Before you know it, you're shooting dragoons!" He dropped her arm and mimed aiming a rifle. "Boom!"

Aimée jumped. "Don't do that! You startled me!"

He grinned at her. She was adorable with raindrops in her long eyelashes and her rosebud mouth puckered in irritation. He took her hand and kissed it. "Forgive me," he said with just the right amount of chagrin.

She sniffed. "I suppose. But I wish you had told me you'd asked the commander for permission to address me. We could have asked Father Henri to post banns yesterday in mass. I was taken all a-fluster when you called me your . . . betrothed."

He couldn't tell if she was gratified or angry at his presumption. "It seemed the expedient thing to do. Bienville doesn't approve of young ladies who take themselves to be more important than they are."

"Yes, he's very angry with Françoise." She

wrinkled her little nose. "But it could be that he's only angry because he loves her and resents it."

He laughed. "What do you mean?"

"A man who wishes to become married must give up all his mistresses."

"Where did you get that peculiar notion?"

She removed her hand from his elbow. "A *good* man would do so."

"Then I am exceptionally relieved not to be a good man." He caught her arm and hauled her close to him again. "*Cherie,* I am teasing you. Never fear, there is only a little more to do, and we will be the happiest and richest married couple on two continents."

She gave him her lovely smile then, and flung her arms around his waist. "Why, what else is there to do? Oh, I know! You're going to intervene for my sister and make sure she doesn't stay in prison."

"I'll do what I can, of course, but that wasn't what I meant. I've intercepted some rather bad news that will mean we must leave the colony for a little while. You must go home and pack your belongings and be ready at a moment's notice." When she looked up at him in wide-eyed fear, he laid a finger over her lips. "But you mustn't tell anyone. Not your sister, not Madame

451

L'Anglois, not *anyone.* Do you understand?"

Nika stopped to catch her breath, turning her face up to the pouring rain. The litter she had made from Mah-Kah-Twah's blanket and rope had been getting heavier and harder to pull, and the rain made it worse. The yoke system she had fashioned from a tree branch braced across her chest had worked well, until her bruised muscles began to scream with pain and fatigue.

She dropped the yoke and walked back to assess Mah-Kah-Twah's condition. She knelt and laid the back of her hand against his cheek. Not long after they staggered away from Azalea's hogan, his skin had started to burn like a winter fire. Soon he descended into delusional conversations with the priest he called Father Mah-Tu, and an hour later he was too weak to walk. Nika didn't know how she was going to drag him another step. If only she had a horse or a boat . . .

But wishes got one nowhere. She had prayed for help, and there had been no answer. If only she hadn't promised to go with him back to the French fort. Leaving her two boys asleep, with only a kiss on each forehead, had brought on pain of life-giving proportions. The knowledge that they remained safe with Azalea, playing with her children, eating well and sleeping soundly, was the only thing that gave her courage to slip away with Mah-Kah-Twah.

Ah, that and watching his face as he first laid eyes upon his children, tumbled together on a sleeping mat like gangly puppies. He had laid his hand first on Chazeh's head, then on Tonaw's, as if in blessing. When she drew him away to rest in another corner of the hogan, he came reluctantly. "I didn't know," he murmured in French as he sank exhausted onto his back. His eyes closed. "Nika, I didn't know."

"Nika, do you have the book safe?"

At first she thought the question came from her swirling thoughts, but when she looked down at Mah-Kah-Twah, she found his eyes open and lucid. She put her hands on either side of his face. Was it cooler to the touch, or did she only imagine it?

"Is it? Do you have it safe?" His voice was hoarse but clear.

She hurried to uncork her gourd, lift his head, and hold the canteen to his mouth. "Drink," she commanded. "Yes, it's safe. How do you feel?"

"Like I've been wrestling an alligator." He smiled a little.

Her tears, near the surface, overflowed. "Mah-Kah-Twah . . ."

"I was joking," he said, frowning. "Don't cry."

"I'm not." She sniffed and wiped her face on her rain-drenched skirt.

"Where are we?"

She sighed and looked around. The forest looked familiar. Maybe. "I'm not sure. I wanted to skirt the Mobile village, so I've had to go off my usual trail."

"I hear running water. We're close to the river."

"Yes, we could save time if we crossed, but the rain has swollen it so — I'm afraid there will be floods. Mah-Kah-Twah, I'm worried. It's getting more dangerous with every step."

He struggled to sit up. She protested and started to make him lie back, but he pushed her hand away. "No, let me — Ah." Grimacing, he propped himself on his good elbow. "How did you pull me so far?" Admiration and something else shone in his eyes.

She blushed. "I had to. Or Azalea would have ended your misery with her corn pestle." When he laughed, she grinned at him. "God has given me unusual strength."

"Yes, he has." He sobered. "But we can't continue this way. You have to let me walk."

454

He looked down at his wound and plucked at the makeshift bandage, which Azalea had re-formed with medicinal herbs and clean leather stripping. It was wet through with rain and seeping blood again. "This feels better."

"You are not a good liar, my friend." Nika sighed. "But at least the rain has slacked off a bit. Maybe we should find a place to shelter for an hour or so."

"No." Stubborn lines bracketed his mouth. "I have to get to the fort and warn them —" He stopped abruptly. "What is that noise?"

She listened. "I still hear the river. Wait. It's — footsteps. Shhh. We've got to hide." She got to her feet and crept to the yoke, bent to pick it up.

But Mah-Kah-Twah rolled off the litter and struggled to his hands and knees. He was going to try to walk.

"No!" she whispered. "No, don't!" She ran to catch him, for surely he was too weak —

But it was too late. He had fainted.

Despairing, she sank down cross-legged and lifted Mah-Kah-Twah's upper body, cradling his head in her arms.

And that was how they found her.

■ ■ ■ ■

Dressed in a man's jacket, breeches, and stockings, Aimée knelt in front of her open trunk, thinking wistfully of her little bedroom above the bakery in Pont-de-Montvert. She had not remembered it in quite a long time, because it always brought to mind the dragoon with sour breath who had taken it and made her sleep with Ginette. That was after he had tried to sleep in her bed *with* her, and Papa had made him get out.

For months on end, she'd had nightmares about that dragoon, often awakening screaming until Ginette sang to her and dried her tears. She had not had those disturbing dreams in weeks — and she could even think of Papa, and home, without experiencing that horrid suffocating sensation.

Now she was going to leave Louisiane and all her friends behind. She looked around at Madame's charming little guest room, with its cheval mirror, damask coverlet, and gilded shepherdesses bracketing either side of the door. Madame would be sad to find her gone in the morning, but it couldn't be helped. One must grow up and take on adult responsibilities.

With a sigh, she fingered her lacy Sunday chemise and the blue mantua that matched her eyes. Julien insisted she could bring nothing with her but a blanket roll and the clothes upon her back. The long overland trip would render female garb impractical. Besides, he added, they would be wise to hide her identity until they reached their destination.

This explanation had mainly served to make her wonder if leaving in such a havey-cavey fashion was a good idea. She and Geneviève had managed to accomplish the journey from the Cévennes all the way to the western coast of France without resorting to disguise. But Julien refused to listen. Perhaps he would become more amenable to her wishes once they were married.

"Mademoiselle, would you like a cup of tea before bed?" chirped a little voice behind her.

Aimée gave a squeak and whirled. "Raindrop! I told you to always knock before you open the door!"

"I thought I heard you call." The child gave her a sunny smile as she inspected Aimée's peculiar garb. "Perhaps you would like company. Wherever you are going."

"I didn't call!" Aimée frowned, then

added hastily, "And I'm not going any-where."

"Madame thought you might be sick, you have stayed in here so long by yourself. She is very easily upset, and I don't believe she would like to think of you walking alone in the dark." Raindrop folded her arms as if daring Aimée to contradict her. "Wherever you are going."

Aimée gave her an annoyed look. "Where I am going you may not come."

"Didn't Jesus say that to somebody?"

"How should I know?" Aimée rolled her eyes. "I'm not the biblical scholar that my sister is."

Raindrop looked wistful. "I love your sister. I wish she was my sister too."

The pang of remorse that pierced Aimée directly under Julien's starched neckcloth was so unfamiliar that she almost didn't recognize it. Geneviève was a good sister, and it was too bad she must stay locked up in the guardhouse long enough for Aimée to escape with Julien.

"You can borrow her," Aimée said. "I will not need her for a while." At least until she and Julien were comfortably situated in Carolina with a baby or two and a house full of servants. Then perhaps she could send for Geneviève to come and live with her. Maiden aunts could be useful, she had heard.

Raindrop giggled. "Mademoiselle, you are funny."

Aimée sniffed. "I'm happy to amuse you." Hoping she'd distracted the child, she waved a hand. "I don't want any tea, and I'm very tired, so please go away." She pretended to yawn.

But Raindrop looked stubborn. "A moment ago you said you are going somewhere."

Perhaps she could take Raindrop into her confidence and keep her from tattling to Madame or Ginette. She crooked a finger. "Come here. I'm going to tell you a secret." When Raindrop's eyes widened, Aimée lowered her voice. "Monsieur Dufresne wants to marry me." That much at least was true.

Raindrop shrugged. "*That* is no secret."

"Yes, but we are going to do it tonight. Monsieur is waiting for me at the little storehouse on the river bluff."

"I knew you were going somewhere!" Raindrop's big eyes suddenly narrowed in suspicion. "But why are you not going to the chapel?"

"Shh! Lower your voice." She leaned in close to the child's ear. "We are . . . going on a trip, and Madame would not like it, so don't tell her. Listen, Julien will be worried, and I'm not quite ready to go. Please run down to the warehouse and tell him I'll be there directly." Julien would think she had gone as far out of her mind as Ysabeau, but on such short notice, Aimée couldn't think of another way to get rid of her little nemesis.

Raindrop looked at her doubtfully. "How much longer will you be?"

"Another fifteen minutes should do it." By the time Raindrop returned to tell Madame, Aimée and Julien would be long gone, and no one could catch her and make her stay. "Hurry! Julien will be watching for me."

Raindrop smiled. "I will run like lightning!"

If Tristan had not believed before that there was a personal God who answered prayer, his faith became a vibrant and glowing thing when he saw his brother lying in the Indian woman's arms — wounded and unconscious, to be sure, but alive — a scant twenty miles outside the walls of the fort.

Now the two Indian boys carried the litter, upon which Marc-Antoine lay still and silent in his pain. Tristan and the woman walked on either side, with Deerfoot guarding the rear.

Nika claimed to be Kaskaskian, though she was dressed in the light Mobilian dress of palm fronds woven with cotton fabric, fashioned in a loose blouse over a skirted girdle about the hips. Her long, black hair had been parted down the middle and plaited into a single tail down the back, and her small ears were pierced and hung with multiple strings of tiny beads that swung against her shoulders. She walked on bare feet beside Marc-Antoine's litter, guarding him as jealously as a lioness with her cubs.

Tristan could all but smell the possessiveness in her reluctance to look away from Marc-Antoine's face, the gentle way she laid the back of her fingers against his forehead every so often.

Most curious of all, she spoke nearly flawless French — simple in vocabulary, but in grammar and pronunciation displaying only a slightly mislaid accent. When he asked which Jesuit missionary had taught her, she gave him an unexpected smile and said it was no missionary, but a very bad boy.

"Do you not remember me, monsieur?" she asked lightly.

He studied the lush mouth, retroussé nose, and black almond eyes. She looked like a hundred other native women he had encountered over the last eight years, including his own wife. He started to shake his head, then a sudden image hit him, and he was leaving fifteen-year-old Marc-Antoine alone in a Kaskaskian village at the northernmost boundary of the Alabama territory. There had been a young maiden standing beside the chief that day — his only daughter, beautiful and exotic as a woodland flower, and already clearly infatuated with the French boy.

Her lips curved as Tristan's eyes widened. "It is true," she said softly. "We taught each other languages . . . and many other things." She looked away. "I had not seen him for a long time, but of course I remembered him. And when I found him wounded so . . ." She shrugged. "Could I leave him to die?"

"You *found* him? How did you happen to be close by during such a massacre?"

She, in turn, studied him. "You are his older brother, are you not? The one he will die for. The one for whom he will leave everyone, including the girl who loves him."

He had no answer for that. He glanced at Marc-Antoine. "I didn't ask him to die for me."

"Of course not. Which is why he would gladly do so." She lifted her chin. "But I think there are others he would give his life to now." Then she grinned at him again. "Though he is much more use to us alive, don't you agree?"

Tristan chuckled. "Yes. Come now. Tell me the story. We have a long walk ahead of us."

And she did, downplaying her own courage and strength. She had watched her husband murder three men and wound two more, but still hadn't left Marc-Antoine to die, even to protect herself.

Tristan tried to understand. "Your husband is Mobilian? But Barraud reported that the attackers were Koasati. How could he possibly confuse the two? And why would Mobilians attack a French peace party? They've been our allies for many years."

Nika was silent for a long moment, staring at Marc-Antoine's face as if willing him to wake up and answer for her. "My husband is a jealous man. He knew — he seems to have become sure, somehow, that — that your brother and I were once very close." She glanced at Tristan, shame in her expression. "You will think that I am a wanton woman, but it is not so. I was a maiden when I gave myself to him, only fourteen summers old, and I was sure that Mah-Kah-

Twah would stay with me, that my father would allow us to marry. But then —"

"I came back for him."

Her eyes were sad. "Yes. After he left, I . . . had to marry my father's choice for me."

"You've been in the Mobile village all this time? Without seeing Marc-Antoine?" That sounded rather far-fetched.

"I was careful." When he did not answer, she blurted, "He didn't want me! I wouldn't follow him like a puppy!"

Ah, pride. That he understood. It had kept Marc-Antoine from reconciling with their father. It had kept Tristan from going home after Sholani's death. "But what were you doing that far north, if you weren't traveling with your husband? And you say you weren't following my brother?"

22

Ysabeau was singing that monotonous song
again. "Raindrop, raindrop, you wet the tip
of my little nose. Fall down, fall down on
the road. Wet is the road, and wet is my
nose."

She wouldn't stop singing. And the rain
wasn't going away either.

Geneviève sat cross-legged upon her cot
with nothing to do but to watch a growing
stream rush under the floor slats of the cell.
She didn't have her Bible or her journal.
She didn't have her tatting. She didn't have
corn to grind. All she had were her anxious
thoughts and prayers.

And if the rain didn't stop soon, more
than the tip of her nose was going to be wet.
She wondered if Noah's wife had looked
over the side of the grounded ark, watching
the waters rise and hoping her husband had
heard God's instructions correctly. She
wondered if the guardhouse would float.

She wished she'd learned to swim.

She was in a cage. Like a canary in a rich woman's house. With another canary who knew only one sad song.

Why had they locked her up? Did they think she would run away? Where would she have gone? What harm had she done, after all? She had written a letter to Jean Cavalier through Pastor Elie Prioleau, but all it said was that she was settling in well among the Catholics (they weren't all papist heathens), the Indians she had met were friendly, and oh, by the way, I married a man who thinks I'm beautiful.

But none of that mattered because it was a crime to communicate with a French rebel, however innocently.

Which made her think of Julien Dufresne, whom she had been trying to push *out* of her thoughts because he made them so angry and bitter. *He* was one of the self-righteous papist heathens she had been taught to fear and distrust. The Bible said that one should test the fruit of a life to determine whether they were of the true faith. She had seen no evidence that Dufresne had committed any part of his life to serving God. He served only himself, and he was dangerous as a roaring lion looking around for a tender lamb to devour.

She *must* get out of here, before he ruined her little sister.

It had been hours since young Foussé had shut her in and then walked away. Nobody had bothered to guard her and Ysabeau. She had called and called for a drink of water, but nobody answered. She had slept a little, but her sleep had been restless and uncomfortable. Waking to the sound of Ysabeau's eerie voice, she'd sat up and started measuring the distance between the water under the guardhouse and the floor.

The floor was now wet on top. The cell was going to flood.

"Ysabeau!" She tried not to sound frightened. "Can you see water beneath your cell?"

"Wet is the road, and wet is my nose."

"Listen to me! Stop singing and look at the floor."

To her surprise, the song halted. There was a wattle-and-daub wall between the two cells, so she couldn't see Ysabeau's movements, but she heard a faint rustling as Ysabeau got off her cot, then a patter of bare feet against the floor.

"Geneviève, the floor is wet!"

"Ysette, I think they've forgotten us. We have to get out before the building floods." Ysabeau might not even be lucid, but maybe

467

if both of them shouted for help, someone would come.

"Help!" Ysabeau shrieked. "Someone open the door!"

Geneviève went to the bars of the cell and joined her shouts and screams until she was hoarse. Even should someone walk past, the rain pounded outside like the roar of a waterfall. Thunder boomed with deafening anger. Into the looming darkness lightning crackled, allowing glimpses of the water which now covered the entire floor, drenching Geneviève's moccasins and reaching the bottom of her skirt.

She sloshed over to the wall between the cells and laid her palm on it. The lumpy oyster-shell-and-mud texture was damp. And soft. She pushed on it, felt it give, then pushed harder. It cracked. Slamming the heel of her hand against the wall with all her strength, she felt it give way, falling in chunks into the other room.

"Ysabeau! Come here! The wall is soft enough to break down. At least we can be together!"

There was no answer. Geneviève waited until the next flash of lightning and peered through the hole she had made.

Ysabeau sat on her cot, arms wrapped around her knees. When lightning lit the cell again, Ysabeau's wide eyes gleamed like a cat's. "No one's coming," she said flatly. "We're going to die."

Marc-Antoine was not going to die. He would not allow it.

Tristan and the Indian boys had carried his brother's litter twenty miles in driving wind and rain with lightning flashing like bolts of fire flung from the heavens. Nika had gone ahead of them to search out the safest trails, dodging swollen creeks and flooded swampland. Then she would circle back and guide them through.

By the time they reached the stockade, evening blanketed the wooded terrain with sluggish, funereal darkness. The entire party dragged themselves forward on strength of will alone. As they stopped before the big oaken gates, intermittent flashes of lightning threw the pickets of the stockade into glaring relief as if the teeth of hell waited to swallow them all. After shouting for the sentry, Tristan glanced over his shoulder and caught a glimpse of his brother's face, wet and twisted in pain. Marc-Antoine twitched about, eyes closed, playing out some feverish dream, muttering nonsense about books and pictures, paintings and the Madonna's child. Perhaps he thought he had already died and faced heaven's gates.

He would give the sentry another minute or two before he ordered his native companions to hack down the gate with their hatchets. Part of him hoped there would no longer be anyone here. Bienville should have taken the inhabitants of the settlement, soldiers and all, and moved them to higher ground, as Tristan had suggested before he left. The fort itself sat on high ground, but the river had swollen outside its bounds, even on this bluff.

He had regretted his decision to leave Geneviève, more with every step. With Marc-Antoine safely within his care once more, her fate became uppermost in his mind.

He signaled to the Indians that he wanted to rest Marc-Antoine's litter on the ground, and they retraced their steps to a little hillock where the river rushed past, leaving a broad muddy knoll above the flood. Leaving Nika to keep watch over his injured brother, Tristan, Deerfoot, and the two boys waded back to the gate. In a matter of minutes they had hacked the rotten gate open. They pulled down the hewn pieces, threw them out of the way, and went back for Marc-Antoine.

As they struggled through the waist-high

stream running along the base of the glacis, holding the injured Marc-Antoine as high as possible, Tristan continued to pray for wisdom, for holy favor, for the safety of his family and his countrymen. Whatever wrongs he had suffered at their hands, he willed no man to die in this enclosed whirlpool.

At last they navigated the ascending glacis and reached the main entrance of the fort, which opened into the guardhouse. Judging by the general state of abandonment they had encountered thus far, Tristan expected the guardhouse to be empty. He signaled for Nika to pound on the locked door with the butt end of Tristan's hatchet. They waited, heard nothing, and Nika banged on the door again. Tristan gestured her aside, took the hatchet, and traded places with her.

This door, being a little more protected from the weather, was harder to chop through than the outer gate, but it finally gave way to three or four of his weary blows with the hatchet. He started clearing away the pieces of the door and immediately saw why it had been so difficult to open.

"Get back!" he shouted as a waist-high wall of pent-up water rushed at him. He turned to grab the litter, but it was too late. The deluge shoved him into Nika, and she dropped her corner of the litter. Marc-Antoine rolled off underwater, while the three Indians shouted in terror as they tried to stay on their feet.

Bracing himself, staggered by the force of the flood, Tristan held his breath and went under for Marc-Antoine. Lungs bursting, he was just about to come up for another gulp of air when his right hand snagged fabric. Blindly grabbing at it, he hauled himself upright and jerked his brother out of the water by his ruined shirt. He caught Marc-Antoine up in his arms and held him fast, both of them coughing and spewing water.

When he could breathe again, he searched for Nika and thought he saw her at the bottom of the glacis, swimming against swirling eddies in an attempt to regain her feet. He didn't see the three Indians, but a sound from within the guardhouse made him look back. The stream of pent-up water from within the building had slowed as the water level subsided, until he could stand without being knocked off his feet. Marc-Antoine was heavy in the best of circumstances, but his wet clothing and unsupported weight tested the limits of Tristan's strength. He needed to find a place of shelter where he could lay his brother down and attend to his injury. Nika, Deerfoot, and the Koasati boys would have to fend for themselves for the moment.

He would have to wade through the dark guardhouse. Maybe someone had left a lantern and flint hanging out of the water's reach. Shifting his brother a little higher in his arms, he turned to edge his way through the door.

Then, as he paused in the hallway between infirmary and guardroom, he heard it again — a hoarse noise that might have been a woman's voice. Frowning at the tricks his mind played upon him in his anxiety, he waited for another shaft of lightning. There! Though he saw nothing but water and the leaky thatched roof overhead, he heard the shout again, a little louder and longer. In the darkness he felt along the wall with his shoulder until he found the guardroom door.

Holding onto Marc-Antoine, he was forced to find the latch with two fingers, crouching to release it. The door, swinging open on another rush of contained water, would have taken him off his feet again if he hadn't hit the infirmary wall with his back. By now he could hear two women shouting for help.

Had Bienville been so cruel as to leave

Geneviève and Ysabeau to drown in this rat hole? "Geneviève!"

"Tristan!" she screamed.

"Hold on — I'm coming!" Galvanized, muscles trembling from his brother's dead weight, he fought his way into the room through the swirling dark water. Even with some of it having rushed out into the hallway and over the glacis, he was in waist-high water. "Where are you?"

"Center cell! Ysabeau's on your right."

"I don't have a key," he said in despair. "Marc-Antoine is injured — I can't break you out." He thought for a precious few seconds. "I'm going to press through to the drill ground — maybe there'll be someplace to leave him out of the storm. Hang on — I'll come back for you!"

With every last ounce of his strength Tristan fought his way back to the hallway. Keeping his back pressed against the wall, he sidled toward the drill ground entrance. When he stepped out into the flooded green, he saw that, though neither moon nor stars lit the weeping night sky, the rain had slackened to a mild drizzle and he could pick out the shadowy shapes of the fort's other three buildings. A wavering lamplight came from headquarters. Murmuring a prayer of thanksgiving, even while he wondered how Nika and the three Indians fared, he waded toward the light.

He accomplished the thirty-foot uphill distance without incident, discovering that by the time he reached his destination he was no longer wading, but splashing through ankle-deep water. Mounting the steps to the gallery, he looked down at Marc-Antoine's face and was startled to find his eyes open.

"This makes twice, big brother," Marc-Antoine said with a wan smile. "You'll never get rid of me now."

Tristan sighed and leaned against the closed door. "We all have our burdens to bear."

Aimée slipped out the side door, which opened onto Madame's chicken yard. She was not overly fond of chickens, but if she went through the front family room, she would face Madame's endless questions. Pausing to assess the chicken detritus she was likely to step in on the way to the river, she shifted the blanket roll tied across her shoulder with a rope. Rain had come down in torrents all day. This was starting out as a very unpleasant adventure.

She stepped out from under the thatching of the eaves. She was almost sorry she had sent Raindrop away. Life was going to be dreary indeed with only Julien for company. It was true that he had beautiful manners, he danced like an angel, and he could be charming and entertaining when he chose. But ever since the night she had taken Geneviève's pastries to him, and allowed him the liberty of kissing her lips, he had developed an annoying habit of ordering her about. As if she were one of his cadets, or — or a kitchen wench even.

If Madame was to be believed, this was an almost universal trait of the male sex. Madame complained incessantly about Monsieur L'Anglois's snoring, his habit of leaving dirty utensils on the table for her to pick up, his refusal to wipe his muddy boots before entering the front door. Aimée had noticed, however, that in the evenings Monsieur followed Madame's movements about the house, anticipating her needs with a sweet devotion that attested to his love for her.

Somehow she could not picture Julien playing "Le Beau Robert" five times in a row on a violin simply because it was her favorite song.

She squared her shoulders under the weight of the scratchy rope. Julien was her choice, and no one was going to make her change her mind.

"Mademoiselle! There you are! Oh, please go back! Do not come!"

Raindrop's escalating shrieks at last penetrated her fog of contemplation. She realized from the stench around her that she stood in Madame's pigsty. "Raindrop? What are you doing back here so soon?"

Raindrop flung herself at Aimée in the dark. "Didn't you hear me?" She grabbed her hand and pulled her toward the house. "You must go back inside at once! He is a very bad man!"

Aimée resisted, digging in her heels. "Stop this at once, you ridiculous child! Let go!"

"Monsieur Dufresne — he killed the Indian man, picked up his gun and —" Raindrop threw her arms about Aimée and burst into tears.

"Julien shot an Indian?" Aimée patted Raindrop's back. "Why would he do that, at this time of night? Did you speak to him as I asked you to?"

"No!" The little girl burrowed her face against Aimée. "I was frightened when I saw that big Indian waiting to jump out at Monsieur Dufresne, so I hid behind the corner of the building and watched. They were arguing about —"

"Arguing? So it was someone Julien knows?" This was getting odder and odder by the minute.

"Yes! The Indian said he had k-killed the soldiers and Monsieur Lanier and the priest — and that Monsieur Dufresne was to pay him."

"That makes no sense. Why would Julien want his own people dead?" Even as she said it, a tiny voice reminded her that Julien had more than once expressed contempt for the Lanier brothers and for the priests.

"I don't know," Raindrop wailed. "I only know what I heard and what I saw. The Indian said, 'I killed them all,' and Monsieur said, 'No you didn't, so I shall have to clean up your mess.' They argued some more. And when the Indian turned to walk away, Monsieur Du-Dufresne, he picked up his musket and — and shot him in the back — Oh, mademoiselle, it was truly horrible, much worse than butchering a hog or wringing a chicken's neck!"

"Shh, shh . . . it's all right, never mind . . ." It wasn't true. It couldn't be true. Julien would never shoot a man in the back. Aimée patted the little girl's back while she gathered her scattered wits. Finally she took Raindrop by the shoulders and shook her a little. "Stop it now."

Raindrop hiccupped. "I'm sorry, mademoiselle."

Aimée yanked the neckcloth from about her throat and mopped Raindrop's face. "I don't know what you saw, but Julien would never pay anyone to murder a priest. Don't say anything to anyone else, while I go and straighten this thing out. Better yet, tell Madame you and I are both feeling poorly and are going to bed. I will see you in the morning."

With that colossal batch of lies, Aimée picked up the blanket roll she had dropped and left Raindrop standing in the pigsty, sobbing into the neckcloth.

She would just see what this nonsense was all about.

Geneviève was still standing on the cot, in water up to her hips, when she heard a noise from the hallway. When she had failed to shake the iron bars loose and found the oaken boards of the outer wall impenetrable, she had tried to find a way to jump high enough to reach the thatching of the roof. She had imagined that if she could create a hole big enough to climb through, she might convince her fellow prisoner to climb on her shoulders, then go for help.

Ysabeau's despondent refusal to get off her cot had put an end to that notion, even if further thought hadn't brought her to realize that the light cane poles to which the thatching was lashed would never sustain the weight of a grown woman. So she had simply stood praying as the water rose and rose. For all her sins, she didn't want to die by drowning. She didn't want to die at all, not right now; but, dear God, if it must be, not in a prison of water.

And then somehow he was here, just like the first time she'd met him, pulling her out of watery terror into a gasp of precious free air. And most blessed miracle of all, he didn't sound angry, he didn't sound sad or disappointed. He'd sounded terrified, as if he loved her and didn't want her to die anytime soon.

I'll come back for you.

Waiting, she'd held the fear at bay with those precious words. *He's coming back for you.*

At first she thought the noise was a fresh onslaught of rain. But then she recognized the sound of someone wading through water toward her. A dark, shadowy form appeared in the doorway.

"Geneviève! Are you all right?"

"Yes! Oh, Tristan, I'm so glad you're here!"

"I have the key. Hang on."

"Ysabeau first. She's very frightened."

Ysabeau released a whimpering sob. "Please! Let me out!"

"I'm coming. Geneviève, I love you." He said it as if the words had been ripped from him, and he couldn't have held them back another moment.

She wanted to say them back to him, but there was too much unsettled between them, not least her charge of treason. So she stood silent, gripping the bars, as he unlocked Ysabeau's cell, all the while speaking quietly to keep her from hysterics.

"Can you see enough to get to the door?" he asked the girl when the door swung open.

"I think so." Ysabeau sounded shaken, but she took a tentative step into the flooded room, then one more. She was halfway to the guardroom door by the time Tristan moved to Geneviève's cell.

He fumbled with the lock and key in the dark. "I will make sure Dufresne is court-martialed. Bienville sent him to release the two of you when the drill green started to flood, but he never came back. The officers have been making arrangements to evacuate the settlement and didn't follow up."

Lacking the energy to form a reply, Geneviève nodded, though she doubted he could see her. When the door opened, she walked into his arms.

He lifted her, held her close, and she clung to him. "I won't leave you again," he said against her ear.

"I'm glad," she choked out. "Is your brother all right?"

"He's very ill, but I left him with Nika. She'd already made it to headquarters." He shifted his grip, slipping an arm under her knees, the other across her back, and began to wade toward the door. "I think I will not toss you over my shoulder this time," he said with a low chuckle.

At that point, she wouldn't have cared, but she kissed his damp cheek. "Tristan, you must know I didn't poison that bread. I would never —"

"I know." He stopped her lips with his, warm and possessive. "There is an explanation, and we will find it. But let's wait until there is less immediate danger." He kissed her again. "Please."

"Yes. All right." He was here, that was enough for now.

Nika sat cross-legged beside Mah-Kah-Twah's bed, keeping vigil while the Frenchmen plotted and planned in the other room. Loud, disagreeable, they reminded her of her childhood, when she had sat in an out-of-the-way corner of her father's hogan, listening to the elders decide on a place to make winter camp. They would come to agreement, and the women and children would be dragged along to make the best of wherever they landed.

Tonight, she was not bound to give counsel to these pigheaded Frenchmen. They were the enemies of her mother's people, whatever their chief, Byah-Vee-Yah, liked to proclaim. She could refuse to go with them, return to the Apalachee village for her children, and wait for battle to seal her allegiances.

She laid the backs of her fingers against Mah-Kah-Twah's forehead, as she did when her boys were ill. Was his skin perhaps a little cooler, or was that wishful thinking? His facial bones were prominent beneath his fine dark beard, his lips cracked. She poured a little water from her canteen onto her fingers and wet his mouth.

Her heart was drawn to this man. She had helped deliver him to his own people, despite her fear of Mitannu. And she did not want to leave him — as he had once left her. Revenge would bring only bitterness.

He claimed he had not taken a white woman to wife. But neither was he likely to take an Indian woman for more than a mistress. And Nika would not share him.

She thought about her conversations with Ginette. She was ashamed now that she had not allowed her friend to pray with her about her deepest desire. Ginette had shyly told her about her marriage to Mah-Kah-Twah's brother. Her respect and affection for Tree-Stah was clear, and he seemed to hold Ginette in equal regard.

Would that God had granted her such a mate.

But, as Ginette had said, sometimes God said *no.* Nika only wished that God would speak with an audible voice so that she could know his will.

She looked down at Mah-Kah-Twah and found his eyes open and clear.

He smiled at her. "I dreamed you were here."

She felt her cheeks heat. "You are better. Your shoulder no longer bleeds."

"Where's my brother?"

"I will get him. He asked to see you when you awoke."

He licked his dry lips. "Could I have a drink of water first?"

"Of course!" Angry with herself that she had become so flustered under the regard of a pair of black eyes, she uncorked the canteen and lifted his head to drink.

"Thank you. My brother. Hurry, Nika."

She corked the canteen, rose and hurried into the other room. The French leaders were all seated around a long oaken table, Byah-Vee-Yah at one end and Tree-Stah at the other. To her relief, she did not see Du-Fren.

Tree-Stah looked up when she approached him. "How is my brother?"

"Awake and asking for you."

He shoved his chair back. "I'll be back." He followed Nika into the side room.

Mah-Kah-Twah had pushed himself to a sitting position. He held his injured shoulder, panting a little.

Nika rushed to him. "No, you must not. You will make yourself black out again."

"I'm better. I have to talk to my brother." He looked annoyed, which was a good sign.

She nodded and stepped back, but she didn't leave the room, and he didn't ask her to. He seemed to accept that she was part of whatever he had to say to Tree-Stah.

Tree-Stah knelt near the bed and searched Mah-Kah-Twah's face. "You're looking better, my brother," he said. "Your nurse has taken good care of that wound. You are very lucky."

Mah-Kah-Twah met Nika's eyes. "I know. I would have died if she hadn't found me right away." Then he looked at his brother.

"She found Father Mah-Tu's book. Have you seen it?"

Tree-Stah frowned. "No. Do you mean the one he had me draw pictures in?"

"Yes." Mah-Kah-Twah caught Nika's hand. "Where is it? Will you get it?"

"Of course." She reached to the end of the bed for the priest's satchel. Loosening the leather string that gathered it at the top, she reached inside for the journal and handed it to Tree-Stah.

He held it in his hands for a moment, his thumb rubbing its scarred leather cover. Pinching his lips together, Tree-Stah opened the book and fanned the pages. "What am I looking for?"

Mah-Kah-Twah's expression was tense. "Father Mah-Tu told me early on in the journey that if anything happened to him, I was to give the book to you, and the painting of the Madonna over his bed to Jon-a-Vev."

"Did he say why?"

Mah-Kah-Twah studied his brother for a long moment. "I assumed he told you."

"That our mother was seduced by a selfish aristocrat when she was just a young girl?" Tree-Stah gave him an odd smile. "You of all people should know that is not so unusual."

Mah-Kah-Twah flushed and gave Nika a guilty glance. "I'm no aristocrat. And if I had known . . . well, if I had thought it possible, I would have stayed or brought her with me."

"Ifs are useless, little brother. And as I told Father Mah-Tu, I don't need an empty French title when my life is here."

"The title might not be as empty as you think — especially since a fortune comes along with it. That's what the journal outlines." Mah-Kah-Twah leaned forward, eyes intent on his brother's face. "The King's support of this colony hinges on decisions he makes in other theaters of war, and our survival hinges on when and to what extent the royal coffers open to support us. As Mah-Tu said, Louis is capricious about who he listens to — and the right man in the right place of influence could make all the difference in the direction France goes as a nation — Louisiane being only one small part of it."

Tree-Stah looked away. "My unwanted father already has a legitimate heir."

"Who is by all accounts a lazy, spoiled spendthrift. He's run through his allowance regularly since he gained his majority." Mah-Kah-Twah leveled a finger at his brother. "Which is why the Comte sent

Father Mah-Tu. He knew, if you were the man he hoped, then you would have to be persuaded."

"I will read the journal," Tree-Stah said reluctantly. "But what is the significance of the painting? My wife is a Reformist, and they're not fond of artistic representations of the saints."

"The document legitimizing you is inside the Madonna's frame." Mah-Kah-Twah lay back with a weary sigh. "Tristan, you must take this opportunity seriously."

Nika stood up then. "Tree-Stah, your brother is very ill. He should rest before you move him."

"You are right." Tree-Stah stood as well. "Will you walk with me to the door, Nika?"

She looked down. Mah-Kah-Twah had closed his eyes and was already breathing deeply.

Tree-Stah stopped just inside the door, blocking her way. "I'm going to ask you again. Why were you following our contingent into Alabama territory?"

She looked at her hands, clasped loosely at her waist. "I was not following you." That was the truth.

"Then why were you there?"

"I was going to visit my family in the Kaskaskian village."

"Without your children." It was not a question. "I don't believe you."

"I left them with my friend. Chazeh had been ill." Also true. She glanced back at Mah-Kah-Twah's sleeping form. She had braved considerable danger to keep him alive. If she did not tell everything she knew, the risk she had endured would be all for nothing, because the French would be overcome by the British — Mah-Kah-Twah and his brother included.

Her fingers twisted. If she told, she might never see her children again.

She looked up into Tree-Stah's eyes, marveling that a countenance could be so hard and so compassionate all at once. He said nothing, only waited for her to decide — *truth* or *lie.* This was a good man, a strong man like Mah-Kah-Twah. A man who considered the safety and well-being of others above his own.

She was tired of being a pawn of cruel and selfish tyrants. "I have Jon-a-Vev's letter. You are right not to trust Du-Fren. *He* is the British spy, not your wife."

"But she wrote —"

She waved an impatient hand. "She wrote a message to the man who saved her life — this Kah-Vah-Yeh — and gave it to me for the father in Carolina. But I also have a letter from Du-Fren to the English commander at Charles Towne." She slipped the priest's satchel off her shoulder, took out both letters and handed them to Tree-Stah. "See for yourself."

She watched him read Du-Fren's letter first, his expression darkening.

At the end of the letter, he looked up. "He tells them that we are short of food, that the powder magazine is depleted and likely to flood in the first hard rain. That the settlement is divided into factions for and against Bienville, and the Crown is losing interest in the colony."

"Yes. So you see what this man is capable of. He thinks to be safely away before the British muster an attack. But not with the Koasati as your commander thinks. They are arming Kaskaskians in the northeast — my own mother's people. When the southern Indian peoples and the French are divided and weakened, the British and their allies will come in and crush you all."

"How do you know this?" he demanded. "Can you prove it?"

"One of my agents at the Apalachee village informed me." She spread her hands. "But do you really need me to prove it? Haven't you known for some time that the English have been working to split and stir up the Indian tribes against one another and against France? Du-Fren thinks to control me by threatening my family. But my children are where he cannot touch them. I will no longer live in fear of cowards and traitors."

Tree-Stah stared at her, his tired, bearded face grim. "How old is this information?"

"As of yesterday."

He absently crumpled the letter in his hand. "Bienville must know," he muttered and wheeled to stride into the main room. But he caught his hand on the doorframe and looked back at her. "Thank you. I'll make sure you and your family are protected."

She nodded as he left, at last feeling some measure of peace. Whether she lived or died, she had cleared her conscience. God would be pleased with this obedience. She turned to take up her vigil beside Mah-Kah-Twah, seating herself cross-legged at his feet. Bending her head, she closed her eyes. The most painful part would be leaving him when the time came. She had already paid a harsh price for giving herself to him, and her heart could not bear to pay it again. Slow tears escaped to drip upon her hands.

God have mercy on me.

23

"I'm not convinced this woman is telling the truth about a British attack." Bienville pushed his hands into his disordered hair. His eyes were opaque with worry, permanent lines of anxiety etched beside his nose and between his brows.

Tristan thought his old friend seemed to have aged ten years in the last twenty-four hours. Indeed he could feel his own weariness pressing like a hundred-pound weight upon his shoulders. Leaving Geneviève curled in an exhausted sleep on an improvised pallet in a corner of Bienville's office, he had slogged across the settlement through the mud and the rain to the priests' quarters. There he found Father Henri and Father Albert occupied in the futile activity of bailing water from their common room. It didn't take much to convince them to abandon their task and retreat to higher ground. Tristan had found Father Mathieu's painting of the Madonna above his bed, escorted the seminary priests to the tavern, and then reported back to headquarters. After nearly forty-eight hours without sleep, he was literally swaying on his feet.

But one glance into the officers' quarters — where his brother sat up eating a little broth from the spoon Nika held to his lips — filled him with fresh courage and determination.

"You have Dufresne's letter, and Nika has no reason to lie," he said. "In fact, every reason to say nothing at all."

Bienville stood, pushing his hands against his knees. "We're settled in this bog because I didn't listen to you four years ago. But if we take no action and the Koasati find us holed up here like sheep in a pen . . ." He grimaced. "I don't have to tell you the massacre upriver will be nothing compared to the bloodbath we can —"

The outer door burst open, and Raindrop, the little Indian slave girl who used to follow Geneviève about, catapulted into the room.

"Monsieur L-Lanier!" Raindrop stood dripping, shivering just inside the door. "Mademoiselle Aimée told me to stay home, s-sir, and I'm sorry to be a disobedient slave — but, but she wouldn't b-believe me!"

Bienville gave the little girl an impatient look. "Why are you out and about at this time of night, girl? Does your mistress know where you are?"

Raindrop shook her wet head. "No sir, but it is an emergency! I had to come before he does something terrible to her!"

Tristan stooped to one knee and beckoned the child. "Come here, Raindrop. Slow down and begin at the beginning. Who is in danger?"

"Mademoiselle Aimée!" Raindrop rushed to Tristan. "She was dressed in men's clothes, so I knew something funny was going on. She finally told me she planned to meet Monsieur Dufresne —" She clapped a hand over her mouth. "Oh, I wasn't supposed to tell that either!"

Tristan covered a smile. "Never mind, you did the right thing to come to me. Continue, please."

Raindrop glanced at Bienville. "You won't put me in the guardhouse, will you, sir?"

The commander's eyes twinkled in spite of his obvious irritation. "Not unless you killed someone."

"Not me — Monsieur Dufresne!"

Bienville's expression darkened. "You had

best explain."

"Yes, sir. Mademoiselle sent me to tell Monsieur Dufresne that she would be there soon, though I think she was just trying to get rid of me. When I got there, I saw him arguing with that big Mobile Indian — I hear him called Mitannu — over money."

Bienville made a chopping motion with his hand. "Dufresne is a supply officer. His job is trading with the Indians."

Raindrop looked confused, but Tristan caught her face to make her look at him. "Never mind, what happened next?"

Her big dark eyes filled with anguish. "Mitannu said he killed Lanier and the priest! Oh, Monsieur — I'm so very sorry. I know he meant your brother —"

"But as you can see, I'm very much alive." Marc-Antoine leaned in the doorway, looking more like Lazarus come from the grave than a decorated officer of His Majesty's marine.

"Marc! Go lie down before you fall down!"

Marc-Antoine gave Tristan a wan grin. "I'm finding it rather difficult to sleep when reports of my demise are being so grievously exaggerated."

Nika glided to his side and took his elbow upon her shoulder. "I will make sure he doesn't fall and crack his head."

"It appears the damage is already done," Bienville said dryly. "Go on, child. As you can see, both Messieurs Laniers are alive and, er, somewhat well. The Indian claimed to have perpetrated the attack on our peace party?"

"That's what he said, sir." Raindrop regarded Marc-Antoine in wonder, then met Tristan's eyes. "Mitannu seemed to think he had killed everybody, but Monsieur Dufresne told him he had not, and that he would not pay him for — for not killing them all. Mitannu was very angry, of course, and threatened to k-k-kill Monsieur Dufresne. Monsieur said he would give him another chance to do the — the job, and then he would pay him double what he promised the first time!"

As Bienville began swearing fluently behind him, Tristan took Raindrop by the shoulders to keep her attention. "And did Mitannu agree to this?"

She nodded. Her little pointed chin began to tremble. "Yes, but as soon as he turned to go, Monsieur Dufresne sh-shot him —" Her mouth went square, and she wailed, "He shot him in the back! Oh!" She covered her face with her hands and sobbed.

Tristan pulled her into his arms. "All

right, little one. You were very brave to come to me. Hush, now, we'll take care of it." Over her head he met Bienville's stunned eyes.

"It's true, then," the commander said hoarsely. "What the Indian woman said — it's all true. Dufresne is a traitor."

Julien was longing for a bath, but he knew he must get to La Salle and his faction before anything else went wrong. He decided not to waste time dragging the Indian's body to the bluff, pushing it into the river, and letting the forces of nature cover his actions. He could always claim that the Indian had attacked him, and he'd responded in self-defense. Not that anyone in command was likely to be concerned about the death of one more savage.

Of course, Bienville was always a wild card. One never knew when he might take it into his head to prosecute the killing of an Indian for political reasons, as he and the Lanier brothers seemed to entertain some insane notion of luring the savages into an alliance — as if Louis the Sun King cared a sou about the well-being of a band of savages.

So he'd simply hauled the body outside and around the corner, then mopped up the remaining puddle of blood with a fallen limb. Carefully wiping his bloody hands on a discarded tarp and laying it over the body, he took up his candle to light his way to the fort.

Meeting Aimée at the chapel entrance of the fort drew him up short. It was a measure of his preoccupation that, in fact, he'd forgotten all about his intention to take her with him tonight.

He summoned a smile. "Aimée! *Cherie,* you ought to be in your bed at this advanced hour." He surveyed her breeches, which fit her curves in a delightfully scandalous way. "I see you are trying on your disguise — but you must hurry and change before someone sees you and recognizes you without your hat."

She halted, her smile fading. "What? But we were to leave tonight. It's well past midnight. I was only coming to find out what had delayed you."

"Tonight?" He chuckled. "My dear, your eagerness is charming, but the river would be much too fast and dangerous in such weather as we have had today. We shall leave this time tomorrow."

Frowning, she walked toward him with what one could only term aggression. "Julien, I sent Raindrop to you a little while ago, in case you should be worried about my delay." She stopped at the foot of the chapel's gallery steps, her small, dimpled chin elevated in pugnacious fashion. "How could you allow a child to witness you murdering a man — even an Indian! — by shooting him in the back?"

Julien pried his tongue loose from the roof of his mouth. "Raindrop? The little Indian orphan?"

"She isn't an orphan! She has seven siblings in the Apalachee village — which you would know if you paid the slightest attention to anyone but yourself."

This non sequitur, which on a good day would have made him laugh, produced in him a strong urge to snatch her by the hair. "Says the common-born wench who cannot walk past a mirror without stopping to admire her own face and form. And who is stupid enough to take the word of a ten-year-old savage over an officer of His Majesty's marine."

"How dare you!" Aimée slapped him.

Nursing his stinging cheek, Julien eyed her coldly. "I shall deal with you later," he said between his teeth. "For the moment, I have more important things to do. I advise you to take yourself back home and pray that I forgive you before the morrow." He turned on his heel and mounted the steps, crossed the gallery, and entered the chapel.

He walked through the empty sanctuary, which was softly lit by a cluster of tallow candles beneath a rather plebeian plaster bust of some bearded saint. A second door opened out onto the interior gallery facing the drill green. Judging by the light streaming from the open windows of headquarters, Bienville would be there, joking and drinking with his cronies, even at this advanced hour.

That an accident of birth had placed such a crude, ramshackle personality in command of this outpost would have driven a less patient man than Julien to rash action. But as one who carefully played the hand he had been dealt — looking for and pouncing upon weaknesses in the enemy, pressing opportunities as they came, milking every advantage — Julien knew it was only a matter of time before he came into his own.

Turning to his right, he approached the door of Commissioner Nicolas de La Salle's office. La Salle, whose contempt for Bienville rivaled Julien's own, would no doubt welcome his intelligence. He rapped sharply upon the door.

"Who's there?"

"Dufresne, sir. May I come in?"

"Dufresne?" La Salle himself lifted the latch and opened the door. He eyed Julien up and down. "What are you doing here?"

Julien hoped he'd managed to eradicate the bloodstains from his clothing. "I came to see if you require anything before I go off duty, sir."

"No, I — wait." La Salle opened the door farther, as Julien had hoped he would do. He scowled. "Did Bienville send you?"

"As a matter of fact . . ." Julien paused, looked over his shoulder in the direction of the lighted windows. "I was hoping you would say nothing of my being here. The commander is a bit, shall we say, territorial these days."

"Yes, you might well say that." La Salle relaxed somewhat. "What do you want?"

"I bring fresh developments in Bienville's delay in retaliation against the attack on our peace contingent. Sir, I . . . cannot remain quiet when this unnatural timidity could result in danger falling upon the settlement."

La Salle shoved at his wig. "Come in, then, but be quick about it. What we are planning must stay in this room until the time is ripe for action."

Julien slipped past La Salle. The room was several feet longer than the commander's cluttered office and seemed even bigger because of its Spartan cleanliness and order. The commissioner's large oaken desk, empty chair, and floor-to-ceiling bookcase took up the far end of the room. Ranged in front of it with military precision sat a line of wooden chairs occupied by perhaps a dozen artisans and merchants of the settlement — all of whom had at one time or another come to loggerheads with Bienville.

Julien knew them all by sight and had had business dealings with many. He followed La Salle and stood back with an assumption of modesty while the commissioner introduced him.

"Gentlemen, Dufresne brings us an update of Bienville's determination to hold the inhabitants of our colony hostage while wild savages, armed by British agents, advance upon us. Please hear him out." La Salle sat down behind his desk and linked his fingers across his paunch.

Julien executed a brief bow. "I regret to inform you that I just intercepted an Indian scout sent in to ascertain the strength of our garrison. Suffice it to say, he did not make it out alive."

As expected, there was an eruption of outrage and fear. La Salle jumped to his feet. "What? You didn't tell me —"

"Wait!" Julien overrode the outbreak of raised voices. "Commissioner, the situation needs to be discussed among cool heads. If Bienville refuses to send out a detachment to demonstrate our strength to the savages, the least we can do is to encourage each man to prepare to defend himself and his household." He lowered his gaze. "I hope you all understand why I cannot directly lead this action — it would be seen as insubordination at the very least; mutiny at worst."

The words were barely out of his mouth before Father Henri surged to his feet. "No need for the aide-major to stand at the forefront of our protest." He laid a dramatic hand over his crucifix. "I am not afraid to show Bienville what I think of his lack of leadership. This very day he has shown leniency to a woman caught in an act of treason! I have corresponded more than once with Minister Ponchartrain about the commander's habit of lining his own pockets at the expense of those he is duty-bound to defend. Gentlemen, citizen-warriors! As Scripture states, the man of God is abjured to stand firm, fully armored against the day of evil." He looked around, fire — or perhaps peevishness, it was hard to tell the difference — in his prominent eyes. "The day of evil is here! Who will stand beside me?"

A chorus of agreement testified that "cool heads" had been superseded by angry ones.

Julien stepped back, more than satisfied. If one must be denied a title of nobility due to an accident of birth, then the next best thing must be military power earned by intellect and cunning. If Bienville fell or was recalled by the Minister, there was no one more qualified to replace him than himself. On the other hand, if the British were to succeed in their campaign to force France out of the southern territories, he had set himself up for guaranty of favor.

Yes, he fancied that he had managed this affair well so far. One more step, and his work for the night would be complete.

"Gentlemen." He raised a diffident hand. "I applaud your decision. And should you need ammunition for the coming battle, I happen to hold the key to the powder magazine."

Geneviève put her arm around Raindrop and led her toward one of the armchairs in a corner of the officers' living quarters. She sat down, drew the child into her lap, and held the thin, shivering body close until Raindrop relaxed and her sobs quieted to intermittent sniffles.

Awakened by the door slamming shut in a gust of wind, then the commander's loud voice, she had peered into the common room at about the same time Marc-Antoine limped to the doorway of the barracks.

Having missed the onset of the conversation, she didn't completely understand what it was about, but clearly Raindrop was overset. When Tristan looked up and saw that Geneviève was awake, he'd looked relieved. Motioning for her to take charge of Raindrop, he'd gone off with Bienville and Marc-Antoine into the commander's office.

She kissed the top of Raindrop's head. "Have you had anything to eat tonight, my dear?"

"I'm not hungry." Raindrop sat up and rubbed the heels of her hands into her eyes. "What's going to happen to Mademoiselle Aimée?"

"What do you mean?"

Raindrop glanced at the closed door of Bienville's office. "She went to meet Monsieur Dufresne. I said she ought not — but she wouldn't listen." She clasped her hands together. "Please, mademoiselle, you've got to make them go after her!"

Aimée would do that, of course. She was both bullheaded and naïve, a deadly combination. Geneviève knew she was going to have to go after her sister, because the men, it seemed, had forgotten about her.

"I will do that," she promised, hugging Raindrop. "But first let me fix you a hot cider, and you can curl up here while I talk to the men." With any luck, Raindrop would relax and fall asleep. She herself felt refreshed after her own nap — strong enough even to challenge the arrogant Julien Dufresne.

Aimée had heard enough. Feeling as if a blindfold had been snatched from her eyes, she slid to the damp floor of the gallery under the window of La Salle's office.

Her first reaction was outrage at Julien's duplicity. Or perhaps one might more accurately call it triplicity. Until tonight, he had been her ardent suitor, the man who called her *cherie* and *belle,* and other lovely words, as if she were a princess straight out of a castle. *Then* he had called her *common born* and *stupid.* She shivered a little, remembering his threat to deal with her later.

Then there was Julien the trickster, who had talked her into defying her sister's wishes, encouraging her to go through Geneviève's trunk and snoop out the Bible with its damning letter from Jean Cavalier.

Julien would never have known about Cavalier if Aimée hadn't babbled to him like a child in her hurt feelings. Then to use her words to pin a charge of treason on Ginette, when Aimée knew in her heart of hearts that her sister simply wanted to be left alone to worship God as her conscience dictated. Almost as bad was this Machiavellian turn on Monsieur Bienville. The commander might be less than tactful at times, but he had seemed to trust and like Julien. So why had Julien betrayed him to the men inside that room? Offered to help them take up arms against Bienville and his officers?

Worst of all . . . Raindrop had seen evidence of his brutality with her own eyes, the killing of that Indian in cowardly fashion. And he had not denied it! In fact, she was quite certain that Julien had poisoned Ginette's bread with the intention of murdering Tristan Lanier rather than that poor Indian boy.

Truth.

She almost gagged on it. She sat under the window, forcing herself to inhale and then exhale, one lungful at a time, until she could formulate her next move. A princess, she supposed, would simply expire from fear, hurt, betrayal, *stupidity,* while she waited for some prince to rescue her.

But she was a common-born wench. And she was not as stupid as Geneviève feared and Julien assumed she was. Fully aware now of the depth of selfishness to which she had descended — traipsing along like a child in a garden, giddy with release from the fear of dying in a fire or rape and execution at the hands of the dragoons — she found herself awake, sober of mind, determined to right the wrongs she had committed.

How? What could she do? It was almost too late. The men in that room were set to take over the arms and ammunition of the fort, usurp the commander's authority, and hunt down and attack the Indians of the upper river villages.

What could one frightened and shamed young girl accomplish, especially one who had tied her own reputation to the biggest liar and villain on two continents?

Geneviève supposed the time must be somewhere past two o'clock — though it was hard to tell, as the night sky was as hard and black as the bottom of a cauldron. She and Nika had left the fort through the outer door of the headquarters building, crossing the gallery and descending its steps without a light and then slip-sliding down the muddy glacis and over the flooded moat. On this side of the stockade, water stood knee deep in some places, the darkness terrifying beyond description. Geneviève shuddered, still feeling the panic of standing on her cot, waiting in the water for Tristan to come for her and Ysabeau.

She prayed that Ysabeau hadn't gotten herself trapped in another dangerous place. No one seemed to know where she'd gone after she left the guardhouse. The commander had sent Foussé to look for her, but he hadn't as yet returned.

Her sister was her main worry now. Aimée's last known location had been outside the L'Anglois home, but Raindrop seemed to think she would be heading for the small riverside warehouse. Geneviève and Nika had almost split up to look for her but decided to stay together for safety. Neither carried a weapon — at least Geneviève did not. Nika likely had a knife somewhere about her person.

"So Dufresne was behind the attack on our men?" Geneviève whispered, following Nika, who was feeling her way along the stockade toward the gate. "Why? What would he accomplish with such a crime?"

"Probably to provoke retaliation against the Koasati." Nika stopped and crouched, pulling Geneviève down with her. "Shh! I think I hear someone coming!"

Geneviève listened, heard nothing, then whispered, "But Raindrop said Mitannu was supposed to attack Tristan Lanier. That Dufresne wouldn't pay him because he shot Marc-Antoine instead."

"What?" Nika's grip on her arm tightened, her whisper intense. "That doesn't make sense. She is mistaken!"

Geneviève shook her head. "It doesn't make much sense either way."

Nika was silent so long Geneviève thought she might not answer. At last the Indian woman drew a breath. "There is an explanation, if Marc-Antoine was Mitannu's target. I knew your husband's brother many years ago. We were both very young and — became lovers. I did not tell Mitannu this for fear of what he would do."

Geneviève tried to hide her shock as several events and chance remarks came together. She had noticed the European cast to the twins' eyes, their light hair. "Are you saying your boys . . ."

Nika's silence told the truth.

"If Dufresne knew this, he wouldn't be above using Mitannu's jealousy for his own ends. . . . Perhaps he thought your lover had been Tristan instead of Marc-Antoine.

Their features are similar."

"Yes. I am grieved that so many died and were wounded because of my foolish choices."

Geneviève touched Nika's arm. "You aren't to blame for your husband's wickedness."

"I tell myself this. But my heart does not believe it." Nika sighed. "Wait, I hear that noise again."

Then Geneviève heard it, a muffled scream. "That's my sister!" She tried to lunge to her feet, but Nika restrained her.

"Wait!" Nika repeated. "We will not help her by rushing in. Follow my lead." She crawled toward the gate, which seemed to be abandoned by the usual sentry.

Geneviève followed on hands and knees. Two women alone. They should have waited. She should have insisted that Tristan listen to her. Almost she stood up to run back into the fort. But Aimée was in trouble, and there was no Jean Cavalier or Father Mathieu to rescue them.

Crouching, Nika slipped through the gate, Geneviève behind her, and then they were outside the fort, standing on the shallow strip of land between stockade and bluff. Nothingness lay beyond the sudden dropoff, blackness so dense that Geneviève felt, bizarrely, she could have stood on it. Panicked, she backed against the stockade. To her left loomed the vague outline of the Le Moyne warehouse, where she had once or twice purchased supplies for Burelle's kitchen.

"Quiet," Nika whispered, "and follow me. Our advantage is surprise."

Geneviève could hear noise of a struggle somewhere beyond the warehouse, noises that sent curdled excitement through her veins. It was the same sort of rush that had given her the courage to pick up a hunting rifle and follow uniformed brutes dragging her father to his execution.

Nika edged along the stockade, and Geneviève lost her grip when she tripped over a fallen pike from the stockade. She bent to move it, then picked it up. It was sharp at the top, splintered and uncomfortable to carry, but not as heavy as she had expected. A weapon.

"Stay close," Nika whispered, then darted across the space between the stockade and the warehouse, Geneviève behind her with the pike.

She prayed they were far enough from the edge of the bluff so as not to slip over.

Nika jerked to a halt with a grunt, and Geneviève slammed into her. "What is it?"

Nika was looking down, both hands over her mouth. A moment later she let out a shaky breath. "It's Mitannu."

Geneviève peered around her. The outline of a muscular body lay sprawled against the warehouse wall. She gripped Nika's shoulder, felt her shivers. They stood that way for a frozen moment before Nika jerked into motion.

Geneviève's eyes had adjusted to the darkness enough to see that the wriggling form toward which Nika had been moving was actually two men, locked together in violent struggle. Judging by the grunts and muffled curses, one of them was trying to subdue the other, who was gagged but not bound.

Confused, she touched Nika's elbow and hissed in her ear, "I thought I heard Aimée. Where is she?"

Nika laughed softly. "That's her. She just kicked Dufresne."

But Dufresne wasn't so easily vanquished. He snarled curses at Aimée as he grabbed her by the hair and slung her toward the edge of the bluff.

In her terror, Geneviève ran toward him with the pike aimed like a battering ram. "Nika!" she shrieked. "Get Aimée and pull her back!" At the last moment she whirled the pike overhead. The soft rotten wood thunked against the side of Dufresne's head. He dropped. Geneviève jumped over his inert body, wobbling as the softened ground gave way beneath her feet.

24

Nika barely gave the prostrate Du-Fren a glance as she jumped over him to grab Jon-a-Vev's hand and haul her back from the edge of the bluff. Collapsing, the two of them sat hugging each other and shaking, while Ah-meh pulled off her gag, gathered herself, and crawled over to join them.

Ah-Meh sat up and looked over her shoulder at the still form of the French officer. "Is he dead?"

"I hope so." Unable to produce the least concern for such a liar and murderer, Nika wiped her tear-wet face.

Jon-a-Vev got up and walked over to him. She stooped down and laid two fingers against the pulse point under his jaw. "He's alive." Her voice was flat, but revulsion laced the words. "We have to go for help." She stood up and looked at her sister. "Are you all right? He didn't hurt you?"

"Just my pride. And he pulled out some

of my hair. But I'm alive. Thank you, Ginette. And thank you . . ." Ah-Meh looked at Nika, wrinkling her nose. "I don't know your name."

"I am Nika. Jon-a-Vev, we have to tie him up, or he will sneak away like the cur that he is. I will watch him while you go back to the warehouse for rope. Little Sister can go back to tell Mah-Kah-Twah and Tree-Stah what we have done."

Jon-a-Vev nodded. "That is a good plan. Come, Ah-Meh, we need to hurry."

Yes, they needed to hurry. She was suddenly desperate to hold Chazeh and Tonaw tight in her arms.

She watched the two Frenchwomen disappear into the darkness beyond the warehouse. With the unconscious Du-Fren sprawled nearby, and Jon-a-Vev's pike across her lap in case he stirred before they returned, Nika had little to do but stare across the river, where a bank of clouds had split to reveal a corner of the crescent moon.

Mah-Kah-Twah had left her without a glance, to hold conference with his brother and the commander. Of course she was a strong woman, who had survived for many years without a man to care for her. She did not really need him.

■ ■ ■

From his earliest memory Tristan had understood that his destiny lay outside established boundaries. If his father had been a more forgiving man, perhaps he might have been reluctant to leap into that destiny. But choices, once acted upon, could rarely be undone.

With Bienville waiting for his answer, he sat looking at the scars across the backs of his hands. Symbols of independence, of sacrifice, of manhood, they reminded him to think before acting.

Almost a year ago to the day, he had made the choice to leave Fort Louis and service to his King. Now Bienville was giving him the chance to come back.

Come back? Leave his plantation? Condemn Geneviève to live in His Majesty's Catholic colony, where she could never openly practice her faith? Yoke himself once more to the vicissitudes of Bienville's decisions?

If he refused, there would be no more offers of grace. He would once more cut himself off from his brother, who needed him perhaps more than ever.

He clenched his hands, widening the scars

to silvery bands. He was not the first man to suffer for the decision to stand alone. Yet not alone, for there was a beautiful woman ready to go with him. And the God who had brought her to him.

He looked up at Bienville. "I'll pray about this decision and give you my answer in two days' time."

"Pray?" If he'd said he would consult the Koasati medicine man, Bienville could not have looked more stunned and offended. "What difference will that make?"

Marc-Antoine, looking like a man come back from death, pushed himself to his feet. "It couldn't hurt. Commander, Dufresne is our real snake in the grass. He must be found and court-martialed before he makes more mischief. And with the storm blown over, I believe we would all make better decisions with a few hours sleep. Time enough to assess the flood damage when daylight comes."

After a moment or two, Bienville rose as well. He stared down at Tristan. "All right, then, but you'd be a fool to turn down my offer, Lanier." He cocked his head and walked over to the open window. "What am I hearing? It's coming from the chapel."

Tristan listened. A faint roar of men's voices grew louder by the moment. "Sounds like a mob —"

But Bienville was already bolting to the door.

Marc-Antoine followed more slowly. After grabbing his musket and powder horn, Tristan caught his brother's elbow to support him down the gallery steps.

Marc-Antoine shook his head. "Go. I'll catch up."

Tristan loaded his gun, gave his brother a brief nod, and took off. A faint lightening of the sky over the river indicated that dawn was not far off. At least he hoped it was dawn, and not a fire.

The chapel was wide open, throwing the men inside into relief. Bienville reached the gallery and pounded up the steps just as a milling crowd of some twenty or thirty poured through the open door. Some carried torches, some muskets, and a few wielded swords and clubs. None were in uniform, so at least this wasn't a mutiny, as Tristan had halfway feared.

Then his heart stopped as the crowd parted and three women — Geneviève, Nika, and Aimée, bound at the wrist — were dragged forward and shoved to their knees in front of Bienville.

"What is the meaning of this?" Bienville roared, even as Tristan passed him to get to

Geneviève.

Nicolas de La Salle seemed to be at the head of the mob. His musket fixed on Tristan. "Stop right there, Lanier, or I'll blow your head off."

Ignoring him, Tristan reached Geneviève and scooped her into his arms. She sagged against him, shaking.

Bienville leveled his own musket. "La Salle, release these women before I have you court-martialed. Have you all gone mad?"

Looking uncertain, La Salle jerked his head toward Father Henri, who stepped forward to speak for the group. Behind him were gunsmith Théo Boyer, shipbuilder André Ardouin, and brickmaker Jean Alexandre — all Frenchmen who had emigrated a year or more before the *Pélican*'s arrival and all allies of La Salle. All three carried raised bayonets.

The priest was of course unarmed, but he puffed out his chest and shook a plump finger at the commander. "I was sent by Minister Pontchartrain himself and the bishop. I defy you to threaten me, Bienville. We caught these women in the act of assaulting one of your officers — after they had sabotaged the powder magazine, leaving it open to flood."

"That's over seven-hundred man-hours of

labor lost," Boyer said belligerently. "It's unforgiveable."

Geneviève wrenched away from Tristan to face her accuser. "None of us had anything to do with it!" She looked at Bienville, an agony of distress in every line of her face. "You cannot believe this, Commander."

Bienville stared at her, doubt hooking his brows together. "I . . . must have the entire story."

"We don't have time for that. We are about to be overrun by the Indians you love so much, Bienville." La Salle pushed the mouth of his gun against the back of Nika's bent head.

She whirled, releasing a spew of Kaskaskian at La Salle. Just as suddenly she switched to French. "There are no Indians coming to attack you — unless you go off to provoke them like the little boys you are! You *brave* Frenchmen, to allow yourselves to be overcome by three women! Oh — you are so stupid that you do not recognize the snake in your own garden."

La Salle hit her with the barrel of the gun, cutting her temple open as she fell unconscious.

Tristan lunged sideways to grab the gun barrel, wresting it from La Salle and throwing him to the ground. "Coward," he panted, standing over him. He glared at the men behind the priest, most of whom had backed away in confusion. "You are no Frenchmen, and you are certainly no Canadians, to attack three defenseless women. Where is your proof of any wrongdoing? Where is this officer who was attacked?"

Father Henri's mouth opened and closed, his chins wobbling. "He was right behind us. Who brought Dufresne?"

"Dufresne?" Bienville barked. "Where is he? I was just about to arrest him."

"My sister felled him with a rotten pike from the stockade." Aimée Gaillain struggled to her feet, flinging her long golden hair back with a toss of her head. "I hope he is dead, but I'm afraid he is not. *He* is your traitor, Commander!"

For the first time, Tristan realized Aimée was dressed in men's clothing. She looked like a beautiful actress in some bizarre theatrical play. She also looked more like a woman than the spoiled child he had last seen pouting in Geneviève's kitchen.

But before he could respond, Marc-Antoine pushed past the clearly flummoxed Bienville and fell to his knees beside Nika. Gathering her up with his one good arm, he looked around at the shuffling crowd of inhabitants. "La Salle," he said betwixt his teeth, "you have just assaulted the woman who kept me alive — after your so-admired Dufresne arranged to have me and the rest of our party murdered by her husband and his band of renegades — and then, by herself, dragged me all the way home on a litter."

La Salle shook his head, raising his shaking hands. "I did not — I did not know, I swear! I only know that this woman —" he gave Geneviève a venomous glare — "was caught in correspondence with the enemy, and she somehow escaped from the guardhouse —"

"You left her there to drown, you fool!" Tristan reached down and hauled the clerk to his feet, shaking him like a rat. "Even if she were guilty — and she is not! — no one deserves to die that way. I hope Bienville will lock you up in her place and see how you like it!" Realizing he was losing control, Tristan released La Salle, who staggered backward into his henchmen, and took Geneviève's hands. He untied her wrists and bent to kiss them one at a time.

He lifted her in his arms and turned to carry her into the chapel, her body a precious weight against his heart. Behind him he heard the roar of voices in dissent, but he cared little how Bienville settled the contretemps or even what happened to Dufresne. His decision had been made. He was not staying in Fort Louis and, legitimate or not, he was not going to France as the Comte de Hayot.

He and his bride were going home.

"And you are sure there are no Indians coming to attack us?"

Aimée, seated in one of Bienville's office armchairs, shook her head. "I told you, he was trying to create conflict where there was none, to discredit Bienville and to make himself more valuable to the British." She allowed her eyes to close and her head to fall back against the wall. When were they going to release her to her bed? Her entire body ached, her scalp was unbearably tender, and she felt like bursting into tears. For some reason, now that she had endured real struggle, she was determined to cover her emotion.

Geneviève was brave. Nika was brave. And Aimée was no longer a child. Therefore she must no longer behave like one.

But, oh, she was tired.

"Mademoiselle," Commander Bienville persisted, "you say Aide-Major Dufresne had planned to leave the settlement with you sometime during the night, but he changed his mind. Why do you suppose he did that?"

Aimée forced her eyes open again to focus on the commander's face. How had she once thought him handsome? His nose was hawkish, there were severe lines radiating from his black eyes, and a streak of gray grew from the center part of his hair and striped down the left side. Why, he was quite an *old* man.

She bared her teeth. "I have no idea. You will have to ask him when he wakes up. All I know is that he is a liar and a brute, and if I ever see him again, I am going to use Nika's tomahawk to cut off all his flaming red hair! If he is lucky, I will leave the scalp." She pushed herself to her feet, swaying a little. "You will excuse me, Commander. I am going to sleep."

She stalked from the office, feeling his wicked black eyes follow her until she had slammed the door behind her.

Nika did not know why she had been called into this meeting. She had given her testimony to Commander Byah-Vee-Yah. She had said farewell to Jon-a-Vev and to Tree-Stah, gathered her meager belongings, and attempted to slip out. A few hours' sleep in the common room had refreshed her for the long walk ahead back to the Apalachee village. Her little boys would be so happy to see her, and she would kiss their faces until they squealed and giggled.

But at the last minute, Mah-Kah-Twah had appeared in the door between officers' quarters and the common room, and insisted she stay "for just another hour." His sleepy black eyes had held hers until she found herself nodding and following him into the office of the commander. Even with an injury that would have killed most men, worn out from lack of food and sleep, he walked like a warrior.

Her heart longed for him. Her mind shamed her for her weakness.

He held the door until she entered the room, then shut it and took her elbow as if she were a French duchess. He hooked a chair with his foot and pulled it in front of Byah-Vee-Yah's desk for her to sit on, then stood behind her, his hand braced upon its back. She could feel his fingers touching her, and she closed her eyes, all but blind with pain, willing him to move away. Opening them again, she forced herself to look around. Jon-a-Vev sat in another chair a few feet away, Tree-Stah standing behind her. The commander sat behind his desk, elbows propped on it, fingers steepled against his lips.

The men began to speak about the scoundrel Dufresne, where he would be sent, how much damage his treachery had brought about, whether he should be shown leniency because of his aristocratic father. Nika remained silent. She did not care what happened to him. She wanted to get out of that room.

Then the discussion shifted to the flooded settlement. All the water that flowed away from the bluff on which the fort stood had collected to form a huge lake in the center of the town. Nika could have told the commander four years ago that the fort and settlement would never last at that location, subject as it was to torrential rains at least twice a year, once in the spring and once in the fall. Now the French faced the decision of when and where to move their little colony.

Again, she remained silent. It did not matter to her where they went, because she must go back to her people. Leaving the Mobile village would be hard, because she had made many friends, including Mitannu's sister Kamala, their mother and their father. But she no longer belonged with them. The Kaskaskians would welcome her back. She was young. Perhaps she could find another husband with whom she could be content. This time, though, she would make her decision based on cold thought, the answers to careful questions.

"Byah-Vee-Yah," Tree-Stah said forcefully, "you know the fort should be moved down to the southern bluff at the top of the bay. You gave the property to me, but I choose to return it to the King."

The commander was shaking his head, but Mah-Kah-Twah spoke behind her. "Commander, he is right, and you know it. We can't stay here any longer. The fort is rotting out from under us, and this last storm was nearly our undoing. If we start planning now, make it through the winter, perhaps we could start rebuilding in the spring and be moved by next summer."

Byah-Vee-Yah sat silent for a long time, gaze cast aside. Finally he spread his hands and looked first at Mah-Kah-Twah, then at Tree-Stah. "All right," he said on a sigh. "Yes, you are right. I have known this for some time. But no one in the settlement is going to like it. And convincing Pontchartrain to loosen the purse strings for a new fort will be all but impossible."

"I think you would be surprised to know how many supporters you have, Commander," Jon-a-Vev said softly. "The women especially — they hate the constant floods, mildew, rotting wood, mosquitoes . . . And they have influence with their husbands. If you *lead* them, with a level head and a good example, you'll find they will follow you anywhere."

The commander stared at her blankly, and for a moment Nika feared he might cast off Jon-a-Vev's opinion. But a slow smile grew in his eyes, spread to his lips, and created a charming grin that suddenly explained his popularity with both men and women. "As you led Aide-Major Dufresne last night, madame? With a stockade pike?"

"Perhaps," Jon-a-Vev said, eyes twinkling. "One makes do with whatever God provides in the moment."

Byah-Vee-Yah laughed. "Yes, Madame, there is much wisdom in your words." His gaze cut to Nika, so suddenly that she flinched. "But there is one more question I would ask of my friend Nika. Do I understand that you are turned from your loyalty to your mother's people? That you will no longer carry messages for British agents planted among the Kaskaskians?"

With an effort, she did not turn to look at Mah-Kah-Twah. But she felt his fingers move to her shoulder. Their gentle touch

sent a message she was afraid to hear. "I . . .
do not want to carry messages for anyone."

"Then you are a woman without a
people." Byah-Vee-Yah's voice was matter-
of-fact but not cruel. "You are welcome
here."

"Welcome?" With nothing to lose, Nika
decided to be equally forthright. "Your
priests would not say so. Many of the
Mobile people are Christian, but Father
Henri and Father Albert resist providing
the sacraments for us — for them, I mean.
'It is so expensive,' they say. And you —"
She felt Mah-Kah-Twah's cautioning
squeeze of her shoulder but laughed and
kept going. "You discourage your men from
marrying our women, even when they make
children together." She rose. "Forgive me,
Commander, if I doubt the sincerity of your
welcome." She turned and looked up at
Mah-Kah-Twah, took a moment to memo-
rize his face — though there had never been
any danger of forgetting it, as it was limned
in her children's eyes — and glided from
the room.

"Nika!"

She was at the gallery steps when she
heard him call her, but she barely faltered.

"Nika, stop! You know I can't keep up

530

with you without starting the bleeding again!"

Her feet slowed against her will, then refused to move another step until he took her by the shoulders. "Let me go," she said, bracing herself.

"No. Not again. Never again." He wrapped his arms all the way around her and pulled her back against him.

She stiffened her body. "Mah-Kah-Twah, I am not your plaything anymore. Did you not hear anything I just said?"

He pulled her hair back and bent his head to press his warm mouth against her neck. "I heard. I heard what you didn't say as well. Nika, I love you. I've waited for you all this time, and I didn't even know it."

She closed her eyes as warmth flooded every part of her, even while her mind screamed that she must get away before it was too late. "I am a Christian woman. I will not live with you in sin."

"But you do love me." There was swagger, confidence in his quiet voice.

"I — do not." She all but choked on the lie.

"Yes you do. And I don't want a plaything. I want a wife. I want one specific wife, the strong one who can dress a wound and tan hides and make baskets and beads and feed a village full of children and still be so beautiful as to break a hundred hearts." He turned her to face him, his sleepy eyes begging her to come in to him. "I want you," he whispered. "Don't go, Nika. Stay with me."

She felt her eyes fill. "All right, I love you," she said angrily, "but Byah-Vee-Yah will never allow you to marry me. Do you want to be an exile like your brother?"

"The commander knows when he has met the stronger man — or woman, as the case may be." A smile crept into his eyes, making him so dangerous that she almost turned to run. "We will go to Father Henri, who will marry us to spite the commander, and Bienville will soon be so busy moving the settlement that he will forget to be angry."

She had one more defense to put up. "I won't leave my children. They are very noisy, rambunctious, and disobedient."

"You mean, like teenage cadets of the marine?" He grinned at her. "Find something else to scare me with, Nika. I laugh at your threats."

To her enduring shame, she could no longer resist burying her face against his chest. "You are a very hard man to argue with, Mah-Kah-Twah."

"You'll find that I am not much like the selfish youth who walked away from you five years ago." His voice left its teasing and went soft and deep with serious intent. "God knows I'm not a perfect man, Nika, and I'll make mistakes, I'm sure. But I'll never intentionally hurt you or abandon you or our children. I promise this from my heart."

She sighed and lifted her face to him. "All right. I give up."

"It's about time," he said and kissed her.

25

It was time, she thought, to tell him.

On the afternoon of Marc-Antoine and Nika's wedding, she and Tristan sat on the gallery steps of Charles Levasseur's house, eating a simple supper of crusty bread and cheese. Bienville had given the house to them to live in until the move to the southern bluff could be completed. Tristan would be useful to the commander as architect and draftsman of the new fort and settlement, which would be called Mobile for its location on the bay.

Cutting her a sliver of cheese with his knife, he had just asked her for the fourth time in as many days if she objected to staying in town. Each of the previous times she had kissed him and said patiently, "Where you are is home."

This time she hesitated.

"What is it?" he asked quickly. "I know there is something bearing on your mind.

You seem happy, but if there is something else you need —"

She stopped the words with her lips, hands on his face. "I have everything I need." She watched his mouth curl up and kissed him again. He seemed to like that she was bold, purring like a lion. Taking a deep breath, she drew back a little. "But there's something in Father Mathieu's journal I want you to see." He had given it to her as a memento of her absent friend.

"I don't want to read right now." He tipped her face up with his thumb.

Geneviève laughed and wriggled away. "It's broad daylight, monsieur, and we mustn't scandalize the neighbors." A pleasant cool snap had followed the spate of rain earlier in the day, and several inhabitants had already wandered past on their way to market, smiling at the two of them sitting so close together. When Tristan sighed and sat back, she reached into her pocket for the little book.

She had enjoyed looking at her husband's drawings almost as much as reading Mathieu's lively descriptions and comments on the experiences of his journey up the river. Now she flipped past them to one of the last entries in the book.

"Here," she said, squinting at the priest's

535

crabbed writing. " 'I pray for my dear Geneviève and her Tristan,' he says, 'that they will find peace together, whatever the outcome of my quest here in New France.' Had you read this?" She glanced at Tristan and found him regarding her, chin propped on his hand, the cheese and bread set aside.

He shook his head. "I've been very . . . busy lately."

"Yes, you have." She teasingly bopped him with the book. "Pay attention."

"Yes, madame. Whatever you say, madame."

She cleared her throat. " 'This peace they will never know, unless they come together as one in Christ, bearing each other's burdens in the mundane as well as the spectacular events of life, as the letter to the Galatians admonishes. There are things about the confessional that Geneviève as a Reformed, and Tristan as a nominal believer, may miss. I pray that they will be freed to uncover every secret so that love may cast out all fear.' " She paused and closed the book on her finger. "Tristan, I —"

"He is wrong about that." Tristan took her hand. "I am no longer a believer in name only."

"I know. And I'm glad." She looked away.

"But he is right about confession. I'm burdened with something I must tell you. You know most of what happened to me in the Cévennes, but the longer I stay, the more I fear that my presence here puts you in danger."

He kissed her fingers. "Then we will leave on the morrow and move to my plantation in Mobile."

"No, this is — something that will follow me as long as we are in a French colony." She clasped his hand between both of hers urgently, letting Mathieu's journal fall into her lap. "Tristan, I am wanted for murder in France. I k-killed that dragoon who arrested my father." Her lips trembled in spite of her determination to be brave. "I shot a man! Do you hear me? I was in prison awaiting sentencing when Jean Cavalier and Father Mathieu got me out of the country."

"My heart, I am glad you tell me these things that worry you." Tristan caressed her face, smearing the tears away with his thumb. "But you must let the guilt go. You know you are long forgiven, and surely you have paid whatever price God asked of you." With a deep groan, he folded her close and held her until her storm of tears had passed. "I've seen your scars, and they are beautiful to me because they brought you to me. As mine brought me to you."

With her head still on his shoulder, she stroked the silvery stripes across the sun-browned hand he gave her to hold. "Will you tell me how?"

He was silent for a long moment. Then, "I came between my father's whip and — my brother."

"Ah, beloved. . . ." She pressed his hand to her lips. "May God preserve us from more of such violence. Surely it grieves his heart."

"And our new family will honor him, I promise you."

As Tristan held her close, she let her lingering guilt and fear roll away like the river that flowed past Fort Louis. Father Mathieu was right — true love cast out fear, replacing it with hope and faith. He had brought her to a man of courage, strength, and honor, a man who would love her in deed as well as words.

I choose joy, she thought with a smile.

A WORD TO THE READER

There is a lot of little-known American history in this book.

I ran across a brief mention of the "*Pélican* Girls" while researching a previous work of fiction set in Mobile; thought, "Hmmm, that's interesting," and tucked it away for later study. When the opportunity came to write a whole series based on the colorful history of my birthplace, the logical place to start seemed to be with the larger-than-life Le Moyne brothers — Canadian explorers, entrepreneurs, politicians, and swashbuckling adventurers, who placed their stamp upon a whole territory in the name of Sun King Louis XIV of France.

Because my storytelling "sweet spot" is romance, my curiosity was drawn to the women who married and civilized those first French-Canadian settlers of Louisiane. Who were they and where did they come from? Why take on a three-month journey across an ocean to what would have been little more than a hostile, mosquito-infested bog for the sole purpose of marrying a stranger? How did these mainly convent-raised young women, teenagers with few practical survival skills, manage to establish homes and raise children? What kinds of relationships did they build with the native peoples, and what influences did they bring to one another?

Those were some of the questions I brought to my initial research. Little did I realize the depth of knowledge required to build that world from the ground up, people it with compelling characters — some of them historical figures with documented biographies, some purely conjured from my imagination — and cast my protagonists and villains into book-length conflict. By the time the basic story line had bloomed into a ten-page synopsis, I had begun to realize the challenges of writing in English about characters who spoke and viewed life through a French and/or Native American lens — over three centuries ago! I found some primary resources — baptismal and burial records, letters, contracts, journals, maps, and the like — plus historical internet sites and a few good nonfiction books (I'm largely indebted to Jay Higginbotham's wonderfully detailed and readable *Old*

Mobile: Fort Louis de la Louisane, 1702–1711).

I visited local museums and read the Higginbotham book before beginning to write the manuscript. Still, I daily found myself stumped by questions about things like refrigeration, funerals, midwifery, baking, grinding corn, shooting a musket . . . and on and on. I'm pretty much the ultimate history geek, so I found myself loading the story with way too much information for the average fiction reader (I suspect I'll have critics on both ends of the spectrum). At my editor's suggestion, I decided to put some of that information here, to keep from bogging down the action in the novel.

The Pelican Bride is essentially a romance, embedded in a particular political, religious, and economic historical climate. So who were the big players on the North American continent in 1704?

England controlled the Atlantic seaboard, from Massachusetts south to Georgia, with the Appalachian Mountains forming the western border. Spain held Florida, Texas, the Caribbean, Mexico, and Central and South America. France had claimed Canada and the Great Lakes. If you look at period maps, it's clear that whichever power could lay claim to the rivers bisecting the continent from the Lakes to the Gulf Coast would gain a chokehold on American commerce. No wonder all three were anxious to find and claim the mouth of the Mississippi River.

The courage, cunning, and sheer persistence of such explorers as La Salle, Levasseur, Iberville, and Bienville — under the leadership of Minister of Marine Pontchartrain — gave the edge to the French. They established Fort Maurepas at present-day Biloxi, Mississippi, then Fort Louis twenty-seven miles up the Alabama River north of present-day Mobile; eventually, New Orleans became the capital of the Louisiana Territory. But at the turn of the eighteenth century, Iberville — commander of the French outpost on the Gulf — found himself a political juggler responsible for maintaining alliance with the Spanish in Pensacola, keeping the British from encroaching from the east, and courting trade with the natives.

The local Mobile Indians were generally friendly to the French settlers, who brought European commodities such as guns and ammunition, farming and building implements, and textiles. However, the French faced constant threat of attack from the more warlike northern Alabama clans who had discovered the value of slave trade with English tobacco farmers. The Indians as depicted in *The Pelican Bride* are as accurate as I could make them from available resources. Records kept by the Catholic Diocese of Mobile indicate that there was a good deal of intermarriage between natives and Europeans at the turn of the eighteenth century, as well as mutual leveraging of resources and economic power.

Religion was another critical factor in the success or failure of French settlements along the Gulf Coast. Even before King Louis XIV took the reins of power in 1661, France had been sending Jesuit and seminary missionaries into Indian villages, both as evangelists and ambassadors. These competing orders of priests sometimes created as much headache as benefit for military commanders.

Since the beginning of the Reformation, cycles of civil war, uneasy peace, and bloody massacre escalated between Protestants (known as Huguenots) and Catholics in France, until Protestant-turned-Catholic monarch Henry IV issued the 1598 Edict of Nantes, which protected those who wished to worship peacefully outside the Roman tradition. Then in 1685, Louis XIV declared himself free from foreign conflict and ready to rid the nation of "the memory of the troubles, the confusion, and the evils which the progress of this false religion has caused in this kingdom" (see the Revocation of the Edict of Nantes). Persecution of the "R.P.R." — so-called reformed religion — renewed and intensified, until the Abbé of Chaila brought the King's forces into the mountainous Cévennes region of southern France to enforce conversions to the Catholic faith. Soldiers were billeted with Reformist families in an effort to make them convert or emigrate. Those who refused to comply were arrested, deported, or sentenced to the galleys, and their property confiscated or burned.

An interesting real-life character, educated young apprenticed baker Jean Cavalier, arose from that conflict in the Cévennes. Cavalier, a natural orator and genius of irregular warfare, led armed Protestant civilians — known as Black Camisards — in resisting the persecution. While winning several pitched battles against His Majesty's experienced and trained military, Cavalier was never captured but managed to negotiate some concessions from the royal commander. After Louis XIV died in 1715, hostilities finally ended, and the Protestant remnant in the Cévennes was left in peace.

Some years later, Cavalier went over to the British and in 1738 was made governor of the island of Jersey.

Those facts were enough to give me an intriguing background for my heroine, Geneviève Gaillain, and I hope historians will forgive whatever details I had to tweak or exaggerate for the sake of story.

Native Mobilians will perhaps recognize character names from the annals of local history. The "Pelican Girls" of 1704 were real people who married, raised children, and died in real time. Little was recorded about most of them, beyond the usual church records, which left me free to use their names and embellish their stories. Gabrielle Bonnet (my Ysabeau), for example, was noted for going mad and walking about in her underclothes. There is no record of her marriage. Other names I changed or simplified (due to the seventeenth-century practice of naming children after saints, resulting in a confusing plethora of Maries, Jeannes, and Catherines) for readability. Geneviève and Aimée Gaillain are products of my imagination, as are Nika, Tristan, Marc-Antoine, Julien, and Father Mathieu. For details on the life of the famous Le Moyne brothers, whose exploits are well-documented, I recommend titles such as

Jean Baptiste Le Moyne: Sieur de Bienville by Grace King, *Colonial Mobile* by Peter J. Hamilton, and of course Jay Higginbotham's brilliant *Old Mobile: Fort Louis de la Louisiane, 1702–1711.*

ACKNOWLEDGMENTS

This is one of my favorite parts of the writing process, where I get to name names. You know, the people who stand behind the author, prodding, praying, and breathing a sigh of relief when it's all over. I'll try to keep it short.

I am as usual grateful for the encouragement, advice, and common sense provided by my husband. Scott puts up with his daydreamy, disorganized, and distractible wife with uncanny grace and good humor. He's also gotten to be quite a good editor. Then there's my best friend, Tammy, who faithfully reads and prays over everything and helps me pitch out bad ideas and replace them with good ones. I love you guys.

Honestly, this book wouldn't have seen the light of day without my longtime friend and agent, Chip MacGregor. Somehow, in the middle of the chaotic swings of turn-of-the-century book publishing, he found a partner for my dream of setting the rich Gulf Coast historical narrative as a fictional family saga, and introduced me to Lonnie Hull Dupont — an editor with experience, insight, and an extraordinary love for the written word. I am blessed beyond expression.

I would also like to thank the faithful friends and family who have prayed for me during the stressful time of first-draft writing, full-time teaching, and trying to stay active in church — especially my choir students at LeFlore High School. Yes, children, Mrs. White has finished that book. Fist bump.

Finally, the job of a novelist is to entertain, but if she can at the same time hold up a mirror to society, so much the better. With that in mind, I would like to thank a few wise and gentle brothers and sisters who, over the past three years, have helped me explore what it means to be free to pursue life, liberty, and happiness. You know who you are.

Mobile, Alabama
June 2013

ABOUT THE AUTHOR

Beth White's day job is teaching music at an inner-city high school in historic Mobile, Alabama. A native Mississippian, she is a pastor's wife, mother of two, and grandmother of one — so far. Her hobbies include playing flute and pennywhistle and painting, but her real passion is writing historical romance with a Southern drawl. Her novels have won the American Christian Fiction Writers' Carol Award, the RT Book Club Reviewers Choice Award, and the Inspirational Reader's Choice Award. Visit www.bethwhite.net for more information.

DATE DUE

CT OCT 2 0 2014	
CO NOV 1 0 2014	
	PRINTED IN U.S.A.